Never had Dana felt so disoriented by passion,

yet so certain that her heart was leading her in the right direction.

Her love for Rick was like a beacon shining in the night, guiding her way.

Surely whatever rocky shores their relationship might have foundered on had been swept away by forces as inevitable as the rise and fall of the tide. Tonight there would be no hidden shoals, no treacherous undercurrents.

Tonight she would surrender gladly to a maelstrom of yearning....

Dear Reader,

Welcome to Silhouette **Special Edition** . . . welcome to romance. Each month, Silhouette **Special Edition** publishes six novels with you in mind—stories of love and life, tales that you can identify with . . . as well as dream about.

We're starting off the New Year right in 1993. We're pleased to announce our new series, THAT SPECIAL WOMAN! Each month, we'll be presenting a book that pays tribute to women—to us. The heroine is a friend, a wife, a mother—a striver, a nurturer, a pursuer of goals—she's the best in every woman. And it takes a very special man to win that special woman! Launching this series is *Building Dreams* by Ginna Gray. Ryan McCall doesn't know what he's up against when he meets Tess Benson in this compelling tale. She's a woman after the cynical builder's heart—and she won't stop until she's got her man!

On the horizon this month, too, is MAVERICKS, a new series by Lisa Jackson. *He's a Bad Boy* introduces three men who just won't be tamed!

Rounding out the month are more stories from other favorite authors—Tracy Sinclair, Christine Flynn, Kayla Daniels and Judith Bowen (with her first Silhouette **Special Edition** title!).

I hope that you enjoy this book and all the stories to come. Happy 1993!

Sincerely,

Tara Gavin
Senior Editor
Silhouette Books

KAYLA DANIELS

FROM FATHER TO SON

Silhouette®

SPECIAL EDITION®

Published by Silhouette Books New York

America's Publisher of Contemporary Romance

For Brian,
my favorite Norwegian Bachelor Farmer

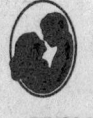

SILHOUETTE BOOKS
300 East 42nd St., New York, N.Y. 10017

FROM FATHER TO SON

ISBN: 0-373-09790-5

First Silhouette Books printing January 1993

Books by Kayla Daniels

Silhouette Special Edition

Spitting Image #474
Father Knows Best #578
Hot Prospect #654
Rebel to the Rescue #707
From Father to Son #790

KAYLA DANIELS

has three great passions: travel, ballroom dancing and Norwegian cuisine. She is currently working her way from Afghanistan to Zimbabwe by reading one book about every country in the world. She takes breaks from writing to play baritone horn with the local college band and to study piano.

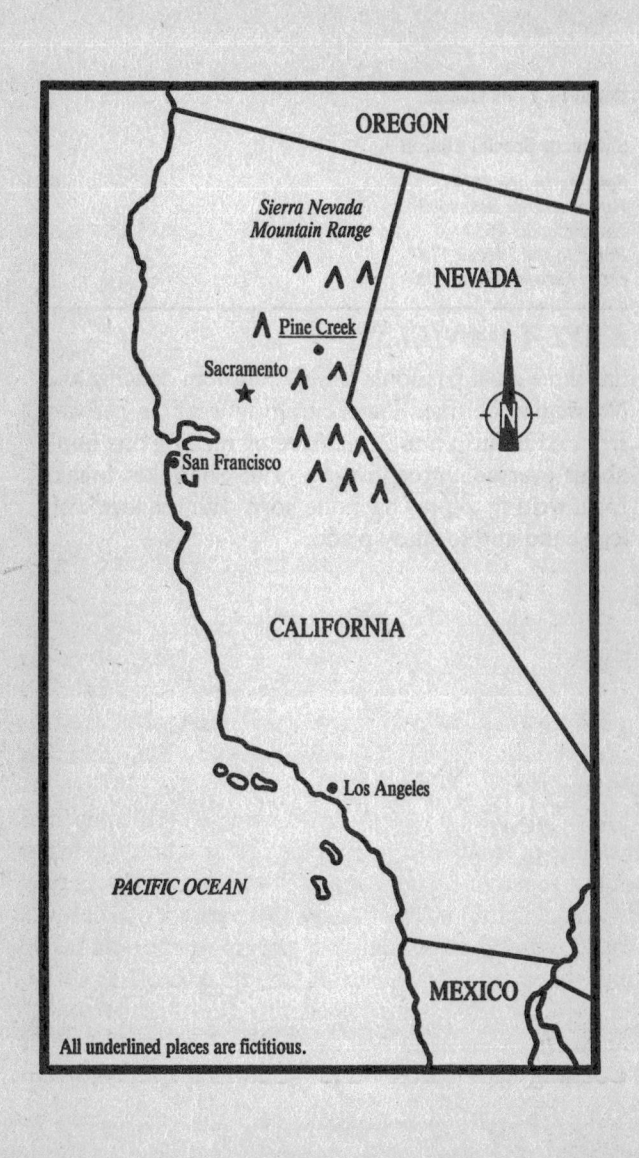

OREGON

*Sierra Nevada
Mountain Range*

^ ^ ^

NEVADA

^ <u>Pine Creek</u>
•

Sacramento ^
★ ^

^ ^ ^
^ ^ ^

San Francisco

CALIFORNIA

N

• Los Angeles

PACIFIC OCEAN

MEXICO

All underlined places are fictitious.

Chapter One

As usual, Dana Sheridan was trying to do three things at once.

In one hand she juggled half the egg-salad sandwich she hadn't gotten around to eating at lunchtime, in the other the telephone receiver. Meanwhile she was hunched over her desk skimming through the tentative list of local talent acts Elaine had scheduled for the upcoming pledge drive.

"Sounds good, Andy," Dana said, her voice muffled by a bite of sandwich. "What have we got lined up in the way of musicals? They always draw lots of viewers during membership week." Andy Gallagher's official title was vice president in charge of programming—an inside joke, since a public television station as small as Channel Five couldn't afford even *one* full-time person to handle programming. Andy doubled as producer of "Cooking with Carole" and "Gabriel's Garden," and also filled in as acting general manager on the rare occasions when Dana wasn't at the station.

Three offices away, Andy said, "I thought we should run musicals by a variety of songwriters—you know, like Rodgers and Hammerstein's *South Pacific,* Meredith Willson's *The Music Man...*"

Dana tucked her dark hair behind her ear, wedged the receiver against her shoulder and began to scribble furiously. "*Match Made in Heaven* . . . okay, that takes care of West and Winslow, and how about *Camelot* for Lerner and Loewe?"

"Hmm . . . I think more people would tune in for *My Fair Lady.*"

Just then Dana's office door swung open and Elliott Ledbetter, the station's accountant, peered cautiously inside. Dana waved him forward. "Come on in, Elliott. Have a seat. Okay, Andy, let's go with *My Fair Lady.*"

Elliott scanned the room for a place to sit down, then finally lifted a stack of file folders off the nearest chair and placed them neatly on the floor next to a pile of videocassettes. Dana rolled her eyes at him and shrugged helplessly, nearly dislodging the phone receiver from her shoulder. She grabbed for it quickly before it tumbled to the floor, and knocked over a half-empty cup of cold coffee in the process.

"Aw, jeez! Andy, I've gotta go. Disaster has struck. I just spilled coffee all over our list of local talent."

Elliott hastily yanked a perfectly ironed white handkerchief from his suit pocket and extended it in Dana's direction. She snatched it gratefully and used it to mop up the worst of the spill. "Go ahead with those musicals, Andy. But check first with Elaine on the local talent schedule. We don't want some harmonica trio playing

'76 Trombones' right after *The Music Man*. Catch ya later.''

She dumped the receiver back in place and scrubbed futilely at the papers on her desk. "Sorry about your handkerchief, Elliott," she said, dangling it between thumb and forefinger as she handed it back to him.

He nudged his bifocals up the bridge of his nose. "Er, uh, no problem." He pinched the wet handkerchief gingerly and looked somewhat at a loss. Then with a sigh he opened his briefcase across his knees, grimacing as he stuffed the damp, stained hankie into one of its numerous compartments.

Dana felt Elliott's gaze following her while she spread the papers across her desk to dry. She liked the fortyish, slightly pear-shaped accountant, even if he *was* the only person she knew who sent his handkerchiefs to the dry cleaners. Today, however, he was making her nervous for some reason.

She plopped herself into her chair, kicked off her high heels and swung around to face him. "What's the matter, Elliott? You look like the price of adding-machine tape just went up."

"You know perfectly well I use a computer, not an adding machine." He squinted at her Snoopy wall calendar. "Do you know your calendar still says March?"

"Does it?" Dana propelled her chair over to the wall, ripped off the offending calendar page and crumpled it into a ball. Rolling back to her desk, she lobbed it at her wastebasket. She missed. "Is that what you came all the way over here to tell me?"

"I wish it were." Elliott removed a file folder from his briefcase, snapped the case shut and set it on the floor. Gosh, he was sure acting like Mr. Doom-and-Gloom today!

"Uh-oh, must be bad news. Come on, spill it!" Dana grinned, recalling her recent disaster.

Elliott continued to regard her with basset-hound eyes. "I'm afraid this is a little more serious than a spilled cup of coffee."

"Hmm . . . I'll bet it has something to do with money, right?"

"Brilliant deduction."

"That's why I'm station manager," she replied cheerfully. But behind her forced smile and lighthearted banter an ominous chill was creeping up Dana's spine. The station had faced financial woes in the past. But the grim expression on Elliott's face was one she'd never seen before.

He scooted his chair closer to her desk and opened the file folder in front of her. "Here are the figures. I also had the computer draw up these charts so it's easier to see what I'm talking about."

Dana's heart sank even farther. "Elliott, I'm no math whiz, but these graphs make it look like . . ."

"If you don't come up with some major funding *fast,* Channel Five is going to go under within the next three months."

Elliott's words stunned her, although now that it was out in the open, Dana had to admit the news didn't exactly come as a surprise. She'd worked in public television since she was a teenager, and understood all too well the financial tightrope most stations walked. Her instincts had warned her for some time that trouble was looming ahead, but she'd had too many other immediate concerns that required her attention first.

"We've had budget crunches before. . . ." she said cautiously, still not quite ready to believe things could be this bad.

"Not like this." Elliott shook his head mournfully. "Those past crises were just a matter of finding funds to tide you over temporarily. But look at these income projections." He spread another graph in front of her—wavy red lines bleeding all over the page. "With government cutbacks and the drop-off in Channel Five memberships, your income is simply drying up, and you've got zero prospects for any major sources of funding in the near future."

"But the annual membership drive is coming up next month...."

Elliott shook his head. "According to these projections, which are based on statistics from the past three years, it won't be enough."

"But—"

"Your viewership has been steadily declining for some time now. People rent videocassettes nowadays, or they watch cable TV or even pull in programming with their own satellite dishes, for Pete's sake." Elliott stuffed the graphs back into their folder. "Public television's piece of the pie is constantly growing smaller with all the competition." Awkwardly he patted Dana's shoulder. "Your station isn't alone, you know. Even the networks are suffering."

But the networks weren't Dana's concern. Her father had started Channel Five almost single-handedly back in the early sixties, back when the idea of viewer-supported television was still a novelty. People had told him he was crazy, that a small community of nine thousand like Pine Creek, California, could never support its own television station—especially one that didn't accept advertising.

But Ben Sheridan hadn't listened. He was a native of Pine Creek, a prominent businessman and a tireless community booster. He was also a man with a vision, and he'd devoted the major portion of his life to bringing quality local television to this remote area of the Sierra Nevada. In the days before cable, even on a clear day Pine Creek television antennas were lucky to pick up fuzzy reception from the network affiliates in distant Sacramento. During stormy weather, TV viewing was impossible—until the day Channel Five went on the air.

When her father died, Dana had been the logical choice to succeed him as general manager. After all, she'd practically grown up around the station, having worked at nearly all the different positions by the time she went away to college. So at age twenty-seven she'd quit her promising job at the PBS station in Los Angeles to come home and take up the reins of Ben Sheridan's dream. In the midst of her grief over her father's death, the challenge of running Channel Five had given Dana something to hang on to, a reason to look forward to the future.

And now a bunch of charts and tables were telling her that Channel Five's airwaves were about to fall silent. "I don't understand," she said, trying to keep her voice from wavering. "How could this have happened all of a sudden? It—it's like an earthquake or an avalanche, coming out of nowhere."

Elliott snapped shut the clasps of his briefcase. "The station's revenues have been steadily declining for some time now, Dana. The final straw was when old Mrs. Merrifield died. After all the generous donations she'd made over the years, it was a real financial blow when her heirs decided not to continue her largess."

"I won't let the station go under, Elliott—I won't!" Stabbing twinges made Dana realize she'd been clenching her fists tight enough to dig her nails into her palms.

She studied the angry red crescents. "I can't let my father down," she said softly.

Elliott ran his fingers through his thinning brown hair. "Times change, kiddo. Technologies change, people's priorities change. You can't blame yourself for that."

Dana catapulted to her feet. "My father built this station out of *nothing,* Elliott! People laughed at him, called him a fool for trying. But he went ahead and did it anyway." She blew her bangs off her forehead with a gust of hopeless frustration. "Now you're telling me I'm not even capable of keeping his dream alive."

"Dana—" he said helplessly.

The door swished open and Elaine Hennessy stuck her red curly head into the room. "Dana, we're having cake for Jenni's birthday over on the 'Cooking With Carole' set—oh, hi, Elliott! You're invited, too, of course." She gave him a dazzling smile. Elaine, a widow with two teenage sons, had never made any secret of her interest in the shy accountant.

Elliott checked his watch. "Thanks, but I have to get back to my office. I've got another client coming in at three."

"Oh, pooh! That's half an hour from now. You've got time for a piece of cake, haven't you?"

"Well..." Absently he rubbed his stomach.

"It's chocolate mocha with raspberry filling...." Elaine teased in a tempting singsong.

Elliott licked his lips. "Did Carole bake it?"

"Who else?"

He checked his watch again. "Well, I guess I could stop by for a second, just to wish Jenni a happy birthday."

"Good! I knew we could talk you into it, didn't you, Dana? Dana?" Elaine snapped her fingers.

"Huh? Oh, yeah...the party." The last thing in the world Dana felt like doing at the moment was celebrating, but the station employees were like family, and Dana would never let family down. The least she could do was paste on a happy smile for a few minutes.

"Shoes." Elaine pointed at Dana's nylon-clad feet.

"What? Oh, gosh." She retreated behind her desk and slipped on her high-heeled pumps. "Okay, let's go."

The kitchen set was at the far end of the building and up a flight of stairs. Dana followed the others in a fog, still reeling under the implications of those damn computer charts Elliott had shown her. Numbers whirled before her eyes like a swarm of taunting insects. There must be *some* way to change those numbers, some way to make the income figures greater than the outgo figures. Maybe she could—

"Surprise!"

Dana clapped her hand to her chest and fell back a step in astonishment. Beneath a festive web of blue crepe-paper streamers, the entire station staff was beaming at her. Elaine lifted her hand and led them in a rousing rendition of "For She's a Jolly Good Fellow." There was a cake all right, but it had Dana's name written in icing, not Jenni's. Above the set hung a gaudy homemade banner that said Happy Anniversary.

Dana's dark brown eyes widened in confusion. "I don't get it!" she cried when the last chorus died away. "What *is* all this?"

"Five years, Dana!" Andy Gallagher stepped forward and planted a big kiss on her cheek. "Five years ago today was your very first day as station manager! Did you forget your own anniversary?"

"I—I guess I did," she replied, slightly breathless. Through the scattered applause and shouts of congratulation she heard the *pop!* of a champagne cork.

Carole wove her way through the crowd, passing out glasses. "A toast!" Andy shouted. "Come on, everyone, gather 'round for a toast!"

Someone stuck a glass in Dana's hand and splashed champagne into it. In a daze she accepted the hugs and congratulations of the people who were her co-workers, her friends, her family. "Speech!" someone shouted, tapping on a champagne glass. "Come on, Dana! Speech!"

Swallowing a huge lump in her throat, she forced her lips to form a wobbly smile. She gazed at all the smiling faces surrounding her, glowing with affection and respect.

This was the perfect moment—if such a moment could be called perfect—to share the disastrous news Elliott had brought her. Dana caught the accountant's eye at the back of the crowd, his expression full of grim sympathy.

She couldn't bring herself to do it. "Thanks, everyone. I—I—well, I know you're not going to believe this, but for once I'm actually speechless!" Her curving lips felt numb as she raised her glass to the sound of scattered laughter. "Here's to the next five years!"

The set echoed with shouts of "Here! Here!" as Dana tilted back her head and downed an enormous gulp of champagne.

It didn't help. Watching that crowd of happy smiling faces, Dana could only wonder what those same faces were going to look like once they found out they were all about to lose their jobs.

* * *

The night air felt cold blowing through the open car window, but Dana welcomed the refreshing chill after all the hot air she'd had to contend with in Sacramento that day.

She hadn't wasted any time wringing her hands and feeling sorry for herself after Elliott had dropped his little bombshell yesterday afternoon. Bright and early this morning she'd been on the road to the state capital, ready to plead, cajole, threaten—whatever it took to wheedle a few measly dollars out of those penny-pinching legislators.

Funding for a tiny public television station would be a mere drop in the huge bucket that was the California state budget. Dana was well acquainted from past fund-raising efforts with the ins and outs of the state capital. She understood the back-room political machinations, the promises and favors exchanged in those corridors of power. She knew how to play the game, and in the past she'd usually emerged victorious.

Not today, though. She'd called in past favors, promised the moon—all to no avail. Where Channel Five was concerned, the state coffers were sealed tight as a drum until next year.

Only, next year would be too late.

Dana was all in favor of balancing the state budget, but surely the pittance she was requesting wouldn't tip the scales. *Probably earmarked those funds for a study on how many angels can dance on the head of a pin,* she thought in disgust.

She'd been so agitated by her failure that she'd cruised right past the usual highway turnoff for Pine Creek. Now she found herself winding along hilly, unfamiliar back roads late at night, exhausted from her exasperating ordeal and the two-hour drive from Sacramento.

The wind whistling through her hair helped a little. She flicked on an oldies radio station, hoping some good old-fashioned rock and roll would help keep her alert. She hadn't driven this route in years, since there were faster, less roundabout ways to get to Pine Creek. If she didn't pay attention, she was liable to miss the road she was looking for and wind up lost in the mountains.

Gosh, but it was dark with no moon out tonight. *Stupid!* she thought suddenly. *What do you think high beams are for?* She was reaching for the headlight switch when a light-colored blur darted into the road in front of her.

Deer! her mind shrieked at the same instant her foot hit the brake. The rear end of her Toyota fishtailed, tires screaming in protest, and Dana frantically cranked the steering wheel in a desperate effort to regain control of the car. Some deeply buried instinct reminded her to turn in the direction of the skid, but she'd been too intent on avoiding the deer and reacted a second too late.

The Toyota careened off the pavement and slammed into the ditch alongside the road.

Sensations filtered back gradually.... The faint stench of burning rubber...the persistent beat of the radio, eerily loud in the otherwise silent darkness...the throbbing pain in her head.

With a groan, Dana delicately brushed her fingers across her forehead. The skin didn't seem to be broken, but she was going to have a whale of a lump there in pretty short order.

She took a quick physical survey, finding no other apparent injuries. Thank goodness she'd been wearing her seat belt. Taking a deep breath, she twisted her head around to look back over her shoulder, praying she wouldn't see a deer lying in the road or hobbling beside it injured. In the dim red illumination from her still-glowing taillights, she saw no sign of the deer.

Dana exhaled a long sigh of relief. She hadn't *felt* the car hit anything, but it all happened so fast....

Now what? Even if the car started, would she be able to back it out of this ditch?

She groped for the key, twisted on the ignition. The engine made a pitiful grating sound, as if gears were grinding painfully against each other. No dice.

Well, at least now she didn't have to worry about how she was going to get the car out of the ditch. The tow truck would pull it.

She peered down the deserted road in both directions, trying to see a light or some other sign of humanity. But the bends in the road prevented her from seeing very far, and what she *could* see was pitch blackness.

Well, the longer she waited for help, the longer she was going to sit here. At this late hour the cars were likely to be few and far between. She would just have to hike up the road a ways until she found a house, preferably with inhabitants who were still awake. Although she didn't exactly relish the idea of tottering up a lonely country road in her high heels late at night, what choice did she have? Besides, she'd never been one to wait passively for assistance.

Dana unbuckled her seat belt, and pulled on the door handle. The door opened about three inches before stubbornly refusing to budge. She craned her neck out the window, trying to see what the obstruction was, but it was too dark to tell if the door was wedged against a rock or if it had been dented in such a way that it simply wouldn't open any farther.

Aha! With a gleeful chuckle she remembered the flashlight in the glove compartment.

Unfortunately, what she *hadn't* remembered was to put any fresh batteries in it recently. With one last series of frustrated clicks, Dana tossed the useless instrument aside. What she *really* wanted was to toss it out the window, but with her luck she'd probably clonk some poor defenseless bunny rabbit on the head.

Before she resorted to crawling out the window, she decided to see if the passenger door was in any better shape. This plan would have been a lot easier if the car's gearshift stick wasn't in the way. With a groan of resignation, Dana hiked up her narrow skirt and attempted to squeeze her five-foot-five-inch frame around it—quite a challenge considering the compact size of the car and the steep angle at which it was wedged into the ditch.

"Ow!" She banged her sore head against the ceiling light. "Damn it...."

"You all right in there?"

Dana froze in her contortionist's position, skirt hiked up around her thighs, rear end in the air. *Oh, God, of all the embarrassing moments for a rescuer to arrive....*

Quickly she wrestled herself backward into the driver's seat again. A high-powered flashlight shining directly into her face nearly blinded her. "Would you mind getting that thing out of my eyes?" she said irritably to cover up her embarrassment.

"Sorry." Her rescuer aimed the beam to one side, but the bright image lingered, making it impossible for Dana to make out his face—even if she *had* wanted to meet his eyes. "Are you hurt or anything?" She thought she detected a hint of amusement mixed with the concern in his voice.

"I just bumped my head," she replied, resenting the fact that he seemed to find her predicament entertaining. "But my door's stuck, and I can't get out."

"So I noticed."

She chose to ignore his ungallant remark. "Can you tell what's holding the door shut?"

He stepped back and swept the flashlight beam across the side of the car. "Hmm, yeah…the front of the door's bashed in. Hang on a sec—I've got some tools in my truck. I'll have you out of there in a jiffy."

Dana drummed her fingers on the steering wheel, telling herself she should be grateful and relieved that someone had come along so soon. If only he hadn't come along just in time to find her in that humiliating, undignified pose. . . .

"Here, hold this." When he handed Dana the flashlight his hand brushed hers, and she felt calluses on his palm.

The beam wavered a bit while she aimed the flashlight where he was working. She was tempted to flick it across his face so she could at least get a glimpse of the guy, but something restrained her.

He certainly seemed to know what he was doing. A few expert levering motions with a pry bar, a couple of whacks with some other mysterious tool, and he pushed himself to his feet. "Let's try it now."

He opened the door with only a brief rasp of metal against metal, swung his arm out with a flourish and bowed.

Dana scrambled out of the car. "Very funny," she muttered.

"Beg pardon?"

"I said, thanks for your help." She tugged her skirt as far down as it would go.

"Yeah, that's what I thought you said." He knelt to the ground and picked up his tools. "Look, can I, uh, take you to the hospital or anything?"

"Hospital? I just bumped my head a little, that's all."

He swung the flashlight beam into her face, then quickly away. "Doesn't look so little to me."

Before she could protest or dodge beyond his reach, he stepped close to touch the lump on her forehead.

"Ouch! Cut that out!"

He had her practically pinned against the car. "Hold still, will you? I'm trying to see how serious it is." His fingers grazed over Dana's skin, making her shiver. She could smell his pleasant masculine scent of sweat and denim.

"I suppose in addition to being an auto mechanic you're also a doctor," she said, uncharacteristic sarcasm lacing her voice. But his gentle inspection was oddly unsettling.

"Wrong on both counts." He dropped his hand from her brow. "But I've seen a few bruises and broken bones in my time. Head injuries are tricky. You could have a concussion and not even know it." He returned to his pickup truck and tossed the tools in back. "I still think I should take you to the emergency room."

"That won't be necessary." His insistent concern flustered her. "But if you could drop me off someplace where there's a phone..."

He braced himself against the cab of his pickup with one hand and regarded her thoughtfully. At least she *thought* that's what he was doing. It was hard to tell in the darkness.

"My place is just down the road," he said finally, jerking his thumb in the direction she'd come from. "You can use the phone there."

Warning alarms sounded in Dana's head. Or maybe her ears were ringing from a concussion.

"Don't worry," he said, somehow correctly interpreting her hesitation. "I'm not some crazed maniac who cruises the back roads late at night looking for beautiful women who crash their cars into ditches."

"I was trying to avoid hitting a deer," she said indignantly. *Beautiful?*

"So you nearly killed yourself instead."

"I didn't exactly plan it that way."

"What are you doing way out here this late at night, anyway? Besides listening to the Beach Boys, I mean."

"Huh? Oh." She ducked back into the car and switched off the radio. "Coming back from Sacramento."

"Kind of dark to be taking the scenic route, isn't it?"

"I missed the regular turnoff, okay? Now if you wouldn't mind giving me a lift to your place..."

"You tried starting your car?"

She nodded. "It's broken."

"Broken, huh?" He rubbed the nape of his neck, rolled his head around in a slow circle as if his muscles were sore. "Well, if it weren't so late and so dark, I'd take a look at it myself. Could probably hitch up the pickup and pull you out of the ditch, too, though it *is* kind of muddy after all the rain we've been having."

"It'd be easier if I just called the auto club," Dana said hastily.

"Yeah, you're probably right. Okay, come on—hop in."

She reached back into the car to switch off the headlights, then groped around on the floor and between the seats until she found her purse. When she stood suddenly upright, a wave of dizziness overcame her, turning her knees to jelly. As she started to buckle like a folding chair, the man lunged forward and flung his arms around her waist to support her. When he tugged Dana's sagging body up against his, his whiskery jaw sanded her cheek, making her skin tingle.

"Easy now," he crooned. "You've had a bad scare, that's all. Delayed reaction."

"I thought you said I had a concussion," she mumbled against his neck, too wobbly to care that a complete stranger was practically embracing her.

"I didn't want to worry you." Before Dana could protest, he scooped her up against his chest and carried her to the pickup.

There *must* be something wrong with her head. Why else would she almost *enjoy* being cradled helplessly in his arms?

He opened the passenger door and set her gently inside. By the time he walked around the truck and got in, Dana's head was beginning to clear. She scooted over against the door, as far away from him as she could get.

He paused with his hand on the ignition key. "You must be feeling better," he said. "You've got that feisty gleam in your eye again."

Dana's chin inched up a notch. "It's too dark to see any gleams," she pointed out, "feisty or otherwise."

"Want me to turn on the flashlight again?"

"No!" she answered quickly. She could just imagine what a mess she must be—clothes in disarray, hair like a haystack, a lump the size of a tennis ball crowning her forehead. Maybe the darkness was a blessing after all.

They rode in silence for perhaps a quarter of a mile. *Thank goodness I didn't have this accident in the city,* Dana thought. Otherwise she would never have dared accept a ride from a stranger. Of course, it was highly unlikely a deer would have leapt in front of her car in the city.

"What are you smiling at?" The sudden sound of his voice made her jump.

"What? Oh . . . nothing." How could he see the expression on her face? Dana muffled the impulse to instruct him to keep his eyes on the road. She could just imagine the crack he would make about her not being in a position to give advice on driving.

Why was she so certain about what he would say? They'd only known each other for what, half an hour now? But there was something . . . familiar about him, as if perhaps they'd met before.

She was about to extend her hand and introduce herself when she had second thoughts about touching him again. Recalling the delicious, tingling sensation she'd experienced each time they'd made physical contact, she decided that shaking his hand would be about as smart as poking her finger into a light socket.

Dana settled her hand back into her lap. This guy might not be a crazed maniac, but there was definitely something about him that set her nerves on edge. The air around him bristled like the atmosphere before a thunderstorm, crackling with electricity, volatile and untamed, full of the sense that something scary and exciting was looming on the horizon.

What nonsense! she scoffed silently. She was dazed from the accident, that was all. It was late at night and she was getting punchy.

The pickup slowed down, then turned into a narrow gravel road beneath a canopy of tall cedars. A small Private Drive sign marked the turnoff, but even in daylight a person could easily miss it unless he knew exactly where he was going.

They followed the drive for several hundred yards before a house loomed out of the trees. The man brought

the truck to a stop beside the front steps. "Here we are."
He climbed out of the pickup and with seemingly effort-
less speed was at Dana's door before she could open it
herself.

He grasped her elbow as she stepped to the ground.
"I'm fine," she insisted, not wanting to seem ungrate-
ful, but anxious to avoid any more unsettling contact
with him.

He released her. "If you say so." With no further
hovering he preceded Dana up the front steps.

She got an impression of wood and stone and wide expanses of glass. Too bad she would never see the house
in daylight, because it seemed like something special.

Dana negotiated the steps to the front porch with no
trouble. She was feeling much stronger now—no more
dizziness, no more spots swirling in front of her eyes, no
more knees refusing to support her.

Inside the house he switched on a light, and for the first
time Dana got a good look at her rescuer. Tousled brown
hair, intelligent gray eyes, sturdy jaw faintly shadowed
with stubble. His rugged, well-tanned features looked as
if they'd been carved from a block of highest quality,
fine-grained wood.

As she tried not to ogle him too obviously, his mouth
quirked into a faintly cynical, definitely sexy half grin.
Even in mud-spattered jeans and a faded blue T-shirt, he
was the most attractive man Dana had ever seen—six feet
of lean, hard-muscled, mouth-watering male.

It took her about three seconds to recognize him.

All of a sudden she felt light-headed again.

Chapter Two

She couldn't believe it was him.

Rick West. He'd been responsible for Dana's nearly flunking tenth-grade geometry. How could she possibly concentrate on trapezoids and triangles when her heart was full of sighs and her head full of daydreams about the absolute dreamiest guy in school?

Only problem was, Rick West hadn't known she was alive. Why would he? He was a senior; Dana a lowly sophomore. He had every girl at Pine Creek High School chasing after him. He was a track star, student-body president and chairman of the honor society. Why would he even *notice* Dana Sheridan, when she got so uncharacteristically tongue-tied around him that she could barely mumble hello when they passed in the hallway?

Well, she wasn't tongue-tied around Rick West any longer. In fact, Dana suddenly became downright chatty, seized by the ridiculous fear that he might somehow remember her or be able to read in her face how she'd once worshiped him from afar. And she'd already suffered more than her share of embarrassment this evening.

"Gosh, did you get that mud all over you while you were working on my car? I'm really sorry. Look, I'll just make a quick phone call to the auto club and then I'll get out of your hair." She reached for the phone. "Don't let me keep you from, uh, whatever you'd be doing if I weren't here. I've caused you enough trouble already. You probably want to go take a shower or something." She punched out the phone number. "I'll be fine waiting here by myself. Really. I promise not to steal the silverware or anything." She gave him an overly bright smile.

Rick was studying her as he would an interesting specimen in biology class. "Do I know you?" he asked finally, a sexy pucker forming between his eyebrows.

Dana cleared her throat. "I, uh, I think we might have gone to high school together or something. Hello, auto club? What? Yes, I'll hold." She tapped her foot nervously and gazed at the ceiling.

"What was your name again?"

"Umm . . . Dana. Dana Sheridan."

"Dana Sheridan. Hmm . . ."

She turned away and squinched her eyes shut. This was so dumb, to worry like this. If she had an ounce of sophistication she would just confess her schoolgirl crush and she and Rick would have a good laugh together.

Oh, God, what if one of my high school friends ever told him how crazy I was about him?

So much for sophistication.

Rick snapped his fingers. "Dana Sheridan! Say, weren't you one of those kids on that homecoming float? The ones who got suspended for squirting grape juice at the visiting team's bleachers during the pregame parade?''

"It was Kool-Aid," Dana muttered, wishing there were a big hole nearby she could crawl into. "It didn't even stain their clothing. I never understood why the principal made such a big deal out of it."

Rick chuckled. "Now I remember you. Weren't you also involved in that prank with the dissected frog, when the vice-principal opened her purse and—"

"What? Yes, I'm still holding," Dana said loudly into the receiver, even though no one had come on the other end of the line. She smiled feebly at Rick. "Gee, high school sure seems a long time ago, doesn't it?"

"Sure does. By the way, in case you don't remember my name, I'm Rick West." He stuck out his hand, noticed how grimy it was and pulled it back. "Guess I did get kind of dirty working on your car. I think I will go hop in the shower and wash some of this mud off." He started to leave, then turned back. "If you're sure you don't want me to drive you to the emergency room, that is."

"I'm positive."

His mouth twitched as if he were trying to keep a straight face. "I won't be long."

Dana heaved a sigh of relief when he finally left the room. It figured. All Rick remembered her for were a few childish escapades. Not exactly the kind of impression she'd once hoped to make on him. Well, if he'd been that oblivious to her other charms, at least he probably had no idea what a crush she'd had on him.

But hoo, boy! He was even more of a dreamboat now than he'd been in high school.

Dana took advantage of his absence to make a quick survey of her surroundings. The living room was all sleek lines and square angles, the furniture constructed of some kind of light-colored wood—white oak, maybe. Large cushions in shades of turquoise, cream and peach were strewn about, and the few well-chosen paintings and select pieces of pottery on display followed a southwestern desert motif. The room was devoid of knickknacks, family photos or any other personal items that would give it a cozy, lived-in feel. It was an attractive, masculine room, but it felt more like an art gallery or a picture in a magazine than a home.

That impression, even more than the absence of a gold band on his ring finger, told Dana that Rick lived here alone.

Well, it was no concern of hers whether he lived alone or with a troop of circus performers. Her only concern should be getting herself and her poor car back into town.

When he finally came on the line, the auto club dispatcher wasn't encouraging. "We had a five-car pileup on Route 49 a little while ago. Most of the local tow trucks are over there. I got one out on a dead-battery call, and one that's outta commission till a new part gets in from Sacramento." Dana could practically hear him shrug. "What I'm sayin' is, it's gonna be a while, lady."

Terrific. Stifling a groan of dismay, Dana gave the dispatcher directions to Rick's house. Meanwhile she was mentally running down a checklist of friends she could call instead to come pick her up. They and their families were sure to be sound asleep at this hour, and although Dana hated to impose on people, she certainly didn't want to remain under the same roof as Rick West any longer than necessary. Even after all these years the man still had an undeniably adverse effect on her nervous system.

She was gnawing on her knuckle with indecision when someone rapped on the front door. Dana could hear the shower running somewhere toward the back of the house. What the heck was she supposed to do now?

With one last dubious glance in the direction Rick had disappeared, she rose from the couch and cautiously cracked open the front door.

She blinked in surprise at the figure revealed in the yellow glow of the porch light. His posture was military, his clothes straight from the army-surplus store. At first glance, the portly old gentleman appeared to be one of those crazy survivalist types who holed up in the mountains waiting for Armageddon.

Either that or the Green Berets were recruiting senior citizens these days.

"Yes?" Dana asked warily.

The man's white walrus mustache twitched in surprise. "I say, is Rick about?" His booming voice carried a British accent.

"Rick? Why, er..." At that moment she heard bare feet thudding across the hardwood floor. Turning, she caught her breath at the vision that greeted her.

Rick, clad only in a clean pair of jeans and a white towel slung around his neck, reached past Dana to pull the door wide open. A whiff of shampoo tickled her nose. Water droplets glistened in the brown curls matting his chest. His hair stood up in damp spikes. He looked and smelled wonderful.

"Come on in," he told the man on the porch.

The visitor's blue eyes darted uncertainly from Rick to Dana. "Don't mean to interrupt," he said, clearing his throat with a loud *harrumph*.

Rick chuckled. "It's not what you think, Pop."

Pop? This quaint old codger was Rick's father?

"I was passing through the woods, saw the light on."
As he marched into the living room, assorted gear jingled from his canvas belt—Swiss-army knife, canteen, flashlight. "I'm on the trail of the elusive northern spotted owl. Been reports of a sighting in these parts, though they aren't usually found this far south."

"My father is somewhat of a night owl himself," Rick said to Dana with a wry grin, "as well as an avid bird-watcher. He lives at the end of this private drive."

"I see," Dana said. Wait a second. Wasn't Rick's father—?

"Thought if you were still awake, we could have a drink together." The older man's eyebrows wiggled like snow-white caterpillars. "Didn't realize you had company."

"I was coming back late from the job site when I found Ms. Sheridan and her car stuck in the ditch just up the road."

"Gadzooks! I trust you weren't injured?" The old man's forehead furrowed with concern.

"Just a slight bump on the head, that's all. Excuse me, but aren't you—"

"She won't let me drive her to the hospital." Rick settled himself into a chair, propped his bare feet on the coffee table and shot Dana a look of exasperation.

"For the umpteenth time, I'm perfectly all right."

"Sheridan…Sheridan…" Rick's father tugged on his mustache. "Any relation to Ben Sheridan?"

"You knew my father?" Dana brightened instantly.

"Not well, though I had occasion to meet him a few times over the years. He was a fine man."

"Thank you." She peered at him closely. "Correct me if I'm wrong, but aren't you Alistair West?"

He doffed his shapeless khaki cap and looked pleased. "Indeed I am, my dear. Been a long time since anyone's recognized me."

Dana had completely forgotten that Rick had a famous father, though it was common knowledge locally that the reclusive songwriter lived out here on Whisper Ridge. She seized his hand and pumped it enthusiastically. "I'm sure you've heard it a thousand times, but it's really a thrill to meet you."

"Very kind of you, dear girl." He lowered his eyes modestly, although his chest puffed up a bit.

"In fact, your name came up at the station just yesterday."

Alistair West looked puzzled. Rick leaned forward and said, "That's right—didn't your dad run Channel Five?"

Gee, at least he remembered *something* about her besides her youthful high jinks. "Yes, he did, and after my father died I took over as station manager." She turned back to Alistair. "We're going to be running one of your musicals during our membership drive next month—*Match Made in Heaven.*"

"Ah, yes! Always been one of my favorites. Fond memories, don't you know." His blue eyes crinkled when he smiled. "That was your mother's first leading role, Rick." He shook his head. "She was the loveliest young woman I'd ever laid eyes on. And her voice?" He bunched his fingertips together and blew a kiss into the air. "Sweeter than a nightingale's."

Dana's jaw dropped. She snapped her fingers. "That's right! You were married to Chloe St. James. And that means..." She wheeled around to face Rick with excitement. "Chloe St. James was your mother!" Dana had been too smitten in high school to give much thought to Rick's parents. Now, however, the fact that his father had been a famous songwriter, his mother a movie starlet, only made him more intriguing.

Rick managed to look bored and annoyed at the same time. He bounded impatiently to his feet and tossed the towel over the back of his chair. "Did you get hold of the auto club?"

The abrupt shift of gears bewildered her for a moment. "What? Oh, yes." Dana's face fell as she recalled her predicament. "They told me they're awfully busy tonight, and it's going to be a while before they can send out a tow truck." She twisted her fingers together in her lap. "I've been trying to figure out someone I can call to come get me."

Rick slicked back his damp hair, wrestling with his conscience. The easiest solution to Dana Sheridan's problem would be to invite her to spend what remained of the night in his guest room. It would be an easy matter to tow her car into town himself when he headed back to the job site in the morning.

But he wasn't sure how he felt about spending the night under the same roof with this stubborn, stranded, sexy intruder. Rick was a man who valued his privacy, and Dana was a woman who asked too many questions. He'd seen the glimmer in her eye when the subject of his mother came up. She'd probably want to sit up all night chatting about the good old days in Hollywood.

Rick nearly snorted. The only things he associated with Hollywood were phony glitter and glamour, bitter tragedy and betrayal. Not exactly the kinds of topics he was eager to reminisce about—even with a woman as charming as Dana.

All right, he admitted it. He *did* find her charming. He liked the way she refused to be coddled or fussed over, the way she hadn't burst into tears after the trauma of running her car off the road. No hysterics, no damsel-in-distress routine.

Well, you didn't get to be general manager of a television station by being a cream puff—especially if you were a woman. Rick still found it difficult to reconcile this confident, capable woman in her natty, professional suit with his hazy memory of a ringleader of teenage mischief-makers.

Yet behind her competent, self-sufficient exterior he detected a hint of something soft and vulnerable. Maybe it was her faintly bruised appearance—the smudge of dirt on her cheek, the undoubtedly painful lump on her forehead. Maybe it was the windswept disarray of shoulder-length brunette hair framing her face, the silky, untamed tresses softening her pretty, strong-willed features.

Or maybe it was something Rick saw lurking in those deep, chocolate-brown eyes, a glint of some secret fear. Unless his instincts were completely off base, Dana Sheridan had a lot more serious worries on her mind than getting her car out of the ditch.

He wished he knew what was really troubling her.

Damn it, that was exactly why he shouldn't ask her to stay here a minute longer than necessary! Already he was drawn toward her, drawn toward all the problems and complications he didn't need or want cluttering up his well-ordered existence.

If he gave her half a chance, Dana Sheridan might very well weasel her way into his life, inch by inch, until she finally consumed him completely.

For God's sake, hadn't he done enough for her already? Extricating her from her car . . . offering to drive her to the hospital . . . bringing her into his home so she could use the telephone. . . .

This wasn't some primitive ancient culture where saving someone's life made you responsible for that person forever. So why did a little voice keep prodding Rick to suggest Dana stay here until morning?

Oh, hell. His conscience wouldn't let him sleep even if he *did* kick her out. "Look, there's no sense in your sitting up till the wee hours of the morning waiting for the auto club to show up." He picked up the towel, snapped it taut between his fists. "Why not spend the night in my guest room? In the morning I can bring both you and your car into town."

Dana looked startled. Rick enjoyed catching her off guard. She shot a self-conscious glance at his father before replying. "Thanks, but I think it would be better if I got out of your way as soon as possible. I've imposed enough as it is."

Rick slung the towel over his shoulder and propped his hands on the back of his chair. "Look, I can't just let you wait out here all by yourself, and I'm dog tired. You'd be doing both of us a favor if you'd call the auto club back and let me tow your car into town tomorrow." He glanced at the driftwood clock on the wall. "Today, rather."

"Well..." She fiddled with the top button of her high-collared white blouse. The stubborn set of her chin was beginning to droop a little.

"I think it's a capital idea," Alistair said, pushing himself creakily to his feet. "My dear girl, if you don't mind my saying so, you look as though you could use some rest yourself." He waved an arm around the room. "Rick has more than enough space here. Positively rattles around in it all by himself. I'm sure you'll be quite comfortable."

Dana swallowed. She felt kind of funny, discussing this in front of Alistair. It was one thing to stay here when she and Rick were the only ones who knew about it. It was another matter entirely for Rick's father to know that she'd spent the night with his son.

Yet the distinguished old songwriter would hardly have given his blessing if everything weren't perfectly proper and aboveboard, would he?

She was silly to worry about what people might think. Besides, if she insisted on waiting for the auto club, Rick would no doubt insist on staying up to keep her company until the tow truck arrived. It *would* make more sense for both of them to get some sleep.

"All right," she said, mentally crossing her fingers and hoping she wasn't making the biggest mistake of her life. "I'll stay, if you're sure it's not too much trouble."

"Excellent!" Alistair rubbed his hands together. "Well, I'll be off, then." He clanked and jangled his way to the front door. Sneaking up on a northern spotted owl was going to take a miracle, Dana thought. Or else an extremely hard-of-hearing owl.

She made a quick phone call to cancel the tow truck. As she hung up, Rick was just closing the door after his father. "I'll stop by tomorrow after work, Pop."

The *click* of the door latching echoed through the room. The sudden silence seemed to emphasize the fact that the two of them were alone now. "What exactly *is* it you do for a living?" Dana asked, a little too brightly.

There she goes, Rick thought, *peppering me with questions already.* He *knew* this was a bad idea....

"I design and build houses."

"You mean like an architect? Or a building contractor?"

"Both." He switched off the overhead light so the only illumination spilled in from the hallway. "Come on, I'll show you to the guest room."

Jeez, prying some simple answers from this guy was like pulling teeth, Dana thought as she followed him down the hall. *I've heard of the strong, silent type, but this is ridiculous.* Funny, but this wasn't the same outgoing kid she remembered from high school.

Rick leaned into the first door on the right and flipped on the light switch. "Here's your room. Towels on the dresser, bathroom down the hall on the left." He jerked a thumb over his shoulder. "See you in the morning. We'll leave at seven."

Well, good night, Clint Eastwood, she thought, closing the door after him. She pressed her ear against the wood, waiting to hear his bedroom door click shut before she scurried down the hall to the bathroom.

Dana's reflection in the mirror almost made her yelp with dismay. No wonder Rick had wanted to take her to the hospital. She looked like a train-wreck survivor. Dirt-streaked face, hair a tangled mess, huge ugly knot above her right eyebrow. And her expensive navy blue suit would never be the same again.

Not exactly cover-girl material for *Career Woman* magazine.

Oh, well. All she needed was a shower and a good night's sleep. If she *could* sleep, that is, knowing that Rick West was snoring happily away just down the hall. She wondered if he slept in the nude.

Ha! Something you'll *never find out,* she scolded her reflection. The bright fluorescent glare threw every bump and bruise, every line of worry and exhaustion into high relief. Dana winced.

She flipped off the light with disgust and tiptoed back down the hall to the guest room. Hopefully she would look less bedraggled after getting some sleep.

No such luck. In the morning Dana yanked a brush through her freshly washed hair, doing her best to arrange her bangs over the fist-sized bump, which had turned a hideous shade of purple overnight.

She'd only gotten a few hours' sleep in the unfamiliar bed before the sizzling smell of bacon had awakened her at the crack of dawn. Dark circles rimmed the puffy eyes that greeted her in the mirror when she stumbled down the hall to the bathroom. After her quick shower, she dressed in the same clothes she'd worn yesterday, hating to do so, but knowing she didn't have a whole lot of choice.

No wonder she was in such a grumpy mood as she followed her nose to Rick's kitchen.

He lowered his newspaper long enough to say, "'Morning. Coffee's on the counter. Help yourself to bacon and eggs."

She found the mug he'd set out for her, took careful aim and managed to fill it without sloshing hot coffee over the sides. "I'm not much of a breakfast eater, thanks."

He set down the paper. He was freshly shaven, clear-eyed and looked ready to take on the world. Dana could just imagine what a lovely sight *she* was to behold. She hid the lower part of her face behind the mug and gingerly sipped her coffee.

"Don't you know breakfast is the most important meal of the day?" he asked, demonstrating his point by forking some scrambled eggs into his mouth.

"Spare me the public service announcement," she replied, grimacing.

"How about some toast?"

"Okay, okay, I'll have some toast. Just one slice, though."

Rick stood and stepped over to a carved wooden bread box. "Are you always so cheerful first thing in the morning?"

"I'm not exactly a morning person," she mumbled.

"Somehow I could have guessed that." He popped two slices of wheat bread into the toaster.

"It's just that I didn't get much sleep, and I'm worried about my car and everything...." Dana's voice trailed off. She knew she was behaving badly, but this setting was too cozy, too intimate. Despite her schoolgirl fantasies, she barely knew the man, and here she was sharing breakfast with him! Maybe subconsciously she was trying to push Rick away with her boorish behavior.

He reached into the refrigerator for some butter and raspberry jam. "You're lucky I came along last night," he said. "Not too much traffic along the road at that hour."

Dana knew he was right, but somehow lucky wasn't exactly how she felt at the moment. She sipped some more coffee. "How come *you* were driving by so late?"

Rick set a plate of toast in front of her. Not even 7:00 a.m. and already she was starting in with the questions. "I'm building a house over on Juniper Street." He noticed she didn't say anything about the extra slice of toast he'd slipped her. "The electrician's behind schedule, so I had to stay late last night and finish up the wiring myself before the drywall contractor comes today."

Against his will, Rick found himself musing on how downright desirable Dana looked this morning. Her damp hair curtained her face, little wisps curling along her jawline. He caught a whiff of his usual brand of shampoo, and wondered why it never smelled that good on him.

Sleep had gently blurred her features, leaving her looking soft and kind of fuzzy in an adorable sort of way. She looked, well . . . cuddly.

The idea of cuddling up with her sent a shaft of desire through Rick's loins. He shifted uncomfortably, refilled his mug and took a huge swig of coffee, nearly scalding his mouth.

"So you're a general contractor?" Dana prodded, rescuing Rick from his own foolish thoughts. "That means you oversee all the workmen building a house, right?"

He cleared his throat. "I also design houses. I started out as an architect." He scraped the leftover bacon and eggs onto his plate, dropped two more pieces of bread into the toaster. "I got tired of watching other builders screw up the houses I'd designed."

"If you want something done right, do it yourself."

"Exactly."

"So where'd you go to college?"

"Berkeley."

She grinned. "Student radical, huh?"

"Hardly," he said with a snort.

Dana propped her chin on her fist and watched him smear jam on another piece of toast. "Do you always eat such a huge breakfast?"

Rick shrugged. "Never know when I'll get a chance to take a break for lunch. Or *if* I'll get a chance."

"I guess building houses is hard work."

"Sometimes." He gestured with his fork. "This house was the first one I both designed and built."

"Really?"

Nodding, he picked up a piece of bacon. "My father still lives in the house where I grew up, just up the hill a ways. I moved back in with him while I was building this place."

Dana's dark eyebrows knit together. "How come you weren't raised in the Los Angeles area? What with your parents being in the movies and all?"

Suddenly Rick's bacon tasted like a mouthful of metal filings. He chewed carefully, swallowed a big lump. How had they gotten on this subject, anyway? That's what happened the minute you started answering questions—people felt as if they had a right to pry into your personal life.

What do you do for a living?

Do you always eat such a big breakfast?

Why do you and your father live like recluses five hundred miles from Hollywood?

He couldn't figure out how Dana had tricked him into opening up as much as he had already.

Rick crumpled his paper napkin into a ball. "My mother was killed in a plane crash when I was five."

Dana's hand flew to her mouth. She set her mug down with a hasty *clunk*.

"She was flying to the filming location of her next movie. My father retired from show business after that, and we moved up here."

"Rick, I'm sorry—I—I'd forgotten how your mother died."

"Guess you're not up on your Hollywood trivia, huh?" He got up and dumped the rest of his food into the garbage.

"Well, I'd hardly call it trivia, but no, I'm not exactly an expert on show biz."

He fixed her with a skeptical look. "I thought you were in television."

"Well, *public* television. Which isn't to say we just show documentaries on the life cycle of the Saharan sand flea or anything—we also show programs that fall into the category of pure entertainment. Like that old musical your father wrote the lyrics for, the one starring your...mother."

Dana could have tied her tongue into a knot. How could she have been so insensitive? Obviously the subject of his mother still struck a painful chord with Rick. And here she was, old Foot-in-the-Mouth, referring to the poor woman again.

Rick's face looked like a thundercloud before all hell broke loose. Wordlessly he gathered up their plates and practically dropped them into the sink. Dana wanted to reach out and touch him, to apologize for her stupid blunder and offer him her sympathy.

But she was at least sensitive enough to realize that would only aggravate matters. At the moment, Rick was as prickly as a porcupine, bristling with resentment. With a pang of regret, Dana realized she would probably never get the chance to make up for her tactlessness. This unexpected reunion was just about over.

Rick wiped his hands on a dish towel, then tossed it onto the counter. "Let's go get your car," he said, gray eyes simmering like molten steel.

As she followed him outside to his pickup truck, Dana couldn't help but wonder if Rick's bad mood was covering up more than the lingering pain of his mother's untimely death. His reaction seemed a bit out of proportion for something that had happened so long ago.

But it looked as though that was *one* question she would never get an answer to.

* * *

The cloying sound of Muzak filtered through the telephone. Dana wriggled her bare toes and drummed her fingers impatiently. How could they take a perfectly good rock-and-roll classic like "Good Golly Miss Molly" and arrange it for strings? A crime, that's what it was.

The secretary came back on the line. "Ms. Sheridan? I'm sorry, but the senator's schedule is all booked up this week."

"What about next week?"

"He leaves to go back to Washington on Monday." The woman sounded smugly delighted to be imparting bad news.

"Isn't there some way I could speak with him? Just for a few minutes? It's terribly important." Dana hated to beg with this officious bureaucrat, but desperate times called for desperate measures.

"*All* of the senator's appointments are important," his secretary replied in a tone suggesting that Dana's business probably wasn't.

"But didn't the senator promise during his last campaign to make himself more available to his constituents?" Dana realized she might as well try to argue with a brick wall, but her irritated frustration, not to mention her inborn stubbornness, wouldn't let her quit so easily.

"Goodness, the senator could hardly meet with *all* his constituents, could he?" His secretary sounded positively shocked at the suggestion. "He wouldn't have any time to take care of his official government duties."

"Gee, you mean the country might have to do without National Dill Pickle Week?"

Click.

Dana studied the receiver. "Guess I just blew my chance for an invitation to the senator's next victory bash." She slammed down the phone in disgust. Good Golly Miss Molly—*now* what? The senator had been her last hope of obtaining some extra federal funding for the station. Obviously the government was going to be no help....

A couple quick knocks and her office door opened. Jenni Carpenter, the volunteer who worked three days a week as station receptionist, secretary and all-around gofer, sent Dana a melancholy look from the doorway. "The auto place called while you were on the phone," she said with a sigh. "Your car's ready to be picked up." She twisted a lock of her long brown hair around her finger.

Dana gritted her teeth and smiled. "Thanks, Jenni. I'll get someone to drive me over there at lunch."

"Well..." Another melodramatic sigh. "...Okay." She closed the door carefully behind her as if she were in a funeral parlor.

With a groan, Dana buried her head in her hands. If she had to look at one more long face today...

She hadn't gotten around to the dreaded task of informing the station employees that Channel Five was about to go under. She hadn't needed to, thanks to the station grapevine's usual speed and efficiency. Word of Elliott's dire prediction had spread like ants at a picnic, and now everyone at the station was moping around in various stages of disbelief, panic or resignation.

First thing this morning it had been Jenni's turn to drift into Dana's office with her tale of woe.

"It's not the money—I mean, I'm not even getting paid for working here, though I'm hoping I'll be able to apply the experience toward my degree. But gosh, Dana..." Poor kid had looked ready to cry. "If Channel Five goes off the air, I won't be able to earn college credits from those televised courses!"

Dana knew what a catastrophe that would be for Jenni, who was the sole caretaker for her aging grandparents. Through arrangements with the state university, Channel Five broadcast a continuing series of courses that could be taken for credit.

"I can't commute to the campus—it's nearly a hundred miles away! And who would take care of Grandma and Grandpa if I moved closer?" Jenni had been raised by the old couple after her parents drowned in a boating accident. Her grandmother was bedridden with arthritis now, and while her grandfather could still get around with a walker, he was far too frail to care for his invalid wife by himself.

"If Channel Five goes off the air, I'll just have to forget about college, I guess. Maybe after my grandparents—" Jenni gulped. "Maybe someday I'll be able to go back. Though I've heard that's pretty hard to do once you've dropped out."

Dana had felt helpless, unable to offer Jenni anything more than a pink tissue and a sympathetic pat on the shoulder. How could she promise everything would be all right, when the way things were going Channel Five was doomed?

Damn it, she wasn't going to think that way! Springing up from her desk, Dana padded back and forth like a caged panther. There must be some way to rescue the station from financial disaster! Maybe if the entire population of Pine Creek realized what they were about to lose...

No, that wouldn't work. If the general public knew Channel Five might be history in three months, they would hardly be likely to sink their hard-earned dollars into one-year memberships. Why throw money into a losing cause?

What Dana needed was a way to drum up financial support, create publicity, make Pine Creek proud of its lone television station. Everybody loved a winner, right? What she needed was some snazzy, sensational, super boffo idea that would capture community interest in the upcoming pledge drive and have people signing up for memberships in droves.

With growing excitement Dana strode back and forth, pounding her fist into her hand. She wanted everyone in town tuning in, she wanted the phone lines swamped, she wanted a frenzy of enthusiasm that would have donations flooding in like . . .

She wanted a miracle.

With a moan of dismay, Dana collapsed into her chair and dropped her head onto her desk. What if she couldn't come up with an idea? What if inspiration didn't strike? What if there were no such thing as miracles?

This whole mess was driving her crazy. Soaring toward the sky with hope, crashing to the ground with despair. It was like being on an emotional roller coaster, and Dana was getting sick of the ride.

She needed something to distract her, something to take her mind off her problems for a while. She tilted her head to one side, resting her cheek flat against the desk. She found herself staring at the spine of the book she'd checked out of the library yesterday.

It was a big, glossy, gossipy book on the history of Hollywood musicals—not at all the sort of book Dana usually checked out. But after her weird encounter with Rick West two nights ago, she'd been . . . curious to learn more about him. And about his father, too, of course. It wasn't every day you met a living legend. Who could blame her for wanting to learn more about the famous songwriter she'd bumped into so unexpectedly?

Dana flipped open the volume, right to the page she'd already bookmarked with a slip of paper.

Poring slowly through the section on the songwriting team of West and Winslow, Dana learned some new facts and refreshed her memory about some things she'd forgotten.

Lyricist Alistair West and composer Jake Winslow had collaborated on their first musical back in the mid-1940s. It was a Broadway play later made into a movie musical, and it brought instant fame and success to the songwriting duo.

Dana's eyebrows flew up in surprise. She hadn't realized that Chloe St. James, the vivacious young screen actress who'd starred in several West and Winslow musicals, had once been engaged to marry Jake Winslow.

Dana scanned quickly ahead. In addition to being a fine composer, handsome, dashing Jake Winslow had also been a talented piano player. In 1951 he'd been on a USO tour, entertaining the troops in Korea, when the group he was traveling with was ambushed by enemy soldiers. Although his body wasn't found, Jake Winslow was presumed to have been killed along with the rest of the group.

A year later, Chloe St. James married Alistair West, who was Jake Winslow's senior by eleven years. The general consensus around Hollywood was that the grief-stricken young actress had married West out of a mutual desire for comfort and companionship after the tragic loss of the man they had both loved.

But when the war ended, Jake Winslow resurfaced, having survived two hellish years in a POW camp. He and Alistair defied the predictions of Hollywood tongue-waggers and resumed their successful partnership for several more years.

Then the year before Alistair and Chloe's son Rick was born, the songwriting team abruptly split up for reasons that were never quite clear. Rumors swirled around about some kind of feud, but both men refused any public comment and had apparently maintained their silence to this day. Whatever their reasons, the legendary songwriters hadn't appeared in public together since the Eisenhower administration.

After Chloe St. James's tragic death in a plane crash, Alistair West had taken his son and left Southern California forever, though, according to the book Dana was reading, Jake Winslow still led a quiet existence in the exclusive hills of Bel Air, overlooking Hollywood.

Dana brushed her fingertips over the brief mention of Alistair and Chloe's son. Knowing who his mother was, it was easy to see where Rick had gotten his sensational looks, not to mention those fabulous gray eyes. They'd been Chloe St. James's trademark.

Though she would rather die than admit it, Dana had dug out her high school yearbook last night and looked up Rick's picture. Then, naturally, she hadn't been able to resist paging through the group photos of all the clubs and organizations he'd belonged to.

Wonder what he looked like as a little boy....

Dana leafed idly through the rest of the chapter on West and Winslow, hoping for an early photograph of Rick. Considering the way he'd turned out, he must have been an awfully cute kid. Probably a little hellion, too.

Nothing. Evidently his parents had done a good job of shielding him from the paparazzi, or whatever they were called back in those days.

Dana thoughtfully tapped a fingernail against her front teeth. Slowly her eyes lit up; the corners of her mouth curved up in a tentative smile. What if she could...?

She licked her thumb, paged rapidly back to a shot of Chloe St. James and the rest of the cast singing the finale from *Match Made in Heaven*. Gears whirred and clicked inside Dana's brain, while excitement rose up inside her like the incoming tide.

Wouldn't it be terrific . . . ?

What a coup it would be if she could persuade . . .

Dana slammed the book shut, wedged her feet back into her shoes, grabbed her purse and headed for the door. She didn't have all the details worked out yet, but she had a glimmer of an idea. A potentially fantastic idea. An idea that just might save Channel Five.

And the fact that it involved seeing Rick West again had absolutely nothing to do with it.

Really.

Chapter Three

Rick picked up his plastic water bottle and dumped the contents over his head.

"Feel better?" asked one of the drywallers as he passed by lugging a huge rectangle of Sheetrock.

"Feel wetter, anyway." Rick grinned back at him.

"Hot for April."

"Yeah." Rick picked up the shirt he'd discarded mid-morning and used it to mop off his face. Now that the drywall was being nailed into place, he could start to see what the house was going to look like when it was finished. Even though he'd drafted the plans himself, spent night after night poring over the details, it was impossible to visualize exactly what a house was going to look like once all those lines on a piece of paper became wood and stone and plaster. There was always that moment of suspense when the house finally took on a character of its own and Rick could finally see how close the reality had come to his imagination.

He paced slowly around the lot boundary, examining the house from all angles. Satisfaction swelled his chest. This was going to be a real showplace, all right. Nothing fancy, but a home built of solid craftsmanship that would last for generations. It blended seamlessly with the character of the surrounding neighborhood, nestling into the slight slope of the hillside as if the setting had been sculpted especially for this house alone.

A few more trees planted alongside the garage, and—

Rick frowned. Shading his eyes, he looked down the hill where a vaguely familiar car had pulled up next to the curb. An elegant pair of legs emerged when the door opened, then a slim female figure in a cream-colored suit stepped gracefully out. She pulled off her sunglasses, tapping them against her chin while she studied the framework of the house.

Rick felt as if someone had just poured another bottle of ice water over his head. What the hell was *she* doing here? Just when he'd managed to stop thinking about her every thirty seconds, just when the memory of her tousled hair and ripe, kissable lips had started to fade...

Dana crossed the sidewalk and strolled up the driveway, her head swiveling slowly as if she were looking for something. Like trouble.

A chorus of wolf whistles announced her approach. She took them good-naturedly, rolled her eyes and made some crack that elicited a hail of raucous laughter from the workmen. Rick strode down the hill and stepped through what would be the back door when the house was completed.

The partially finished den fell silent as the stony look on Rick's face registered. Dana ignored his expression, switching her smile to high beam, focusing the sparkle in her eyes directly at Rick. Even in this heat she looked as fresh and cool as morning dew. She smelled like the first lilacs of spring.

Damn it. She was even more gorgeous than he'd remembered.

As if on cue, hammers started banging away again, drills whirred, saws grated. Dana cringed at the deafening din and Rick motioned for her to follow.

He led her beneath an ancient oak tree that spread its leafy branches over the backyard. "Gee, it's noisy in there!" she said, wrinkling her pert nose. "Louder than a Rolling Stones concert."

Rick leaned back against the tree trunk and hooked his thumbs through the belt loops of his jeans. "How did you find me?"

"What? Oh. Elementary, my dear Watson." She slipped into a British accent that reminded Rick of his father's. "That's, uh, supposed to be a joke," she said when he didn't respond. "You're supposed to laugh."

"Ha, ha."

"That's it!" She tucked her hands into the pockets of her linen blazer. "It wasn't hard. You mentioned the other night you were working on Juniper Street. Fortunately Juniper Street isn't that long. I started at one end and drove till I found a house under construction."

"Very clever."

"I recognized your pickup truck parked out front, too."

Rick peered past her shoulder. "I see you got your car fixed."

"Yup. They did a pretty good job with the bodywork, considering what a mess it was in. Then they had to fix some thingamajig that got knocked loose from the engine.''

"Thingamajig, huh?"

Her coffee-colored eyes twinkled. "I think it's connected to the whatchamacallit."

Despite Rick's intention to resist her charms, the corners of his mouth tugged upward. "How's that bump on the noggin?"

Her hand darted toward her forehead, then changed direction to twirl a lock of dark hair around one finger. "Fine. No dizzy spells, no amnesia, no hallucinations."

"Glad to hear it." His gaze wandered to where she'd hooked her gold-rimmed designer sunglasses over the neck of her blouse. Then it wandered a little lower to where the glasses snuggled between her breasts. Quickly he averted his eyes.

"I wanted to thank you again for rescuing me the other night." Dana rocked back and forth on her heels like a willow swaying in the breeze.

Rick brushed her gratitude aside. "Don't mention it."

"And—" she took a deep breath "—I want to ask you a favor. Well, ask your opinion, really."

"About what?"

Dana tried to focus her thoughts on the matter at hand. Not easy, when Rick stood propped up against a tree three feet away, bare chest dappled by leafy shadows, muscular thighs encased in tight faded jeans. A leather tool pouch was slung low across his flat hips, reminding her of a gunslinger's holster.

Darn it, she couldn't afford to blow this! She dug her nails into her palms, forcing her eyes to meet his instead of surveying his splendid anatomy.

But gazing into Rick's eyes was like sinking into soft gray velvet. His damp hair was slicked back, emphasizing even more strongly the rough-hewn planes and angles of his face. The sensual slash of his mouth made her wonder what it would feel like to...

Dana gave herself a good, swift mental kick in the rear. Darn it, she was acting like a moony-eyed teenager again! People were depending on her to save the station, and here she was practically drooling over some handsome hunk who'd made it plain he wasn't exactly thrilled to see her. His body language, a certain tension in his posture, conveyed the message loud and clear. He was wary, alert, on guard. Against her? Strange...

"I was wondering what the chances might be of persuading your father to appear on TV during our pledge drive next month."

Rick looked even less thrilled, if possible. He looked, in fact, as if a coiled rattler had sprung at him.

"I would have approached him directly," Dana continued hastily, "but I wasn't sure how he felt about public appearances. I know he's avoided them for years, and I thought maybe you could give me some advice on the best way to persuade him."

Rick inspected his close-cropped nails. "My father's retired from all that show-business hoopla."

"Yes, I know, but this is a special situation, and I thought maybe he might make an exception."

He glanced up at her from beneath tautly knit brows. "What's so special about it?"

Dana hesitated. The last thing she wanted was for word to leak out about the station's desperate financial straits. She decided not to reveal her plight to Rick except as a last resort. "It's our annual membership drive," she said. "We're going to be showing one of your father's old movies, and I thought he could sort of introduce it—you know, reminisce a little about the old days, make a pitch for more pledges. Lots of people would tune in to see him, and I'm sure our membership numbers would sky-rocket." Inside her pockets she crossed her fingers.

"In other words you want to exploit him, huh?"

Dana fell back a step as if Rick had taken a swing at her. "*Exploit* is a pretty strong word."

"How about 'use'? 'Take advantage of'?"

"You've got it all wrong." Dana licked her lips. "I admire and respect your father's work. So do a lot of people. I don't see anything wrong with asking him to help support a worthy cause." What on earth was Rick getting so bent out of shape for? She could understand his being protective of his eighty-three-year-old father, but it wasn't as though she were inviting Alistair to dem-onstrate bungee jumping on national television.

A tiny flame of fear licked at Rick's belly. Up until now, the only threat Dana had posed was to Rick's peace of mind, to his calm, orderly life. But now she posed a threat—however remote—to his father's happiness. Not Dana directly, of course, but the possible end result of what she was proposing. Rick was all too aware the ac-tions could have disastrous, unintended consequences farther down the line. He had to quash Dana's bright idea before it went any further.

He had to keep his father out of the spotlight—no matter what the cost.

"It's out of the question," he said, folding his arms across his chest and fixing Dana with a stern look he hoped would quell any protest.

He should have known better.

Her chin jerked upward, her eyes flashed as if in re-sponse to a challenge. "Don't you think that's up to your father?"

"You came here to ask my advice, didn't you? Or was it only to flirt with my workmen?"

She made a noise that was half gasp, half laugh. "*Flirt* with your workmen? You're accusing me of—listen, buddy, *they* were the ones whistling at *me,* not the other way around."

He raised, dropped one shoulder. "You didn't seem to mind."

She stared at him as if he'd gone plumb loco. Maybe he had. "What did you want me to do, send a telegram to Gloria Steinem?" She propped her hands on her waist. "Getting mad doesn't solve anything. Besides, I used to baby-sit one of those guys, for gosh sakes! It's a little hard to get my feminist hackles raised by a guy whose diapers I used to change."

Well, at least he'd managed to distract her from her plan to parade his father in front of the cameras. "Look, I don't have time to stand here yakking with you," Rick said. "I've got deadlines to meet."

"Yeah, well, you're not the only one. I didn't drive all the way over here so you could make ludicrous accusations." Her eyes narrowed. "What's the matter—are you jealous because I'm not flirting with *you?*"

Rick snorted. "In your dreams." He turned his back on her and strode uphill to the house, tool pouch slapping against his thigh. He could feel Dana's outraged stare boring into his back. What the hell had come over him, anyway? Acting like an obnoxious jerk wasn't his usual style. It was almost as if fear had turned him into another person.

And he hadn't succeeded in discouraging Dana one bit.

"Fine, if you won't help me, I'll ask your father my-self." She'd put her snazzy sunglasses back on by the time she caught up with him. "Even if he says no, I'm sure I'll get a more gracious reaction than I got from you."

Rick halted, nearly overcome by the urge to shake Dana by the shoulders and forbid her to speak to his father. He ground his nails into his palms, knowing that putting up too much opposition would only make her even more determined.

"Fine, suit yourself," he said, forcing himself to sound indifferent as he picked up a roll of electrical tape. "But you'll only be wasting your time. My father hates publicity."

"But it would mean so much to—it could make all the diff—oh, never mind." She tossed her head as if shaking off her doubts. "I'm sure I'll be able to persuade him to make one little appearance for a good cause."

Rick shrugged, pretending to lose interest in the whole matter by pulling out his tape measure to check the height of an electrical outlet. But the sick churning in the pit of his stomach increased.

Dana watched him for a few moments, tapping her toe. "Well, thanks for the advice, if not the encouragement. See you around."

When she started to leave, Rick called after her, "Just one question."

She paused, turned around.

"Did you stage that whole car accident the other night as a way of getting to meet my father?"

Rick couldn't see her eyes behind her sunglasses, but he could easily imagine the furious indignation flaring in them right now. Her lips pursed together in disgust. "Well, I sure didn't stage it to meet *you,*" she retorted before pivoting on her heel and marching back to her car.

Rick watched the Toyota roar off in a cloud of angry exhaust. Dana wasn't the only one disgusted by his remark. What self-destructive impulse had prompted him to make such a stupid, insulting insinuation? Well, now he'd certainly blown any chance he might have had with her.

Chance? What chance? Rick nearly swallowed the row of nails he was now clamping between his lips. He'd never had any intention of pursuing Dana Sheridan.

Had he?

He plucked a nail from his mouth and began to hammer in a slow, emphatic rhythm.

Bang...bang...

Dana was stubborn...inquisitive...bossy....

Funny...charming...intelligent. And sexy as hell.

Not that it mattered now. Rick suspected he'd done a pretty thorough job of alienating her. He could only hope she would be so mad at him that she would forget the whole idea of putting Alistair West on television.

He had to keep his father and Dana Sheridan as far apart as possible. And that meant steering clear of her himself.

If only visions of her mischievous smile and her alluring dark eyes didn't keep dancing in front of his—

"Ouch! Damn it!" Rick jammed his throbbing thumb into his mouth. He tossed the hammer aside in exasperation.

Next time he came across a beautiful woman stuck in a ditch late at night, he was going to drive right on by.

Dana strode back and forth across her office like a duck in a shooting gallery.

She was so darn furious with Rick! Not only because he'd behaved so rudely, but because he'd tried to dash cold water on her fabulous idea.

A ribbon of doubt wavered in her mind. It *was* a fabulous idea, wasn't it? Using Alistair West to promote membership week? Well, not *using* him ... Dana had no intention of *using* anybody, no matter what Rick West might think.

But what a coup it would be if she could persuade Alistair to lend his support to Channel Five's pledge drive! Contributions would certainly soar, hopefully high enough to save the station from financial ruin.

Dana was fast running out of alternatives. With the doors to government funding slammed shut at the moment, her only chance was to capture viewer interest by giving Pine Creek something sensational, something to talk about, something they could be proud of that would drum up community support to record levels.

And Pine Creek's own resident celebrity seemed just the man to do it....

If his unreasonable, pigheaded son didn't stand in the way, that is.

Dana tapped a pencil against the palm of her hand, trying to decide on the best way to approach the reclusive songwriter. She certainly respected his privacy, so she could hardly drop by unannounced. The man had every right to live like a hermit if he wanted to.

Okay, phone first. But wait ... he was bound to have an unlisted number. And something told her that asking Rick for it would be about as useful as dialing numbers at random.

Maybe she should disguise herself as a yellow-bellied sapsucker and hope to encounter Alistair on one of his bird-watching expeditions.

Then she snapped her fingers, remembering a friend in Los Angeles who worked in the musicians' union office. Surely *they* would have Alistair's phone number on file, or at least know where to look it up. And luckily, this particular friend just happened to owe Dana a favor.

She snatched up the phone and punched out a number, cheerfully whistling a tune from *Match Made in Heaven,* feeling smugly pleased with herself for discovering a way to outwit Rick.

Now if she could only discover a way to stop dreaming about him at night.

The afternoon breeze was whispering through the pines when Dana pulled up in front of Alistair West's well-maintained Victorian home. There were lots of restored Victorians scattered along streets in the older section of Pine Creek, but it was unusual to find one so far out in the country. The original builder must have enjoyed his solitude as much as the current owner.

Dana inhaled deeply as she stepped out of the car, filling her lungs with the crisp woodsy fragrance that always reminded her of fresh pencil shavings.

The house where Rick grew up was like something out of a fairy tale—all cupolas and gables and turrets festooned with gingerbread ornamentation. To a small boy it must have seemed almost as much fun as playing in King Arthur's castle.

Not that Dana was the least bit interested in Rick West's childhood exploits.

Alistair had graciously agreed to see Dana as soon as she called, and welcomed her with an Old World hospitality she found charming and rather endearing. Too bad none of it had rubbed off on his son.

He insisted on plying her with tea and crumpets while they talked. "I was only a lad when I immigrated to this country," he told Dana while he poured tea into delicate porcelain cups, "but this is one British custom I still treasure." He circled the steaming cup beneath his luxuriant white mustache, breathed in the fruity scent of Earl Grey, sipped, then sighed with pleasure. "Delicious," he pronounced, smacking his lips and reaching for a buttered crumpet.

Today he'd abandoned his army-surplus garb for somewhat more conventional and definitely more colorful attire. Green-and-orange plaid trousers, lime-green turtleneck shirt, gleaming white loafers with little tassels on them.

He was certainly easier to talk to than his son. Before she knew it Dana had practically told him her life story. "After my mother died when I was four, it was just my father and me. Kind of like you and Rick." Funny, but she'd never realized that before.

"The two of you were close, then?"

"Oh, yes. My father was quite a busy man—running the station, participating in local service organizations, but he always made time for me. When I was older I worked at the station after school and on weekends, so we spent lots of time together there." Dana paused, swallowed some tea to wash down the lump in her throat. "I—I really miss him." Even after five years, her first instinctive thought was still "Wait'll I tell Daddy!" each time she heard an amusing anecdote or accomplished something she was proud of.

Alistair's sympathetic blue eyes took on a faraway glow. "Yes, eventually the pain fades, but we never stop missing them, do we?" He was referring to his beautiful young wife, of course—Rick's mother. "At least I have the consolation of being able to watch Chloe on film, to hear her lovely voice, to see her precious smile again...."

Dana was never one to pass up opportunity when it came knocking on her door. Besides, this conversation was going to make her cry pretty soon if she didn't change the subject. "Speaking of your wife's films, Mr. West..."

"Do call me Alistair, my dear."

"Alistair." She gave the old gentleman a warm smile. "As I mentioned the other evening, Channel Five is going to show one of your wife's movies during the week of our membership drive, and I was wondering..."

"...And that's my idea, Mr. West—er, Alistair. So...what do you think of it?" Dana tried to look as if she weren't holding her breath. She reached for another crumpet, hoping her hand wouldn't tremble. Everything was riding on Alistair's answer.

He set his cup down, folded his gnarled hands and scrutinized her for a few moments from beneath his bushy eyebrows. "My dear, are you certain you aren't perhaps overestimating my popularity?" he said finally. "After all, I've been out of the public eye for over thirty years—people don't remember me anymore, they don't watch the kind of movies Jake and I used to create."

"Oh, but they do!" Dana leaned forward eagerly as hope flickered inside her. At least he hadn't come right out and said no, had he? "People *love* to watch old musicals—they're still enormously popular. That's why we always run them during membership week. The more people who tune in, the more pledges we get."

Alistair continued to regard her skeptically. "And you think people want to watch an old has-been like me?"

"You're not an old has-been! And of course people will want to watch you! You're part of the history of Hollywood, you're a—a living legend right here in our own backyard!"

Alistair chortled. "Gadzooks, I never thought of myself like that before."

"Well, other people do. Myself included—so there." Dana took a deep breath, eager to press her advantage but not wanting to push too hard. "Will you at least consider the idea?"

"Hmm." He stroked his chin. "It's been a long time since I appeared before an audience. What if I pass out from stage fright or something?"

Dana grinned. She could tell he was only teasing her now. "Think how much *that* would boost the ratings!"

Alistair slapped his knee. "Har! Har!" He wheezed so hard, Dana was afraid he might start to choke. At last he knuckled a tear from his eye and said, "Good glory, I haven't laughed like that since the time Jake and I..." His voice trailed off. "Ah, well, never mind." For a moment the lines of his face converged into a web of sorrow.

Like a burst of fireworks, a bolt of comprehension exploded inside Dana, revealing with dazzling clarity that Alistair West wasn't only mourning the loss of his wife. So there *had* been some kind of terrible rift between him and Jake Winslow!

Another idea began to nudge its way into Dana's brain. But some sixth sense warned her this wasn't the right time to bring it up. First let Alistair get used to the idea of appearing in public again. If he would agree to do that, maybe Dana could persuade him to—

A door slammed somewhere. Footsteps pounded briskly in their direction. Then Rick strode into the parlor, filling it with his overwhelming masculine presence. Suddenly the antique furniture seemed too small, the delicate china too fragile.

Eyes blazing, he switched his suspicious stare back and forth between his father and Dana. "Well, well, what's this?'' His words were deceptively mild, but he didn't fool Dana for one minute. He was scowling at her as if she were the villainous landlord in some Victorian melodrama. His fists clenched and unclenched as if he were fairly twitching to pick her up and toss her headlong out the front door.

"Dana and I were having tea." Alistair's eyes narrowed, giving him a speculative look as he studied Rick. "Would you care to join us?" He glanced at the ormolu clock on the mantle. "Didn't realize it was this late already. Time flies when you're talking to a pretty girl, eh, son?"

Rick sprawled into an ornately carved brocaded chair, completely dwarfing it with his long, powerfully built body. He wrapped his big fingers around a cup of tea and drained half of it in one swallow.

"Crumpet?" Dana offered sweetly, pushing the plate in his direction. Triumphant in her minor victory over him, inside she was quivering from something besides nervousness or fear. The strange mingling of emotions made her giddy.

Rick's unbuttoned shirt fell open across his broad chest, sleeves rolled up to his elbows. Muscles bulged along his tanned forearms as he continued to knot and unknot his fists. He swiped a crumpet from the plate and wolfed it down in two bites, keeping his ferocious gaze pinned on Dana the whole time.

He noticed a tiny smear of butter at the edge of her lips and was seized by a lusty urge to lick it off. Damn it, this was no time for such adolescent nonsense! He crossed one leg over the other and silently swore to keep his hormones under control.

He forced himself to uncurl his hands and drape them over the chair arms. "And what is it the two of you were talking about that made time pass so quickly?'' Already his fingers were drumming against the polished cherry-wood.

Dana set her teacup down with a rattle and sprang up from the sofa. ''Goodness, I really must be on my way— I just realized I'm late for a meeting with the station's board of directors.'' She extended her hand toward Alistair as he rose stiffly to his feet. ''Thank you so much for the tea and crumpets. I'll be in touch soon, after you've had a chance to think about—'' she flashed Rick an uneasy sidelong glance ''—about what we talked about.''

She kept up a steady stream of chatter while Alistair escorted her to the door, Rick trailing them like a bloodhound. ''See you again soon!'' She waggled her fingers in their direction before opening her car door.

It so happened that Rick had once set a still-unbroken school record for the hundred-yard dash at Pine Creek High. Otherwise Dana might have made good her escape. He sprinted down the steps, along the front path and across the driveway as if intending to break his own record.

''Not so fast,'' he said, gripping the top edge of the car door to prevent Dana from closing it.

She slid her sunglasses down her nose and peered at Rick over the tops. ''Would you mind letting go of my car? I'm late for a meeting.''

''You're going to be even later.''

''Hey!'' she squawked when he grabbed her wrist and pulled her out of the car.

''I don't want Pop to overhear our conversation.'' He towed Dana down to the end of the driveway, giving his father a reassuring wave over his shoulder.

"What conversation? You and I have nothing to talk about." Frowning, Dana tugged on the sleeve of her suit to straighten it, then brushed imaginary dirt off the fabric.

"That's what you think." Rick folded his arms. Although he was trying to act like Mr. Tough Guy on the outside, inside, his guts were clenched up with the anxiety that had gripped him from the minute he'd arrived home, glanced out his bedroom window and spotted Dana's car parked in his father's driveway. "Did you barge into Pop's house and pester him with that ridiculous scheme of yours?"

Dana stuck her hands on her hips and swayed the upper half of her body toward Rick. "For one thing, I did not *barge* in. I was invited. And for another thing, my *scheme,* as you call it, is not ridiculous." She beamed an innocent smile at him. "At least, your father didn't think so."

Rick's stomach plunged toward the center of the earth. "Are you saying—" His mouth was dry as sawdust. He swallowed. "Are you telling me my father agreed to appear on television?"

Her victorious smile faltered. "Well . . . he hasn't said yes, *yet*. But I'm sure he will."

"Don't be so certain." A layer of calm settled over Rick. The situation wasn't as bad as he'd thought, then. As long as his father hadn't promised to appear, Rick was confident he could talk him out of it.

Fairly confident, anyway. For Pop's sake, he couldn't let this scheme go any further.

A pinecone fell from the tree they were standing beneath, landing nearby with a soft *plop!* that tugged Rick's attention back to Dana.

"...And that's when it dawned on me," she was saying.

Rick blinked. "Huh?"

She threw her hands in the air. "Haven't you been listening? I said something came up during my conversation with your father that gave me an even better idea."

"What?" Rick asked cautiously, not really wanting to hear any more of Dana's brilliant ideas.

"I want to convince both your father *and* Jake Winslow to appear on TV. Together."

When Rick first started working in construction, he'd taken a careless step one day and toppled twelve feet off a roof. He'd been stunned, the wind knocked out of him, his skin alternately hot and clammy while he waited for his heart to crawl down from his throat and his bruised body to start screeching in protest.

He felt the same way now.

"Pop hasn't spoken to Jake Winslow in over thirty years." Rick's mouth was numb, as if he'd just received a shot of novocaine.

"And he's miserable about it," Dana said with a curt bob of her head.

"What are you talking about?" The frozen gears in Rick's brain were beginning to creak into motion again, trying to figure out a way to avert the disaster that now loomed even closer on the horizon.

"You should see the look on his face when he talks about Jake Winslow." Dana bit her lower lip. "Your father misses him, Rick. He misses him terribly."

"You're crazy," he scoffed with more assurance than he really felt. "The two of them had a falling-out years ago. Pop never even mentions his name anymore."

"Well, he mentioned it today and it nearly broke my heart." Dana's voice snagged in her throat a little.

"Whatever they fought about, surely it's not worth holding a grudge for over thirty years."

"It's none of your business what they fought over." The sweet relief that had flowed through Rick only moments ago had turned to acid.

Dana replied as if trying to explain things to an exceedingly slow person. "I didn't *say* it was any of my business. I'm not interested in digging up dirt from the past. What I *am* interested in is seeing your father reunited with a man he obviously misses and still cares about."

"What you're interested in is raking in more money for your TV station." Rick hoped the harsh note he forced into his voice would disguise his fear. One thing he had to give Dana credit for—she was extremely perceptive, sensitive to the hidden thoughts and emotions people often tried to mask.

Could that mean she was right about Pop wanting to mend fences with Jake?

Rick shoved the possibility aside. Pop might not know it, but he was better off never speaking to Jake again.

Dana poked her tongue into her cheek, bowed her head for a moment, then faced Rick again with that stubborn, uptilted chin of hers. "Okay, you're right. I *am* interested in raising money for the station. But if in the process I can reunite two old men who once meant an awful lot to each other, what's the harm?"

Rick smothered a groan. If she only knew! If the truth ever came out, his father would be shocked, griefstricken, devastated. And an emotional blow like that might very well kill him at his age.

Rick didn't for a moment believe that Dana was some heartless businesswoman who only cared about profit-and-loss statements. Her concern for his father was genuine—he could see it in her eyes, hear it in her voice. No one was *that* good an actress.

But what Dana didn't realize was that in this case her compassion, her good intentions might end up destroying the very people she was trying to help.

For a moment Rick was tempted to tell her why he was so anxious to keep his father and Jake Winslow far apart for the rest of their lives, how fearful he was of what might spill out into the open if the pair ever got together again and started apologizing, sharing memories of the old days, asking forgiveness for past transgressions.

Rick had seen how softhearted Dana was—look at the way she'd practically totaled her car to avoid hitting a deer, for God's sake! He could tell she was one of those rare people who were as beautiful on the inside as they were on the outside. Even against his better judgment, Rick had been reluctantly attracted by her obvious compassion and integrity from the very first. He knew instinctively that Dana would never betray a secret or exploit it to her own advantage.

Yet...

Alistair West had trusted his young wife with every fiber of his being, hadn't he? And though Chloe hadn't deliberately set out to betray him, in the end she'd chosen to follow her heart, even though it meant violating her husband's trust and her own wedding vows.

Rick's family history had taught him a bitter lesson: that even the purest motives, the most noble intentions could result in disastrous consequences. Dana was cut from the same cloth as his mother—in the end she would always follow her heart. And Rick couldn't take the risk of discovering where that road might lead.

He wasn't about to reveal to anyone—even someone as sympathetic and well-intentioned as Dana—the secret he shared with Jake Winslow. It was a secret Rick had sworn to take to his grave.

Because the devastating truth was that Jake Winslow, not Alistair West, was Rick's natural father.

Chapter Four

The meeting broke up with the sounds of scraping chairs and empty cardboard coffee cups hitting the metal wastebasket. Andy Gallagher followed Dana out into the hall, fingering his mustache in a way that meant he was worried.

"What do you really think your chances are of persuading Alistair West to go along with your idea, boss?"

Dana crossed her fingers, both for luck and because she was about to tell a lie. Well, not a lie...more of an exaggeration. "It'll be a piece of cake, Andy." *I hope...I hope...I hope...* her heels pounded down the corridor.

"I don't know...building a whole publicity campaign around someone we're not even sure will cooperate seems kind of risky to me."

"My sentiments exactly." Elliott Ledbetter caught up with them as they veered around a corner. "Dana, are you sure you know what you're doing? What if you go ahead with all your plans to promote the membership drive, and then West decides not to appear?''

''We only have three weeks until membership week,'' Dana pointed out. ''It might take a while to convince him. We can't afford to twiddle our thumbs until I get a definite yes or no out of him.'' She made a quick, slashing motion with her hand. ''I mean, a definite *yes.*''

''Shouldn't we come up with some alternative strategy? Just in case he gives us a definite *no?*''

''Andy's right,'' Elliott said. ''You need a backup plan, an alternate source of funding in case this doesn't work out.''

''I've tried everything else I can think of! Government agencies, philanthropic organizations, private individuals... Money's tight everywhere. I suppose I could buy a lottery ticket, but that seems like kind of a long shot.''

''So's this idea of yours,'' Andy said. ''Even if West does agree to appear, there's no guarantee that the membership drive will bring in enough money to save the station.''

''That's why I intend to go after Jake Winslow, too.'' Dana swept her hand across invisible headlines in the air. ''I can see it now, guys—'West and Winslow, Together Again!' 'Publicity Coup of the Century!' 'Tiny Station Scoops Networks!' ''

''Even so...''

''Elliott, don't you dare start waving that calculator at me. We're committed to this course of action now.'' She halted so suddenly, the two men nearly bumped into her. ''That is, unless either one of you has a better idea.'' She swiveled her head back and forth between the two of them. Elliott shuffled his feet. Andy tugged on his mustache and studied the ceiling. "No, I didn't think so," Dana said, resuming her brisk pace.

Good old Elliott gave it one more shot, anyway. "Dana, as the station's accountant I feel duty-bound to advise you that putting all your eggs in one basket is a very poor business decision."

"Elliott," she replied as they reached the reception area, "it's the only basket we have."

Her old friend locked glances with her for a long moment. His expression alternated between sympathy and reluctant agreement, underscored with grudging admiration. "I'll do anything I can to help," he said finally. "Good luck."

"Thanks, Elliott." She touched his sleeve in farewell.

Andy emitted a sound halfway between a sigh and a groan. "Guess I'd better get to work on this promotion campaign—though I still think we're putting the cart before the horse."

"Think of it as a challenge, Andy." Dana watched him disappear into his own office. Goodness, if he kept plucking at his mustache like that, he wasn't going to have any mustache left!

At the reception desk, Jenni Carpenter was positively bubbling with suppressed excitement. Dana hadn't seen that kind of sparkle in her eyes since word of this financial crisis had leaked out. "Good heavens, Jenni! I bet if I pricked you with a pin you'd pop like a balloon! What's up?"

"You've got a visitor," she replied, tilting her head toward the closed door of Dana's office.

"Who is it? Elvis?"

"Who? Oh, him. No." Jenni's puzzled frown vanished, replaced by a smile that made Dana think of a cat with a bowl of cream. "See for yourself."

"Isn't identifying visitors part of your job?" Dana grumbled as she twisted the doorknob. Jenni twined a strand of long hair around her finger, managing to look smug and mysterious at the same time.

Dana rolled her eyes and plunged into her office. "Good morning! What can I do for—oh, it's you."

Backlit by bright sunshine, Rick glanced up from the open book he held in his hands. It was only an optical illusion, of course, but the golden rays angling through the window appeared to form a halo around his head.

Some illusion, all right.

"What did you do to my secretary?" Dana asked, marching briskly past him to her desk. "Ooze some of that famous Rick West charm at her?"

"Nah. I saved it all for you." He snapped the book shut and wedged it back onto the shelf. "Have you actually read all these?" He gestured at her father's extensive library of books on business management and television production. Dana's philosophy had always been that you learned best through hands-on experience, not by reading some boring manual.

No need to let Rick know that, however. "Only once or twice," she replied, trying to look modest.

"I'm impressed."

So was Dana—with the way his burgundy-colored polo shirt clung to his chest, emphasizing the well-developed outline of his pectoral muscles. Goodness, he'd certainly filled out since high school! She couldn't help noticing how nicely he filled out his snug jeans, too. He was certainly a walking advertisement for the benefits of physical labor.

"I'm sure you didn't take time off from work to discuss my reading habits," she said abruptly, wondering why it suddenly felt so warm in here. "What do you want?"

"Mind if I sit down?" Without waiting for her reply, Rick scooped up a stack of videocassettes from the nearest chair and set them carefully on the floor. Dana lowered herself behind her desk, watching him the same way she would watch a hooded cobra poised to strike. What new obstacle was he about to throw in her path to keep her plan from succeeding? .

Rick sat down, crossed one leg over the other, folded his hands across his chest, then recrossed his legs. For some odd reason he seemed reluctant to meet Dana's gaze. "Wow, is that an Emmy Award?" he asked, shifting forward to get a better look at the gold statuette on the bookcase behind her.

"When I worked at a public television station in L.A., I was involved in the making of a documentary that won an award. All of us on the production team got one."

Was that a gleam of new respect she detected in his eyes? Surely Rick must have grown up in a house surrounded by similar awards, considering who his parents were. Maybe it gave him a special appreciation of such things.

He bounced to his feet, making Dana wonder why he'd bothered to sit down in the first place. "I suppose I should have called for an appointment, but your secretary said you could squeeze me in before lunch."

An unfortunate choice of words, she thought. *And thanks a lot, Jenni.*

"I know that you and I kind of got off on the wrong foot, but..."

Dana drummed her fingers impatiently, wishing he would get on with it, though she had a pretty good idea of what was coming.

"I'd like to ask you..."

Here it comes. She whipped open her file drawer, dumped in her stack of meeting notes and slammed the drawer with a bang. Rick blinked in surprise, but Dana was in no mood to pussyfoot around anymore. She'd just spent an hour trying to convince herself and a room full of people what a snap it would be to persuade Alistair West to appear on television. The last thing she wanted to face now was another go-round with his uncooperative son.

She folded her hands on the desk in front of her. "What's the point of this discussion? You've made your position clear. I don't have time to keep arguing with you about it."

"No, you don't understand—"

"No, *you* don't understand." Dana yanked open another drawer and rummaged through it for something to soothe her stomach, which had been fluttering strangely ever since she'd walked in here and found Rick waiting for her.

Nausea, she decided.

"I don't know what your problem is," she went on, "or why you're so dead set against your father helping out with the pledge drive." She found a bottle of bright pink stuff and brandished it at Rick. "But I've got a station here on the brink of financial ruin, and you can damn well bet I'm going to do everything I can to save it."

Oops!

She'd just revealed far more than she'd intended. Oh, never mind—what difference did it make if Rick knew what a pickle she was in? Rumors about the station's financial trouble were bound to leak out soon, anyway.

Rick's eyes shifted rapidly back and forth, as if he were assessing this new information and trying to figure out a way to use it to his advantage. He dashed back a lock of hair that had fallen across his forehead. "I didn't realize how serious your financial situation was."

"Yeah, well, now you know." Dana unscrewed the bottle and took a long swig of the stomach-coating medication.

"Maybe we could discuss it further...over dinner?"

She slammed the bottle down, sending droplets of pink goop flying everywhere. The bottle cap skittered off the desk and rolled to a stop at Rick's feet. "What?"

He cleared his throat, gave her a crooked smile, which under other circumstances would have made her knees melt. "Actually, that's why I came here. To ask you out."

Dana gawked at him in disbelief. "On a *date?*"

"Uh, yeah." Rick felt sweat crawling down the back of his neck. Damn, he *knew* this was a stupid idea, but how else was he going to get a chance to talk her into leaving Pop alone?

He felt like a virus under a microscope, the way she was staring at him. He knelt to the floor and retrieved the bottle cap. "Here."

She ignored his outstretched hand, rising slowly to her feet. "Let me get this straight." She pressed her hands together in front of her as if praying for understanding. "You came over here to ask me out on a *date?*" She pronounced the last word as if it were *liquor-store heist*.

Rick raked his fingers through his hair, feeling as if he were fifteen again and had just asked pretty, popular Margie Courtland to go ice skating with him. Except that Margie's reaction had been a lot less incredulous and far more enthusiastic. "I thought we could have dinner, take in a movie...." Maybe he didn't deserve any points for originality, but then neither did he deserve the daggers of indignation Dana was shooting at him with those fiery brown eyes.

Incredible, Dana thought. Really incredible. How stupid did he think she was?

"Look, if you don't want to go out with me, that's—"

"What kind of cheesy ploy is this?" she demanded, bracing her knuckles on her desk and leaning forward.

Irritation began to lick around the edges of Rick's discomfort. If Dana didn't want to go out with him, fine, but he didn't need this kind of abuse. He flipped the bottle cap onto her desk. "You must have one terrific social life, if that's how you react when someone asks you out."

"My social life is none of your business. How transparent can you get? The only reason you're asking me out is so you can wine me and dine me and sweet-talk me into forgetting about my plans involving your father." She propped her hands on her hips and glared at Rick as if challenging him to deny it.

There was enough truth in what she said to prick at his conscience and annoy him even further. "I'd sooner try to sweet-talk a shark out of its dinner," he retorted, heading for the door. "Come to think of it, I'd rather ask a shark out to dinner in the first place."

Dana stomped around the desk and charged out of her office after him. "I pity the poor shark!" she yelled.

Her only response from Rick was the swish of the glass entrance doors as they closed behind him. Jenni and Elaine, however, both stared at her as if she'd gone crazy.

Maybe she had.

"And what was all *that* about?" Elaine propped herself on the edge of Jenni's desk, folded her arms and studied Dana with a lively speculative gleam in her eyes.

"If that guy ever comes back, tell him I'm in a meeting," Dana instructed Jenni.

Elaine leaned over and whispered confidentially to the receptionist, "Send him to my office instead." She met Dana's glare with a wicked smile. "So what did Mr. Gorgeous Hunk want, anyway?"

Dana's simmering outrage finally reached the boiling point. "He had the nerve to ask me out!" she exploded.

Elaine pressed a hand to her chest in mock horror. "Dear Lord, Jenni, did you hear that? Good heavens, you'd better dial 911 and report a date invitation in progress."

Jenni giggled behind her hand. "Gosh, Dana, if that's the kind of guy you reject, I'd be happy to accept your hand-me-downs from now on."

"No way," Elaine said. "I've got first dibs."

"I wouldn't wish him on either one of you," Dana grumbled. "He's arrogant, conniving, self-centered—"

"Yeah, but he's got a great body," Elaine said with a sigh. "Not to mention that face. Did you see those fabulous gray eyes?"

"It's in his genes," Dana muttered.

"I'll say! In his jeans, his shirt, those sexy red briefs I bet he wears..."

"Genes, not jeans! As in chromosomes? His mother was Chloe St. James. Honestly, Elaine, get your mind out of the gutter."

Jenni squealed. "Chloe St. James? You're kidding! Wasn't she some kind of famous old-time movie actress?"

Elaine arched her eyebrows. "And you turned him down?"

"I told you, he's an obnoxious jerk."

Elaine slid off the desk and slung an arm around Dana's shoulders. "Kid, you've got a lot to learn. So he's not perfect!" She leaned close and whispered loudly in Dana's ear, "Who cares?"

"Elaine, if I didn't know how crazy you are about Elliott, I'd think you were a shallow, superficial schemer who only cared about the size of a man's wallet and the size of his—"

"Dana!" Jenni clapped a hand over her mouth.

Elaine blushed like a schoolgirl, but her eyes sparkled at the mention of Elliott's name. "Okay, okay, you've made your point." She gave a long, theatrical sigh. "Now, if I could only figure out a way to get a certain teddy bear of an accountant to ask *me* out."

Dana poked Elaine repeatedly on the arm and said to Jenni, "See that? A shameless manipulator. Don't let this happen to you."

Jenni shook her head solemnly, clamping her lips together to repress her mirth.

Dana returned to her office with good humor restored. But the minute she was alone again her thoughts boomeranged to Rick. The nerve of that man! Thinking he could manipulate her, bend her to his will by...

She refused to allow her thoughts to proceed any further along that provocative path. But before she slammed the door shut on any more suggestive images, a vivid picture of sexy red briefs pranced through her mind.

With a moan of exasperation she grabbed the pink bottle and chugged down another dose.

* * *

Rick curled his fingers around a long-necked beer bottle and imagined it was Dana's pretty little throat.

Not that he was the violent type. Never had been. That was one of the reasons he'd gone out for track instead of football in high school and college. He'd never understood the sense in a bunch of guys trying to pummel each other's brains out, all in the name of good clean fun.

But for some reason Dana seemed to bring out the worst in him. Look at how ready he'd been to stoop to deception in order to derail her plans. The fact that she'd seen through him immediately made Rick even more disgusted with himself.

He recalled how her eyes had glittered with anger, shooting out shards of dark brown glass the same color as the bottle he held in his hand. A rosy flush of indignation had warmed her animated features, staining the high arches of her cheekbones. She'd practically *glowed,* she was so mad, her full lips curved into an arc of disdain.

Just like the old cliché—she was beautiful when she was angry. Ah, hell. Never mind. Rick scooped up a handful of peanuts from the dish in front of him and tossed a couple into his mouth. A big cheer went up when one of the Giants hit a home run on the wide-screen TV at the far end of the bar.

"All *right!*" Harry Conway, Rick's drywall contractor, slapped him on the back. "Looks like we might have a chance at the World Series this year, huh?"

Rick nodded automatically and refrained from pointing out that baseball season had barely started. The next batter struck out. Just as Rick had struck out with Dana this morning.

Damn it, there he went again, thinking about her when he was supposed to be enjoying himself! Having a few beers with the guys after work . . . watching the game on TV . . . soaking up all that good old male camaraderie the way his clothes were absorbing the smell of cigarette smoke.

In a way, this was kind of a special occasion. Certainly an unusual one, at least. Rick hardly ever palled around with the guys he worked with, sensing somehow that he didn't really have much in common with them. They all had wives, kids, even dogs that barked a welcome when they got home.

All Rick had was his work. And Pop, of course. No one was waiting for *him* at home. And today when five o'clock had rolled around, for some odd reason he'd found himself dreading the long, empty evening that stretched ahead of him.

Not that he envied the guys he worked with, though. Over the years, Rick had purposely cultivated his isolation, his privacy, erecting a protective wall to keep out intruders who might accidentally stumble upon his carefully guarded secret.

An intruder like Dana, for example.

Just look at the way she kept intruding into his thoughts! It was just as well his despicable, shameless scheme to manipulate her hadn't worked. He had no business getting involved with a woman like her, a woman he could get serious about, someone smart and funny and compassionate. Ever since college, Rick had made it a policy to keep his romantic relationships strictly lightweight, with the clear understanding on both sides that this was only a temporary fling.

He kept his affairs neat and tidy, with no loose emotional ends dangling afterward, no messy hurt feelings to deal with. The fact that his affairs were also few and far between didn't bother Rick a bit.

What did love get you, anyway? Heartache, lies, betrayal...

He signaled for another beer.

"Haven't seen you in here for a while." The bartender set another icy bottle in front of Rick and mopped off the wet ring where the first beer had stood. "Construction business must be booming."

Rick took a swallow, backhanded a speck of foam from his mouth. "Not so's you'd notice, but I manage to keep busy." He was busy, all right. Busy keeping himself disconnected from the human race.

Funny... this was the first time he'd ever looked at it that way.

He forced himself to pay attention to the game, where the Giants' pitcher was in the process of striking out the side. When the inning ended and a commercial for the beer Rick was drinking came on, he watched the laughing, attractive couple cavorting on the TV screen and wondered why *he* wasn't having as much fun as they were. He was drinking the same beer, wasn't he?

The woman bore a faint resemblance to Dana, though her smile was too artificial, her figure too pencil-thin in that emaciated way that Madison Avenue evidently considered appealing.

Personally, Rick appreciated a few more curves on a woman. Take Dana, for instance. Now *there* was a figure *he* found appealing. Soft, well-rounded breasts, slightly flared hips, shapely calves...

She was probably out on a date right now, having even more fun than the couple on TV. Surely an attractive, vivacious woman like her wouldn't be sitting home alone on a Friday night. No doubt her date was some rising young junior-executive type. They'd go to a highbrow chamber-music concert, then have a late supper at whatever the hottest new trendy restaurant happened to be....

Damn it, what did *he* care whom she dated or where they went?

Would the guy kiss her good-night? Or were they already on more intimate terms than that....

Rick tilted back his head and poured a long stream of beer down his throat. Dana's accusation this morning had rankled—that was why he couldn't stop thinking about her. He *had* had an ulterior motive in asking her out, and that made him feel guilty.

But some other emotion was lurking in the shadows— an emotion that felt strangely like disappointment. Maybe his motives in asking Dana out had been a little more complex than he cared to admit. For the first time in a long, long while, Rick found himself wishing things could be different. If only he weren't burdened with this terrible secret . . .

If.

How could such a tiny word have such enormous consequences?

If he hadn't gone on that college ski trip to Squaw Valley . . .

If a novice skier hadn't plowed into Rick and landed him in the hospital with a broken leg and assorted internal injuries . . .

If Pop hadn't rushed to his side and donated blood for the surgery he required . . .

And *if* the doctor hadn't mentioned in passing that Pop's blood turned out to be a type incompatible with Rick's . . .

During the long, exceedingly dull weeks of recuperation, Rick had quickly grown tired of books, television and jigsaw puzzles. One afternoon, desperate for some mental challenge to combat the excruciating boredom, he'd constructed a little chart to figure out how he'd inherited his blood type.

He was taking biology that term, so he knew his genetics chart was correct. He remembered his mother's blood type, and now he knew his father's, but ... something was wrong.

Rick drew the chart over and over again before coming to the completely incomprehensible yet inescapable conclusion that his parents couldn't *possibly* have produced a child with Rick's blood type.

But that must mean ...

For weeks afterward Rick struggled to forget his discovery, struggled to make sense of it, struggled to contain his impatience until he was well enough to get out of bed and start looking for some answers. Maybe he was adopted, maybe there was *some* logical explanation other than the one that relentlessly taunted him.

He'd gone back to L.A., where he'd been born, started talking to people who'd known both his parents back in the old days and who were only too happy to pass along long-buried gossip and not-so-idle speculations. Rick pieced together each fact, each rumor, each tidbit of gossip, until the puzzle formed a picture he recognized.

Jake Winslow.

A loud burst of applause jarred Rick from his morbid reverie. Apparently the Giants had just won the game. All of a sudden the cigarette smoke was stifling, the noise deafening, the crowded bar too confining. Rick plucked a few bills from his wallet and tossed them onto the bar. As he shouldered his way through the crowd, he recalled the mind-numbing, gut-wrenching moment when he'd finally confronted Jake Winslow and learned the truth.

For the thousandth time since then, he vowed that Pop would never have to go through the same trauma.

Dana put the finishing touches on the painted backdrop, then stepped back to squint a critical eye at her work. "Hmm, not too shabby, if I do say so myself."

Shabby was a good word to describe the general condition of the Channel Five parade float, which got hauled out of mothballs once a year for Pine Creek's annual Gold Rush Days celebration. Dana's father had started the tradition of sponsoring a float in the parade, both as a way to support the community and—hopefully—to drum up some support from the community in return.

It wasn't really a float, just a plywood-and-papier-mâché tableau fastened onto the bed of an ancient flatbed truck. The historical scene it depicted was the old Celebration Mine, which had produced millions of dollars in gold during the nineteenth century and served as the mainstay of Pine Creek's economy until the last owner shut it down some sixty years ago.

Dana studied the rickety mine building, the rusted ore car and the sagging papier-mâché mule. "Darn, I wish we could afford to rebuild this whole thing," she said to Carole Westlake, who was busy dusting cobwebs off an artificial pine tree. "But with our financial situation the way it is, I guess we'll just have to make do and spruce it up the best we can."

Carole sat back on her heels and wiped a sheen of sweat from her forehead. "Not to sound like a gloomy Gus, but this might be the last year we drag this thing out, anyway."

"Don't remind me." Dana found another chipped spot and bent forward to dab at it with her paintbrush. "By the way, I sure appreciate your coming in on a Sunday to help me work on this. I can't believe that Gold Rush Days is only a week away. Don't know how it snuck up on me.''

"Well, you've had a lot on your mind lately." Carole adjusted the blue bandanna covering her pale blond head. "Don't worry, we'll have this ready in time for the parade."

"Who's watching your kids this afternoon?" Carole was a single mom with a three-year-old girl and a little boy who'd be starting kindergarten in the fall.

"My neighbor. She's really a doll, won't even let me pay her. She's like a grandmother to Amy and Christopher." Carole's smile faded. "I don't know what I'll do if the station closes and I have to find another job. Day care's so expensive, and I know I'll never find another job where I can bring my kids to work." She swept briskly at some cobwebs. "You don't know how much I've appreciated your letting me do that."

Dana brushed her gratitude aside. "Amy and Christopher are terrific kids. They never get in the way, and everyone loves having them around. Matter of fact, I think they liven the place up."

"That's one way to put it." A dimple flashed in Carole's cheek. "Remember that time we were taping my show, and I opened that box of graham crackers to make a cheesecake crust?"

"And Christopher had eaten every last one!"

They both burst into giggles at the memory. Carole wiped a tear from her eye. "We had to stop taping while I dashed out to the market to buy another box."

"Ooh, Andy was so furious, remember?"

Carole's smile evaporated, and her thin shoulders slumped. "Honestly, Dana, sometimes I just don't know how I'm going to manage. It's so expensive raising kids—they grow out of their clothes so fast, and good, nutritious food isn't always cheap. Then there's the pediatrician's bills, and now if I have to start paying a babysitter..."

"What about Russell?" Dana gnashed her teeth. The name of Carole's no-good, abusive ex-husband always left a bad taste in her mouth.

Carole shrugged halfheartedly. "I can't afford to hire a detective to find him, and until then there's no way I can force him to pay child support."

"Even so, you're better off without him." Dana usually avoided pronouncing judgments on other people's personal lives, but Russell had been such a creep....

"Oh, you're right. I know that. I'm proud of the way I've managed to hold things together since he ran out on us, but it's so frustrating sometimes! Just when I think I've finally got things under control, some disaster happens. Something like—like this!" She shook her dust rag at the Channel Five parking lot as if it represented the station's financial crisis.

Her expression grew alert, then curious as she gazed past Dana.

"Carole, I'm not going to tell you not to worry, because we've all got plenty to worry about, believe me."

"Dana..."

"But we're all in this together, and if we pull together as a team—"

Carole cleared her throat loudly.

"—we have a good shot at surviving this little, uh, challenge."

Carole was making peculiar shifty motions with her eyes, as if maybe a speck of dust was irritating one of them.

"Besides, once I talk Alistair West and Jake Winslow into reuniting on the air, we're going to be flooded with donations." Dana dunked her paintbrush into a can of turpentine and brushed her hands together. "And I'm sure I can do it, too," she said, pressing a hand against her sore lower spine and arching backward. "If it weren't for that interfering son of a— Carole, what *is* the matter? What's wrong with you? Your face is all red, you look like you just swallowed a goldfish and—and—"

Dana spun around to discover the cause of Carole's strange behavior.

Rick lounged against the truck cab, arms folded across that massive chest of his. "Don't let me interrupt," he said with an innocent smile that didn't fool Dana for a minute. "Please, do go on. I believe you were about to refer to me as a son of a—?"

Chapter Five

"Son of a—A-Alistair West! That's what I was about to say." Dana grabbed Carole's dust rag and busied herself tidying up the poor old papier-mâché mule. "Besides, how do you know I was talking about *you*, anyway?"

"You just told me." Bracing himself against the side, Rick vaulted easily onto the flatbed and looked around with a mildly astonished expression. "Going into the antiques business?"

"This is Channel Five's float for the Gold Rush Days parade." Goodness, maybe she'd been working too hard. Her heart was thumping a mile a minute.

"Oh, yeah—that's right. Next weekend, isn't it?"

Dana picked up a hammer and started pounding a nail into a loose board on the roof of the blacksmith shop. Rick poked an exploratory finger at the mule. "Oops."

He looked at the resulting hole with a chagrined expression.

"What have you done to Sparky?" Dana cried, tossing down her hammer.

Rick's eyebrows arched. "Sparky?"

"My dad let me name him when I was a little kid," she muttered, inspecting the damage.

"I'd say that old mule's about ready to be put out to pasture."

"No thanks to you."

"It was an accident! Here, let me—"

"Keep your hands off him!"

"Damn it, Dana, I'm only trying to—"

Snap.

They both stared, horrified, at the ear that had broken off in Rick's hand.

"I, uh, I think I'll be going now," Carole said, jumping off the truck bed. "I gotta go pick up my kids." Carole, like everyone else at the station, had no doubt heard about Dana's little run-in with Rick the day before yesterday. She looked torn between the desire to stay and watch the fireworks, and a suspicion that maybe she ought to get out while the getting was good. "See you at work tomorrow," she called, backpedaling across the parking lot to her car.

"Coward," Dana said under her breath. She snatched the broken ear from Rick. "What do you want, anyway? Besides to destroy our float."

"That wasn't why I—*aarrggh!*" He plowed his hands through his hair. "You are the most exasperating, impossible, unreasonable—"

"Flattery will get you nowhere." Dana gave him a sugary smile.

"Maybe not, but I'm running out of ideas." He rasped his hand across his jaw. "Look, I came over here to make a deal with you."

"Oh, really?" She pressed the tip of her index finger against her chin and batted her eyes at him. "Let me guess. If I cancel my plans to put your father on television—" her eyes narrowed and she thrust the broken ear under his nose "—you won't give me the same treatment you gave poor Sparky!"

Rick jammed his hands in his pockets to keep from wrapping them around her neck. Why did that image keep recurring? "That's not the deal I had in mind," he said, forcing his voice to stay level.

"I'm not interested in making any deals with you." She picked up the hammer, turned her back on him and started attacking the broken board again.

Rick couldn't resist taking the opportunity to sneak a quick, unobserved survey. He'd never seen Dana in anything but a business suit before, and couldn't help regretting what he'd been missing—like the way her slender thighs tapered gracefully into strong, sleek calves. She'd knotted her T-shirt at her waist, and as she raised her arms to wield the hammer and nail, a teasing band of smooth skin peeked out between her shirt and the waistband of her shorts. His gaze slid a few inches lower, to the pert curve of her denim-clad derriere. His fingers fairly itched to give it the spanking it deserved, but then other, more interesting possibilities crept into his imagination.

Squelching his traitorous desires, Rick shifted his position to a safer perspective. Though it turned out this was no better. Now he could see the seductive bounce of her breasts each time she struck a clumsy blow with the hammer. The T-shirt had a V-neck, and with each abrupt movement he caught a glimpse of white lace, the hint of lush curves, the slope of a shadowy valley that promised secret, endless delights.

His hands balled into fists as he tore his gaze from that tempting vision and tried to reason with her. "Look, here's the deal." Her dark-chocolate hair was tied back with a ribbon, but wasn't quite long enough for a proper ponytail. Wayward strands kept escaping to form a wispy fringe around her face.

"From now on I'll be up-front with you," Rick continued, wrestling to keep his attention on the matter at hand, "and I'll explain why I'm so opposed to your plans. In exchange, you'll sit down with me someplace where we won't be interrupted and hear me out."

"Why should I—"

Bang!

"—listen—"

Bang!

"—to you?"

Bang!

"Because you're a fair, open-minded person?"

Dana paused to give him a wry look, then continued pounding. "Remember what I said about flattery?"

"Look, I know you and I got off on the wrong foot—"

"You can say that again," Dana interjected.

"Can't you give me another chance?"

Her face remained screwed up with concentrated effort. "You've used up all your chances. Only ten to a customer."

"What have you got to lose just by talking to me? All I want is—oh, for Pete's sake, let me do that."

"I'm perfectly capable—"

"You're bending the nail!"

"No, I'm—"

"Hold the hammer closer to the end of the handle. Look, just give me that!"

Rick seized the wooden handle, but Dana refused to let go. They grappled over the hammer, both red-faced and grinding their teeth in frustration. Finally Rick gave a mighty tug that pulled Dana up against him.

Their faces froze inches from each other. What began as an attempt to stare the other down became something else, as both searched each other's eyes, then found what they were looking for.

They stood like statues for what seemed a motionless eternity, until Rick slowly lowered his head and crushed Dana's mouth beneath his.

Her lips resisted at first, then softened, melding gently yet eagerly with his. He sampled her as he would an indescribably wonderful treat he'd been putting off tasting, just so anticipation would make the eventual act even more enjoyable. Though their mouths were the only point of physical contact between them, Dana was so close, Rick could feel her radiant heat, inhale the mysterious womanly fragrance of her. All rational thought fled from his brain, leaving only the overwhelming desire to prolong this moment for as long as he could, for hours, days, months...forever....

Despite all the times she'd once imagined this, despite all the vivid fantasies she'd woven, nothing could have prepared Dana for the stunning reality of Rick's kiss. His mouth was hard yet tender, taking and giving at the same time. When he lazily nudged his tongue between her lips she met him tentatively at first, knowing she was crossing a line from which there would be no turning back. Either she called a halt to this right now, or she might very well spend the rest of her life lost in this kiss, dreaming of it, aching with the knowledge that there would never be more.

Recklessly she sought his tongue with her own, savoring the exquisite, impossible pleasure of him, finding consolation in the thought that at least once, just once, her fantasy had come true and was even more heavenly than she'd imagined. Whatever the eventual price she would have to pay, surely this moment was worth it.

She felt Rick's hand pressing against her bare lower back, pulling her gently, insistently against him. Every bone in her body seemed to melt, every muscle seemed to quiver....

The hammer, forgotten, dangled from their hands and then fell.

The loud *clunk!* when it landed, jolted them apart.

They stared at each other, chests heaving, lips glistening, hearts thudding. Stunned.

Rick stepped toward her, but Dana ducked under his arm to retrieve the hammer and took the opportunity to back farther away from him. "Oh, gosh, look at that! Darn thing made a big dent in the ore car."

"Dana..."

"I know I should just drive this whole float over a cliff into Pine Creek Ravine and start from scratch, but unfortunately the station can't afford to—"

"Dana..."

"You know, if you're really willing to help, we *could* use your expertise in fixing it up. We'd pay for the materials, of course—"

He grasped her forearm and silenced her.

She glanced quickly at the spot where his fingers seemed to scorch her bare skin.

"I'd be glad to help," Rick said quietly. "But can we go someplace to talk first?"

Dana swallowed. "Sure." She extricated herself from his grip, feeling as if she were leaving part of herself behind. "There's a café across the street where some of us at the station hang out and drink coffee. They have great lemon meringue pie, too." Not that she could have eaten a bite, what with her stomach doing somersaults and her heart lodged in her throat.

"Sounds great." Rick was studying her with a peculiar intensity that Dana found vaguely unsettling yet somehow exhilarating.

"I, uh, have to cover the float with a tarp before we go." She jumped to the ground and fumbled with the unwieldy canvas cover.

With Rick's help she soon had the tarp fastened in place over the float. She'd managed to avoid meeting his gaze the whole time, and by the time they finished she felt seminormal again, back in control of her emotions.

Who am I kidding? she thought as they walked across the street, carefully maintaining a good four-foot separation. *All he'd have to do is crook his little finger at me and I'd fling myself into his arms.*

Fortunately, Rick made no beckoning gestures at all, unless Dana counted the nod he gave the waitress when they were ready to order. Maybe he was having second thoughts about that kiss. Dana was already up to her fifty-seventh thought about it.

Suzy, the waitress, kept shooting curious looks at Rick and smirking at Dana while she scribbled down their orders. Good grief, it wasn't bad enough everyone at the station was so fascinated by Dana's private affairs—now even casual acquaintances seemed eager to eavesdrop on her love life! *Personal* life, rather.

"Let's put our cards on the table," Rick said after Suzy brought their coffee and sashayed off with a thumbs-up gesture to Dana.

Dana's defenses instantly went on red alert. What was this, confession time? She had no intention of revealing that once upon a time she'd had the world's biggest crush on Rick.

"You and I each have a goal, and unfortunately those goals are mutually exclusive."

Despite her resolve to remain nonchalant about that kiss, Dana's heart sank. She hadn't expected Rick to pledge undying love or anything, but still, he seemed awfully cold-blooded about what had just passed between them. Hmph. If that was his attitude, she would darn well show him the meaning of the word *indifferent*.

"Goal? I don't have any goal. It was just one of those things, that's all." She tossed her head with all the disdain of a queen dismissing a peasant.

He paused with the coffee cup halfway to his lips and frowned. "You mean you've changed your mind about using Pop to promote your pledge drive?"

All of Dana's lofty unconcern came tumbling down like a house of cards. She felt like an idiot. Talk about being on different wavelengths! Rick hadn't been referring to their personal relationship at all.

"Oh, that," she said. "No, I haven't changed my mind. We're still going forward with the promotion."

A tight grimace flashed across his face, followed immediately by a puzzled expression. "What did you think I was talking about?"

"Never mind. Could you pass me the artificial sweetener, please?"

His gray eyes reflected a hint of amusement, but he tossed her a couple of packets without saying a word.

"Thanks." Dana tore one open and dumped the contents into her cup. Normally she drank her coffee black, but Rick had her so flustered, she barely knew what she was doing. She took a sip, made a face. "Go on, say your piece. I'm all ears." She would show him she could be all business—that their brief, accidental kiss had meant nothing to her, either. She could be as calm and cool as the next guy.

Behind his composed facade, Rick was still staggered by the effects of that kiss. He hadn't meant to do it, hadn't intended for it to happen, but all of a sudden they were standing so close, and he found himself drowning in those big, dark eyes. . . .

He could tell Dana had been powerfully affected, as well, that she'd felt the incredible chemistry flowing between them as something intense and exciting had sprung to life. She was trying to play it cool, but she wasn't as good at masking her hidden thoughts and feelings as Rick was. No wonder, considering he'd had years of practice. It was easy to see Dana was used to wearing her heart on her sleeve.

And I hope she never changes, he thought. *I hope to God I never do anything that causes her to change.*

He had to resist his attraction to her, couldn't let it stand in the way of his goal of protecting Pop. He forced his thoughts away from her lush, kissable lips, her trim, shapely curves and back to the matter at hand.

Despite his proclamation of honesty, he had no intention of revealing the whole truth to Dana. But maybe they could work out a compromise. "As you know," he began, "my father hates publicity."

Dana traced the edge of her cup with the tip of her little finger and frowned. "He seemed willing enough to consider the idea when I discussed it with him."

"Unfortunately, he also has a hard time saying no when people ask him for favors."

Dana flipped her hands palms up. "What am I supposed to do? He's a big boy, Rick. I can understand your being protective of him, but it *is* for a worthy cause."

"How about this?" Rick took a deep breath. "You forget the idea of reuniting Pop and Jake Winslow, and I'll talk Pop into appearing during your pledge drive—alone."

Dana chewed her lower lip. She hated being so hard-nosed about this, but there was simply too much at stake to change course now. "I'm sorry, Rick, but I'm counting on that reunion. Channel Five needs all the publicity it can get, because publicity translates into donations and new memberships, and without a big infusion of money—"

She hesitated. Well, Rick was being straightforward with her, so the least she could do was be candid with him. "The truth is, the station's in big financial trouble. We need every dime we can scrape up if we're going to stay on the air. Please believe me that I wouldn't be so determined about this if I didn't have to."

"You'll never be able to persuade them to appear in public together," Rick said, trying another tack. "They had a falling-out years ago, and haven't spoken since." He'd never known for sure what their feud was about, and Pop had never talked about it. But in light of the secret he'd discovered years ago, Rick had a pretty good idea of what had destroyed their friendship.

"I don't know about Jake Winslow, but anyone can see your father misses his old partner."

"I've never seen any sign of that."

Dana shrugged. "Maybe you've never bothered to look."

Maybe it was true, Rick thought. Maybe his sense of betrayal and anger at his mother and Jake had blinded him to Pop's change of heart. Was it possible that after the mellowing passage of all these years, Pop might actually be ready to let bygones be bygones?

God, he hoped not! Because if Jake and Pop reconciled, Jake might let something slip, or take it into his head to claim Rick as his son. Or what if, seeing Rick and Jake together for the first time, Alistair saw a resemblance and realized the truth?

Sweat popped out on Rick's brow. Dana set down her cup and peered at him closely, lines of worry etched across her pretty features. "Are you all right?" she asked. "You look like you've just seen a ghost."

"I'm fine." He glanced down and noticed to his surprise that he'd crumpled his paper napkin into a tight wad. He forced his fingers to uncurl and his voice to sound calm. "I just think you're wasting your time, is all . . . trying to get the pair of them back together."

Dana hesitated. "Not that I'm trying to pry, and I'm certainly not fishing around for all the gory details, but . . . do you happen to know which one of them instigated the breakup?"

"Pop did." Rick at least knew that much, from little snippets he'd heard as a child, while his mother was still alive. "That's why I have a hard time believing he'd go along with this scheme. You'd be much better off focusing on some other way to drum up donations."

Dana shook her head. "I've been over this with my staff, our accountant, the station's board of directors." Regret clouded her eyes. "Please believe me, Rick. I don't enjoy meddling in other people's lives, but I—I'm simply desperate."

To Dana's surprise, Rick drew a checkbook out of his shirt pocket. "How much?" he asked calmly.

"I . . . beg your pardon?"

"How big a donation will it take to keep you on the air without Pop's involvement?"

"You can't be serious." But she could tell by the steely gleam in his eye, the rigid set of his jaw that he was.

Throwing her hands helplessly in the air, she gave him her best estimate, based on all those depressing charts and figures of Elliott's.

Rick's face fell. "That much, huh?"

"I told you we were in trouble."

He gazed at Dana thoughtfully for a moment, then began to write.

"Rick, for heaven's sake, you can't afford to—you can't possibly mean to—"

He tore off a check with a flourish and handed it to her. "Here."

She saw the amount. "But—"

"You're right, I can't afford the kind of money you're talking about." He stuck the pen into the checkbook, tucked the checkbook back into his pocket and folded his hands on the table. "But this check will cover a year's membership, won't it?"

"More than that, but why—?"

He shrugged his broad shoulders. "I don't watch a lot of TV, but a lot of what I do watch is on public television. And I'm as lazy as a lot of people are about paying their fair share. So there's mine."

"This is very generous of you." Dana pinched the check between thumb and forefinger and waved it slowly in front of his face. "In fact, if I didn't know better, I'd think this was a bribe." She fixed him with a stern look, although her eyes were twinkling.

"First flattery, now bribery?" He made tsk-tsking sounds with his tongue. "You certainly have a low opinion of me."

That statement could hardly have been farther from the truth, but Dana wasn't about to enlighten him. "Don't forget, you also tried to wine me and dine me."

He shrugged. "Can't blame a guy for trying." The half-joking, half-serious expression he gave her over his coffee cup sent a little thrill rippling up her spine.

For heaven's sake, have a little pride! she silently chided herself. *He just as much as admitted the only reason he asked you out was so he could sweet-talk you into leaving his father alone!*

The faint glow of excitement Dana had felt only moments ago was doused by this self-administered dose of reality. Inside, she felt empty, let down. How dumb to think a man like Rick West would be interested in her, when he could have any woman he wanted.

Just look at the way Suzy was practically drooling over him while she set their orders on the table!

"Is that all you're going to eat?" Rick quirked a sandy eyebrow at Dana's slice of pie. "It's nearly dinnertime. Why don't you let me buy you a hamburger or something to go with that?"

Dana forced herself to give him a breezy smile. "I'm onto that ploy, remember?" She shook a scolding fork at him.

He snapped his fingers. "Oops! That's right, I forgot." He gave Suzy a friendly smile. "That's all for us, I guess."

"I'll bring you some more coffee," she replied, sounding a little more breathless than usual. She sent Dana a cheeky grin over Rick's shoulder and mouthed the words, "Hubba-hubba!" before hurrying off.

Dana rolled her eyes and stuffed a bite of pie into her mouth to stifle a groan. As if she needed any more reminders about Rick's devastating masculine charms!

Rick dug into his burger and fries and considered his options. Forcing the issue—any issue—with Dana would obviously be nonproductive. He had a feeling that if she were backed into a corner she'd fight like a wildcat.

What was left after flattery, bribery and seduction had failed? Threats?

He hadn't sunk *that* low yet, thank God. Not that he would ever dream of harming a hair on her lovely head—despite his occasional impulse to throttle her.

He watched her dissect her pie and push it around her plate. With no makeup on and her hair in that ponytail, she looked all of eighteen. A ridiculous, crazy, tenderly protective instinct welled up inside Rick. Ridiculous because he'd never met a woman more capable of fending for herself than Dana was.

Crazy because he'd spent his entire adult life walling himself off from this kind of feeling. The only person he wanted to protect was Pop. Once he let cracks form in that protective wall, it would be all too easy for someone to gradually infiltrate his peaceful, self-sufficient existence, until finally she took over his life entirely, filling his thoughts, his dreams . . . opening his heart to all sorts of risks.

Someone? Why mince words? He wasn't wary of just *any* someone, some hypothetical woman who might be lurking in his future. The woman who made him edgy as a groom on his wedding day was sitting right across the table from him.

Rick didn't believe in fairy tales, the kind you saw up on the movie screen with singing and dancing and happy endings. His parents' marriage had taught him all too well that relationships were like quicksand. They might seem safe on the surface, but if you were fool enough to trod across the shifting sands, all kinds of secrets, lies and hidden motives lurked below, just waiting to clutch you and suck you into their treacherous depths.

He wasn't about to leave himself open to that kind of pain. Love, honor, good intentions counted for nothing. Where the whims of the human heart were concerned, there was no such thing as a safe bet.

Which was why he was a fool to sit here trying to prolong this conversation when obviously Dana had no intention of changing her mind. Every minute Rick spent with her he discovered something else about her that appealed to him.

Like the way her eyelashes—dark and lush as velvet—dusted her cheeks when she gazed down at her plate. Or the way one corner of her mouth twisted into an adorable pucker whenever she gave him one of those disgusted looks he seemed to earn with amazing frequency.

She had turned quiet all of a sudden. On impulse Rick reached across the table and tilted her chin up with his knuckle. "Hey, why so talkative?"

Her lips curled into a little half smile. Rick's gaze dropped to her mouth, and to his consternation he found himself remembering what it had felt like pressed against his, all soft and molten and eager, the way he knew Dana would be if they ever made love.

Damn it! Where did *that* insane notion come from? As if he would ever be fool enough to get that involved with her, with *any* woman who haunted his every waking moment the way Dana had lately.

And what really worried him was that he'd never even *met* any other woman who'd affected him like this.

Rick tossed his napkin onto his plate and pushed back his chair. "Come on. Let's get out of here."

Astonishment flared in Dana's eyes as he peeled off a few bills and tucked them under his coffee cup. Something in his face must have cautioned her, because she rose to her feet and remained uncharacteristically silent while Rick escorted her from the café, his hand hovering near the small of her back without actually touching her. He caught some kind of quizzical facial interchange between Dana and their waitress, but he was past caring how strange their abrupt departure might appear.

Once out on the sidewalk Dana could contain her curiosity no longer. "What was all that about?" she demanded. "Did you just remember you were parked in a tow-away zone or something?"

"I think I left the water running in my bathtub."

She bit down on her tongue to cut off a smart-aleck response. If Rick had suddenly grown tired of her company, fine. She could take a hint.

The western sky was an artist's palette of pinks, peaches and lavenders, with gauzy rags of clouds draping the far horizon like tattered hopes and dreams. Dana folded her arms and rubbed her shoulders. Shorts and a T-shirt had been fine for an unseasonably warm April afternoon, but the spring evenings were still nippy once the sun dipped low in the sky. Now she felt chilled outside as well as inside. At least her mood and skin temperature matched.

Rick couldn't help noticing the goose bumps on her arms, the way she shivered the whole way back to the station parking lot. He muffled an oath. He wanted to wrap his arm around her shoulders, hug her against him and warm her with his body heat.

But it would be safer to throw himself in front of a speeding locomotive.

"I'll walk you over to your car," he muttered.

Dana paused by the station entrance. "That's okay. I've got work to catch up on." She rubbed her arms some more. "Thanks, uh, for the coffee."

"Don't mention it." Good grief, were her teeth actually chattering? "Will you at least think about what we discussed?"

She shrugged slightly, or maybe it was only an especially strong shiver. "Sure. But I won't change my mind."

"I appreciate your hearing me out, anyway."

She nodded.

Rick felt as if he were back in high school, loitering at some girl's front door at the end of a date, both of them wondering, *Will he or won't he?*

Leave her alone, or you'll regret it later....

I just want to hold her for a moment, that's all.

You're playing with fire, you idiot!

Then why does it feel so good, so right, so...ah, the hell with it!

Rick grabbed Dana's shivering shoulders and hauled her against him more roughly than he'd intended. To make up for it he began to kiss her gently, ever so slowly, but the feel of her in his arms sent desire coursing through his bloodstream, washing away his self-restraint, drowning his intentions.

In contrast to the rest of her, Dana's lips were warm and pliant beneath his. She tasted like sugar and coffee and smelled like spring lilacs. Rick tangled his fingers in her hair, then drew back long enough to growl, "I've been wanting to do this all afternoon," as he tugged one end of her hair ribbon until her dark silken strands at last tumbled free of the ponytail.

He sifted his fingers through her hair, pressed his lips to its satiny, fragrant texture, inhaling as if trying to imprint the memory of her scent on his brain forever.

As he moved his mouth back to hers, he saw Dana staring up at him with wonder, her eyes deep and dark and wide as a midnight sky. Rick cradled her face in his hands and let himself drown in the kiss for a brief moment, just a little while longer....

When his kiss deepened, all trace of her surprised resistance began to melt away, and her body seemed to flow into his, filling his hard angles and hollows with her soft curves. She was tender and responsive and exciting, and a pang of yearning sliced through Rick as pure and crystalline as a mountain stream. An empty place began to echo inside him, an empty place he hadn't even realized existed before. His heart seemed to expand, to reach out for something he couldn't begin to identify.

Now he could no longer tell where his own pounding heartbeat stopped and Dana's began, as if the melding of their lips had spread to encompass their entire bodies. Her soft breasts nuzzled against him; her arms encircling his neck clasped him even closer. Rick could have gone on like this forever, and the sudden shock of that knowledge finally gave him the strength to disengage from their embrace.

He brushed back a wisp of hair that had drifted across her cheek. There was so much he longed to say to her, and so many reasons for holding back.

Dana's wide-eyed gaze skittered over his face, bewildered and questioning. Rick dragged the pad of his thumb slowly, thoughtfully along the delicate yet stubborn line of her jaw, lingering for the briefest of instants on the soft underside of her chin.

"I'll be in touch." Without another word he turned away and strode determinedly back to his truck, resisting the urge to break into a run and hightail it out of there as fast as he could, as far away from those strange yearnings and unsettling desires as he could get.

Dana stood immobile, watching Rick drive off and listening to the roar of his pickup fade finally into the distance.

She took a deep, quavering breath. Well, she certainly wasn't cold anymore. Her skin felt hot enough to scorch her clothing, sizzling with the memory of Rick's mouth, his hands, his broad, sturdy chest. Good heavens, these feelings went far beyond anything her fevered imagination had concocted in high school!

Hot and cold—certainly an apt way to describe Rick's behavior. Even as dazed as she'd been by the overwhelming pleasure of his embrace, Dana had sensed conflict within Rick, though she couldn't understand its source.

She brushed her fingertips over her lips, reliving the kiss and all that had preceded and followed it. Behind the undeniable passion in that kiss, she'd sensed anger...worry.

Anger at her? At himself?

And gut-deep worry bordering on fear.

And one other powerful emotion buried beneath the others.

Pain.

Someone or something...somehow...somewhere... had once hurt Rick very badly, Dana suspected. He'd tried to bury the pain, but it was obvious that deep inside him the wound had never healed.

She felt a throb of compassion, a wave of tenderness. Wistfully she longed to be the one who could banish the pain, who could heal whatever emotional wounds Rick had suffered and erase the lingering scars forever.

But that was unlikely, considering how he locked it all up inside, how he closed himself off and managed to keep Dana at an emotional arm's length even while his arms were wrapped tightly around her.

And unfortunately, she didn't have time to play therapist even if the patient were willing. For the next several weeks she had to devote all her time, effort and concentration to saving the station. People were counting on her, people whose jobs and dreams and futures depended on her.

Rick didn't need her. Channel Five did.

Shivering, Dana turned to go inside. All of a sudden she was cold again.

Chapter Six

"What in tarnation is all that racket?"

Dana had been sitting in Andy's office two full minutes before the repetitive clanking noises from outside finally registered on her distracted brain.

"See for yourself." Andy gave her an odd, teasing smile. "He's been at it all morning. I'm surprised you haven't heard him before now."

"I've been shut up in my office on the other side of the building since 7:00 a.m." Dana skirted Andy's desk and spread the venetian blinds apart with her hands. She peered through the opening and frowned. "What the...who on earth? Oh." To her astonishment, Rick was up on the parade float, busily hammering down a loose section of the ore car's metal track. She let the blinds fall back into place and gave Andy a sickly grin as she returned to her seat. "Looks like we have some extra help getting ready for Gold Rush Days."

"Friend of yours?"

"Not exactly."

"He the guy you had that knock-down-drag-out fight with in the reception area last week?"

"Jenni has a big mouth," Dana muttered. "Besides, it wasn't a fight—more like a difference of opinion."

"That's not what *I* heard." Andy twirled his mustache like a villain in a melodrama. "And don't blame Jenni. The janitor told me."

"How the heck did *he*—oh, never mind. Can we get on with these timetables, please?"

Outside in the parking lot, Rick was surprised to find himself actually whistling. Well, why not? It promised to be another gorgeous April day after the wet March they'd had, the sun felt good on his back and the spring breeze tickled the hairs at the nape of his neck. He felt like a bear coming out of hibernation after a long winter.

He pushed himself to his feet and surveyed the progress he'd made on the float. He experienced that same surge of pride that always came to him when he gazed upon the results of his labor, whether it be a house he'd designed or simply a smooth pine board he'd skillfully sawed and sanded so it was perfectly straight. Both were equally pleasing to his eye.

Today, however, the satisfaction he took in his work felt a little hollow and incomplete, as if something were missing. For the first time in his life he wished he had someone to share his achievement with.

He stole a glance at the two-story gray brick building where Dana would be at work now. No doubt she was holed up in her office plotting some new mayhem that would cause Rick problems. He could just hear her trying to persuade the information operator to give her Jake Winslow's unlisted phone number.

Jake.

His natural father.

Whom Rick had only laid eyes on once in his whole life.

The memory of that one occasion sent a chill crawling up his spine, as if winter had suddenly returned. He recalled every minute detail with razor-sharp precision, as if the details of their encounter were etched in acid on the photographic plate of his memory.

He remembered Jake's home, with its thick-beamed ceilings and hardwood floors, resembling a hunting lodge for a prince more than the typical millionaire's mansion one would expect to find in the exclusive Los Angeles suburb of Bel Air.

He remembered a huge piano the size of a mobile home parked before the sliding glass doors that opened onto the flagstone terrace.

He remembered the look on Jake's face when he'd opened the front door and found Rick waiting there unannounced, practically dancing from foot to foot with impatience, dread and a lot of unanswered questions.

Actually, Rick had had only one question that really mattered. And the fact that Jake had instantly recognized him with no introduction should have been answer enough. It was almost as if he'd been waiting all those years for Rick to show up on his doorstep.

A rapid succession of expressions had filtered over Jake's rugged, weathered face—recognition, shock, joy, wariness.

''Rick,'' he'd said, pronouncing the word like a bene-diction. ''To say that this is a surprise would be a vast understatement." He stood aside and opened the door wider. "Please, come in."

He offered his hand, and Rick was surprised by the iron strength of his grip. He'd expected a musician, a pianist, to have delicate wrists and long tapered fingers he would take great care not to bruise. "We finally meet after all these years," Rick mumbled. His father and Jake had split up before he was born.

Jake rubbed his jaw and studied Rick as if weighing what to say. Despite the seams that time and sorrow had stitched across his face, he was still a strikingly handsome man who looked a good ten years younger than his real age. "Actually, we've met before, though you wouldn't remember it." His eyes took on a faraway cast as if he were gazing back across the years. "I saw you once when you were just a baby. Your mother brought you to see me."

This statement, with all its implications, was consistent with the terrible suspicion Rick had come here to force Jake to either confirm or deny. It wasn't long until he could no longer hold the question inside him.

They had moved out onto the flagstone terrace with its panoramic view of the city. Rick's fingers clutched the glass of cola Jake had brought him. With the directness of youth he'd finally blurted out, "Are you my father?"

Jake hadn't flinched. Carefully he'd set down his own glass on the stone terrace wall and shifted his eyes in the direction of the ocean for the longest minute in Rick's life.

Then he turned back to meet Rick's half-accusing, half-terrified scowl head-on. "Yes," he said. "I am."

Despite his mental preparation for the truth, Rick felt as shocked and disoriented as if an earthquake had suddenly struck. For one sickening instant his stomach plummeted with despair and he wished the ground beneath him *would* open up and swallow him.

Dimly he was aware of Jake's words. "Chloe made me promise never to tell, but since you figured it out on your own, I guess it's—"

"How could you?" Rick breathed. "How could *she?*" His knuckles turned white as he gripped the glass. "My mother—the adulteress!" His bitter laugh echoed harsh and brittle against the flagstones.

"Now just hold on there." Jake took a step forward, then halted in the face of Rick's expression. His dark brows drew together like storm clouds. "I won't put up with any talk like that about your mother."

Rick laughed again, and even through his shock and pain he was startled by the raw sound of his own voice. "That's what she was, wasn't she? An adulteress? She was married to my father—my *real* father, and she betrayed him! You both betrayed him!"

Jake's face darkened several shades. He jammed his fingers into his shaggy gray-and-brown hair. The muscle twitching along his jaw betrayed his struggle for control. When he finally spoke, his voice was low and level. "We were in love, we were to have been married. Your mother thought I'd been killed...she married Alistair out of grief." A spasm of pain contorted his features. "We never meant for it to happen, but—"

"But it did, right? Just one of those things? *Oops!*"

"It only happened once."

"And that makes it all right, I suppose?"

"No." Jake bowed his head for a moment, then raised it to fix Rick with a probing, intense gaze. "Have you ever been in love?"

His question took Rick by surprise. He thought of all the girlfriends he'd had, going way back to junior high school. "Sure," he replied with a shrug. "Lots of times."

Jake studied him thoughtfully. "No," he said finally with a slow shake of his head, "no, I don't think you have."

The wistful regret softening Jake's roughly hewn features almost touched Rick. But not quite. "You make me sick," he said in a burst of self-righteous contempt. "There's no excuse for what you two did."

"No...no excuses. Only a reason."

"My father loved both of you! He *trusted* you!"

Jake stepped closer. "Look, son, if you'll just let me—"

"I am not your son!" Flecks of spittle flew from Rick's mouth. He felt as if his head were about to explode.

"I didn't mean—"

"I'll never be your son, do you hear me? Never!" With an abrupt, violent gesture Rick flung his glass aside against the terrace wall. It shattered, sending shards of glass hurtling through the air. Brown liquid dripped down the gray stones like blood.

Jake stood his ground, eyes dark with compassion. Rick hated him for that compassion.

"Alistair West is my father, and always will be." He felt a brief surge of satisfaction at the pain slashing across Jake's face. "If you ever, *ever* breathe a word about this to him, you will never see or hear from me again. Got that?"

Jake nodded, shoulders sagging slightly as if something vital had leaked out of him.

"My father is never to know the truth. Don't get any funny ideas about telling him, because if you do, I'll take him away someplace where you'll never find us."

Jake closed his eyes. "If that's how you want it."

Then a moan of anguish erupted from Rick's chest and he fled from Jake Winslow's house as if the hounds of hell were nipping at his heels. As he ducked into his red sports car, he caught one last glimpse of the man who had given him life.

Jake stood in the front window, staring after him with such longing, such despair, that for an instant Rick almost felt sorry for him. Now Jake Winslow looked his age and then some.

To this day, the taste of cola still made Rick queasy, though the hatred and bitterness consuming him that day had faded over the years. His determination to protect his father, however, remained as strong as ever.

Jake had kept his part of the bargain, even though he had little to lose by breaking their deal. He'd kept his silence, but the result was the same as if he'd taken out a billboard on Sunset Boulevard proclaiming Rick his son.

He still hadn't seen or heard one word from Rick since the day of that terrible scene.

Sometimes Rick felt guilty about that, but what was he supposed to do? Become pen pals with the man? If Pop ever discovered Rick and Jake were corresponding, he would know immediately that something funny was going on.

Besides, Rick had nothing to say to Jake anyway. He'd pretty much said it all that long-ago afternoon.

Jake's question still chimed in his ears: *Have you ever been in love?*

Rick gave the bolt he was tightening one final twist with his wrench. At the time, he'd scoffed at the notion that he didn't know what love was. Now from the perspective of added years, with the wisdom and self-awareness forged by maturity, Rick had to admit that Jake had at least been right about one thing.

He *had* never been in love.

And if I have anything to say about it, he thought, pushing aside the fleeting image of a certain gorgeous station manager, *I never will be.*

As soon as her meeting with Andy was finished, Dana sped back to her office, dumped her notes on her desk and made a beeline for the parking lot. By the time she got there, Rick was shoring up the sides of the dilapidated mine building with some new lumber.

"What are you doing here?" she demanded, shading her eyes against the sun's glare as she squinted up at him.

He stepped back from his handiwork and wiped a sheen of sweat from his brow with the rolled-up cuff of his sleeve. "I told you yesterday I'd help repair the float, remember?"

Had he? With all that had passed between them, it was hard to remember a minor detail like that. "Don't you have a house to build or a bridge to design or something?"

Rick eased himself down to the edge of the truck bed to sit with his legs dangling over the side. "I don't design bridges," he said, reaching for a half-empty bottle of mineral water, "and today there's a whole mob of subcontractors swarming all over the house I'm working on." He unscrewed the bottle cap and took a long, cool draft. "I decided it would be prudent to take the day off and stay out of their way."

"This doesn't look like taking the day off to me."
Dana watched, entranced, the way the cords of his throat
flexed when he swallowed.

He wiped his mouth, gestured at her with the bottle.
"Seems to me this is how you spend *your* days off."

"That's different. This float is my responsibility, not
yours."

"Consider my labor a donation. I'll deduct it off my
tax return, if it makes you feel any better."

He was perched less than a yard from her, muscled
thighs spread tantalizingly apart, leaning back to brace
himself against the same tanned forearms that had held
her less than twenty-four hours ago. Through the gap in
his unbuttoned shirt, curly brown hair glinted in the sun.

As if to punish her for wondering how it would feel to
run her fingers through those wiry curls, a little imp inside Dana prompted her to say, "This sudden philan-
thropy of yours doesn't change anything, you know. I'm
still determined to bring your father and his former
partner back together again."

Rick's face darkened as if a shadow had passed in front
of the sun. The minute the words escaped her lips, Dana
wanted to snatch them back. Too late.

He pushed himself to his feet, recapped the water bottle with an exaggerated deliberation that only emphasized his effort to control his anger. "If this is how you
thank everyone who contributes time and money, no
wonder your station's in trouble."

Ouch! Touché.

Rick turned his back on her and returned to his hammering as if Dana's words had glanced off him with no
effect. But the tense posture of his shoulders betrayed
him. She searched for the right words to apologize. Darn
it, when would she ever learn to think before she spoke?

Despite the narrow, constricting skirt she wore, Dana managed to wriggle up onto the float. "I'm sorry. I didn't mean that the way it sounded." She grimaced with frustration. Take two. "I mean, I *did* mean it the way it sounded." When Rick kept pounding away, she confessed in a quiet voice, "I guess I was mad at you."

That finally got his attention. "What?" He held the hammer poised motionless in the air.

"I said, I guess I was mad at you, and that's why I made that stupid remark." She glanced nervously over her shoulder, hoping none of the station busybodies were hovering next to an open window eavesdropping. "I was out of line, and I'm sorry."

Rick probed his cheek with his tongue, then cocked his head slightly to one side. "Why were you mad at me?"

Oh, Lord, she just kept digging herself in deeper and deeper....

"Because ... because ... Oh, all right." She forced herself to stop wringing her hands together like some damsel in distress. "I was mad because of the way you've been treating me."

His eyebrows soared skyward. "And what way is that?"

What did she have to lose, what with her pride lying in ruins at her feet? "One minute you're—you're kissing me, and the next minute you look like—like you want to run me over with your truck!"

It was so accurate a description of his ambivalence that Rick had to smile. "Maybe I'm the one who owes you an apology," he admitted.

"I'm not trying to pry into your personal business, but you *have* been sending me these mixed signals...."

Rick set down the hammer. To Dana's surprise he took both her hands in his. "I don't want to hurt you," he said gruffly, his callused palms creating a delightful friction against her skin, ''but...''

''But what?'' Amazing how steady her voice sounded when her knees were practically knocking together. She wasn't such a romantic dreamer she didn't know a brush-off when she heard one coming. But she wasn't a coward, either. Whatever Rick had to say, she wanted to hear it.

He raised his hand to her face, toyed with a stray lock of her hair. ''The smartest thing you could do would be refuse to have anything to do with me.''

The mixture of yearning and regret in his voice made Dana's breath catch in her throat. ''Well, I never claimed to be an *A* student,'' she murmured, remembering that geometry class she'd nearly flunked because of her obsession with Rick.

''If we pursue this relationship, you're going to be sorry.''

''Life is full of regrets.'' Dana tilted her cheek against his palm, closed her eyes. Had he actually used the word *relationship?* She could hardly believe this was happening, that Rick West could truly be interested in her. For so long he'd represented the unattainable, the impossible.

His breath heated her face. ''Dana...you don't know what you're getting into....''

When her lashes fluttered open, she found herself gazing dreamily into the turbulent gray depths of his eyes. She lifted her hand to run her fingers daringly down the front of his chest. ''Show me,'' she whispered.

With a groan Rick seized her, claiming her mouth with his. She was a vixen, that's what! A sorceress, a siren luring him onto the rocks of destruction.

He'd fully intended to keep her at arm's length from now on, yet here he was doing just the opposite. He should push her away; he wanted to pull her even closer. She was a threat to his emotional balance; he wanted to teeter on this exhilarating brink forever.

He marveled at the differences between them. In his arms, sturdy and solid as oak, Dana felt as slim and delicate as a willow. She was silk to his steel; she was a fire warming the icy reaches of his heart.

Rick dragged his lips from hers and branded a chain of kisses across her face to bury his mouth in the sweet, warm curve of her neck. This was only the beginning—he wanted to learn every inch of her soft, sensual body....

His heated caresses were like kerosene poured on Dana's smoldering desire. Like a match set to dry kindling, his lips against her skin ignited a wildfire of excitement that crackled in her ears and seared her nerve endings.

She felt achingly alive, as if her entire life had been a prelude to this very moment, this explosion of joy, this incredible, wondrous shock of knowing that Rick wanted her.

And there was no doubt he wanted her. The hard evidence was pressing against her, spreading waves of arousal through the very core of her being.

Dana's head lolled to one side as Rick nuzzled her neck, sending delicious little thrills ricocheting up and down her spine. She inhaled a long, quavering breath. He smelled like sweat and spice and fresh-cut lumber, and he felt like—like... heaven. There was no other word to describe the sensation of nestling in his arms, feeling the pounding drumbeat signal of his heart to hers, hearing his tortured breath so close to her ear....

It was as if they were the only two people in the world, as if no one else—

"Oh my God!" Rick's shoulder muffled her cry of dismay, but Dana repeated the general message by wedging her hands between them and pushing against his chest as hard as she could.

"Dana, what the hell—?" His eyes were as glazed, his lips as kiss-swollen as her own must be.

Dana tugged down her skirt and did her best to discreetly tuck her loosened blouse back into her waistband. She jerked her head toward the building. "Little pitchers have big ears, and the people I work with have very big eyes." She shot a nervous glance over her shoulder. "Not to mention long noses."

Rick's eyes darted past her. "Oh."

"Not that we have anything to hide—it's just that, well, I'm the boss. I have to set a good example and maintain discipline." With trembling fingers, she adjusted one of the clips holding back her hair. She could picture the entire station staff crowding behind the blinds in Andy's office. *Hey, everybody, come look at this!*

"I understand." Rick leisurely rubbed the nape of his neck. "I wouldn't want the people who work for me to catch me smooching on the job, either." He gave her a knowing wink, and instantly Dana felt better. Even though she could already hear the scuttlebutt being dished up at the office coffee machine along with the jelly doughnuts.

"I, um, guess I'd better let you get back to work." She knelt to the edge of the truck and prepared to jump, but Rick was quicker. He bounded to the ground and lifted her down as if she weighed no more than a feather.

He held her a moment longer than necessary, his strong hands spanning her waist, his hypnotic eyes scanning hers for a sign of—what? He seemed wistful, troubled somehow. Dana wished she could give Rick whatever it was he sought. She longed to brush her fingers through the sweat-dampened curlicues plastered to his temples, to reassure him that life wasn't nearly as grim as his expression would have her believe.

Once again she sensed the unmistakable impression of pain—long buried but never far from the surface. Would they ever grow close enough for Rick to share the emotional burden he was carrying around?

Dana hoped so. She was discovering a whole multitude of things she was eager to share with Rick. She was tired of the dusty old memories of him she'd stored in her heart all these years. More than anything, she wanted to create a whole bunch of new memories.

It was too soon to put a name to this strange longing she felt. She might be guilty of leaping before she looked, a few times in her life—okay, more than a few—but Dana was no fool. Rick might indeed want her, but wanting was a far cry from needing or caring...or loving.

The fulfillment of her schoolgirl fantasies wasn't enough anymore. She was a full-grown woman now, with a woman's needs, desires and expectations. Beneath his brusque, often exasperating exterior, was Rick really the decent, compassionate and infinitely exciting man she perceived him to be? Or were her perceptions skewed by the distorting filter of that long-ago infatuation?

When he finally released her, Dana felt bereft, as if suddenly, unfairly deprived of something precious and rare. When he stepped away, she sensed him retreating emotionally, as well, and had to crush the urge to call him back. His eyes were distant, almost absent now, as if he'd forgotten the passionate embrace they'd just shared and was focusing instead on the best way to brace up the wobbly backdrop on the float.

It was probably just as well. Otherwise she might be tempted to stand out here in the parking lot all day making goo-goo eyes at him.

"Well...thanks again. For working on the float, I mean."

"Don't mention it." As she turned to leave, Rick halted her with one final warning. "I meant what I said, Dana."

Her eyebrows arched into question marks.

"Getting involved with me is a big mistake."

She chewed her lower lip. "You know, usually when someone tries to discourage me from doing something, that only makes me want to do it more."

Rick boosted himself back onto the truck bed and looked down at her, feet planted apart, hands propped on his narrow hips. A slow smile spread across his face, finally cracking into a flash of white teeth. "Yeah," he said. "That's what I figured."

Dana felt his gaze drilling into her back as she crossed the parking lot.

It was a relief to reach the shelter of the building.... Even if Jenni was singing, "Somebody's got a boyfriend," under her breath as Dana passed by.

Dana punched the doorbell for the third time and shifted anxiously from foot to foot, waiting for Alistair to answer the door. Concern began to fray the edges of her impatience. She told herself there was nothing to worry about—she'd spoken to him less than half an hour ago when she'd phoned him for an appointment, hadn't she?

But it only took a split second for an elderly person to slip and fall, for a stroke or heart attack to claim its victim....

Good grief, now she was getting positively morbid! Still, she couldn't shake the frightening image of him lying incapacitated at the foot of a staircase.

Maybe the doorbell was broken. Dana jabbed it again as she pressed her ear against the thick door. Damn. Loud and clear. And she knew from previous encounters that his hearing was sharp as an owl's. She rapped the brass knocker for good measure.

A sudden sense of urgency seized her, propelling her off the front porch and around the side of the house to peer through a window. Nothing but an empty dining room, the table formally set with sparkling crystal and elegant china, waiting for guests who would never arrive. Strange...and sad....

"Mr. West?" she called. "Alistair?"

She heard a muffled cry from somewhere behind the house and tore into the backyard, her heart pounding even faster than her footsteps.

Relief flooded her bloodstream. "There you are!" was all she could think of to say.

Alistair glanced down at Dana from his precarious perch on top of a wobbly wooden stepladder that looked old enough to be the one Romeo had used to elope with Juliet. "Sorry, dear girl—were you waiting at the front door? Of course you were. What a damn fool question." He thumped the heel of his hand against the side of his head, the sudden movement sending the ladder teetering back and forth like a broken metronome.

Dana jumped forward to steady it. "What on earth are you doing up—oh, my." She stared at the birdhouse hanging from the branch of the large maple tree. Bird mansion was more like it. There was enough room inside for a flock of geese.

"Do you like it?" Alistair beamed proudly at the elaborate, hand-carved monstrosity. "Had it specially made by a local craftsman. Fellow just delivered it a few minutes ago, and I'm afraid I simply couldn't wait to hang it up."

"It's certainly... unique," Dana said carefully, privately thinking that any bird with an ounce of sense—or good taste—would be terrified to go near the thing.

"One of a kind! And worth every penny, I might add. As you may have guessed, bird-watching is one of my fondest pursuits."

"I suspected as much," she replied dryly. She couldn't help thinking what a shame it was that Alistair had chosen to give up human companionship for that of his feathered friends. "But you shouldn't be trying to hang it all by yourself."

"Nonsense! I'm fit as a fiddle."

"Maybe *you* are, but that ladder's not. Besides, you're not supposed to stand on the top step like that. Didn't you read the warning label?"

"Bah! What label?"

"Probably wore off decades ago," Dana muttered under her breath. "Here, let me help you down."

Alistair grumbled something, the only part of which she caught was "... mere slip of a girl...." But he did bend over and take a step backward down the ladder.

Dana was reaching for his arm when his foot slipped suddenly. He would have toppled to the ground if she hadn't grabbed him and braced him up with all her strength. "Easy now... careful..."

When at last Alistair set foot on solid ground again, they were both breathing hard. Dana kept hold of his arm and helped him move to the weathered wooden deck. "I warned you about that ladder," she scolded good-naturedly as he lowered his stiff, quavering form into the nearest chair.

Then alarm wiped the teasing smile from her face. Alistair's normally ruddy complexion was pale as the moon, his broad forehead beaded with sweat. "Are you all right?" she asked anxiously, kneeling on the deck beside him.

He pressed a trembling hand to his heart. "My chest," he croaked, ". . . pain in my chest."

Dana struggled to remain calm in the face of her worst nightmare coming true. "You're going to be all right," she said in what she hoped was a reassuring voice, praying that statement was accurate. "You've just had a scare, that's all."

Alistair's rapid breathing chilled her to the bone. "I'm going to get you a glass of water," she said, bounding to her feet and sliding open the glass door that she discovered led to a breakfast nook off the kitchen.

She fumbled through cupboards, found a glass and filled it at the sink. *Dear God, the man's having a heart attack and I'm trying to cure it with a glass of water!* Never had she felt so helpless, so useless.

She sloshed about half the water out of the glass before she got back to Alistair. To Dana's relief, his color seemed much better now, his breathing easier. "How do you feel?"

"All right . . . I think."

"Still have pain in your chest?"

"No." He sipped the water, frowned. "Couldn't you find anything stronger than this?"

Dana gave him a shaky grin. "I don't think that's such a good idea right now."

"Tommyrot!" He thrust the glass at her. "I made some lemonade right after you called. It's in the refrigerator."

"Oh, *lemonade*. Sounds wonderful. I'll be right back." Dana's heart was singing with relief when she returned with a pitcher and an extra glass. She set the tray on the patio table and poured their drinks before settling back into a chair next to Alistair.

He took a swallow of lemonade, but Dana was willing to bet he hadn't tasted it. His eyes were aimed in the direction of the maple tree and that godawful birdhouse, but she could tell by the expression on his face that he was seeing something far, far beyond it. His first glimpse of his own mortality, maybe?

The lemonade was tart, just the way she liked it. She was amazed by how thirsty she was, and was reaching for the pitcher again before Alistair had emptied even a third of his glass. Nothing like a heart-stopping scare to parch the old throat.

As if reading Dana's thoughts, Alistair set down his glass and gave an embarrassed *hmph*. "Must apologize for frightening you, my dear. Sometimes a decrepit old man like me doesn't like to admit he's not as spry as he used to be."

"You needn't apologize. And you're *not* old and decrepit."

"Nice of you to say so." He sounded unconvinced. A spasm of pain crossed his face and Dana tensed, her pulse racing until she comprehended it wasn't physical but emotional pain that was troubling Alistair.

He exhaled a long, drawn-out sigh and for a minute *did* look old and decrepit, although Dana would never have admitted it to him. "A man gets to the end of his life and he starts to look back over the things he's done...the

▲ DETACH AND MAIL CARD TODAY! ▲

BUSINESS REPLY MAIL

FIRST CLASS MAIL   PERMIT NO. 717   BUFFALO NY

POSTAGE WILL BE PAID BY ADDRESSEE

SILHOUETTE READER SERVICE
3010 WALDEN AVE
PO BOX 1867
BUFFALO NY 14240-9952

NO POSTAGE
NECESSARY
IF MAILED
IN THE
UNITED STATES

GOOD NEWS! You can get
up to FIVE GIFTS—FREE!

If offer card is missing, write to:
Silhouette Reader Service, 3010 Walden Ave., P.O. Box 1867, Buffalo, NY 14269-1867.

FIND OUT **INSTANTLY** IF YOU GET
UP TO 5 FREE GIFTS IN THE

LUCKY

CARNIVAL WHEEL

▼ **SCRATCH-OFF GAME!** ▼

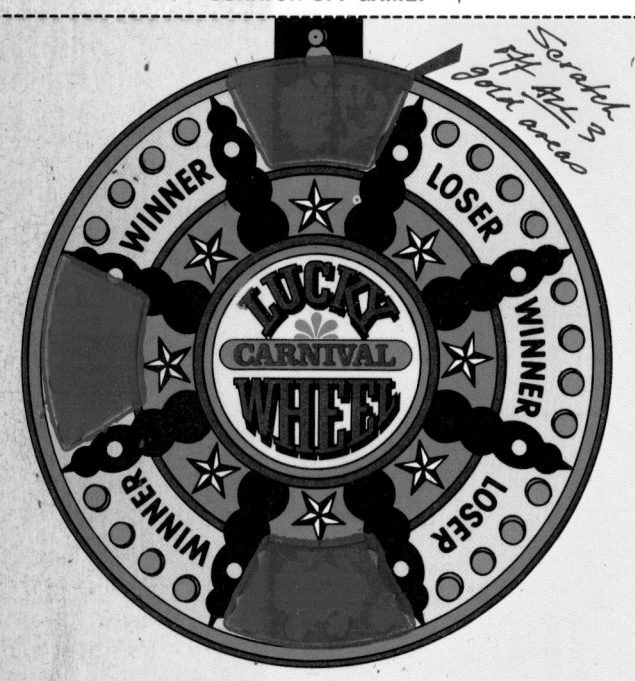

YES! I have scratched off the 3 Gold Areas above. Please send me all the gifts for which I qualify. I understand I am under no obligation to purchase any books, as explained on the opposite page.

235 CIS AG45
(U-SIL-SE-01/93)

NAME

ADDRESS   APT.

CITY   STATE   ZIP

HOW TO PLAY:

1. With a coin, carefully scratch off the 3 gold areas on your Lucky Carnival Wheel. You could get one or more free Silhouette Special Edition® novels, and possibly another gift, depending on what is revealed beneath the scratch-off areas.

2. Return your Lucky Carnival Wheel game card, and we'll immediately send you the books and gift you qualify for ABSOLUTELY FREE!

3. Then, unless you tell us otherwise, every month we'll send you 6 additional novels to read and enjoy, months before they're available in stores. You can return them and owe nothing. But if you decide to keep them, you'll pay only $2.71* each plus 25¢ delivery and applicable sales tax, if any*. That's the complete price, and—compared to cover prices of $3.39 each in stores—quite a bargain!

4. Your satisfaction is always guaranteed and you may cancel at any time just by dropping us a note or by returning any shipment at our cost. Of course, the FREE books and gift remain yours to keep!

No Cost! No Risk! No Obligation to Buy!

PLAY THE
LUCKY
CARNIVAL
WHEEL
GAME...

**GET AS
MANY AS
FIVE GIFTS
FREE!**

**PLAY FOR FREE!
NO PURCHASE
NECESSARY!**

mistakes he's made, the business he's left unfinished...."

Dana's first impulse was to try to tease and cajole Alistair out of his melancholy, but then she realized he needed to say these things, to reflect out loud, to share his thoughts with a sympathetic listener. Dana vowed to be exactly that. She sensed that for some reason he was unable to confide in his son like this.

"We all have things we wish we could change about our lives, things we wish we could do over," she said.

"Yes..." Alistair shifted uncomfortably. "You might not know it to see me now, but I was somewhat of a hothead in my youth."

"You were?" Dana smiled, thinking of Rick. It wasn't really so hard to believe.

"Stubborn, opinionated, always sure that my way was the only way to do things...." He chuckled. "There are still one or two directors in Hollywood who could tell you stories, I'm sure."

She grinned. "Temperamental, were you?"

"Oh, I had a ferocious sense of right and wrong. And I'm ashamed to admit, I wasn't always as forgiving as I should have been when things didn't go my way."

Dana nibbled her lower lip, sensing the perfect opportunity to approach the subject she'd been trying to figure out a way to bring up. But first she needed to know one thing. "The reason I asked to see you today was to find out if you've made a decision about appearing during our pledge drive."

"What? Oh, yes, of course. Matter of fact, I'd consider it an honor."

"You would? I mean, you will? Help us promote our membership drive?"

"If you still think I can really be of any help."

Delighted, Dana pumped his gnarled hand enthusiastically. "You can't know how much this means to me—to the station and to the whole community."

She took a deep breath, ready to gamble all her marbles. "Actually, since last we spoke, I've come up with another idea I'd like your reaction to."

Alistair patted the back of her hand. "You remind me of my dear wife—always so full of enthusiasm and ideas." He winked. "And pretty as a picture to boot."

"Why, Mr. West, if I didn't know any better I'd think you were trying to flirt with me!"

He slapped his knee and chortled with laughter. "My dear, if I were forty years younger, you'd be right!"

A wave of fondness for the old man engulfed her. He reminded Dana of someone, too. Her father. Whom she still missed every single day of her life.

Knowing what a gaping hole losing her father had left in her life gave Dana a special sympathy for Alistair. It was too late for him to get his wife back. But there was still time to get back the best friend he'd ever had.

"I don't want to step on any toes here, or pry into your personal business...."

Alistair's eyes were riveted on Dana with lively curiosity.

"But how would you feel about appearing on television...with Jake Winslow?"

She braced herself for an outburst of indignation, curses and refusals. But though Alistair looked startled at first, he didn't reject the idea out of hand.

Dana crossed her fingers.

At last he cleared his throat and said, "Jake and I haven't laid eyes on each other for over thirty years."

"I wouldn't dream of asking what split up your partnership and ruined your friendship, but whatever it was, surely thirty years is long enough for old wounds to heal, isn't it?''

"At one time I wouldn't have thought so, but now..." Alistair rubbed his hand over his balding pate as if it could help clarify his thoughts. "It isn't only up to me, you know."

Hope flared in her heart. "Then you'll consider the idea?"

"I can't make any promises, but yes, I'll give your proposal some thought." His eyes took on that faraway glow again. "Fact is, I've already given it some consideration. Oh, not specifically in regard to your membership drive," he said in response to Dana's surprised expression. "But I have found myself wondering lately whether or not it might be time to set aside old disagreements, to patch up ancient grudges that don't seem nearly as important now as they once did."

"Would...would you mind if I approached Mr. Winslow with this idea?"

"No..." Alistair gave a resigned shrug. "Can't imagine how he'll react, really. You see, it was I who was responsible for the breakup of our partnership. I could hardly blame him for still holding that against me."

"I'll see if I can't convince Mr. Winslow to let bygones be bygones."

Alistair wagged a crooked finger at her. "I'll wager if anyone can do it, it'll be you, young woman." He shook his head. "I can hardly believe you've already talked me into appearing in public again." He pushed himself creakily to his feet. "Mind now, I haven't said I'll go along with this new idea of yours, but I shall give it some thought. After you've spoken to Jake, we can discuss it again."

"That's all I ask." Dana's head was spinning with excitement, plans and possibilities. She would have Jenni make an airline reservation right away, and talk to Andy and Elaine about working this new development into their promotional spots. They would have to put together a news release and publicity packet to distribute to all the major news media just before the reconciliation took place....

On impulse she stood on tiptoe and planted a kiss on Alistair's wrinkled cheek. As much as this reunion would mean to Channel Five, it could have an even greater, more emotional impact on Alistair. "I won't let you down," she promised.

As she slid into her car Dana called to him, "And from now on, no more hanging birdhouses by yourself—do you hear me?"

He made a crisscross over his heart and waved while she backed out of the driveway.

She wondered if she should mention Alistair's attack to Rick. She hated to meddle, but darn it, she would never forgive herself if anything ever happened to that delightful old man.

Rick. As usual, the thought of him sent shivers of excitement zipping up Dana's spine. But this time she felt a little frisson of dread, too.

What would he say when he found out his father had not only agreed to appear on television but that he might very well be standing next to Jake Winslow at the time?

Chapter Seven

Dana had finished reading the in-flight magazine before the plane had even backed away from the gate at Sacramento's Metro Airport. She was stuffing it back into the pocket on the seat in front of her when a late-arriving passenger flung himself into the seat next to hers. At that moment the plane started to move, and she snuck a sideways glance at whoever had nearly missed the commuter flight to Los Angeles.

Instead of a harried businessman, Dana found herself gaping at a wild-eyed, breathless and—from the looks of him—altogether furious Rick.

"That seat's reserved for someone else," she said quickly.

He speared her with a withering look. "Open seating on this flight," he said between gasps. "I asked the stewardess."

"Gee, whaddaya know."

"I know I nearly killed myself making the drive from Pine Creek in record time! I know I had to park about three miles from the terminal and by the time I bought my ticket, had to run like a maniac to make this flight."

"Tsk, tsk," she clucked. "Poor planning will catch up with you every time."

"I didn't have time to plan anything! Not after I dropped by Pop's before work this morning and found out what you were up to." Impatiently he dashed a fallen lock of hair from his eyes. "Then when I tried to call you at the station I had to sweet-talk your secretary into telling me what flight you were on."

"I bet *that* was real difficult," Dana muttered. No doubt Jenni would consider Rick's frantic pursuit of her highly romantic. And what woman could resist Rick's sweet-talking charm?

Besides her, of course.

"I suppose you think you can talk me out of seeing Jake Winslow," she said, just as the pilot announced they'd been cleared for takeoff.

"I'm certainly going to do my damnedest," he said through clenched teeth.

As the engine whine crescendoed to a deafening pitch and the plane began to accelerate, Dana saw to her surprise that Rick was gripping the armrests as if he planned to lift the aircraft off the ground himself. His eyes squinched shut and his well-tanned face turned several shades lighter. "Well, I'll be a monkey's uncle," she said, leaning over and speaking loudly to be heard above the roar of the jet engines. "You're afraid of flying!"

"No, I'm not," he retorted, peeling one eye half open to glare at her as best he could. "I'm afraid of crashing."

Instinctively Dana covered his hand with hers. "There's nothing to worry about," she said, oddly touched by this unexpected vulnerability. "Look, we're already up into the clouds. Most plane wrecks occur during takeoff, so the worst is over already."

"Somehow that doesn't make me feel any better." But his death grip on the armrest loosened and he opened his eyes.

"Statistics show that flying is far safer than driving," Dana pointed out.

"Thanks for the pep talk," Rick said. "It's your fault I'm here in the first place."

"In the first place, I hardly think *I'm* responsible for your mad impetuous actions. And in the second place, I don't know what you're talking about."

"Can I get you something to drink?" The flight attendant leaned over Rick's shoulder.

"I'd like some orange juice," Dana replied. "And he'll have coffee." She bent forward and explained to the woman confidentially, "He's very grouchy in the morning until he has his caffeine."

One good thing about Dana, Rick reflected as he accepted the plastic cup of coffee with a sour smile. She was so exasperating that he forgot about being nervous.

He declined the offered packet of peanuts with a shake of his head. "I'll take his," Dana said quickly. She tore open a packet, popped a couple of nuts into her mouth and munched cheerfully.

"How can you eat those things so early in the morning?" Rick asked, wincing as he scalded his mouth on his first sip of coffee.

"Didn't have time for breakfast." *Crunch, crunch.*

"That makes two of us."

"You shouldn't have turned down your peanuts," Dana said, opening the second packet.

Rick decided to ignore her until they were safely on the ground again. He had no intention of starting a meaningful dialogue at thirty thousand feet. They might miss an emergency announcement by the captain or something.

But somehow his glance kept sliding to his right, where Dana was chomping away and gazing out the window as if she didn't have a care in the world. She looked like any one of the dozens of other business executives on this flight.

Correction. She was infinitely more attractive than anyone else on the plane. Her elegant linen suit was snug fitting yet professional, giving her a look of cool competence and assurance. The fabric's peachy hue flattered her, casting a delicate reflection of color onto her alabaster skin. With her dark hair pulled up into a neat twist, she looked as tasty as peaches and cream.

Rick had to chuckle to himself, knowing what an irrepressible hoyden lurked behind that prim facade. Dana had been a real mischief-maker in high school, and that much about her hadn't changed. She was still wreaking havoc—at least in Rick's life. Who would think that behind that sedate business-executive façade was a woman who ate peanuts for breakfast, who would throw a temper tantrum over a papier-mâché mule named Sparky?

Rick's smile faded. Just another example of how appearances could be deceiving, how you couldn't trust people to behave the way they were supposed to. They would disappoint you every time.

Dana studied the tops of the clouds, trying to be annoyed by Rick's surprise appearance. Talking to Jake

Winslow was going to be tricky enough without Rick there to sabotage her.

Yet her innate honesty wouldn't let her deny the fact that her stomach had taken an exhilarating swoop when he sat down beside her. And the thrill of anticipation she'd felt had had nothing to do with their impending takeoff.

No matter how often Rick tried to throw a monkey wrench into her plans, Dana simply couldn't help being glad to see him, no matter what the circumstances. She wasn't sure why; each time they met they seemed to wind up in either a shouting match or sulking silence. And his presence had given Dana's co-workers the most they'd had to gossip about since one of the married camera operators had run off with her sound man.

Just look at the way he was hogging the cramped space right now! His broad shoulders encroached on space that rightfully belonged to Dana. He'd stretched his long legs in front of the empty aisle seat next to him. The poor flight attendant was liable to trip on his booted feet when she passed by.

But the most annoying infringement was the way he had his forearm planted securely on *her* armrest! The sleeve of his denim jacket kept brushing against her, making the hairs on her arm stand up. And did he have to lean so close to her? The seductive scent of after-shave and coffee was positively unnerving. How was she supposed to plan her strategy with this big, grumpy, sexy distraction intruding on her thoughts as well as her space?

When she leaned across Rick to catch the flight attendant's attention, Dana's breast accidentally grazed his arm, sending a rush of sensation racing through her. Without thinking, she quickly glanced at his face, and found his eyes simmering like molten steel with the explosive heat of their intimate contact. Hastily she averted her eyes, but not before a flood of warmth spread across her cheeks. "C-could I please have some coffee?" she stammered.

"I'm sorry, ma'am, but we're beginning our descent into Los Angeles."

"Oh." Dana leaned back, careful to give Rick a wide berth this time. "Guess that means it's too late for a Bloody Mary, too," she said to herself, her voice drowned out by the changing pitch of the engines.

Rick could have used a drink himself, she realized the next time she snuck a peek at him. He was going into that rigid, zombie-eyed routine again. Poor guy. He must really want to stop her to put himself through this.

But Dana wasn't the kind of person to hold it against him. He needed something to take his mind off the landing. She could provoke an argument with him...that would certainly make him feel on safe, familiar territory.

"I don't suppose when your father mentioned my visit yesterday that he mentioned his...uh, attack, did he?" Though it seemed cruel to raise the subject at a moment like this, having someone else to worry about would undoubtedly take Rick's mind off his own fears. Besides, Dana really thought he ought to know about what had happened.

She'd guessed right. Rick pounced on her immediately. "What attack? What are you talking about?" His forehead crinkled with deep concern.

"*Attack* might be too strong a word. He was up on a ladder, and slipped coming down. I caught him, but he was awfully short of breath and complained about chest pains for a few minutes."

Rick uttered something inaudible, but Dana could tell it was a curse—whether at her, himself or fate was unclear. "What was he doing up on that damned ladder, anyway? I've warned him about using that old thing."

"Hanging the ugliest birdhouse I've ever seen."

A grim smile flickered across his lips. "Pop's taste *is* somewhat . . . baroque."

"He seemed fine by the time I left. A little quiet, maybe."

"Thank you for helping him." Rick squeezed Dana's hand briefly, surprising her. She'd been afraid he might blame her for his father's attack. "I've been trying to drag him to the doctor for a checkup for over a year, but he can be pretty stubborn once he gets his mind set on something—or against it."

"So he told me."

"He did?" Rick looked taken aback.

"We talked about a lot of things, including the past."

"Really?" He frowned. "Pop's never wanted to discuss the past with me."

"Maybe you never wanted to listen."

Dana held her breath, certain that her blunt remark was about to provoke an outburst. Instead, Rick nodded thoughtfully. "You might be right about that. It's just that—"

Horrified, he nearly bit off his tongue. Good grief, he'd been about to explain his aversion to discussing the past as casually as he might explain the blueprint of a building! Telling Dana everything he'd kept locked inside for so long felt as easy, as natural as making love.

Images of making love with her came crashing through his brain, and the urge to share himself with her—physically, emotionally, completely—nearly took his breath away.

He shook himself out of his daze. It must be the high altitude draining his brain of oxygen or something. How could he even consider risking his own happiness—much less his father's—on something as ephemeral, as fleeting, as unreliable as love?

Panic rose even higher inside him. No, not love—that was ridiculous, that wasn't what he was starting to feel for Dana. Rick realized he was still clasping her fingers in his and dropped her hand as if it had seared his skin. She gave him an odd, questioning look.

He had to banish the fear in his belly, the growing suspicion that somehow he'd been trapped in a spider web, entangled in something he wasn't ready for, would never be ready for. "Don't you see what you're doing?" he asked, not sure exactly what he was accusing her of.

Dana's eyes clouded with confusion. "What I'm doing? What do you mean?"

"My father," Rick replied flatly.

"I still don't—"

"Can't you see how this TV appearance has got him all riled up?"

"No, I don't. He seemed very pleased—"

"It's too much excitement for him. His attack yesterday could be a precursor to something far more serious."

"He nearly fell off a ladder, for Pete's sake! I'd have heart palpitations, too, if the same thing happened to me."

"He's eighty-three years old," Rick plowed on relentlessly. "He's too old for the stress of appearing in public again. If you hadn't railroaded him, he never would have—"

"*Railroaded* him? I never railroaded anyone, buster."
Though she could think of someone she'd love to tie to

the tracks right now. "Your father is an intelligent, vital man who's perfectly capable of making his own decisions. He doesn't need your overprotective mollycoddling."

"*Mollycoddling?* Why, you—"

"Oh, look," she said with a saccharine smile. "We're on the ground already."

Rick blinked, then his jaw clunked open in astonishment when he peered out the window past Dana's shoulder. "How did we—I mean, I didn't even feel . . ." He pinned her to her seat with a stern glare. "You did that on purpose, didn't you?"

"Did what?" she asked, batting her long lashes at him in perfect innocence.

"Picked a fight with me so I'd forget we were landing."

"I never have to pick a fight with you on purpose," she said, retrieving her purse from beneath the seat in front of her. "It happens all by itself. Like spontaneous combustion."

But Rick had completely forgotten about the plane's descent and knew that Dana had deliberately distracted him. She could have tortured him with a play-by-play commentary of the fast-approaching sights on the ground. Instead, she'd pretended to be as oblivious to their landing as he'd been.

Why did she have to keep doing such damn nice things when he was trying so hard to stay mad at her?

He stuck close while Dana bulldozed her way through the airport crowds to the rental-car counter. "I hope you have a reservation," he said when they found themselves at the end of a long line. The other rental-car counters were just as busy.

"*I'm* not the one who doesn't plan ahead, remember?"

"Good, then since you're so organized, I'm sure you won't mind giving me a lift to Jake's house."

With only the briefest hesitation, Dana gave a long-suffering sigh. "I suppose there's no use in my asking you to turn around and go home."

"Not a chance."

"Oh, all right. But *I'm* going to drive."

"Just so long as you watch out for any deer leaping across the freeway."

She couldn't resist returning the friendly, teasing grin that spread across Rick's face like a break in the clouds. He was such fun to be around sometimes.

Too bad she was going to have to play such a dirty trick on him.

Finally they reached the head of the line and Dana got the keys for her compact rental car.

Rick pointed ahead when they reached the parking lot. "That must be it—that tan one over there."

"Gosh, it's parked awful close to the car on the passenger side."

"No problem, there's room to get in."

"I'll back out first so you can get in easier."

"There's really no need for you to—"

The slam of her car door muffled the rest of his sentence. Dana turned the key, praying the car would start right away.

Like a charm.

Smiling broadly and ignoring Rick's impatient gestures to unlock his door, Dana backed out of the parking space. She revved the engine, gave Rick one final wave and took off with a screech of rubber.

She could see Rick chasing after her in the rearview mirror as she pulled out of the lot and into the congested flow of airport traffic.

A faint twinge of guilt pricked her conscience. Very faint. After all, Rick had had a lot of nerve, following her to L.A. like this. He had no one but himself to blame for the predicament he was in now. Besides, her decision to ditch him was strictly business, nothing personal. She would like nothing better than to spend this glorious spring day cruising around L.A. with Rick, windows rolled down, the wind rustling through their hair, visiting all her favorite old haunts from her college days....

Dana nosed her way onto the crowded San Diego Freeway, sparing a glance at her watch. Rick would have to wait in line at the rental-car counter all over again, and with any luck all their cars would be reserved anyway. Furthermore, as far as she knew he hadn't lived in L.A. since early childhood and wouldn't be nearly as skillful at navigating the freeways as Dana was. She'd spent four years at UCLA and five years working at a PBS station in Hollywood, during which time she'd learned the ins and outs of the freeway bumper-car game as well as any native.

She spotted an opening in the fast lane and zipped neatly into it. She also knew a few shortcuts between here and Bel Air. Add that advantage to her head start, and unless Rick chartered a helicopter, she should have a good fifteen minutes to present her case to Jake Winslow, uninterrupted by Rick's unreasonable objections.

Assuming Jake Winslow was home, that is. Dana's instincts had warned her that she would have a better chance of persuading him if she didn't give him advance notice of her visit. That way he wouldn't have time to think up a bunch of reasons to refuse her.

She exited the freeway at Sunset Boulevard and was soon cruising the broad, curving streets looking for the address she'd pried out of her contact in the musicians' union office. She prayed Jake Winslow wouldn't have a locked gate barricading his driveway the way lots of his neighbors did. Not that she couldn't talk her way through it eventually, but she didn't want to waste any of her precious time before Rick showed up.

She found his home. Ah, bless the man! Dana turned into the circular driveway and parked near the front door. Giving herself a quick once-over in the rearview mirror, she hopped out of the car and mentally rehearsed the speech she'd prepared for Jake Winslow's butler or whoever answered the door.

She pressed the doorbell, straightened her skirt and glanced anxiously over her shoulder, half expecting to see a helicopter landing on the broad front lawn.

The door opened. "Hello, my name is—Mr. Winslow!"

The handsome older man grinned in a way that was somehow familiar. "That's funny—that's my name, too."

Dana laughed, flustered by his unexpected appearance. No barred gate, no butler answering the front door... Did the man do his own laundry, too?

She took an instant liking to him. Now that she'd overcome her initial surprise, she could understand why he'd looked so eerily familiar. She'd seen pictures of him when he was much younger, but the man had aged incredibly well. He had to be over seventy now, but really, he was quite attractive....

She halted her woolgathering and introduced herself properly. As soon as she mentioned Alistair's name, an undecipherable look crossed Jake Winslow's craggy features. "Why don't we go out on the terrace?" he said. "I was just having some coffee. Perhaps you'd like some?"

His house was impressive in an understated sort of way, very masculine with lots of wood paneling, broad expanses of glass and a stone fireplace in the living room. It was the kind of house where you'd expect to find dead animal heads mounted on the wall, and Dana was relieved to discover that Jake Winslow's tastes apparently didn't run in this direction. Indeed, the place was remarkably devoid of knickknacks or memorabilia of any kind, as if the owner had no interest in being reminded of the past.

He led her through what appeared to be a music room, with an enormous piano in one corner and bookshelves full of sheet music. When he left her alone on the terrace to fetch a second coffee cup, Dana scanned the hillside below for any trace of her pursuer.

"Nice view, isn't it?" She jumped when her host returned. "The view is what made me decide to buy this place years ago." He set a pink cardboard box on the table next to the coffeepot and gave her a sheepish grin. "This isn't exactly what you'd call a healthy breakfast, but would you like one?"

Dana peeked into the box. "Ooh, I'd love one!" She helped herself to a buttermilk doughnut covered with maple frosting and smacked her lips. "This is my favorite kind."

"Yes, they're one of my guilty pleasures, too, I'm afraid." He winked as she bit into her doughnut, instantly banishing her nervousness by making her feel like a coconspirator in the war against health food. No matter what kind of grudge Alistair and Rick held against this man, Dana found him charming.

He poured her a cup of coffee. "Now, just what can I do for you, Ms. Sheridan?"

She washed down a mouthful of doughnut and launched into her idea for reuniting West and Winslow during Channel Five's membership drive.

"...And after we air *Match Made in Heaven* we'll bring you and Alistair out in front of the cameras. The two of you will shake hands, then sit down with one of our interviewers and reminisce a bit about the old days in Hollywood. Then you and Alistair will give a brief pitch supporting public television and ask viewers to call in their pledges."

Dana paused, completely uncertain what Jake's reaction was going to be. She'd been unable to glean the slightest clue from his expression during her spiel. He'd listened with a neutral look of polite interest frozen on his face.

Now he rose to his feet and braced himself against the stone terrace wall, staring out at the smog-blurred horizon. Finally he turned around and dragged his fingers through his dark gray hair. "You talked about this with Alistair yet?" he asked, studying her from beneath his shaggy brows.

Dana swallowed. Well, at least he hadn't thrown her out on her ear yet, or asked for his doughnut back. "We've discussed it," she replied. "He's already agreed to help us promote our membership drive, and he's agreed to consider appearing with you."

"Hmm." He shook his head, sending Dana's heart plunging to the pit of her stomach. "I must say, I'm amazed he would even consider the idea. You see..." His voice trailed off, then he shrugged. "I was responsible for the breakup of our partnership."

"That's not what Alistair says."

"No?" His eyebrows shot up in surprise.

"He says *he* was responsible."

"Does he now...?" Jake stroked his chin thoughtfully.

Dana decided to press her slight advantage. "Mr. Winslow, I'm not interested in raking up dirt from the past and turning your private life into fodder for the tabloids. But the truth is, I'm desperate."

He sat down again and raised his cup. "Go on."

She took a deep breath. "Channel Five is on the verge of bankruptcy. This plan to reunite you and Alistair is my last chance to drum up the publicity and support we need to keep the station going." She leaned forward, clasping her hands in her lap. "You have the power to make an awfully big difference in the lives of a lot of people. With your help, people will be able to keep their jobs, continue their education, observe local government meetings...."

Dana broke off at the amused twinkle in Jake's eye. "I'm sorry," she said with a reluctant grin. "Guess I sound like a public service announcement myself."

"That's *my* job, remember?"

Her heart fluttered with excitement. "Then you'll do it?"

He held up his palms. "Hold on a second, now. You've given me an awful lot to think about before I make a decision."

On impulse, she reached across the table to touch his hand. "Mr. Winslow, Alistair would probably kill me if I told you this, but he misses you terribly."

She felt his fingers tremble. "Did he tell you that?"

"He doesn't have to! It's written all over his face plain as day every time your name comes up."

Jake closed his eyes for a moment. "Did he tell you what caused our falling-out?" he asked in a voice so quiet, she had to strain to hear.

"No, and I don't want to know. It doesn't matter to me, and what's more important, I don't think it matters to Alistair anymore, either."

Jake patted her hand and curved up one side of his mouth in a skeptical smile. "I wish I could believe that."

"Then *talk* to him, for heaven's sake! It's obvious you're as anxious to patch up your differences as he is. What could be worth—"

The doorbell rang, followed immediately by a barrage of furious pounding. "What the Sam Hill...?" Jake's chair scraped on the flagstones as he rose to his feet.

"Probably just some pesky encyclopedia salesman," Dana said quickly. "Maybe an aggressive Girl Scout selling cookies?" She scurried after her host, not about to let Rick have one minute alone with him if she could help it.

The doorbell rang twice in quick succession just as Jake reached the front entryway. "Good grief, hold your horses." He swung open the door. "What the hell's going—"

Dana was astonished by the rapid drain of color from his face. When he spoke, the word was a barely audible croak. "Rick."

"Hello...Jake." Rick was bouncing from foot to foot like a boxer spoiling for a fight. When he spotted Dana trying to hide behind Jake, his eyes sparked with anger like two pieces of gray flint. "You!" he shouted, pointing an accusing finger like a judge at the Salem witch trials. "You left me standing there like some kind of—"

"It's your own fault," she retorted past Jake's shoulder. "You shouldn't have followed me in the first place."

"All the rental cars were taken, so I had to grab a taxi." He stepped forward, fists knotted at his sides. "Do you have any idea how much cab fare all the way up here from the airport is?"

"You should have thought of that before you tried to interfere."

"Interfere?" Rick's face was a glowing shade of red. "*You're* the one who's interfering, barging into my life with your crazy schemes...."

Jake's head had been swiveling back and forth like a spectator's at a Ping-Pong match. "This is just a wild guess," he said finally, "but do you two know each other?"

Rick blew out a long, frustrated stream of air like a collapsing balloon. "Unfortunately."

"We're old friends," Dana elaborated with a fond smile.

"Who needs enemies?" Rick muttered.

"Let's all go out on the terrace," Jake said.

Dana was careful to keep Jake between her and Rick as they trooped back through the house. Strange...Jake kept staring at Rick as if he were a ghost.

Outside, Jake grasped the coffeepot. "Coffee?" he offered Rick. Dana noticed his hand shook slightly.

"No, thanks." Rick sprawled into a chair, avoiding Jake's eyes.

Dana nudged the pink box in his direction. "Doughnut?"

He made a face that seemed directed at both her and the doughnuts. Then he turned to Jake. "What's she been telling you?"

Rick had been so aggravated by Dana's treachery, he hadn't really had a chance to prepare himself for his first glimpse of Jake in more than a dozen years. Now that he was actually face-to-face with his natural father, an un-expected flood of emotion swept through him. Feelings tumbled over him in a complicated jumble he couldn't even begin to sort out.

The resentment he'd felt since learning his mother's secret was still there, but mixed in with it was guilt—guilt that he hadn't bothered once in all these years to drop Jake a note or pick up the phone to call him.

He couldn't help wondering to what degree he himself was responsible for the new, deeper network of creases etched in Jake's face. Jake had kept his silence the way he'd promised, and what had Rick given him in return?

Zilch.

Jake was all alone in the world, for God's sake! As far as Rick knew, he was Jake's only living flesh and blood, the only link to the woman he'd once loved. How much would it have hurt Rick to send the man a damned Christmas card once a year?

He hadn't expected to feel this way, didn't *want* to feel this way. But no matter how much he tried to deny it, he and Jake shared a biological bond that wasn't just going to disappear. Though he tried to fight it, Rick felt a pull toward Jake that was as inevitable as the tug of the moon on the tides.

He'd stayed away for nearly thirteen years, but even that span of time hadn't been long enough to make him indifferent.

In the eyes of the man who was his father Rick detected caution, uncertainty…and something else he didn't dare to identify. "Ms. Sheridan has brought me an interesting proposition," Jake said slowly.

"I'll bet." Rick fired an accusing glance at Dana. "I suppose you had time to tell him everything before I got here."

She shrugged with maddening calm. "Not quite everything. I didn't get around to explaining that you're dead set against the whole idea."

"Just slipped your mind, huh?" He turned back to Jake. "I need to speak to you—alone." He aimed a meaningful glare at Dana.

"I can take a hint," she said, rising gracefully to her feet like a queen from her throne. "Mr. Winslow, I'll be in touch. Please believe that I'm not trying to *exploit* anyone, no matter what anyone else says." She shook his hand, sliding her gaze in Rick's direction.

"And don't you dare try to leave without me," Rick warned.

Her eyes widened into an expression of wounded innocence. "I wouldn't dream of it. No, please sit down, Mr. Winslow. I can see myself out." She picked up her purse and gave Jake a final dazzling smile before sashaying out of sight.

"Nice girl," Jake said. "Pretty, too. Not that it's any of my business, but are you and she ... ?"

"*No,*" Rick said with far more vehemence than he'd intended. "She drives me crazy."

"So I see." Jake was regarding him with a shrewd, perceptive expression.

"I didn't come here to discuss my love life," Rick said quickly. "I came to warn you—I mean, to *ask* you not to participate in this ridiculous public reunion Dana's planning."

Jake traced the rim of his cup with the pad of his thumb. "She says Alistair's receptive to the idea."

"That's because he doesn't know what could happen!"

Jake didn't respond right away, apparently measuring his words before he spoke. "And what exactly is it you're afraid will happen, Rick?" he asked finally.

"I'm afraid the truth will come out! I'm afraid you'll decide to tell him, or that once the two of you start strolling down memory lane, you might accidentally let something slip." Rick bounded to his feet and propped his hands on the terrace wall, his back to Jake. "I'm afraid if he sees the two of us together he might notice a resemblance between us or something."

"Would it be so terrible if he learned the truth?" Jake's words were spoken softly, almost hesitantly, but they hit Rick right between the shoulder blades with the force of an artillery barrage. In Jake's voice he heard the loneliness, the suppressed longing of a lifetime—*his* lifetime. He hunched his shoulders as if to protect himself from the guilty, bittersweet sympathy he couldn't help feeling for the man.

He studied the skyline, wishing the horizon were studded with lofty pine trees instead of towering skyscrapers. "It would kill him," Rick said, unable to keep the quaver from his voice. "He's an old man—he idolized my mother. The shock would destroy him."

"It might not be as great a shock as you think."

Rick spun around. "What are you talking about?"

It would be hard to imagine a man who looked more miserable than Jake Winslow at that moment. "Did Alistair—your father—ever explain to you why our partnership broke up?"

"No, and I don't want to hear it!" Rick's ears roared with an ominous rumbling, the way an avalanche must sound as it comes crashing down the mountainside, sweeping away everything in its path to destruction.

"Rick—"

"No!" He managed to resist the childish urge to clamp his hands over his ears, but just barely. "Stay away from us," he said, doing his best to ignore the tormented anguish in Jake's eyes. "Just stay away!"

Rick stormed from the terrace, knocking over a patio chair in the process. The clatter echoed in his ears along with Jake's pleas to wait. A horrible sense of déjà vu seized him as he recalled fleeing from this same house over a dozen years ago, leaving in his wake the same shattered hopes, the same painful wreckage.

Dana was adjusting her hair in the rearview mirror when Rick flung himself into the passenger seat beside her. "Done so soon?" she asked in surprise. "What'd you do, threaten to break his arms if he makes up with your father?"

"Just drive."

Evidently she detected some peculiar quality in his face or voice, because she put the car in gear and sped off without another word.

It took every ounce of Rick's self-control not to look back to see if Jake was standing in the front window, watching them drive away.

Chapter Eight

"Look, no hard feelings, right?" Dana switched her gaze from the roller-coaster curves of Sunset Boulevard just long enough to sneak a peek at Rick again. Ever since they'd left Jake Winslow's, he'd been strangely silent. Not once in the past ten minutes had he berated her for stranding him at the airport, or argued about her plans for the reunion or even made a rude comment about her driving.

She'd never thought she could actually *miss* sparring with him. "I mean, I have my reasons for wanting West and Winslow back together, and you have your reasons for *not* wanting them back together." She made a racing last-minute turn through a yellow light. "Though I'll be darned if I can figure out what they are," she added under her breath.

"What's your point?" Rick asked, relinquishing his grip on the dashboard.

Aha! At least he was speaking to her again. "My point is that I don't blame you for trying to stop me."

"That's mighty big of you."

"And you shouldn't blame me for trying to do what *I* have to do."

"Somehow your logic escapes me."

She gave an airy wave of her hand. "Guess you'll just have to trust me."

"That's what they all say. And would you mind keeping both hands on the steering wheel?"

Dana rolled her eyes, but did as he requested. "Just to show there are no hard feelings—at least on *my* part, I'm going to buy you lunch at one of my favorite restaurants."

"Don't we have a plane to catch?"

"*I* do, but not till early this evening. I was going to look up some of my old pals while I was down here, so I booked a later flight back." She braked with a lurch at a stoplight. "As for you, I assume you were in such a hurry this morning that you didn't bother making a return reservation. Or were you planning to take another taxi all the way back to Pine Creek?"

Her teasing tone was rewarded with the barest glimmer of a smile. "I'll buy a ticket when we get back to the airport."

"Good!" The light changed, and Dana zipped into the congested traffic so characteristic of the Westwood Village area of Los Angeles. "Then we have plenty of time for a bite to eat. I discovered the greatest little hole-in-the-wall Mexican restaurant while I was a student at UCLA...." She drummed her fingers impatiently on the steering wheel, waiting for a mob of college students and well-heeled shoppers to cross the street.

Rick didn't exactly share her enthusiastic appetite at the moment. His encounter with Jake had left him shaken, guilty and more worried than ever. He felt boxed in, imprisoned by walls that were slowly closing in on him. There was no place to go, no one to turn to, except . . .

He stole a sidelong glance at Dana, who was busily scanning the street for a parking place, like a shark cruising for its dinner. Maybe if he told her the real reason he was opposed to this reconciliation . . .

Forget it. He took a deep breath and coughed because of the exhaust fumes. He *wanted* to trust Dana, *wanted* to believe that if she knew the whole story she would call a halt to her plans and find some other way to save her station.

But there was something inside him, an immutable, unyielding core that wouldn't quite allow him to trust or believe in anyone. Not even the woman he had reluctantly come to care about.

It was as if there were a titanium shield encasing his heart, protecting it from any further pain or disillusionment. It had served its purpose well over the years, never allowing anyone to get too close to Rick. Never allowing him to reach out.

Suddenly he was thrown against the passenger door as Dana made a highly illegal U-turn and dived neatly into the first empty parking space Rick had seen since they'd entered Westwood Village. "Don't you ever worry about getting sued for whiplash?" he grumbled, yanking on the door handle.

Dana slammed her door shut and joined Rick on the sidewalk. "Quit being such a baby." She linked her arm companionably through his and led him around the corner. "Here it is, just the way...I...remembered it." Her face fell.

"Doesn't look much like a Mexican restaurant."

She pinched her lips together in disgust. "I can't believe it's been turned into a frozen-yogurt-and-gourmet-cookie shop."

"Just what Westwood needs another one of, huh?" They'd passed half a dozen similar establishments while hunting for a parking space. Dana looked so crestfallen, Rick gave in to the impulse to plant a quick kiss on those adorable, pouting lips.

Her eyes grew round as the huge fudge cookies on display in the window behind her. "What brought that on?" she asked, lifting her hand to brush distractedly at a wisp of dark hair that had worked its way loose from her stylish twist.

"Can't I kiss you in the middle of a crowded sidewalk if I feel like it?"

"As far as I know there's no local ordinance against it." She cocked her head to one side and studied him with an expression that made her look as young as the college students passing by. "Does this mean you're not still mad at me?"

Mad *about* her was more like it. Rick drew his forefinger along the delicate slant of her jaw in a quick, affectionate gesture. "No hard feelings, remember?"

"Good." She licked her lips with an unconscious sensuality that sent a bolt of desire through him. "Now, what are we going to do about lunch?"

Rick wasn't sure who was more surprised when he threw back his head and laughed—Dana or he, himself. "Has anyone ever told you you have a one-track mind?"

"Constantly." She gave a haughty toss of her head. "And don't you forget it."

They ended up grabbing lunch at a Middle-Eastern take-out food place and walking over to the botanical gardens at UCLA.

"What's this?" Rick asked with a dubious tilt of his brows when he unwrapped a lumpy pita-bread sandwich.

"Haven't you ever had a falafel before?" Dana's voice was muffled by a mouthful of the same.

"What are these little nuggets inside?"

"Mashed-up chickpeas mixed with spices and deep-fried in oil."

"Yummy."

"You haven't even tried it yet!"

"What about this weird-looking paste?"

"It's called tahini. For Pete's sake, have a little adventure in your soul."

Rick took an experimental bite. "Hmm. Not bad."

"Told you." Dana popped open a can of diet soda. "I used to practically live on these things when I was going to college here."

"I thought you ate at that Mexican restaurant all the time."

"There, too."

He took a swig of root beer. "How did you ever manage to get your degree when you spent all your time eating out?"

She crumpled up her empty paper wrapper and threw it at him. Rick ducked out of the way, then leaned back on his elbows and surveyed their surroundings. The botanical gardens consisted of half a dozen acres of subtropical trees, shrubs and plants, including both native species and more exotic imports. Winding footpaths curved through the hilly, uneven terrain.

There was a cool, soothing hush here, almost like a library's. It was hard to believe they were at the edge of a lively college campus, or that the tall, glass-walled sky-scrapers of bustling Wilshire Boulevard were only half a mile away. It was a pleasant place to bring a picnic lunch, to commune with nature or simply with one's own thoughts. Lengthening shadows indicated it was well past the noon hour now, and except for the birds overhead, a few squirrels and an occasional passerby, Rick and Dana had the place pretty much to themselves.

He rolled over onto his stomach and studied her over the rim of his soda can. She was leaning slightly to the side, one arm propped against the slope to brace her up-right, her shapely legs tucked neatly beneath her. Her peach-colored jacket lay folded beside her on the grass. Rick had expected her to head for a bench when they first got here, but instead she'd forged ahead down the hill and found them a secluded, shady spot beneath a eucalyptus tree.

She seemed completely unconcerned about whether her skirt got dirty or her nylons snagged. It was as if now that she'd accomplished her business she wasn't about to let her clothing restrict her in any way.

"What are you staring at?" she asked suspiciously.

"Just trying to figure out what makes you tick, that's all."

"Ha! That's a good one." She tilted her head back to drain the last few drops of her soda, then tossed the can into the paper sack that served as their trash bag. "My life's an open book compared to yours."

"Is it?"

"You know what my goals are, and my motives." She plucked a blade of grass and twirled it between her slen-der fingers. "On the other hand, I know what *your* goal is, but you won't tell me why you're so all-fired anxious about it."

Rick pushed himself up to a sitting position. "I told you. I want to protect my father from the stress of all that publicity, from having to face a man he doesn't want to see again."

"I don't believe he never wants to see Jake again, and neither do you." Dana tossed the blade of grass aside. "That's why you're so worried."

She was too damn perceptive. She had an uncanny knack for reading his innermost thoughts and fears, almost as if she were clairvoyant. It was a novel, unsettling sensation. Rick had never allowed himself to get close enough to another human being to share this kind of unspoken, intuitive communication.

It wasn't an altogether unpleasant sensation. But it did scare the hell out of him.

"What did you do after graduating from UCLA?" he asked, intending to divert her attention away from himself.

"Got a job at a PBS station in Hollywood. I started out as sort of a glamorized gofer, then worked my way up to associate producer after a few years." The shadow that crossed her face had nothing to do with the leafy boughs overhead. "I'd just been promoted to producer when my father died and I moved back to Pine Creek."

Rick slid closer to her. "You gave up a lot to go back and take over his job, then."

"No." She shook her head. "I make less money now than I would have if I'd stayed in L.A., and maybe the productions I'm responsible for now aren't as glamorous or prestigious. But what I've gained at Channel Five is worth far more."

"It must be pretty satisfying to run your own station."

"What I meant was that I feel as though I can really make a difference in people's lives in Pine Creek. Here I was just another cog on a very big wheel." She shrugged. "Besides, I've never considered Channel Five *my* station, since it's really owned by the members. Though I admit to feeling kind of proprietary about it, since it was my father who founded it."

"And now you're following in his footsteps."

Dana averted her eyes as if she'd spotted something she didn't want to see. "Sometimes I feel like my father's shoes are just too big for me to fill."

Her confession of self-doubt surprised Rick. She always seemed so confident, so sure of herself. "You've done a great job," he assured her. "And from what I've seen, you certainly have the respect and devotion of your employees."

She brushed his praise aside. "If I were doing a decent job, the station wouldn't be on the brink of financial ruin."

"That's not your fault! It's the fault of people like me, who watch public television but don't pay their fair share."

"You've paid more than your share." Dana tilted forward and touched Rick's hand. "Can't you understand why I'll do anything to save the station? I *hate* pushing forward with something you're so opposed to, but I simply have no other choice!"

She scanned his eyes as if searching for a trace of understanding. Reluctantly, Rick had to concede she had good reasons for concocting this scheme of hers. He could be ruthless and pigheaded, too, when something this important was at stake.

If only he could make Dana understand that *he* had no choice, either.

"I don't want to make your life miserable," she said softly.

He grasped her fingers tightly. "You haven't made my life miserable," he said, unable to choke back the words that sprang from his throat as if of their own volition. "You've made it challenging, exciting, happy—oh, the hell with it."

He pulled her roughly into his arms, as if he could drag her away from all her problems and all the secrets that kept them apart. He cradled her in his lap and lowered his head slowly to hers, enjoying the astonishment and anticipation glowing in her eyes. When he was mere inches away he noticed their dark brown depths were flecked with gold and felt himself drowning in her dreamy, beckoning gaze.

When their lips met at last, a radiant warmth filled him, melting the hard shell around his heart, making him forget the reason for its necessity. Dana was soft and sweet and eager, and it seemed to Rick that the outside world had ceased to exist, leaving only the two of them alone in their own private paradise, their own Garden of Eden.

He nudged her lips apart with his tongue and she opened to him like one of the lush, exotic flowers nearby. Her alluring fragrance filled his senses while her tender, ardent response filled the empty, aching place inside him. Her tiny, hesitant whimpers of passion stirred a fierce longing in him, a mixture of protectiveness and desire.

He fumbled with the clips holding her hair in place, and somehow managed to release the dark, silky tresses from their confinement. Drawing back, he gazed down at her, savoring the way the moisture of his kiss glistened on her lips, the way her hair was strewn carelessly around her face as if she'd just awakened in his bed. He sifted his fingers through the soft tendrils, sampling and memorizing their texture.

Her eyes drifted shut with a sensual languor, then flared open in shock when Rick boldly slid his hand down to caress her breast. He half expected her to slap him aside, and part of him hoped she would.

But another part knew that this incredible thing happening between them was right, that Dana couldn't help but share these powerful feelings, this overwhelming passion.

Indescribable pleasure spread from the touch of Rick's hand, sending pulsating surges of desire throughout Dana's body. She'd been surprised when Rick kissed her, even more surprised by the strength and hunger of her own response. But now the feelings he was igniting with the mere touch of his hand went far beyond anything in her experience. Suddenly her clothes were too tight, the shady garden too hot, their time together too short.

Impatience and excitement swept through her, even as a distant voice inside her head was cautioning her that this was impossible, that she and Rick were bound to hurt each other.

She'd never been any good at listening to little warning voices and she certainly wasn't about to start now, not with Rick's lusty, appreciative gaze sweeping her like a torch, not when she could feel the wild thumping of his heart and tense excitement pouring through his bloodstream as swiftly and surely as it poured through her.

Above her his face filled her vision, framed by a tracery of green branches against blue sky. His eyes were smoky with passion, his handsome, boldly carved features thrown into even higher relief by the interplay of shadows and sunlight.

Dana drew in a long, quavering breath, filling her lungs with the pungent, spicy scent of eucalyptus. Then she lifted her arms to encircle Rick's neck and pull him down even closer to her.

A mixture of joy and satisfaction flared briefly in his eyes until the moment when his lips claimed hers once more. Then Dana forgot about everything but the exquisite, unfamiliar sensations Rick was arousing inside her with his hands, his mouth, his whispered words.

"So long..." he muttered against her lips. "For so long I've wanted to do this, to be with you like this...." His breath was hot against her face, fanning the flames that already raged throughout her body.

For once in her life Dana could think of nothing to say, and was reduced to incoherent moans that described her feelings far more vividly than any words. She strained against the solid shelter of his chest, silently urging him on, resolutely ignoring that maddening little voice inside her skull.

She sucked in her breath with a sharp hiss when Rick tugged her blouse free from her skirt and slid his hand against her bare skin.

"You're so soft," he said gruffly, running his callused hand across her midriff.

Dana opened her eyes to find him staring down at her with frank adoration, a look that pierced her heart as swiftly and cleanly as an arrow. She raised her hand to caress the bristly plane of his cheek. Beneath her fingers she found his jaw muscles as taut and tightly woven as steel cable. "Rick," she whispered, though the sound was lost in the rushing whirlwind that filled her ears. "Oh, Rick..."

He was so strong, so handsome, yet with a mysterious vulnerability that touched her profoundly. More than anything she wanted to discover the source of the secret pain she sometimes saw lurking in his shadowed gray eyes, to share the emotional burdens that seemed to weigh him down.

Even through her besotted daze, Dana could sense cracks in the wall Rick had erected around his secret, private self. She could see a glimmer of something on the other side. . . . Hope? Sadness? Longing?

Then he drove all questions from her mind when his roving hand found her breast again, this time with only a filmy wisp of lace between his fingers and the straining bud of her nipple. He teased her gently, mercilessly until she thought she would go mad with the ecstasy of his touch.

He raised her off his lap, showering her cheeks, her eyelids, her temples with kisses while he reached behind to undo the clasp of her bra and release her swollen, throbbing breasts from their lacy prison.

When he repositioned her across his lap, Dana could feel the hard proof of his desire, and rejoiced in the knowledge that—at least physically—she had affected him as much as he'd affected her.

Then his mouth was on hers, greedy, insatiable, while his hand slipped beneath her bra to knead her soft, bare breast, rolling the rosy nub between his fingers, inflaming her desire to a fever pitch.

Oh, God, she was on fire, and there was only one thing that would—

Voices penetrated Dana's befogged senses, only they weren't just inside her head this time. She flung herself off Rick's lap and prepared to dive headfirst behind the nearest hibiscus bush if necessary.

Rick drew himself up onto his knees and positioned himself in front of her to shield her from the view of any intruders. Dana hadn't realized she'd been holding her breath until the voices faded into the distance and she caught a glimpse of white coats receding through the trees.

"Medical students," she said, emptying her lungs with a whoosh. "The botanical gardens are right next to the medical school." She sank from her panicked crouch into a sitting position. "I don't think they saw us from the path, do you?"

"If they did, at least we have the consolation of knowing they're used to seeing naked bodies."

"We're not naked," Dana scoffed. "Oops! At least not more than half naked." She quickly refastened her bra and stuffed her blouse back into her waistband. "There, that's better."

"A matter of opinion," Rick said, extending his hand to help her to her feet. "I liked your clothes better the other way."

When their eyes met, a moment of embarrassed silence lingered in the air. Then Dana pressed her fingers to her lips and giggled, her eyes twinkling with mirth. "Good heavens, I feel like we just got caught making out in the back seat of your father's car."

Rick dusted off his jeans. "I'm getting too old for this," he said ruefully.

"Just goes to show, you're never too old to fool around."

"Is that what you call it? Fooling around?"

Dana stooped to retrieve her jacket and purse from the ground. When she lifted her eyes to meet Rick's, she found him scrutinizing her with a peculiar, curious intensity. "I don't know," she said slowly, running her hands through her disheveled hair. "What would *you* call it?"

Rick picked up the bag containing their trash and punched it so all the air escaped with a loud *pop!* "Maybe there are some questions," he said carefully, "that are better left unanswered."

And suddenly Dana felt that damn wall crash back into place as loudly as a dungeon door slamming shut. The jolt reverberated inside her, knocking loose that warm, delightful sense of closeness she and Rick had shared only moments ago. Amazing how quickly the old self-defense mechanisms could spring back into place.

She almost wished she'd listened to her own self-defense mechanisms when they'd warned her about getting too involved with Rick. But Dana wasn't one to deny her true feelings. Hide them from others, maybe. For a while, and only if she had very good reasons.

But in the end she always followed her heart, which so far had never led her astray.

There's a first time for everything, taunted that annoying little voice inside her head.

Sadly, Dana had to admit that Rick fluctuated like the tide, the way he kept flowing hot and cold where she was concerned. Time and again he would draw close to her, only to reach a point where he inevitably retreated.

And everyone knew it was impossible to hold the tide against the shore.

"Come on, let's get out of here," she said abruptly. "We've got a plane to catch."

Delicious smells filled the air—popcorn and hot dogs and fresh-baked cinnamon rolls. It seemed to Rick that every single one of Pine Creek's nine thousand residents must be crammed into this six-block stretch of Main

Street, eagerly craning their necks for their first glimpse of the Gold Rush Days parade.

He wasn't sure what the heck had possessed him to join the ranks of this boisterous, exuberant crowd. After all, if he were spending this sunny Saturday afternoon the way he usually did—putting in a few extra hours on the job site or catching up on his architectural journals—he wouldn't be getting his feet stepped on or his elbow jostled every few seconds.

Oddly enough, he didn't mind the unfamiliar commotion. Lately the peace and quiet he'd always enjoyed within the solid walls of his home had come to seem more like a sentence in solitary confinement. Now, when he was alone, he was restless. More often than not he found himself ready to climb those very walls with boredom.

It was easier while he was at work. He could joke around with the work crew, and lately he'd gotten into the habit of joining them for a beer after work. But inevitably the clock inched its way toward the moment when he would arrive home alone, open his front door and listen to the sound echo dimly through the empty silence.

He was on edge, dissatisfied these days. And his mood had nothing to do with the trouble he saw looming on the horizon where his father and Jake were concerned.

No, Rick laid the blame for this restlessness, this vague sense of frustrated yearning squarely at the doorstep of a certain lively, aggravating, completely unforgettable station manager. Dana had somehow got under Rick's skin in a way no woman had before.

Like itching powder, he thought.

Out of the blue, he'd awakened one morning with this crazy, inexplicable urge to rejoin the human race.

Well, he'd certainly rejoined it with a vengeance today. The steady simmer of voices rose to a boiling roar when the lead car carrying the grand marshal finally came into view. The crowd surged forward as if intent on spilling into the street.

"Mommy, I can't see!"

Rick had gravitated to the rear of the throng of spectators, making room for people not as tall as he was. He glanced down now in the direction of the unhappy child's voice. Beside him stood a young blond woman with an infant in a stroller and another child sleeping in her arms.

"Samantha, honey, I'm sorry, but I can't pick you up right now."

"But Mommee-e-e . . ."

Rick touched the woman's shoulder. "I'd be happy to hold her up so she can see."

The woman glanced up at him, her harried expression replaced first by uncertainty, then by gratitude. "Would you? That's awfully kind of you. Samantha, this nice man is going to lift you up."

Rick scooped up the little blond girl and hoisted her onto his shoulders. "There, how's that?"

"Mommy, look! Clowns!"

The woman rolled her eyes and gave Rick a sheepish smile. "I sure do appreciate this. I meant to get here early enough to find a spot up front on the curb, but my car broke down, and..." She gave a resigned shrug as if such disasters were an everyday event in her life.

To his surprise, Rick enjoyed Samantha even more than he enjoyed the parade. He hadn't had much experience with children, and he'd certainly never planned to have any himself. Before you had children you had to commit yourself fully to another human being, which meant making yourself vulnerable, setting yourself up for a fall.

But there was something so pure and innocent about Samantha's uninhibited delight. Her bouncing enthusiasm was a little rough on Rick's shoulders, but it also touched something tender and wistful inside his chest, making him wish he were still young and innocent enough to believe in magic and fairy tales and happy endings.

"Look, mister! Horsies!"

A few minutes later Samantha was using the top of Rick's head as a bongo drum, keeping time as the high school marching band passed by.

And here came the Channel Five float at last. A brief, illuminating flash of honesty forced Rick to acknowledge the real reason he'd come to the parade. He spotted Dana instantly among the dozen costumed station employees who were waving wildly and tossing handfuls of hard candy at the crowd.

She was wearing a full-length calico dress with a white apron, and somewhere she'd dug up a colorful sunbonnet that dangled down her back by its ribbons. Her hair was pulled back into an old-fashioned bun, but in all the excitement, half the strands had escaped to frame her face with a cloud of wispy dark tendrils.

She looked the very picture of the pioneer woman she represented—undaunted by life's hardships, unafraid to face the challenges of life in a new, unsettled land. Proud, eager, hardworking...the same qualities Dana herself possessed in abundance. Rick could easily imagine her snatching up a rifle to defend her family from a grizzly bear, or whipping off that apron to beat out the flames of a prairie fire.

Watching her unobserved, he felt a strange, strong emotion well up inside him, filling his belly, his lungs, constricting his throat. He wanted her. Not just in bed, but in ways that transcended mere physical desire. He wanted to see her across the breakfast table every morning. He wanted to watch her eyes light up with pride when he brought her to see one of his newly completed houses. He wanted to spend quiet evenings in front of the fire with her, sharing the minor defeats and triumphs that made up the fabric of everyday life.

He wanted to grow old with her.

Then Dana's searching glance snagged on Rick's and their eyes met above the heads of the crowd. Suddenly it was as if they were the only two people in the universe.

The strangely intimate contact took Dana's breath away. It wasn't until that very instant that she admitted to herself there was only one face she'd been searching for, one figure she'd been hoping to spot among all those spectators.

She was so dazed, so pleased to find him, that it took her a few seconds to realize he had an adorable little blond girl propped on his shoulders. Now who on earth could that be? Was there some secret romance in Rick's past, a child? For all Dana knew, he might have a whole family stashed away somewhere. He was so darn secretive....

But his eyes... Even from this distance Dana could see desire smoldering in those slate-gray depths, underscored by a peculiar intensity that made her shiver despite the warm May sunshine. She couldn't have ripped her gaze from Rick's if she'd wanted to.

His longing for her was unmistakable—it bridged the distance between them, spanning the crowd like a blinding beam of light, dazzling her with its blazing power. A surge of pure joy shot through her. She didn't care about his past—he could have a whole passel of children stashed away someplace and Dana would adore every one of them just because they were his.

A glorious smile burst across her face. She plunged her hand into the brown paper sack she held and drew out a fistful of candy. Then she flung it as hard as she could in the direction of Rick and the child. A rainbow of lime green and cherry red and lemon yellow exploded in the air like fireworks. Dana saw Rick's fist dart out, watched him hand his prize to the little girl and then wave enthusiastically in her direction.

Then the float passed beyond sight of him. Dana continued to call out to familiar faces on the sidewalks below, to scatter candies and smile and wave in all directions.

The smile was real, although her thoughts were not on the parade but on the man who stood head and shoulders above the crowd, who'd somehow managed to reach out and touch her heart across all the obstacles that lay between them.

Dana didn't know if she could save the station. She hadn't the faintest idea what kind of job she should look for if she couldn't.

But one thing she knew as surely as she knew the sun would rise tomorrow.

She was falling head over heels in love with Rick West.

Chapter Nine

Dana felt like a salmon swimming upstream. Everyone else on the sidewalk seemed to be heading the opposite direction. The chances of her finding Rick in all this post-parade chaos were probably hopeless, but instinct whispered in her ear that he was waiting for her, somewhere in this mob scene.

There he was! He wasn't *that* much taller than most of the other men in the crowd, but to Dana that chiseled profile, those broad shoulders and compelling gray eyes guided her as surely as a lighthouse beacon.

"Rick!" she called, stretching up on tiptoe. "Over here!"

He spotted her at once, and within seconds his hand reached out of the crowd to grasp hers. He squeezed it tight, pulling her after him through the worst of the foot traffic until they found shelter in a relatively secluded storefront on a side street.

"Where's your friend?" Dana asked, brimming with curiosity and a whole bunch of other emotions she hadn't had a chance to sort out yet.

Rick frowned. "Who? Oh, you mean Samantha." The creases across his forehead smoothed. "I just happened to be standing next to her during the parade. She couldn't see, so I asked her mother if I could boost her up. Never saw either of them before in my life."

"Oh." Dana brushed stray hair from her eyes. "I thought maybe you had a secret past you were hiding from me."

A funny look that could only be described as indecipherable swept over his handsome features. But all he did was lift a hand to finger the loose ribbons of her sunbonnet. "I like your costume."

Dana groaned. "I know it's kind of silly, but..."

"No, really. It...suits you." He raised her skirt a few inches and grinned. "And those purple running shoes are really the pièce de résistance."

She flashed him a saucy smile in return. "You don't expect me to wear authentic shoes with this getup, do you? Have you ever seen a pair of nineteenth-century women's shoes in a museum? I couldn't even fit my feet into them, much less walk in them." She shook her head with wonder. "Either feet were a lot smaller back then, or those poor pioneer women had it a lot rougher than people think."

Rick's eyes twinkled with amusement, then dissolved into something softer. "You could wear combat boots and still look beautiful to me."

Dana had never been very secure about her looks, but Rick's words and the obvious sincerity with which he spoke them banished her usual embarrassment and filled her with a warm glow. "Gosh, as long as we're slinging compliments back and forth, I want to thank you again for doing such a terrific job on our float."

Rick drew her arm through his and they strolled down the sidewalk, past the food and craft booths stationed along both sides of the closed-off street. "Does that mean you're not still mad at me for breaking Sparky's ear off?"

Dana elbowed him in the ribs. "Oh, come on. I wasn't mad at you."

"Oh, no? You looked like you were ready to take a swing at me with your hammer!"

"Well . . . okay, maybe I did fly off the handle a bit. I should have known you'd fix old Sparky up so he'd look good as new."

"Hmm . . . even when he was new, I doubt that mule ever looked—"

"Okay, okay, you've made your point," Dana said, rolling her eyes. She inhaled noisily. "Don't those cinnamon rolls smell delicious?"

Rick cupped a hand to his ear. "Is that thunder I hear, or are you hungry again?"

She punched him good-naturedly on the shoulder. "Just for that, *you're* going to buy."

He pulled out his wallet with a melodramatic sigh. "Anything to get back into your good graces."

They ambled slowly along the street, chewing their sweet, gooey rolls, stopping to admire the various arts and crafts on display.

This is almost like a real date, Dana marveled silently. *It feels like we're a real couple, spending another in a long series of weekends together.* And oh, what a nice feeling it was. . . .

They managed to find a couple of empty folding chairs in front of a makeshift outdoor stage where a local band was performing. Dana had never seen Rick so relaxed. His foot was beating time with the music, one arm was draped casually along the back of her chair and she could almost swear he was humming.

Gone was that worried, almost haunted look she'd seen so often on his face. For once she didn't have the feeling she was sitting next to a coiled spring or a burning stick of dynamite. The tension seemed to have flowed out of him—temporarily at least—erasing the harsh lines that often marked the carved angles and planes of his face.

He looked years younger, and it was easy for Dana to fantasize that she was back in high school and actually on a date with Rick West, big man on campus, every girl's dream boyfriend.

Oddly enough, the fantasy failed to send even one delicious shiver through Dana. Maybe because she'd finally met someone even more desirable than the boy Rick had once been.

The man he'd grown up to be.

"Something tells me you're not a big fan of country music."

"Huh?" She whipped her head around to face Rick.

"You've been sitting there with a faraway look in your eyes, as if you're a million miles away." He drew his arm around her shoulders, and this time she *did* feel a delicious shiver.

"More like a million *years* away," Dana murmured.

"Beg pardon?"

"Er, I said I like country music just fine. Of course, it's not exactly rock and roll...."

"Come on, let's dance." The words were out of Rick's mouth before they'd fully registered on his brain.

Dana looked as surprised as he was, but then her eyes filled with that familiar gleam that meant she saw something fun heading her way. "Okay, you asked for it." She took Rick's hand and followed him to the area in front of the stage that had been cleared of chairs so people could dance. "I'm warning you, though, you'd better not have anything more complicated than the twist in mind, or we're in trouble."

What the hell did *he have in mind?* Rick wondered frantically as he took Dana in his arms and tried to mimic the simple two-step he saw other couples doing. He couldn't believe he'd actually volunteered to come up here and make a public spectacle of himself in front of all these people. He'd spent his entire adult life trying to stay out of the spotlight, and here he was, hopping around like a clumsy kangaroo for the whole world to see.

Dana didn't seem to mind. He might have been Fred Astaire, the way she moved so effortlessly in his arms, following his every stumbling step as if she could read his mind and anticipate his movements.

"You're a good follower," he said, amazed to discover it was possible to talk and do the two-step at the same time.

Dana's eyes sparkled mischievously. "Only when I dance," she replied.

As he started to relax, Rick actually began to enjoy himself. There was something so liberating, so exhilarating about letting the music flow over you and set the beat that carried you around and around the floor....

Best of all, he held the prettiest woman in Pine Creek in his arms. No, that hardly did Dana justice. She was the loveliest woman he'd ever seen, on or off the movie screen.

The unintentional rhyme and rhythm of his thoughts inspired Rick to even trickier steps. Dana followed him without missing a beat, her laughter swirling around the dance floor, making his heart soar with pleasure. He never, ever wanted to let her go....

Then all too soon the music ended so the band could take a well-deserved break. Reluctantly, Rick released her and they joined the appreciative round of applause for the musicians. Dana's face was flushed a delicate pink, her chest rising and falling rapidly as they made their way through the dispersing audience.

"You've been holding out on me!" she said, gasping. "I had no idea you could dance like that."

Neither did I, Rick thought. "You were pretty fantastic yourself. I thought you said you couldn't dance."

"I can't! Not really, anyway. But somehow...the way we moved together...it was like—oh, I don't know." She shrugged. "Somehow I could just sense what your next move was going to be, that's all." *Now if I could only figure out your moves when we're* not *on the dance floor,* she thought.

As they walked back toward Main Street, Dana replayed over and over the feeling of dancing in Rick's arms, recalling the delightful sensation of his strong hand splayed against the small of her back, the warm caress of his breath on her face, the exquisite pressure of his hips molded to hers.

They moved so well together, swaying and turning in perfect synchronization as if they were two halves of a whole. Why, oh, why did they have to be at such contradictory cross-purposes—stepping all over each other's toes like mismatched dancers—once the music stopped and real life took over?

Then Rick twined his fingers with hers again, and Dana vowed not to let any more gloomy thoughts intrude on this perfect day. Rick West had always been an unattainable dream for her, and there was no reason to assume that would change. That made it even more important not to spoil this precious time with him by dwelling on problems she had no control over.

But it was hard to keep her spirits from sagging, so it was a welcome distraction to spot the commotion up ahead. "Come on," she cried, tugging on Rick's hand to speed him up. "It's nearly time for the donkey race!"

"I think even your pal Sparky could have finished at least second or third in *that* race," Rick said.

"Donkeys aren't very competitive," Dana explained. "That's why each one needs a pusher and a puller, in addition to the rider." They were on their way back to the Channel Five parking lot, where Dana had left her car. She pressed her fingertips to her lips, unsuccessfully muffling a giggle. "Remember the one who was leading near the end until he stopped dead in his tracks, just before the finish line?"

"I doubt his rider could see the humor in the situation."

"Not while she was flying over his head, anyway!"

"Hey, Dana, aren't you going to stay for the awards ceremony? Oh, hello..." Carole Westlake and her two children were heading in the opposite direction. Carole's eyes gleamed with interest when she noticed Rick was with Dana. "Kids, simmer down, all right? I want to talk to Dana for a minute." Her attention, however, was focused exclusively on Rick. "Hi, I'm Carole Westlake. We met the other day, sort of."

Rick shook her outstretched hand. "While you were working on the float."

"Right! Christopher, quit pulling your sister's hair."

"She took my candy!"

"Did not!"

"Did, too!"

Carole mustered a feeble smile. "Sorry. It's been a long day."

Rick knelt so he was child-level, then dug into his pocket and produced two pieces of hard candy. "Here you go, kids. That is, if your mom says it's all right." He glanced upward at Carole.

She clasped her hands together. "Bless you, dear man. Of course it's all right. Amy, Christopher—what do you say?"

"Thank you," they chorused, the words nearly drowned out by the eager crackle of cellophane being torn off the candies.

Rick levered himself to his feet. "By the way, in all the commotion I forgot to introduce myself. Rick West."

"Oh, I know who you are. And I must say, we're so excited about your father appearing during our pledge drive! If anyone can save the station, it's..." She blanched, then swallowed. "Oops, sorry—I mean, uh..."

Dana crossed her fingers and sent up a silent prayer for a meteorite to land in the middle of Main Street or for Elvis to be sighted at the drugstore—*anything* to distract attention and extricate her from this unbelievably awkward situation.

Rick's pleasant expression didn't change, but his eyes grew cold and hard as stone. "How nice of you to say so," he said to Carole in a bland voice that didn't fool Dana for a moment.

"Gosh, Dana, I didn't mean to—I forgot that—oh, heck," Carole finished lamely, blowing her bangs up off her forehead. "Kids, it's time to go." She touched Dana's arm briefly and threw her another sheepish, apologetic look before towing her kids away down the still-crowded sidewalk.

Dana kept up a stream of cheerful chatter the rest of the way back to the station, but for all the response she got she might as well have been talking to Sparky. Rick didn't *look* furious, but his back was stiff and straight as if his spine had been replaced by a length of metal pipe. All the tension that had dissipated during the course of the afternoon was back in full force. Dana had the feeling if she touched him he'd snap like a rubber band.

The sun was dipping low on the horizon, brushing strokes of pink and orange across the canvas of the sky, casting long, distorted shadows across the sidewalk. Dana's spirits were setting along with the sun. Everything had been so perfect today, until one careless comment ruined it.

Not that she blamed Carole. It was common knowledge around the station that Rick was against the idea of his father's appearance. But seeing him with Dana, relaxed and smiling, anyone could have forgotten that it was a touchy subject.

Andy must have been in a hurry to get somewhere else after the parade. Instead of returning the float to its storage shed across town, he'd left it in the station parking lot. As Rick and Dana approached, it loomed dark and mysterious against the backdrop of the vivid sunset—eerie mine buildings...brooding mountains...in the shadows even Sparky looked like some strange mythical creature.

"The old Celebration Mine." Rick's voice made Dana jump. They were the first words he'd spoken since the encounter with Carole, unless you counted noncommittal grunts. "I haven't been up there in ages."

"I went to the opening ceremonies after they restored it and turned it into a state park, but that was years ago."

"I haven't been there since high school." Rick leaned back against the front fender of Dana's car and crossed one ankle over the other.

"Hmph. Guess I don't need to ask what you were doing up *there*." The grounds of the abandoned mine had been a popular high school necking spot—until the state coughed up the money to turn it into a tourist attraction.

The corner of Rick's mouth curved upward in a lazy, rueful smile. "Ah, the follies of youth."

Dana sniffed. "I'm sure I wouldn't know."

Rick's jaw dropped. "Come on, are you trying to tell me you never went up there while you were a teenager to—uh, look at the view?"

"I believe it's called 'watching the submarine races.' And, no, I never went up there for that particular purpose."

He continued to stare at Dana in a way that made her squirm. "I find that hard to believe."

"I was sort of a . . . late bloomer."

"Were you?" He reached out and tugged playfully on a lock of her hair. "That must be why I never noticed you."

"More likely I was completely hidden behind your huge crowd of admirers. God knows, I did everything I could think of to get you to notice me." Oops! Now how did *that* manage to slip out?

"You did?" Rick's eyebrows flew up in amazement.

By now Dana had twisted her bonnet ribbons into thin cords. "I, uh, had sort of a crush on you in high school."

"You're kidding!" For some reason, Rick was absurdly pleased by her admission. He rarely thought back to those days when he could have had his pick of any girl at Pine Creek High School. In light of later events in his life, such reminiscences seemed meaningless, and brought him no satisfaction.

But Dana's obviously reluctant confession touched him. He couldn't imagine her hanging back in the crowd, watching him date his way through a steady procession of cheerleaders and homecoming princesses. The Dana he knew would have hired a skywriter, or arranged for the two of them to be stranded alone on a deserted island together.

Then he remembered the few times when he *had* taken notice of Dana—all the pranks she'd pulled and the mischief she'd stirred up. Had she really just been trying to get his attention?

Both of them had sure come a long way since high school.

"Come on," Rick said, pushing himself away from her car. "Let's go."

Dana's eyes widened in bewilderment. "Go? What are you talking about? Go where?"

He gestured impatiently at the float. "There, of course. The Celebration Mine."

Her expression radiated pure astonishment. "Are you crazy? What on earth for?"

Rick threw up his arms in mock exasperation. "Dana, if I have to explain it to you, you're even worse off than I thought."

She bristled at that, just the way he'd expected her to. Folding her arms across her chest, she fixed him with an indignant glare. "Oh, and I suppose the great Rick West is just the man to cure me of my tragic deprivation?"

He shook his head sadly. "Dana...Dana...you're thirty-two years old and you've never been up to the Celebration Mine with a man." He wagged a scolding finger at her. "This could be your last chance. If you don't come with me tonight, I have a feeling you'll never go."

She batted his finger aside. "Oh, *please*—didn't I see this scene in *The Music Man?* I suppose next you'll be giving me that line about putting things off till tomorrow and winding up with a lot of empty yesterdays."

Her words rang true in his ears. Not that they applied to Dana—Rick knew she wasn't the type to stand on the sidelines and watch life pass her by. But while Dana had spent the years since high school wringing every ounce of enjoyment and satisfaction from life, Rick had wasted those same years brooding about the grave injustice he and his father had suffered, shying away from any meaningful relationships, doing his best to shut out the world and hold himself above any real involvement in it.

And what did he have to show for it? A whole pile of empty yesterdays.

He was tired of considering the consequences of every move he made, tired of letting the guardianship of his secret dictate the way he lived.

For once in his life he wanted to follow his heart. And his heart knew exactly where it wanted to go.

"Come with me," he said in a voice halfway between a growl and a whisper. He bridged the distance between them and slid his hand alongside Dana's face, so that his fingers just barely brushed the nape of her neck. With deep male satisfaction he felt the rapid flutter of her pulse against the side of her throat, saw the provocative mixture of anticipation and anxiety that leapt into her eyes.

He lowered his head till his face was mere inches from hers, drew the pad of his thumb slowly across the lush fullness of her lower lip. "What's the matter?" he asked softly, his question trapped between their lips. "Chicken?"

A beat of silence, then her eyes narrowed, her chin jerked upward in that defiant gesture Rick knew so well. She swatted his hand away. "Chicken?" she repeated in an incredulous tone. "You actually think I'm *afraid* to go up there with you?"

Rick shrugged one shoulder, casually inspected his fingernails. "It would seem so."

"I'll show *you* who's afraid," Dana muttered, whipping off her dangling sunbonnet. "Lead on, Casanova. I just hope you know what you're doing."

So do I, Rick thought. *Sweetheart, so do I.*

When would she ever learn to resist a dare? Dana wondered, watching the headlights of Rick's pickup truck forge a path along the winding gravel road.

She remembered the first time she'd ridden with him in this truck, the night he'd rescued her from the ditch. It had been dark then, too, but otherwise everything was different now—their relationship, her plans to save the station....

Impossible to believe how much her life had changed in only a couple of weeks. Before that, Rick West had been only a bittersweet memory, a faded remembrance she took out and examined about as often as her high school yearbook.

Now he was flesh and blood, a living, breathing adult male whose skin had warmed hers, whose pounding heart had echoed her own. Rick was every inch a real live man, not some teenage heartthrob Dana could conjure up and then dismiss whenever the memories grew too sad.

She couldn't dismiss her feelings for him any longer, either. What she felt for Rick went far, far beyond a simple schoolgirl crush.

Swallowing, Dana twisted her fingers together, discovered her palms were damp. Her feelings for Rick might be adult, but she was nervous as an adolescent on her first date. She rubbed her hands along her thighs, wishing she'd never agreed to this crazy idea.

When the pickup pulled into the mine's parking area, a mixture of relief and disappointment rushed through her. "Aw, too bad," she said quickly. "The gate's locked up for the night. Guess we'll have to come back some other time."

Rick spared her a withering glance as he switched off the ignition. "Not to worry. I'm sure we can find a spot where we can climb over the fence."

"Uh, don't the rangers take a rather dim view of trespassing?"

"It's a state park, right? Belongs to everyone? So how can we trespass on our own property?"

"Well . . ."

"Besides, the park staff goes home after the gates close."

"How convenient." Dana considered her options, then sighed. She couldn't back out now; Rick would never let her forget it. And with his determination, he would insist on traipsing around the perimeter of the park, dragging her through poison oak and prickly bramble bushes and God knows what else until he found someplace they could sneak in.

"Start the truck," Dana said, resigned to her fate. "I think I know where we can get in. . . ."

"I'm impressed," Rick told her a few minutes later when they were inside the park. "How did you know this back gate would be unlocked?"

"The road we took back here is the fire road. In case of emergency when the park is closed, the fire trucks can get in that way without waiting for someone to unlock the main gate.''

''That doesn't explain how *you* knew about it.'' Rick took her hand and started off down one of the hiking trails.

''I have my sources,'' Dana replied, trying to sound a lot more smug and confident than she felt. ''Don't forget, I'm in the information business.''

For a few minutes the only sound was the crackle of their footsteps on fallen leaves, the occasional rustle of an animal in the bushes, the gentle swish of the evening breeze through the trees. When they reached the large clearing where the old mine buildings stood, the setting was so silent and forlorn, Dana felt the urge to tiptoe, so as not to disturb the ghosts drifting through the ruins. ''Where are we going?'' she whispered.

Rick must have felt the somber aura of the place, too, because he whispered in return. ''Up to the old cottage.''

Cottage was hardly the word for the imposing stone mansion constructed at the turn of the century to house the mine superintendent and his family. Ever since the government had taken over the property, the stately but dilapidated building had been undergoing the slow process of restoration before being opened to the public.

''If you think we're going to break in there, you're crazy,'' Dana said when they reached the cottage and paused to gaze up at the massive stone walls. ''There's liable to be spiders and rats and all sorts of creepy crawly things inside.'' She shivered, wishing she'd brought along a sweater to protect her from the cool mountain air.

''That wasn't my intention,'' Rick said, wrapping his arm around her shoulders and drawing her close to him. ''Come on.''

Instantly Dana was warm all over. Rick led her through what had once been a large formal garden. Now it was little more than a maze of overgrown shrubbery and a wild tangle of fragrant flowers. "Mmm, smell those roses," Dana said, inhaling deeply to fill her lungs with their heady scent.

"There used to be a spot right over here—" Rick halted, looked around in confusion for a moment before his face brightened. "There it is! It's been so long, I nearly forgot how to find it."

Dana caught her breath. The place Rick had brought her to was a secret, secluded clearing at a point where the gradual slope suddenly fell away to a ravine. Below them spread a broad, panoramic vista of the Sierras. Mountains surrounded them in all directions, stretching as far as the eye could see. The pale grays and lavenders of twilight tinted the western sky like a watercolor wash. To the northwest twinkled the lights of Pine Creek, its buildings strewn haphazardly along the slopes like toy houses.

The spiky outline of pine trees studded the horizon. And above the trees rose a luminescent three-quarters moon, dazzling bright against the dark, velvety backdrop.

"Oh, Rick," Dana said when she could speak again, "I had no idea this place even existed! How on earth did you find it?" The minute the words were out, she wanted to yank them back and clap her hand over her mouth. What an idiot she was! This had probably been his favorite spot to bring his girlfriends.

Rick knelt to the ground and drew Dana down beside him. The grass was cool and slightly damp. As if reading her mind, he said, "I've never brought anyone else here before, if that's what you're thinking."

"No? Gee, I bet this would be a perfect place to—uh, you know."

"Watch the submarine races?" Through the deepening darkness Dana saw his teeth flash white when he grinned. "I suppose it would have been, but I always felt there was something...special about this place. Something I didn't want to share with anyone else." He circled her with his arms. "Until now."

Dana tilted her head up to study Rick's face, searching for signs that he was teasing her, pulling her leg. But in the glowing gray depths of his eyes she saw that he was telling the truth. She lifted her hand and pressed it against his cheek. "I'm flattered, Rick...really, I am. But I—I don't understand. Why me?"

He angled his head to bury his lips in her palm. Dana's eyes closed as a flood of heat spread outward from his touch. When she instinctively drew her hand away, Rick captured it in his and studied it as if it were the most fascinating object he'd ever beheld.

"I want to share everything with you," he said. "I've never known anyone like you before. You make me forget—" he paused, blinking as if he couldn't quite believe it himself "—everything but the sight of your face, the sound of your voice, the smell of your perfume."

His words paralyzed Dana, left her numb with pleasure. Her heart expanded with joy until she was sure it would burst through her chest. Could it be...? Was it possible Rick felt the same way she did?

But if he didn't...

Slowly...inexorably...like an anesthetic wearing off, the potential consequences of becoming even more deeply involved with Rick began to penetrate Dana's brain. It was as if she could already feel the pain in advance, anticipate the heartbreaking grief she would suffer if she were misinterpreting his words, his intentions.

She jerked her hand from his and scrambled to her feet. "I don't wear perfume," she said in a shaky voice.

Rick rose more slowly. "Don't you?" He moved to stand behind her, traced the curve of her earlobe with one knuckle. "You always smell like lilacs to me."

"It's probably just my dishwashing detergent. Now cut that out!" Against her will, an electric current of pleasure shimmered along her nerve endings. She stepped away from Rick and his seductive hands.

There was plenty of light from the moon for Dana to make out the exasperation scrawled across his rugged features. "Correct me if I'm wrong," he said, plowing his fingers through his hair, "but you seem to be losing your enthusiasm for our little adventure."

"That's all this is to you, isn't it? A little adventure."

A shadow crossed his face. "You're wrong."

"Am I?" Dana paced back and forth across the clearing, her long skirt dragging in her wake. "The only reason I came up here with you was because you tricked me into it."

"I did no such—"

"All right, maybe it wasn't exactly a trick, but you practically dared me to do it, knowing I wouldn't turn down a challenge like that."

"Just because you can't stand being called a coward doesn't mean I don't—"

"I'm tired of playing games, Rick." Her short bark of laughter was laced with something close to hysteria. "Sometimes I feel like that's all our relationship is, one game after another. We each have a goal, and the winner of the game is the one who keeps the other person from reaching his. It's like some stupid soccer match, for heaven's sake!''

Rick folded his arms across his chest and tapped his foot impatiently. ''I assure you, I have no intention of playing—''

Dana rushed on, ignoring him. ''You chase me to Los Angeles, I ditch you at the airport. You double-dare me to come up here with you, I take your dare.'' She flung her arms skyward and wailed, ''We're not kids anymore, Rick! We're too old for hide-and-seek or tag or double dares.''

She faced him squarely and said sadly, ''We're too old to play make-believe.''

Rick scowled at her. ''Is that what you think this is?''

''What would *you* call it?''

He closed the distance between them in one long, swift stride. ''Insanity,'' he growled, just before he hauled her into his arms and crushed his lips to hers.

Chapter Ten

Slowly...slowly...they sank to the ground, lips melding, hands entangled in each other's hair, the lengths of their bodies pressed tightly together as if they were already joined in the ultimate act of intimacy.

Like sinking into a sweet, warm pool of honey, Dana thought.

Like being sucked into quicksand, was Rick's last thought before an overwhelming wave of tenderness swept away the last of his caution.

Then there was only sensation...desire...and an outpouring of some intense, powerful emotion Rick was afraid to identify. As their legs folded beneath them, he propped his back against a nearby oak tree and cradled Dana across his lap.

She was all soft curves and silky skin. So delicate, he was afraid he would crush her. So desirable, he wanted to ravish her thoroughly with all the hot, fierce urgency boiling up inside him.

He forced himself to hold back, to take it slowly, knowing that for once they weren't constrained by time or the fear of interruptions. When he deepened their kiss, seeking the sweet recesses of her mouth with his tongue, a whimper of pleasure escaped Dana's lips. She tasted like cinnamon and every forbidden pleasure Rick had denied himself over the years.

Now the throbbing ache in his loins was making his present position uncomfortable, so he shifted his body to lie beside her. ''Damn this dress,'' he muttered when the long folds of fabric tangled around his legs.

Her quiet laughter fell on his ears as musically as wind chimes. ''I thought you liked my costume,'' she said, lips pursing into a pretend pout.

He found them irresistible and kissed them. ''I'd like it better off you than on.'' He managed to free himself from the clutches of calico and braced his head on his elbow to gaze down at her lovely face. ''Now, where were we?''

Her eyes were wide and dark and sparkling as midnight sky. When Rick lowered his head to claim her lips again, her eyelids drifted closed, dusting her high, perfect cheekbones with long, thick lashes.

He felt a tremor shake her body when he slid his hand to the gentle, seductive swell of her breast. ''Rick...'' She whispered his name as if it were a magical incantation. A surge of satisfaction welled up inside him when her nipple beaded beneath his palm. ''Mmm...yes...''

Her moan of pleasure nearly drove him mad with impatience. Raising her slightly off the ground, he reached behind her to unfasten the buttons of her dress. After a moment of useless fumbling, Rick groaned in frustration. "Do you have any idea how tiny these buttons are? And how many there are of them?"

"Believe me, I know. I had to fasten them all myself, remember?"

"Sit up." He swung both of them into an upright position before Dana had time to comply with his abrupt command. "Now, that's better." With her back to him, he had free access to the long row of buttons. They were still too tiny to be easily opened by his big fingers, but Rick was sure he could manage. If not, he could always rip the infuriating dress open with one fell swoop.

After the first couple of buttons, he got the hang of it. The back of the dress fell open to expose a tantalizing V of creamy skin. "Now we're making progress," he growled. "First one... then the next..."

As each button fell apart at his touch, he branded his lips to each newly bared inch of her back. "And another... and another..."

Dana's head fell backward. "Oh... Rick..." As his mouth blazed a trail of pleasure, inch by agonizing inch down her spine, she thought for sure she was going to melt into a puddle at his feet. He reached her bra, unclasped it, then continued his maddening journey down her back.

"Lower... lower... oops, this one's stuck—there we go...." His voice was muffled against her skin, the heat of his breath only adding to her delicious torment.

At last he reached her waist, but she was to have no respite from his wandering, pleasuring hands. She felt him loosen the bobby pins that held her hair in place.

"There... that's much better." Her hair cascaded to her shoulders. Rick combed it out gently with his strong, sensitive fingers, then dropped his head to nuzzle the curve of her neck and send a heavenly prickling sensation spreading through her limbs. "Turn around," he said in a tone that was as much a plea as a command.

Dana twisted around slowly, afraid to meet his eyes, afraid she would see in them the reflection of her own naked need. Then their glances met . . . locked . . . and for a moment there was no power on earth that could have torn them apart.

Rick reached for her, and when she would have tumbled into his arms he held her shoulders back. Then he slid his hands down to tug gently on the sleeves of her dress. The cloth slipped slowly off her shoulders, down her arms, baring her inch by inch to his ravenous gaze.

With one final sweep of his hand he brushed the last strip of lace, the last fold of calico from her breasts. His Adam's apple bobbed as he swallowed convulsively. "You're so beautiful in the moonlight. . . . Your skin gleams like ivory. . . ."

Dana swayed forward to meet his touch, reveling in the exquisite sensations Rick stirred inside her by the kneading caresses of his hand, the teasing flick of his thumb. Dizzy with desire, she felt the universe whirling around her, the earth spinning on its axis, reeling along its orbit around the sun.

Never had she felt so disoriented by passion, yet so certain that her heart was leading her in the right direction. Her love for Rick was like a beacon shining in the night, guiding her way. Whatever rocky shores their relationship might have foundered on in the past had been swept away by forces as inevitable as the rise and fall of the tide. Tonight there were no hidden shoals, no treacherous undercurrents waiting to knock them off course.

She surrendered gladly to the maelstrom of yearning and emotion that swirled through her, lifting her to greater heights of passion. Rick laid her on the ground with one swift yet strangely gentle motion.

"Are you comfortable?" he asked, concern furrowing his forehead.

Dana cleared her throat. "*Comfortable* isn't exactly the word I'd use to describe how I'm feeling right now."

A lazy smile crept across his mouth as understanding dawned. "Maybe you'd be more comfortable with fewer clothes on."

"What about you?" she protested.

He arched one roguish eyebrow. "You don't expect me to do all the work myself, do you?"

With that less-than-subtle invitation, Dana reached for his belt buckle, shyly at first, then more eagerly as shirt, jeans and shoes came flying off and were tossed aside. Soon the hard, nude length of his body was snuggled next to hers.

Dana ran her hand experimentally along his muscled limbs, the sturdy ridge of his spine, acquainting herself with every square inch of him. To her amazed delight, he seemed as affected by her touch as she was by his.

At last, with a tortured groan, he captured her roaming hand in his. "Sweetheart, if you keep that up, this is going to end awful quickly."

"Mmm..." She turned her head to nibble on his shoulder. "I never was much good at self-restraint...."

"Oh, yeah? Well, two can play at that game."

"I thought we weren't going to play anymore ga—oh, sweet heaven! Oh...Rick...ah, darling..."

Rick felt himself slipping closer to the brink, dangling from the edge of a very tall cliff by his fingernails. Always before, when he was with women, he'd been able to hold a part of himself back, to isolate a detached corner of his brain and use it to maintain control.

But with Dana he felt about as controlled as a runaway train. She was driving him crazy with desire, making him reckless, blotting out all his very good reasons for keeping part of himself distant and aloof.

He was delirious with fever, aching with hunger for her—and worse yet, he had a strong suspicion that no matter how many times they made love, he would never be able to get enough of her.

He tried to focus on her pleasure instead of his own, lowering his head to her breast and swirling his tongue around the hardened peak of her nipple. But when she arched her back and cried out, tangling her fingers in his hair to pull him closer, Rick discovered he could no longer separate her pleasure from his own.

It was as if they were already physically joined, connected somehow so that each time he stroked her, elicited a moan of ecstasy, he was heightening his own pleasure, as well.

"Dana... sweetheart..." He buried his face between her breasts, kneading, suckling, caressing—losing himself in the indescribably sweet, scented softness of her.

Dana's heart thudded a mile a minute next to his ear; her skin was moist and warm, quivering in response to the brush of his hand, the heat of his mouth. When her fingers closed around the hardened evidence of his desire, Rick thought he would explode. "Sweetheart," he gasped into the delicate hollow below her ear, "I warned you...."

Through the rush of excitement roaring through his head he barely heard her urgent whisper, "Rick... yes, darling, now..."

He hoisted himself above her, poised on trembling arms to watch her face while he joined his body to hers. Her gaze locked onto his, her eyes filling with wonder and joy as he eased himself inside her. He fought for his last tattered remnants of self-control, bending the sheer force of his will to make this moment last as long as possible.

As she sheathed him with her velvety, moist heat, passion erupted inside him and he drove himself all the way inside her with one desperate thrust.

Dana barely recognized the guttural moan that sprang from her own throat. She was on fire, every cell in her body aflame with longing. Only Rick had the power to extinguish those flames, yet with each smoldering kiss, each rhythmic thrust, he stoked the inferno higher and hotter.

His face moved inches above hers while he rocked back and forth with a gradually accelerating tempo. His silvery gray eyes shone like a mirror, glowing with the same intensity of emotion and purely physical sensation that also consumed Dana.

"You feel so wonderful," he managed to grind out through gritted teeth. "I could make love to you all night long...."

His words, the tender, tortured expression in his eyes, his throbbing, rhythmic strokes combined to ignite something molten in the very core of Dana's being. Beyond pleasure, beyond name or description, it spread outward to envelop her in a roaring blaze.

Rick watched her face contort with rapture, felt the vibrations rocket through her body. Then the pulsing contractions jolted him past all rational thought, self-control or sanity.

Something snapped deep inside him, and at long last he broke free of his self-imposed restraint and the emotional chains that had shackled him to the ground for so long. In wild, glorious abandon he burst free and soared upward to unimaginable heights of ecstasy, finding a release and a kind of joy whose existence he'd never even suspected before.

Somewhere during that brief yet endless flight he realized he loved her.

He waited for the emotions that were sure to follow—regret that he'd made himself vulnerable, fear for the anguish he would have to endure one day when their relationship inevitably turned sour.

But all he felt was happiness... peace... contentment.

He drew Dana's head against his shoulder and kissed her hair.

She exhaled a long, happy sigh. "Well, that's one dare I'm sure glad I took."

Rick chuckled. "I want you to know, I had no idea this was going to happen when I suggested we come up here."

"Oh, sure. I bet you said the same thing in high school when you ran out of gas driving your date home."

He angled his head to give her a wounded look. "Dana, I'm shocked that you have such a low opinion of me."

"Don't misunderstand—I'm not complaining."

"*You* were the one who found a way to break into the park."

"Only because I didn't feel like climbing a tree to get over the fence!"

"You just can't believe I only wanted to show you my secret spot, can you?"

She batted her long lashes at him. "Secret spot? Is *that* what you call it?"

"Why, you..." He grabbed her and tickled her ribs.

"Stop! No!" She squirmed with laughter, then retaliated.

Rick hadn't even known he was ticklish, but Dana managed to find a spot that drove him crazy. "Truce!" he yelled finally.

They collapsed on the ground, gasping with laughter. Dana slung her arm across Rick's chest, weaving her fingers through the thick mat of curls.

The ground beneath her was hard as a rock, the night air had turned decidedly chilly, and Rick's shoulder wasn't exactly the most comfortable pillow in the world. But she couldn't imagine any other place on earth she'd rather be.

The sky was filled with stars, the air with the mingled scent of pine and roses. And her heart was filled with love for the man who lay beside her, cradling her in his arms.

A perfect day, all right.

How could she possibly spoil this beautiful aftermath by telling Rick that Jake Winslow had called her this morning and agreed to appear with Alistair?

Rick was singing in the shower the next morning when the phone rang. As he hopped out and snatched a towel, he realized he'd been singing the title song from *Match Made in Heaven*.

He dripped his way into the bedroom, amazed he could still remember the words when years ago he'd made a deliberate effort to forget the song that his father—and Jake—had written for his mother.

When he picked up the phone, he heard the panic-stricken voice of his best friend from college.

After that he forgot all about silly love songs and romantic moonlit interludes. . . .

An hour later he was pulling up in front of Dana's home. He'd never been here before, and was surprised to discover she lived in a small house he'd often noticed in passing.

It was a fine example of Queen Anne architecture, with its steeply pitched roof and gingerbread ornamentation. A porch with a spindlework balustrade ran along the front. Obviously well maintained with an eye for historical integrity, the house was painted a bright sunshine yellow with white trim. Rick decided it suited Dana perfectly.

As he hurried up the front walk, he could see a wooden swing hanging from a beam at the far end of the porch. The Sunday paper was scattered across it, several sections spilling to the ground.

His foot had just reached the bottom step when the front door swung open and Dana emerged, balancing a mug of coffee in one hand and a piece of toast in the other. Her eyes flared wide in surprise. "Hi!"

She was barefoot, wearing some kind of flowery robe that came to midthigh. Her hair was still damp from the shower. Mixed in with the smell of coffee and orange marmalade, Rick detected a familiar fragrance. Damn it, she *did* smell like lilacs, no matter what she said!

"How did you know where I lived?" Immediately she rolled her eyes. "Dumb question. I'm listed in the phone book."

Rick hesitated for a moment, awkward as an adolescent arriving at a girl's front door at the end of their first date. Then he stepped forward and quickly pressed his lips to Dana's temple. When he drew back, her face shone softly with happiness. Suddenly she glanced down. "Oops! Sorry! I'm dribbling coffee on your shoe."

She backed away and settled herself on the swing. "I was just about to start my second cup," she said. "Want some?"

"No time." Rick swept the newspapers aside and sat down next to her.

"What are you in such a hurry for?" Dana bit into her toast. "It *is* Sunday, after all." She swallowed. "I thought maybe we could go for a picnic, what with the weather being so nice."

"Wish I could."

"You could show me some more of your secret spots." She winked at him.

Rick threw back his head and laughed. "Sweetheart, you make it sound awfully tempting, but—"

"Rick, we have to talk." Dana set her mug on the ground and balanced the half-eaten piece of toast on top of it. She'd spent the night dreaming of Rick, reliving the wonder of their lovemaking, recapturing every rapturous touch, every tender word they'd shared.

Upon awakening this morning she'd basked in a deliriously happy glow for about thirty seconds before her conscience began to nag her, jabbing at her with little pricks of guilt. She should have told Rick about Jake's call, should have warned him that all systems were go for the televised reunion. Now that Jake had agreed to bury the hatchet, convincing Alistair to go along with the idea would be a snap.

She wanted to believe that the news wouldn't wreck her relationship with Rick, that what they had shared was too strong to be destroyed by a mere difference of opinion.

But deep inside, Dana couldn't help worrying that maybe their romance was too new, too fragile to survive this test. If only Rick weren't so stubborn! If only he could admit that her plan would benefit everyone concerned.

But the longer she kept the truth from him, the worse it would be when he found out. She took a deep breath. "There's something I have to tell you."

Rick draped his arm along the back of the swing. "I know that after last night there are a lot of things that need to be said." He smiled tenderly and brushed a damp lock of hair out of her eyes. "Believe me, I have things to say to you, too."

"But—"

"Unfortunately, we'll have to put them on hold for a while." He checked his watch.

"Rick, you don't understand what I'm—"

He squeezed Dana's shoulders. "I have to catch a plane in less than three hours. That means I should have left for Sacramento already."

Her forehead crinkled in puzzled confusion. "But where—what—?"

"That's what I came over here to tell you." Rick pulled Dana to her feet and clasped both her hands in his. "I got a call an hour ago from a guy who was my best friend in college. He's an architect, too. Lives in Houston."

"From the expression on your face, I'd say he didn't exactly call with good news."

"Hardly. He's currently overseeing construction of a controversial new office complex. The whole project's been plagued with missed deadlines, cost overruns...." Rick shook his head in disgust. "Yesterday his building contractor ran off to Brazil with most of the remaining funds."

"Oh, how awful!"

"Hank's really in a jam. Now the financial backers are screaming, government investigators are crawling all over the place and everyone involved in the project is pointing his finger at everyone else."

"So... Hank wants you to help him out?"

"He needs someone he can trust right now, someone who's an architect but who's also had contractor experience. Hank's a real good guy, and he's done me a favor or two over the years. I can't let him down."

"No, of course not." Dana chewed her lower lip. Obviously this wasn't a good time to bring up the subject of Jake and Alistair's imminent reconciliation. "How... long would you be gone?"

Rick's mouth curved into a sexy smile. "I'll miss you, too," he said, misinterpreting Dana's train of thought. "But it won't be for very long. A week at most. Hank just needs someone who can oversee things at the building site while he's off trying to placate his investors and find a new contractor to complete the job."

"Maybe he'll want *you* to finish it."

Rick shook his head. "I build houses. I can hold things together for a week or so, but Hank will have to hire someone more experienced in office construction."

Gears were whirling around inside Dana's brain. She *would* miss Rick, of course. She loved him, for heaven's sake! And that was one more thing for them to talk about when he got back. But this unexpected trip might turn out to be a blessing in disguise. While Rick was gone, she could set up the final arrangements for the West and Winslow reunion without having to fight him every step of the way.

If he ended up staying in Texas longer than planned, he might even miss the whole thing! And once it was over, he would see that Dana had been right all along about reuniting the two old friends.

The entire problem would vanish, would never even become an issue in their new, more intimate relationship....

Yes, good old Hank's phone call might turn out to be a real boon. When Rick returned, he and Dana could start this new phase of their relationship with a clean slate. And after last night, she could hardly wait to see what the future held.

Dana wrapped her arms around Rick's neck and kissed him in full view of the neighbors, people driving by on their way to church and whoever else might be watching.

"Hurry back," she whispered against his lips. "I can hardly wait to explore some more secret spots with you."

Only the thought of missing his plane gave Rick the strength to wrench himself from her embrace, to leave her behind when all he wanted to do was sweep her into his arms, haul her into bed and spend a long, luxurious Sunday afternoon making wild, sweet love to her.

Halfway to his car he paused and looked back. "Sweetheart, about this thing with Pop and Jake Winslow..."

He probably only imagined the troubled look that flitted briefly across her face. "I'd never do anything to hurt you, Rick." Dana's voice was so soft, it barely carried across the yard.

But with that reassurance echoing in his ears, Rick blew her one last kiss, dashed to his pickup and hopped inside. By the time he sped past the city limits he was whistling.

Everything was happening so fast, Rick hadn't really had time to sort out these strange, newly discovered emotions of his. Fortunately the long plane ride to Houston would give him ample opportunity to examine his feelings, to think about the future in light of this astonishing new development called love.

Funny, but the thought of five hours at thirty thousand feet didn't even faze him. After all, he'd conquered an even greater fear, hadn't he? He'd fallen in love without even realizing what was happening. And look! No bruises, no broken bones. In fact, Rick had to admit the feeling was pretty damn wonderful.

Nothing could mar his good mood this morning—not Hank's troubles, not this unavoidable but temporary separation from Dana, not even anxiety about what would happen if Pop and Jake ever came face-to-face again.

That prospect seemed pretty unlikely now. After last night the game had changed; the ground rules were different now. Falling in love, making love with Dana had turned Rick's life topsy-turvy, and he was sure it was the same for her. Overnight his priorities had changed as well as his perspective. He would never, *ever* do anything to hurt Dana, but the amazing part was that Rick actually trusted her not to hurt *him*, either.

Considering the new twist their relationship had taken, Dana was bound to drop this reconciliation scheme. Maybe he hadn't told her he loved her in so many words, but she was certainly perceptive enough to realize it, wasn't she?

And if Dana truly cared for Rick in return, she couldn't possibly go ahead with her plans to reunite Pop and Jake, knowing how opposed he was to the idea.

Could she?

The next week flew by for Dana in a flurry of preparations. Sure enough, once she informed Alistair that Jake had agreed to a reconciliation, Alistair had embraced the idea with an enthusiasm that further reassured Dana she was doing the right thing.

Channel Five began airing promotional spots that promised to kick off pledge week with a joint appearance by the famous songwriting team of West and Winslow. Community interest was roused to a fever pitch, and the upcoming membership drive was the main topic of conversation in bars and beauty shops all over town. The *Pine Creek Gazette* ran a retrospective series of articles on the careers of both men, and one of the major wire services even picked up the story. Calls for information and requests for interviews began to jam up the station's phone lines, and Jenni Carpenter threatened to quit if she didn't get some extra help.

Five days before the big event, a row of red lights was blinking like a Christmas display on Jenni's phone when Dana rushed past the reception desk on the way to her office.

"Please hold, someone will be right with you." Jenni punched a button with the eraser end of her pencil and added another blinking light to the display. "Dana, wait!" Jenni flagged her down with a sheaf of yellow message slips. "There's another pile of these on your desk, plus a reporter from one of the Los Angeles papers came by to see you, and Andy needs to talk to you about finalizing the schedule for pledge week."

"Where's the reporter now?" Dana flipped quickly through her messages.

"Across the street getting a bite to eat." Jenni pulled out a mirror and fussed with her hair. "I told him you didn't have time to see him today, but he said he'd come back after lunch." She scowled at her reflection. "Dana, these people are driving me crazy!"

"Hmm...I must say you do look a little frazzled. Tell that reporter absolutely no interviews until after the West and Winslow reunion. And tell Andy I can fit him in at three-thirty today. Oh, and Jenni—" Dana paused in her office doorway "—keep up the good work."

Jenni threw her a disgusted glance, then clapped her hand to her forehead. "Oh, gosh, I almost forgot. Rick West is on line three for you."

Dana's smile froze. "Thanks." She ducked into her office and quickly shut the door. Rick had called twice before during the week he'd been gone, and each time Dana had meant to tell him that the reunion was all set.

But each time she couldn't quite bring herself to do it, using the excuse that it wasn't something she could tell him over the phone. She forced a cheerful note into her voice. "Hello, Rick? Sorry to keep you waiting for so long."

Even through two thousand miles of long-distance phone lines, his voice could still make her heart pound, her knees turn to oatmeal. "Sweetheart, what's going on around there, anyway? The line was busy for over an hour, then once I finally got through, your secretary put me on hold for fifteen minutes."

Dana fiddled with a lock of hair. "We're, um, having some trouble with the phones today." Well, it wasn't exactly a *lie,* was it? "Rick...when are you coming home?"

His response was a cross between a growl and a sigh. "That's what I'm calling about. Looks like I'm going to be stuck here at least another week."

Dana sank into her chair, abruptly relieved. Rick was going to miss the reunion anyway, so what was the point of telling him about it? It would be cruel, in fact, to upset him when he already had so much on his mind. "Is that the *only* reason you called?'' she teased in a low, suggestive voice.

When he chuckled the vibrations tickled her ear. He then proceeded to explain in great detail all his plans for celebrating his homecoming.

''Rick, I don't think you're allowed to say that on the telephone,'' Dana warned him with a giggle. ''It might burn up the wires or something.''

And by the time he hung up, the long-distance lines were indeed sizzling.

God, it was good to be home!

Rick slung his suitcase onto the bed and peeled off his shirt. He was dog tired from the eighteen-hour days he'd been working and his exhaustion was compounded by jet lag. But he wasn't about to waste time napping, not when he could take a hot shower, jump in his truck and be on Dana's front doorstep in less than half an hour. He grinned, imagining her surprise when he showed up two days ahead of schedule.

Good old Hank had finally pried out the reason for Rick's foul mood, for his impatience at all the delays in getting the office project back on track. Once he heard about Dana, he'd insisted that Rick pack his bags and catch the next flight back to California.

''You've been a lifesaver, old buddy, but I've taken advantage of our friendship long enough.''

''Hank, it's no problem for me to stay longer. Really!''

Hank shook his head. ''Never thought I'd actually see the day when the old Lone Wolf would fall this hard for someone. I'm sure not about to stand in the way of true love!''

''But you haven't found a new contractor yet.''

"Tomorrow I'm talkin' to a fellow from Dallas who looks like he can do the job." Hank slapped Rick on the back. "You git on back to that sweet l'il gal of yours, y'hear? I ain't takin' *no* for an answer!"

For once Rick had been glad Dana was two thousand miles away, where she couldn't hear herself referred to as his "sweet l'il gal." He could just imagine what she'd have had to say about *that*.

When Rick stepped out of the shower, he flipped on the TV in his bedroom. Even though Dana never appeared on camera—she'd once confessed to him her terrible stage fright—somehow watching Channel Five would be a way of reestablishing a connection with her.

And Rick could hardly wait to reestablish other more intimate connections with her.

He pulled on a clean shirt, humming to himself and wondering which she would prefer—flowers, chocolate or champagne. All three, he decided.

He snapped his watchband around his wrist. All of a sudden he recognized a familiar tune and realized *Match Made in Heaven* was playing on the television. An ominous prickling crept over his skin. Then the movie was interrupted by a pledge break. Rick listened with growing horror. His blood turned to ice. And a sense of betrayal, of outraged disbelief congealed around his heart.

He didn't even take time to switch off the TV. He had less than twenty minutes to get to the station, less than twenty minutes before his life came crashing down around his head.

If he wasn't already too late, that is.

Chapter Eleven

Dana's palms were sweaty and a convention of butterflies was holding session in her stomach. She was as nervous as if she were going in front of the cameras herself, for heaven's sake!

Soon it would all be over—the weeks of planning, the careful negotiations, the tricky choreography that had shielded Alistair and Jake from reporters and kept both men apart ever since Jake's arrival in Pine Creek yesterday.

In nine—no, eight—minutes, Andy would step in front of the cameras, introduce West and Winslow, and the two former partners would meet face-to-face for the first time in over thirty years.

It would be a touching reunion that would no doubt bring tears to many eyes—Dana's included.

She scanned the checklist on her clipboard for the hundredth time, then stepped to the phone bank to see how many new members had called to sign up during the past hour. One of the volunteers grinned and gave Dana a thumbs-up sign.

Wonderful! The pace of new memberships was running well ahead of their last pledge drive, and West and Winslow hadn't even appeared yet.

Dana spoke to the camera operator and director one last time to make sure they understood the plan. "Mr. West is in the greenroom with Carole, and Mr. Winslow's waiting in Makeup with Elaine. When Andy finishes his introduction, Carole will nudge Alistair in front of the cameras, then after Andy shakes his hand, Elaine will give Jake his cue to come out."

Both the camera operator and the director were bobbing their heads up and down like toy dogs in the back window of a car. "Dana, we've been over this a thousand times. Don't sweat it."

"I just want to make sure that nothing goes wr—"

The door to the set flew open with a loud bang that made Dana cringe.

All of a sudden she felt as if someone had punched her right in the stomach. The air rushed out of her lungs in a whoosh, and spots began to dance before her eyes. "Rick," she managed to choke out, "what are you doing back so—"

"Where are they?"

Jenni hovered anxiously in the background, wringing her hands. "I tried to tell him no one was allowed on the set, but he wouldn't listen, he just barged right—"

"It's okay, Jenni. Go on back to your desk." Dana drew in a deep quavering breath, but before she could come up with anything to say, Rick repeated his question.

"Where are they?"

His voice was perfectly level, his features arranged in a controlled expression. But Dana had never seen Rick so angry before. Come to think of it, she'd never seen *anyone* this angry before.

"Rick, please, I can explain—"

"Are you going to tell me where they are, or do I have to tear this studio apart to find them?" His eyes blazed at her with sparks of molten steel. A muscle rippled along his square jawline, warning Dana that he was exerting a great deal of effort to maintain control.

His arms were corded with tension wires as he clenched and unclenched his fists. A film of sweat sheened his forehead, and it wasn't from the hot studio lights. Dana was suddenly afraid, not that Rick would physically assault her, but that she'd gambled their relationship to save her station—and might have lost him forever.

To hide her fear, she jerked up her chin and met his furious gaze head-on. "It's too late," she said. "Everything's ready. They go on in five minutes."

Amazingly, she saw something like her own fear shimmer in Rick's eyes and then vanish. When he spoke, it sounded as if the words were wrenched from deep inside his chest. "My God," he said quietly, "do you have any idea what you've done?"

Dana stared at him in dismay. "Look, I know you don't like the idea of your father appearing on television, but you're making too big a deal out of this."

His eyes, which had drifted away to stare at some distant, terrible vision, focused sharply on Dana again. "Have they spoken to each other yet?"

"Your father and Jake? No, we decided the emotional impact of their reunion would be greater if—"

"Maybe it's not too late," he muttered. Then he seized Dana's arm and dragged her off the set, out into the hallway.

"Let go of me! Somebody call Security! If you think you can get away with—"

Rick clamped his hand over her mouth. "Listen to me, will you? Just hear me out."

Well, it was really the least she owed him.... Dana nodded her head.

Rick pulled his hand away and spoke rapidly. "You want to know why I can't let my father and Jake patch things up? All right, I'll tell you. Because I'm afraid if they do, Jake will tell Pop the truth. And the shock of hearing the truth could kill him!"

Dana's eyes darted back and forth across Rick's feverish face. "Truth? What truth? What are you talking about?"

Rick grasped her shoulders and gave her a little shake to emphasize every word. "The truth about who my real father is."

"Your real—? But isn't Alistair—?"

Rick's fingers dug into her arms. "Jake Winslow is my biological father."

Dana gasped. *"Jake?"*

"I discovered it years ago. Jake swore never to tell Pop, but if they start talking again, rehashing old memories..."

"You're afraid the truth will slip out."

"Or that Jake will decide it's time to claim me as his son." Rick spat out the words as if he couldn't bear the taste of them. He gripped her shoulders more tightly. "I can't take the chance he'll tell Pop the truth!

I can't!'' He punctuated his last statement with another shake.

As the stunning shock of Rick's revelation wore off, Dana's eyes grew wide with horror. "But that means we can't let them—oh my God!" She clapped her hand over her mouth. "Come on, quick!"

Flinging open the door she dashed back into the studio. "Your father—Alistair—is in that room over there with Carole. You get him out of here—make up some excuse, tell him anything. I'll handle Jake."

Andy Gallagher's worried frown evaporated when he spotted Dana. "There you are! I was afraid we were going to have to start without—"

"Everything's off, Andy—the whole thing. When the movie ends and you go on camera, you'll have to announce that the West and Winslow reunion has been canceled due to unforeseeable circumstances."

Andy's jaw just about hit the floor. "Are you crazy? The movie ends in two minutes! What the hell are you—"

"Just do it," she snapped. "I'll explain later. Doug, get that barbershop quartet out here to perform right after Andy's announcement."

The director shook his head uncertainly. "I don't know if they're ready to go on yet."

"Then put on a pair of tap shoes and *improvise,* for Pete's sake!" Dana paused to catch her breath. This couldn't be happening.... What would her father think if he could see what a mess she'd made of things?

Andy had turned pale as a ghost. "You're blowing our last chance to save the station, Dana. If we call off this reunion after all the publicity—"

She held up her hand like a crossing guard to halt the flow of his words. No one knew better than she did what this decision was going to cost her. But she wasn't about to ruin Rick's and Alistair's lives. Human beings were more important than television stations. "No arguments," she said. "I know what I'm doing."

Andy looked highly skeptical of that, but his attention was diverted by Doug's frantic gestures indicating that Andy was on in thirty seconds.

Just then Rick hustled his father out of the green-room. Carole was hot on their heels, yanking on Alistair's other arm as if he were a wishbone she and Rick were fighting over. "You can't do this," she whispered fiercely. "He's about to go on!"

"It's okay, Carole. Let him go."

Carole stared at Dana as if she'd lost her mind. "What are you talking about? If he doesn't go on, we're sunk!"

Dana clamped her lips into a tight line. "I know. Alistair, I'm so sorry about all this, but—"

"My dear, I don't understand! And Rick here simply refuses to explain...."

Dana's gaze met Rick's over the top of Alistair's shiny pink head. She searched his eyes for a clue to his feelings, but that damn wall had slammed shut with all the force and finality of a guillotine, effectively severing his emotions from her. She might as well have tried to see through lead shielding.

"Rick can explain later," she said softly, unable to tear her gaze from his. "I'm sorry—for everything." Her last words weren't really directed at Alistair, and she saw a flicker of acknowledgment in Rick's eyes.

Then he broke contact and hurried Alistair toward the studio exit. The door swung silently shut behind them, but it clanged inside Dana's head as loudly as a prison gate. Only she was being locked out, not in.

Her heart felt brittle enough to shatter into a thousand pieces if anyone so much as looked at her the wrong way. Fortunately Andy and the others were too busy scrambling to cover for the last-minute change in plans. A load of guilt settled on Dana's shoulders, compounding the shock and pain that already weighed on her. She might have averted disaster for the Wests, but she'd also let a lot of people down—loyal, dedicated people who didn't deserve to see this station and their jobs go swirling down the drain.

Her feet seemed encased in concrete overshoes as she trudged wearily down the hall. The nightmare wasn't over yet. She still had to face Jake Winslow.

He didn't make it any easier for her. When Dana opened the door to Makeup, he leapt eagerly to his feet and straightened the bow tie she knew must be choking him. He looked about as comfortable in that tuxedo as he would wearing chain mail, but the excited sparkle in his eye told Dana how much he was looking forward to this reunion.

"Show time, huh?"

"Mr. Winslow, there's something—"

"Boy, I'll tell you—I can't believe I'm about to finally see Alistair after all these years!"

"Jake—"

"You won't believe this, but I'm as nervous as I was the night we won the Academy Award! But it'll be worth it once I—"

"Jake, there isn't going to be any reunion. The whole thing's been called off." It was one of the hardest things Dana had ever had to say.

Elaine's hand flew to her heart. "Dana, what's wrong?" she gasped.

"Would you mind if I spoke to Mr. Winslow alone? I'll explain later."

"Okay, but I—I hope everything's all right." Elaine's face was flushed nearly as red as her hair. She gave Dana's arm a sympathetic squeeze as she left the room.

Dana avoided Jake's bewildered stare, searching for the right words to explain what had happened.

He saved her the trouble. "Rick stopped it, didn't he?" It wasn't really a question.

Dana's first instinct was to soften the truth, to try to ease the pain and sorrow she heard in Jake's voice. But there had already been too much deception, too much unhappiness caused by trying to gloss over the truth. She was tired of lies.

"Yes," she said. "He came back to Pine Creek before I expected him. He—" She swallowed, then forced herself to look Jake squarely in the eye. "He told me you were his father."

Jake lowered himself into a chair as if his legs would no longer support him. His complexion was ashen, and he loosened his tie like a man having trouble breathing. "Did he, now?" His voice was filled with wonder and sadness. He bowed his head. "Then you've heard him say something I've been waiting more than thirty years to hear him say to me."

Dana's eyes brimmed with tears. She'd lost a lot today—the station, her father's legacy and very likely the chance of any future with Rick.

But Jake had lost a lot, too. His dearest friend. His son.

Dana knelt down and put her arms around him. Then her tears finally spilled over, and after that she wasn't sure who was comforting whom.

Rick reread the same paragraph of his architectural journal for about the twentieth time. With a snarl of disgust he finally hurled the magazine across his living room. He strode into the kitchen, scanned the refrigerator shelves for something interesting, then slammed the door shut without taking anything.

He slumped into a chair, drummed his fingers on the table. Unbidden came the memory of how he'd once shared breakfast with Dana here. Fool that he was, he'd once even thought he wanted to share breakfast with her every morning for the rest of his life!

But that was before he'd found out what a conniving, underhanded vixen she was. If he hadn't come home ahead of schedule yesterday, that damned reunion would have taken place as planned. Jake and Pop would have had time for a nice long chat, and Pop might very well be in the hospital right now. Or worse.

Rick shoved back his chair so hard, it nearly toppled over. How could Dana have done this to him? He'd given her his love, and in return she'd betrayed him—or would have if he hadn't arrived in time.

Dana was no better than his mother.

He'd been a fool to trust Dana, to hope for even one instant that she might be different. He'd wisely kept up his emotional guard all these years, and the first time he let it down, *wham!* A sucker punch right to the gut.

He'd learned his lesson, by God. Never again would he stop to wonder if keeping the world at arm's length was the right thing to do. From now on he would keep himself detached from any emotional entanglements. No more risks, no more reckless forays into that treacherous quicksand called love.

He had one consolation, anyway. At least he'd found out what kind of woman Dana was before he'd done something stupid. During that interminable separation while he was in Houston, he'd actually decided to propose when he got back.

Really, everything had worked out for the best. Although he was pretty sure Pop hadn't believed his cockamamy excuse for dragging him out of the studio at the last minute. The only explanation Rick could come up with was that their appearance had been called off due to technical difficulties.

And of course, by the time Pop started to wonder why the reunion wasn't rescheduled, Channel Five would probably be off the air.

Rick paced back and forth across the kitchen. Damn it, why did he feel so guilty about that? Dana had had no right to pin all her hopes on one do-or-die plan. He'd told her over and over again not to count on Pop and Jake to save the station.

Maybe there was still something he could do, some way to help. Maybe the pledge drive would still bring in enough money to rescue Channel Five from ruin.

Rick returned to the living room and switched on the TV. On the screen an accordion trio was wailing away on a rather unique rendition of "Yesterday." Behind them a row of bored-looking volunteers sat at telephones, none of which were ringing. The giant thermometer that monitored the pledge drive's progress toward its financial goal showed a decidedly chilly forecast.

He flicked off the set with a frustrated curse. This was exactly why it was a mistake to care too deeply for people. Before you knew it, their problems became your problems, their worries your worries. Who needed all that aggravation?

He ought to be rejoicing with triumph, basking in the glow of relief. His secret was safe and he'd narrowly escaped making the mistake of his life—asking Dana to marry him.

Why, then, did he feel so rotten? Why couldn't he quit worrying about Dana and how she would deal with the loss of her TV station? Why couldn't he stop wondering what Jake was feeling right now?

Why did he feel as if his heart had been ripped right out of his chest?

He'd succeeded in preventing the dreaded reunion, which was what he'd wanted all along. But everything felt wrong, as if his life had been turned topsy-turvy and inside out. Perversely, the one person who might have helped him make sense of his feelings was—

The doorbell rang.

Rick peered cautiously through the drapes, expecting to find some nosy tabloid reporter skulking around his front porch.

Adrenaline flooded his bloodstream, sending his pulse into overdrive. It was Dana.

When he opened the door, they stared wordlessly at each other for a minute. She looked tired, as if she'd been awake all night making phone calls, going over financial figures, scrambling for a way to scrape up enough money to keep the station going.

Her eyes were clear but red-rimmed—whether from tears or exhaustion Rick couldn't say and didn't want to think about. She wore a one-piece tailored jumpsuit whose vibrant blue color only emphasized the paleness of her skin.

Her mouth twitched slightly, as if she'd been about to offer him a smile but found it too much effort. "May I come in?" she asked in a husky voice.

Rick turned and walked away, but left the door open. He heard her feet tap across the hardwood floor as she followed him. "I'm on my way to pick up Jake at his hotel and drive him to the airport in Sacramento," she said.

Rick retrieved the magazine he'd flung to the floor earlier. What did she expect him to say?

"I thought you might want to say goodbye to him first."

Rick nearly dropped the magazine again. "Well, you thought wrong."

She moved toward him, then his expression stopped her in her tracks. "Rick, he's your father! He's devastated by all that's happened. Can't you at least spare a few minutes to talk to him?"

"Haven't you interfered enough already?"

Dana recoiled visibly from his words. "I didn't mean to interfere," she said slowly, as if she were making an enormous effort to control her voice. "If you'd only told me the truth, explained to me why you—"

"It was none of your business."

Her eyes widened. "None of my business?" she repeated incredulously. "After everything we've shared, how can you say it was none of my business?"

"After everything we shared, how could you go behind my back like that? You just couldn't wait for me to turn around so you could stick the knife in, could you?"

He wouldn't have thought it possible for her to grow paler, but she did. Her eyes drifted closed, and for an instant Rick was afraid she would faint. "I guess there's no point in discussing this," she said, swaying slightly. "But there's no reason why you can't call a truce with Jake now."

"I don't owe him anything."

"Only your life."

Rick hurled the magazine aside. Dana's words had hit him with stunning force, and for a moment he simply couldn't think of a response.

"How can you be so cold-hearted and callous about your own father? This isn't like you, Rick." Dana's voice had risen to a high pitch that bordered on hysteria. She paused to get a grip on herself. She saw now that she'd lost Rick, but maybe she could salvage at least one relationship. "Maybe Jake didn't raise you or give you his name, but that wasn't *his* choice. I just don't see what he's done that's so wrong."

"What would you know about it?" Rick demanded angrily.

"Because I've spent a lot of time with Jake since that fiasco yesterday. He told me how much he loved your mother, how guilty he felt when Alistair found out about them—"

"I don't want to hear any more about it!" he roared.

"Maybe it's time you did, son."

Rick and Dana whirled toward the front door. Dana's heart dropped like a stone at the sight of Alistair. Rick let out a low moan of anguish. "Pop, how long have you been standing there?"

"Long enough to realize there are some matters we need to discuss." He marched stiffly across the room and plunked himself down on the couch. Once again he was clad in his bird-watching regalia.

Rick threw Dana a tormented glance and rubbed his jaw nervously. "I don't know how much you heard, Pop, but I hope you didn't misunderstand—"

Alistair waved his hand in an impatient gesture. "I didn't hear anything I didn't already know, or at least suspect."

Rick's Adam's apple bobbed sharply up and down. "What are you saying?"

Dana backed slowly toward the door. "I think I'd better leave the two of you alone."

Alistair beckoned to her. "Stay, my dear. You got tangled up in this mess through no fault of your own, and I think you deserve to hear how it all comes out."

"It's really none of my business...."

"Nonsense! You care about my son, don't you?"

Without looking at Rick, she nodded. "And about you."

"Then sit down and let's get on with this, shall we?"

"Pop, maybe we shouldn't. You look tired. I'm concerned about your—"

"Oh, tommyrot! When are you going to realize I'm not some frail old invalid who's going to fall apart if someone says *boo?*"

Rick's jaw clenched stubbornly. "You had an attack not more than three weeks ago."

Alistair's bushy white eyebrows bunched together. "Attack? What attack? You mean the day I nearly fell off the ladder?" He snorted. "That was sheer clumsiness, boy, not a medical emergency. You aren't going to use my health as an excuse for tippy-toeing around the truth any longer."

"I don't know what you're talking about."

"No? Then I'll do some more talking." He shifted the paraphernalia attached to his belt and settled himself more comfortably on the couch. "Let's talk about your mother—what a wonderful woman she was."

Rick gritted his teeth. "Pop..."

"No, it's my turn to do the talking, remember? As I said, Chloe was a wonderful woman, Rick. Human, of course, like all the rest of us. But that's why I loved her. She was so full of life, so eager to be happy."

Alistair sighed. "I married her, knowing she still loved Jake—at least his memory. I could hardly believe such a talented, pretty young thing would agree to be my wife, even if she didn't love me the same way I loved her."

Dana lowered herself into a chair, while Rick remained standing, fists knotted at his sides.

"When Jake returned from the war, your mother and I were just so happy he was alive, for a while that was enough. But as time went on, I could tell that was changing. They'd get this certain look in their eyes whenever they were in the same room together." He shook his head sadly. "I felt like a man trying to bail out a sinking ship with his fingers. No matter what I did, no matter how hard I tried, there was simply no way to prevent the inevitable."

"You make it sound as if Mother had no will of her own, no control over her actions." Rick's voice was edged with bitterness.

Alistair, however, had obviously come to terms with his late wife's infidelity long ago. "Your mother loved me, son. But she loved Jake, too. It's not so easy to turn your back on the person you love. Even when you feel they've betrayed you."

His meaningful glance wasn't lost on Dana. She could only hope it wasn't lost on Rick, either.

"When I dropped by Jake's house unannounced one day and discovered him and Chloe together, I was furious. I felt betrayed, deceived. I wanted to turn my back on both of them, to kick them out of my life forever."

Rick folded his arms across his chest. "Why didn't you?"

"Because I loved her. And so I forgave her."

"But you didn't forgive Jake."

Alistair shook his head slowly. "No. I broke off our partnership and refused to speak to him again. But I've missed him every single day for the past thirty-five years."

Dana touched his sleeve. "It's not too late, you know. Jake's missed you, too."

"I believe before I straighten out matters with Jake, there's something Rick and I must straighten out first."

Caution clouded Rick's eyes. "What exactly are you referring to?"

"I'll answer your question with another. How exactly did you find out that Jake was your father?"

Rick's lungs emptied with a rush of air. He gripped the back of a chair to steady himself. "You knew all along," he whispered.

Alistair shrugged. "Not for certain. But it didn't matter, so I never worried about it."

"Didn't matter? How can you say that?" Rick's face flushed a deep crimson.

"You were my son, regardless of the biological technicalities."

"Biological techni—how can you dismiss this so lightly?"

"Because the day you were born was the happiest day of my life. Because you were part of the woman I loved, and that would have been reason enough to love you even if I'd had proof that I wasn't your natural father."

Rick turned away and plowed his fingers through his hair. "I can't believe this. All these years I've tried to protect you from the truth, and it didn't even make any difference to you."

Alistair climbed to his feet and rested his hand on Rick's shoulder. "I suppose we should have had this talk long ago. But I didn't know until today that you already knew the truth. Fact of the matter is, I was a bit afraid to bring it up, for fear you might abandon me for your real father."

"Pop," Rick said, his voice clogged with emotion, "you *are* my real father."

Then he reached for Alistair and blindly pulled him into a huge bear hug. His father patted Rick fondly on the back, sniffing loudly.

Dana stumbled from the living room, tears misting her vision. Unnoticed, she closed the front door softly behind her, leaving father and son alone.

She was so happy for Rick, that at last his terrible secret burden had been lifted from his shoulders, paving the way for an even closer relationship with Alistair.

But that didn't ease the agonizing pain in her heart. Rick had deliberately shut her out of his life for good this time. And she couldn't begin to imagine the bleak future she now faced without him.

Channel Five would soon go bankrupt, but how insignificant that loss seemed compared to the loss of the man she loved. And yet, would she have done anything differently if she had it to do all over again?

No. Rick hadn't trusted her enough to tell her the real reason he'd been so opposed to the West and Winslow reunion. Under the circumstances, Dana had had no choice but to do everything in her power to save the station.

If only he'd trusted her, believed in her! She saw now that without trust there could be no love. She'd loved Rick—*still* loved him, would *always* love him. But whatever he'd felt for her wasn't in the same category.

Would she have fallen in love with Rick if she had to do it all over?

He'd stirred feelings inside Dana she'd never even suspected existed. He'd opened her eyes to all the wonderful possibilities of life. How ironic that a man who fought so hard against love would be the one to show her its splendor.

Surely the ultimate cost in heartache would be worth that brief, blissful interlude. . . .

Driving away from Rick's house for the last time, Dana muffled a sob. Right now it was a little hard to believe that falling in love had been worth it.

Jake had his suitcase all packed and ready to go when Dana rapped on the door of his hotel room. He peeked out cautiously, then smiled faintly when he saw it was her.

"Come in," he said, opening the door wider. "I was afraid you were another reporter."

"Have they been bothering you much today?"

"The hotel staff has been doing a pretty good job of keeping them away. But I did catch one trying to hide himself in the maid's laundry cart just before she got to my room."

"I'm so sorry for all this ruckus," Dana said. "After all the ballyhoo we stirred up before the reunion, the media's curiosity has been aroused even higher by its sudden cancellation."

"That wasn't your fault."

"No, but if I hadn't set the whole thing up in the first place, none of this would have happened."

Jake patted her hand. "I'm sorry about your station."

She mustered a feeble smile. "It's not the end of the world."

"Couldn't tell by the expression on your face." He chucked her under the chin.

A wave of affection enveloped her. She'd spent a lot of time with Jake since his arrival in Pine Creek two days ago, and had become very fond of him. It was going to be hard to say goodbye.

She wondered if she should tell him that Alistair knew Jake was Rick's father.

No. She'd interfered enough in this family's private affairs, caused enough emotional trauma. Better to let Rick and Alistair tell him—or *not* tell him, as the case might be.

"We'd better be on our way," Dana told Jake instead. "It's a long drive to Sacramento."

"Believe me, it won't seem nearly as long as the flight itself." Jake picked up his suitcase. "For all the miles I've flown in planes, I've never gotten used to the damn things."

"That's funny—Rick doesn't like to fly, either." She gave herself a swift mental kick as soon as the thoughtless words had escaped her lips. "I'm sorry," she said, touching Jake's arm. "I—I wish things could have worked out differently for you—for *all* of you."

A grimace of pain slashed across his craggy features. "So do I, sweetie." He opened the door. "Boy, so do I."

"My car's waiting in the alley out back." Dana led him down the corridor. "I figured we could make our escape easier if the press didn't spot us."

"Good thinking."

They stowed Jake's suitcase in the trunk and hopped into the car. Wasting no time, Dana headed for the highway.

She was lost in her thoughts, distracted by the emotional turbulence whirling through her heart when Jake said, "I think someone's trying to catch up with us."

"Darned reporters," she grumbled, stepping hard on the accelerator. "I'll see if I can lose them." She made a sharp ninety-degree turn down a side street, then another, flinging Jake against the passenger door.

"I feel like I'm in a spy movie," he yelled over the roar of the engine. His eyes twinkled with the first spark of humor he'd shown since yesterday.

Dana wrestled with the steering wheel as she glanced in the rearview mirror. "I think we lost them back there. Just to be safe, I'm going to take a shortcut—oh, rats!''

The long black luxury car that had been tailing them pulled out from the corner ahead and blocked their path. With a squeal of rubber Dana spun her car around in a spectacular U-turn and floored it.

"Wait!" Jake shouted.

She threw him a puzzled look.

"I think it's Rick."

Dana slammed on the brakes, throwing them both toward the dashboard. Thank heavens for seat belts. Craning her neck out the window, she saw that it was in fact Rick, with Alistair in the front seat beside him. The unfamiliar car must be Alistair's.

She coasted to the curb and rolled down her window as Rick got out of the car and approached. He ducked his head and gave her a sour look. "I see your driving technique hasn't changed any."

"I didn't know it was you," she retorted, bristling despite her cautious pleasure at seeing him.

"No? Funny, I figured that was why you were driving like a getaway man in a bank robbery."

"What do you want, anyway?"

"I want," Rick said, suddenly looking uncomfortable, "to talk to Jake."

Gladness surged through her, making her limp with relief. Surely this meant he was ready to straighten things out with Jake, to come to a new understanding with his natural father. And the fact that Alistair had come along for the ride must mean he was ready to end their old feud, too.

Dana was so happy for them, she didn't even care that Channel Five's cameras were nowhere in the vicinity to capture this historic moment.

Then her heart took another one of those roller-coaster plunges. Rick might be ready to make peace with Jake. But he hadn't said a word about making peace with her.

And Dana could tell by the look in his eyes—or rather, by the way he avoided looking at her at all—that as far as she and Rick were concerned, the hostilities definitely continued.

Chapter Twelve

"Dana, you haven't heard a word I've said!"

She tore her gaze from the window and looked at Elliott in surprise, as if she'd just realized he was sitting across the desk in her office.

"What's to hear, Elliott? You're telling me Channel Five is sunk financially, aren't you? The only thing I don't already know is exactly how much time we have left."

The accountant drew off his glasses and pinched the bridge of his nose in exasperation. "That's what I've been trying to tell you." He slid his glasses back on and shoved another chart in her direction. "According to my latest projections, which take into account the rather abysmal results of your recently concluded pledge drive..."

Dana winced.

"... You can continue to operate until the middle of next month."

The pencil she'd been absently twirling between her fingers snapped in two. "That's it, huh?"

"That's it." He rustled through his briefcase. "I've drawn up some papers for you to go over with the board of directors—all the legal and financial mumbo jumbo you need to complete before you shut down."

"We can't even go out of business without filling out paperwork, huh?"

He pressed his lips together and shook his head sympathetically. "'Fraid not."

She gave an idle wave of her hand. "Just leave that stuff with me, then. I'll pass it along to the board."

Elliott frowned, opened his mouth as if he were going to say something, then clamped it shut. He tapped the stack of papers on the desk, neatly straightening the edges before returning them to their folder. Dana leaned back in her chair and stared at the ceiling.

Finally Elliott burst out, "Dana, are you all right?"

She sighed. "What do you mean?"

"Well..." He fidgeted with his tie. "I've never seen you act so—so—*defeated* before! It's like all the fight has gone out of you."

Even shrugging her shoulders required a major effort. "What more can I do, Elliott? I gave it my best shot, but it wasn't good enough. Time to throw in the towel."

"It's not like you to give up so easily. I expected you to have one more secret weapon, one more ace up your sleeve. Don't you—" He fluttered his hands helplessly. "Don't you have someone you could blackmail or something?"

That brought a faint smile to her lips. "If you know anyone with a deep dark secret and lots of money, I'd be willing to try it."

He snapped his briefcase shut, then aimed a disgusted look at her. "It's that Rick West guy, isn't it?"

"Elliott..."

"He's the reason you're just sitting there like a bump on a log."

"I don't want to discuss my personal—"

"Where's your gumption, that famous Sheridan feistiness? I know breaking up is hard to do—"

"Thank you, Neil Sedaka," she muttered.

"—but you can't let it get you down like this!"

"That's easy for you to say," she nearly shouted. "You haven't had your heart clawed out of your chest and stomped on!"

Elliott blinked at her outburst. For a few moments her voice echoed through the room. "That bad, huh?" he said finally.

Dana nodded miserably. "That bad."

"I'm really sorry, kiddo. If there's anything I can do..."

His woebegone expression of sympathy nearly made her cry. She nodded her appreciation, unable to speak around the lump in her throat.

"Maybe I could talk to him, explain why it was so important to arrange that reunion...."

"Thanks, but it wouldn't do any good. He'd probably be furious that I even mentioned such a personal matter to you."

Elliott snapped his fingers. "Look, I have two tickets to that new community theater play that opens tonight. What d'ya say we go together? I'll even spring for dinner."

"You're a true pal, Elliott. But I don't feel much like socializing tonight. Maybe some other time."

He rubbed one shoe against the other, studied the floor, then blurted out, "Do you think Elaine would go with me?"

For a second Dana nearly forgot her own troubles. "Elaine? Go out with you? Why, Elliott, I bet she'd be tickled pink."

"Really?"

"Why don't you ask her?"

Elliott brightened. "I think I'll just do that." He grabbed his briefcase and headed for the door. "Yes, that's exactly what I'll do." His smile could have lit up a darkened room. "Thanks, Dana." Hand on the door-knob, he frowned. "You sure you're going to be all right?"

She nodded, though she didn't believe it for a minute. Nothing would ever be all right again. "You two have a good time tonight. Tell Elaine I'll understand if she's late for work in the morning."

"Really, Dana..." Elliott's face was red as his tie. "What kind of a guy do you think I am?"

"I was thinking of Elaine, actually. Now go on, get out of here and catch her before she leaves for the day."

Elliott's indignant muttering followed him out of her office. Dana's lips twitched into a hint of a smile. At least true love was still working its magic for *some* people.

Her lips quivered again, but not with amusement this time. It had been three long days since she'd seen Rick, three long days since he'd nearly driven her off the road and practically kidnapped Jake from right under her nose.

And three long sleepless nights.

Pine Creek was a small community, and even though most of the press seemed to have gotten their story and gone home by now, Dana managed to stay apprised of Rick's comings and goings through the local grapevine.

She knew, for example, that Jake had been staying at Alistair's house. She knew that Rick had taken a few days off work, apparently to spend some time with both men. She even knew that all three had shown up for dinner last night at the most expensive restaurant in Pine Creek and consumed two bottles of champagne between them.

But Dana's most painful awareness was that Rick seemed to have finally put his life in order—without her in it. He was doing just fine without her, it seemed. He'd become quite the social gadabout, if half the stories she'd heard were true.

She was delighted the three men had sorted out their differences, mended their old relationships and forged new ones. But, oh, she was so sorry her own relationship with Rick had been destroyed in the process.

If only—

A quiet knock disturbed Dana's melancholy thoughts. She turned toward the open doorway, blinked, and despite her better judgment was filled with sudden wild hope. "Hello, Rick," she said softly.

"I didn't know if you'd still be in your office," he said. "Everyone else seems to have gone home."

She glanced at her watch, surprised to see how late it was. "Guess I lost track of time." Her pulse was racing a mile a minute, and beneath her desk she wiped her damp palms on her skirt. She couldn't think of any reason for Rick to have come here—unless he was having second thoughts about terminating their relationship.

"Sit down," she told him, managing her first genuine smile in several days. He was dressed as if he were going out to dinner, in dark slacks and a gray corduroy blazer with suede patches on the elbows. The gray matched the color of his eyes.

"I can't stay long." He hovered near the doorway, and Dana's hopes slipped a couple of notches. He certainly didn't *act* like a man who'd come here to make up.

"How are your father and Jake?" She kept her smile resolutely pinned on her face. "I hear the three of you have become fast friends."

"You could say that." Rick scratched his head. "Funny, all these years I pictured Jake as some kind of devil incarnate, but it turns out he's really a pretty nice guy."

"I liked him a lot myself."

"Apparently the feeling's mutual. Both he and my— Pop have been asking about you, wondering why you haven't been around."

Dana's spirits soared again. "Is that why you're here?"

Rick frowned in confusion, then shuffled uncomfortably from foot to foot. "Uh, no, actually. I came about something else."

"Oh." This time it simply required too much effort to keep up her smiling facade. "What can I do for you?" she asked wearily.

"It's more what Pop and Jake can do for *you.*" Worry edged over his handsome features. "If it's not too late, that is."

"I—don't understand."

Rick lowered himself cautiously into the nearest chair, as though afraid Dana might have rigged it to trap him. "Pop and Jake feel terrible about the reunion being, uh, canceled at the last minute."

Dana waited.

"Fact is, uh, I feel bad about it, too."

"What happened was certainly . . . unfortunate."

Rick lurched forward, gripping the chair arms. "You understand why I had to stop it, don't you? I didn't realize how calmly Pop would take learning the truth, I didn't know that Jake—"

Dana dismissed his explanation with a curt chop of her hand. She could tell by the unyielding set of his jaw, by the wary look in his eye that Rick hadn't come here to apologize or ask her to resume their relationship where they'd left off. Making small talk with him under the circumstances was simply too painful. "Just tell me what you came here to say and get it over with."

He gnashed his teeth as if he had plenty else to say, but then mercifully returned to the subject. "Pop and Jake want to make a donation to Channel Five."

So that's what this was all about! Disappointment gave a chilly edge to Dana's voice, despite her warm feelings about the two old songwriters. "That's very generous of them, but I'm afraid it *is* too late. I met with the station's accountant today, and he tells me we'll be off the air by the middle of next month."

For the first time since he'd entered her office, Rick looked truly disturbed. "What if—what if they went ahead with the reunion after all? Even though they've already ended their feud, the public still hasn't seen them together yet. I know they'd be willing to make a special appearance—as a Channel Five exclusive, of course."

In spite of her determined acceptance that saving the station was a lost cause, a glimmer of hope flared inside Dana. Against her will, ideas and possibilities whispered in her ears. What if she . . . ? How much would . . . ? Maybe there was a chance. . . .

"No," she said firmly, mentally clamping her hands over her ears. "The pledge drive is over, and we couldn't possibly schedule another one within the next month."

"But if Pop and Jake's donation could keep you going for a while..."

"Even so, we'd still have fundamental money problems. We can't depend on a one-time windfall to bail us out. Once that money's gone, we'd be right back to square one financially." Dana could hardly believe the defeatist attitude she heard coming out of her own mouth. Not that she didn't relish the role of devil's advocate, but she'd never expected to find herself playing it where her own station was concerned. It was as if losing Rick had destroyed her self-confidence, her determined, never-say-die stubbornness. The old Dana Sheridan would have clutched at any straw, jumped eagerly at any chance—however slight—of saving the one thing in life that meant most to her.

Maybe the problem was that Channel Five wasn't the most important thing in her life anymore.

"I haven't told you everything," Rick said.

"Gee, that's a first," she mumbled.

"Pop and Jake want to sign over their royalties from *Match Made in Heaven*."

That perked her up. "What do you mean?"

Rick relaxed a little, apparently relieved to have finally got a rise out of her. "Well, every time that movie is shown anywhere or any performer uses one of the tunes from it, Pop and Jake still get a little money."

"It can't be much, after all these years."

"You'd be surprised how it adds up. As you yourself are so fond of pointing out—" here he paused to drum his fingers in remembered exasperation "—West and Winslow musicals still have a lot of widespread appeal."

"And they want to sign a percentage of those royalties over to Channel Five?" Dana asked, still not able to believe this could actually be true.

"They want to sign over *all* the royalties."

She gasped. "Rick, I—I'm overwhelmed by their generosity, but—but why?"

"They're grateful."

"What on earth for?"

At least Rick had the good grace to lower his eyes and look embarrassed. "For bringing them back together. They're convinced if it hadn't been for you, they'd have gone the rest of their lives without seeing each other again." He shook his head in wonder and regret. "And if I'd had anything to say about it, they'd have been right."

"You were just trying to protect Alistair," Dana murmured. Heavens, look how the tables had turned! Now she was actually defending Rick's pigheaded actions.

If he appreciated the irony of the situation, he didn't show it. "So what do you say?" he asked eagerly. "With an initial donation to tide you over, a big publicity drive spearheaded by West and Winslow and the promise of a steady income from those royalties, surely you can manage to keep Channel Five on the air." He peered at her hopefully. "Can't you?"

Exactly the same question Dana was asking herself at that moment. And she was amazed to discover that she still cared about the answer. "I'm not sure," she said slowly. "I'll have to discuss this with Elliott, have him confer with Jake and Alistair about the numbers...."

She glanced sharply at Rick. "Which raises another question."

His expression turned quizzical.

"Why didn't the two of them come over here and make this fabulous offer in person?"

Rick flushed. "Uh, well..." He twiddled his thumbs and pressed his lips together as if his chair was a witness stand and he was about to take the Fifth Amendment. "If you want to know the truth, I think they're plotting to get us back together."

Bless their hearts, Dana thought. Channel Five wasn't the only lost cause they were willing to devote their efforts to.

"I guess they figured that by insisting I be the one to present their proposal, you and I might get to talking about more personal matters, and..." He flipped his palms up helplessly. "Well, you know."

Dana shoved back her chair and rocketed to her feet with a suddenness that startled them both. "No, I don't know, Rick. I haven't the faintest idea why you're giving me the cold shoulder, considering that everything between you and Jake and Alistair worked out fine in the end."

Rick's eyes darkened like gathering storm clouds. "That was just luck. Things could have turned out a nightmare instead."

What did I do that was so wrong? Dana pleaded silently. But she refused to let the words pass her lips. Pride might be a mighty poor companion during those cold lonely nights, but it was the only companion she had left. "If only you'd told me the truth, been honest with me from the beginning..."

Her implication that he'd been dishonest rankled. *Dana* was the one who'd used *him,* who'd taken advantage of his feelings for her in order to achieve her own goals. Look at the way she hadn't breathed one word about the reunion to him all the time he'd been in Houston! She'd practically shoved him onto the plane, so anxious had she been to get him out of the way so she could pursue her plans without interference.

A referee inside Rick's head cried, "Foul!" Another voice berated him for being a fool—that he was throwing away a precious chance for happiness as casually as he might discard a used candy wrapper.

But over the years Rick had grown accustomed to ignoring such voices. Love was a trap, and happily-ever-after an illusion. No matter how much losing Dana felt like a knife twisting in his guts, he couldn't risk letting himself fall victim to such magic tricks again.

He hated himself for hurting her, for hurting himself. But it was better to get the pain out of the way now than to have it hanging over his head like Damocles's sword for the rest of his life. He'd made the mistake of letting his emotional guard down once, and the result had nearly been catastrophic. He wasn't a man to make the same mistake twice.

So why did freezing Dana out of his life feel as though *that* was the mistake?

Rick could barely endure the bewildered misery he saw etched in her face, heard laced through her voice. If he'd thought he could escape it by leaping out of his chair and fleeing from her office, he'd be halfway across town by now. But the past few days and nights had taught Rick that no matter what he did to forget her, Dana's face, her voice, her touch were going to haunt him for a long, long time.

Though he'd tried to erase from his mind the memory of their one passionate night of lovemaking, its images kept taunting him, growing even more vivid and poignant with each reliving. Never had he felt so alive, so *whole* as when he'd been joined with her, sharing pleasure and laughter and tenderness and all the things that lovers were supposed to share.

No matter how much he tried to deny it, Rick's fundamental honesty forced him to admit he still loved her. Ironically, with each day, each hour, each minute they were apart, his longing for her grew stronger.

But surely his obsession with Dana would fade in time, wouldn't it?

That lame assurance echoed hollowly inside his head. All the self-defensive axioms Rick had chosen to live by, all the internal warnings that had kept him detached, protected him from any emotional involvements, rang in his ears like meaningless platitudes.

Telling himself that love was a fraud, a cheap trick created by Hollywood dream-makers to sell movies, did nothing to lessen the anguish that clenched his heart like a fist and filled his chest with sorrow.

And he found absolutely zero consolation in the reminder that he'd been lucky to escape the trap of love before stumbling into an even more dangerous trap.

"I did what I had to do," Rick said, injecting into his voice a certainty he was far from feeling. "Just like you did."

Dana nodded, probing the inside of her cheek with her tongue. "I guess that's it, then."

"Guess so." Rick rose to his feet, his words strangely at odds with his feeling that there was much more to say, that this business between them was far from finished.

He'd been through so much emotional turmoil during the past few days, so many ups and downs, sometimes he didn't know left from right. He'd had to revise his opinions so many times, it was hard to separate fact from fancy.

His mother, whom he'd considered a prime example of female treachery, he now saw in a far more sympathetic light, as a woman who was as much a victim of her own heart as her husband had been.

Jake, whom Rick had once viewed as some kind of monster, had turned out to be a pretty decent guy whom he'd already started to care about. And instead of posing a threat to Pop's happiness, Jake had put a spring in his step and a sparkle in his eye that Rick hadn't seen for years.

If he'd been wrong about those people, wasn't it possible he was also wrong about Dana? Maybe she *hadn't* set out to deceive him, maybe loving her *wasn't* a mistake.

Everything had happened so fast lately, events swirling by in a confusing rush that left Rick no time to sort out his feelings, much less reexamine the assumptions of a lifetime.

He only knew he was being torn apart inside, that he wanted to seize Dana in his arms and ask her to marry him....

That he wanted to run away from her as fast as he could before his love for her grew even stronger, more impossible to escape....

A blurred figure came flying through the office door. "Dana, you'll never believe what just happened! I was on my way out to my car when Elliott practically ambushed me in the parking lot and asked me to go—omigosh, I didn't see you standing there, Rick! I'm sorry to interrupt, but I was just so excited...."

Dana's co-worker Elaine blushed to the roots of her red hair. "I know it's ridiculous for a woman my age to get so flustered about being asked out on a date, but I've been hoping for so long that Elliott—oh, never mind, you

don't want to hear about my personal life.'' She couldn'
restrain a sheepishly pleased grin.

Rick decided to take advantage of the interruption. He
had some serious thinking to do, and he couldn't concentrate while in the same room with Dana's sad, accusing eyes...those trembling lips he so longed to kiss...tha
brave expression that failed to conceal her unhappiness.

"I was just leaving anyway," he said, unable to resist
stealing one last glance in Dana's direction. She met his
gaze, stiffened her back and inched up her chin. "I'l
leave the two of you alone to talk."

"Oh, Dana and I can talk...later." But by the time
Elaine finished, Rick was gone.

Her porch swing made a monotonous *creak, creak,*
creak as Dana prodded herself back and forth with her
toe. She'd come out here to study the new projections
Elliott had drawn up based on Jake and Alistair's incredibly generous donation. Instead, her attention had
drifted to the magnificent sunset.

She was easily distracted these days, though she'd certainly paid attention when Elliott had brought her the
good news that Channel Five now had the financial resources to continue operating.

Under other circumstances that news would have sent
her straight to cloud nine, but considering the gaping hole
Rick had left in her life, her spirits had only managed to
reach about cloud three.

Dana let out a long, heavy sigh. The next weeks would
be busy ones indeed, filled with preparations for the long-
awaited West and Winslow reunion. Jake was only too
happy to extend his visit to Pine Creek until after their
televised appearance, and Alistair was perfectly delighted to have his old friend as an extended houseguest

Everything was working out just peachy keen for all concerned.

If you didn't count one little case of terminal heartbreak, that is.

Dana grasped the chain holding up the swing and pressed her cheek against its cold metal links. She had a lot to be grateful for but somehow, without Rick, none of it seemed to matter. She felt a bout of tears coming on again and squinched her eyelids tightly shut, determined not to succumb this time.

A car door slammed. Elliott most likely, come to pick up the papers Dana hadn't even glanced at yet.

She gathered up her false bravado, pasted an artificial smile on her face and opened her eyes.

Rick was striding up her front walk.

Dana's pulse went haywire, her stomach did flip-flops. Rick wore his usual jeans with a freshly ironed burgundy shirt. His sun-streaked brown hair was neatly combed, and when he bounded up the front steps and curled his arm around one of the porch columns, she caught a whiff of pine-scented after-shave. He looked and smelled like a man with a mission.

From the look in his troubled gray eyes, he'd probably come to tell her Jake and Alistair had changed their minds about the royalties.

Dana crossed her fingers anyway. Always the hopeless optimist.

Rick lounged against the porch column, trying to look a lot more self-assured than he felt. Sometime during the past few days he'd come to the conclusion that he'd been a complete jerk about everything. He'd been wrong to condemn Dana for following her heart. He realized now that hers had been the right course all along.

After all, in the end her heart had chosen saving someone's happiness over saving her station. It had finally dawned on Rick that, in effect, Dana had sacrificed the most important thing in her life for him.

But wait...didn't that mean *he* was the most important thing in her life?

For once Rick decided to follow his heart. And his heart had led him straight to Dana's doorstep.

He could only hope she would be more forgiving than he had any right to expect.

"You're good at bringing people back together," he said without preamble. "Maybe you can help me with a problem I'm having."

Her eyes widened in surprise, then narrowed with suspicion when his words sank in. "That depends," she said slowly, plucking at the buttons of her pale blue blouse. "What did you have in mind?"

Rick unwound his arm from the porch column and stepped closer. So far so good. At least she hadn't hurled any heavy objects at his head. "I have this friend," he went on, "who's behaved like a total idiot. He was stubborn, wouldn't listen to reason, went flying off the handle when things didn't go his way. And the worst of it is, he hurt someone badly in the process. Someone he cares deeply about."

Dana swallowed. The muted rays from the setting sun slanted across her face, setting her cheeks aflame, highlighting her exquisite features. Rick had never seen her look more beautiful. Or more scared.

She came slowly to her feet, her brown eyes enormous. "He really cares about her?"

Rick stepped close, tilted up her chin. "He loves her," he said gruffly.

Dana's lashes fluttered shut, and she swayed slightly toward him. Rick grasped her shoulders to steady her. Or maybe to steady himself. "He does?" she asked, her mouth barely forming the words. If he hadn't been standing so close, he wouldn't have caught them.

He lowered his head and claimed Dana's mouth with his. Kissing her felt like coming home. Her lips opened like the petals of the first blossom of spring, eagerly seeking the life-giving warmth of the sun's kiss. Her arms slid slowly around him, not like the jaws of a trap but like the welcoming embrace of forever.

Rick drew back and sank willingly into the bottomless depths of her bewitching dark eyes. "I love you," he said.

Dana's heart filled with the same wonder she heard in Rick's voice, and for the same reason. Neither had ever thought to hear those words spring from his lips. Her soul expanded with joy until she thought she would burst with happiness.

"I love you, too, Rick West," she said in a low voice. "I always have, and I always will."

He hugged her tight, feeling the last traces of tension, of bitterness and fear seep from his limbs forever. How could he have doubted for one instant that he belonged here, here in the loving arms of the most wonderful woman on earth?

"Marry me, Dana," he said, his voice muffled in her silken hair. To his dismay, she stiffened and pulled back. Her eyes were clouded with caution when she stared up at him, searching his face.

"What brought on this sudden turnabout?" she asked. "I mean, a few days ago I got the impression you couldn't stand the sight of me. Now all of a sudden you want to spend the rest of your life with me." She disengaged his hands from her waist and stepped back. "Why?"

Frustration itched at Rick like poison oak. "Don't you want to marry me?" he asked. "Didn't you say you loved me?" He was new at this, for Pete's sake! Had he forgotten something, left out some magic words?

Dana flinched. "Of course I love you," she replied softly. "And I used to believe love was enough. But lately I've discovered it isn't."

"What more do you want of me?" Rick flung his hands in the air, feigning exasperation to hide the fear that he'd misread the situation after all, that Dana wasn't as eager to spend the rest of their lives together as he was. After everything he'd been through, the possibility of losing her was unbearable.

She gathered up the scattered papers and lowered herself onto the porch swing as if all the strength had ebbed from her limbs. But her voice was firm when she spoke. "Love doesn't mean anything without trust, Rick."

"I trust you!"

Dana shook her head. "How can you say that, after everything you kept secret from me?"

"I had to protect Pop!"

"What did you think I would do—go blab the truth to him as soon as you told me?" If possible, Dana looked even sadder. "You didn't trust me enough to guard your secret, Rick. You didn't trust me at all."

He raked his fingers through his hair. "It wasn't that I didn't trust you, it was just that I couldn't take the chance—oh, hell." He pounded his fist on the porch railing and bowed his head.

Dana waited silently. Part of her was screaming not to blow it—that Rick had asked her to marry him, for heaven's sake! What more could she possibly want?

But despite her love for him—or maybe *because* of her love for him—something deep inside Dana's heart wouldn't let her settle for second best. With Rick it had to be all or nothing. Either he loved her enough to trust her, or he didn't love her enough.

When at last he raised his eyes, Dana held her breath.

"You're right," he said. "I didn't trust you." He moved to sit beside her on the swing, and when his warm fingers touched hers she realized how cold her hands were.

They rocked quietly for a moment. "You see," Rick said finally, "I've spent my entire adult life not trusting people. I knew how my mother and Jake had betrayed my father, and it destroyed my trust in everyone, my faith in human nature."

The swing creaked. "I had to learn how to trust all over, sweetheart, and in the beginning I'm afraid I wasn't very good at it. But somehow you taught me to trust again, to believe in people." He squeezed her hand. "To believe in love."

Dana squeezed back, unable to speak for the knot of emotion in her throat.

"So you see, I'm asking you to believe in *me* this time. To believe that I've finally learned how to trust again, how to love someone with all my heart." He pulled her against his shoulder, and his voice grew rough with feeling. "Because I do, Dana. Love you with all my heart."

She pressed her eyelids shut, but tears seeped out anyway. "Oh, Rick," she whispered. "I *do* believe in you. In us." She lifted her head and framed his face with her hands. "Marrying you is going to make me the happiest person in the world."

"Second happiest," he growled a split second before their lips crushed together and they forgot about the rest of the world for a while.

Later, as the sunset's fading splendor cast an amber glow over the two figures rocking contentedly on the porch swing, Dana fondly poked Rick in the ribs. "Something I've been meaning to ask," she said, luxuriating in the heavenly feel of his strong arms wrapped around her. "Can I borrow one of your fathers to give me away at the wedding?"

His shout of laughter soared to the sky, echoing across the mountains and through the pines.

* * * * *

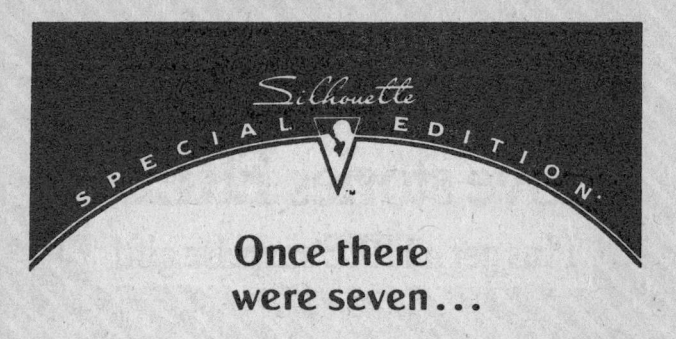

Take 4 bestselling love stories FREE

Plus get a FREE surprise gift!

Special Limited-time Offer

Mail to Silhouette Reader Service™

3010 Walden Avenue
P.O. Box 1867
Buffalo, N.Y. 14269-1867

YES! Please send me 4 free Silhouette Special Edition® novels and my free surprise gift. Then send me 6 brand-new novels every month, which I will receive months before they appear in bookstores. Bill me at the low price of $2.71* each plus 25¢ delivery and applicable sales tax, if any.* I understand that accepting the books and gift places me under no obligation ever to buy any books. I can always return a shipment and cancel at any time. Even if I never buy another book from Silhouette, the 4 free books and the surprise gift are mine to keep forever.

235 BPA AJCH

Name	(PLEASE PRINT)	
Address		Apt No.
City	State	Zip

This offer is limited to one order per household and not valid to present Silhouette Special Edition® subscribers. *Terms and prices are subject to change without notice. Sales tax applicable in N.Y.

USPED-93   ©1990 Harlequin Enterprises Limited

Silhouette Books
is proud to present
our best authors,
their best books...
and the best in
your reading pleasure!

Throughout 1993, look for exciting books
by these top names in contemporary
romance:

CATHERINE COULTER—
Aftershocks in February

FERN MICHAELS—
Whisper My Name in March

DIANA PALMER—
Heather's Song in March

ELIZABETH LOWELL—
Love Song for a Raven in April

SANDRA BROWN
(previously published under
the pseudonym Erin St. Claire)—
Led Astray in April

LINDA HOWARD—
All That Glitters in May

When it comes to passion,
we wrote the book.

Silhouette®

It takes a very special man to win

She's friend, wife, mother—she's you! And beside each Special
Woman stands a wonderfully *special* man. It's a celebration of
our heroines—and the men who become part of their lives.

Look for these exciting titles from Silhouette Special Edition:

January   **BUILDING DREAMS** by Ginna Gray

February   **HASTY WEDDING** by Debbie Macomber

March   **THE AWAKENING** by Patricia Coughlin

April   **FALLING FOR RACHEL** by Nora Roberts

Dont miss THAT SPECIAL WOMAN! each month—from your
special authors.

AND

For the most special woman of all—you, our loyal reader—we
have a wonderful gift: a beautiful journal to record all of your
special moments. See this month's THAT SPECIAL WOMAN!
title for details.

TSW1

"But now the path divides. I see
"Inchoate, dark reality
"Twin-struck from ancient Unity
"—And I, my Brother's enemy! . . ."

—*The Enchanted Tower*
by Hal Mayne

NECROMANCER

GORDON R. DICKSON

SF
ACE BOOKS, NEW YORK

NECROMANCER

An Ace Book

ISBN: 0-441-56852-1

First Ace Printing: April 1981
This Printing: August 1982

Published simultaneously in Canada

Manufactured in the United States of America

Ace Books, 200 Madison Avenue, New York, New York 10016

CONTENTS

Book One: ISOLATE

And now, through double glass, I see
My brother's image, darklingly.
Now, aid us, Thor, who prisoners be.
Come—hammer, Lord! And set us free.

The Enchanted Tower

Chapter 1

The mine, generally speaking, was automatic. It consisted of some hundred and eighty million dollars' worth of equipment, spread out through three and a half cubic miles of gold-ore-bearing rock—granite and quartz—all controlled by the single console where the shift engineer on duty sat.

Like some ponderous, many-purposed organism, the mine walked in the layered rock. On various levels it gnawed out the gold-bearing ore, ground it up to pebble-sized chunks, and sent it by the carload up six hundred feet or more to the open air and the equipment above. As the mine machinery moved, it created and abandoned surface shafts, elevator tubes, new exploratory levels and stopes; and extended the vast central cavern through which the heavier machinery and its controlling console slid with the work in progress, laying down rails before and taking them up behind.

The single engineer on shift at the time controlled all this. And a touch of megalomania did him no harm on the job. He was seated before the control panels of the console like the identity before the brain. His job was the job of ultimate control. Logical decision, and the facts on which to base decision were supplied by the computer element in the equipment. The logically optimum answer was available at the touch of a button. But it had been discovered that, like the process of living itself, there was more to modern mining than logic.

The best engineers had *feel*. It was a sensitivity born of experience, of talent, and even of something like love, with which they commanded, not only the mountains, but the machine they rode and directed.

Now this too was added to the list of man's endeavors for which some special talent was needed. Less than ten per cent of the young mining engineers graduating every year turned out to have the necessary extra ability to become one with the titan they directed. Even in the twenty-first century's overcrowded employment marts, mines were continually on the hunt for more shift engineers. Even four hours at a time, and even for the talented ten per cent, was a long time to be the faultless god in the machine. And the machinery never rested.

Six hundred feet overhead of the man at the console, Paul Formain, on his first morning at Malabar Mine, stepped from his small individual quarters of white bubble plastic, and saw the mountains.

And suddenly, there it was again, as it had been time and again since his boating accident of five years before, and had been more recently, lately.

But it was not now the open sea that he saw. Or even the dreamlike image of a strange, shadowy figure in some sort of cape and a high-peaked hat, who had seemed to bring him back to life after he had died in the boat, and returned him to the boat to be finally found and rescued by the coast guard.

This time, it was the mountains.

Suddenly, turning from the white, plastic door, he stopped and saw them. Around him was a steep slope with the other white buildings of the Malabar Mine. Above him the fragile blue of a spring sky spoke to the dark blue of the deep lake below, which filled this cleft in the mountain rock. About him in every direction were the Canadian Rockies, stretching thirty miles in one direction to the British Columbia city of Kamloops, in the other to the Coast Range and the stony beaches touching the salt Pacific Ocean surf. Unexpectedly, he felt them.

Like kings they stood up around him, the mountains. The surf sounded in his blood, and abruptly he was growing, striding to meet them. He was mountain-size with the mountains. With them, he felt the eternal movement of the earth. For a moment he was naked but unshaken to the winds of understanding. And they blew to him one word:

Fear.

Do not go down into the mine.

". . . You will get over this, this sort of thing," the psychiatrist in San Diego had assured him, five years before, after the accident. "Now that you've worked it out for yourself and understand it."

"Yes," said Paul.

It had made sense then, the way he had explained it to himself under the psychiatrist's guidance. He was an orphan, since the time of his parents' simultaneous deaths in a transportation accident, when he was nine. He had been assigned to good foster parents, but they were not the same. He had always been solitary.

He had lacked what the San Diego psychiatrist called "protective selfishness." He had the knack of understanding people without the usual small urge to turn this understanding to his own advantage. It had embarrassed those who might have been his friends, once they understood this capability in him. They had an instinctive urge to put a protective distance between himself and them. Underneath, they feared his knowledge and did not trust his restraint. As a boy he felt their withdrawal without understanding the reasons behind it. And this, said the psychiatrist, gave him a false picture of his own situation.

". . . After all," said the psychiatrist, "this lack of a desire to take advantage of a capability, amounted to a disability. But no worse than any other disability, such as blindness or loss of a limb. There was no need to feel that you could not live with it."

But that was the way, it seemed, that unconsciously he had felt. And that feeling had culminated in an unconscious attempt at suicide.

". . . There's no doubt," said the psychiatrist, "that you got the bad-weather, small-craft warning put out by the coast guard. Or that you knew you were dangerously far offshore for any weather, in such a light sailboat."

So the storm had driven him out to sea and lost him. He had been adrift, and in the still days following, death had come like some heavy gray bird to sit perched on the idle mast, waiting.

". . . You were in a condition for hallucination," said the psychiatrist. "It was natural to imagine you had already died. Then, when afterward you were rescued, you automatically searched for some justification of the fact that you were still alive. Your unconscious provided this fantasy of having been brought back to life by a father-like figure, tall and mysterious, and wrapped in the garments that denote magical ability. But when you had fully recovered, your conscious mind could not help finding this story somewhat thin."

No, thought Paul, it couldn't help thinking so. He remembered, in the San Diego hospital, lying there and doubting the whole memory.

"So to bolster it, you produced these moments of extreme, almost painful sensitivity. Which filled two needs. They provided support for your delirium fantasy of having been raised from the dead, and they acted as an excuse for what had caused the death-wish in the first place. Unconsciously you were telling yourself that you were not crippled, but 'different.' "

"Yes," Paul had said at that point. "I see."

"Now that you've dug out the true situation for yourself, the need for justification should diminish. The fantasy should fade and the sensitivity moments grow less frequent, until they disappear."

"That's good to hear," said Paul.

Only, in the past five years the moments had not dwindled and disappeared. They had stayed with him, as the original dream had stuck stubbornly in the back of his mind. He thought of seeing another psychiatrist, but then the thought would come that the first had done him no good at all. So what was there to expect from a second?

Instead, in order to live with his problem, he had anchored himself to something that he had discovered in himself since the accident. Deep within him now, something invincible stood four-square to the frequent gusts from the winds of feeling. Somehow he thought of it as being connected to, but independent of, the dream magician in the tall hat. So when, as now, the winds blew warnings, he felt them without being driven by them.

Fear: said the mountains. *Do not go down into the mine.*

That's foolish, said Paul's conscious mind. It reminded him that he was at last hired for the work to which all his education had pointed him. To a job that in the present overcrowded world was the dream of many and the achievement of few. He reached for that which stood unconquerable in the back of his mind.

Fear, it replied, is merely one more in the multitude of factors to be taken into account in moving from point *A* to point *B*.

Paul shook himself free from the winds of feeling, back to the ordinary existence of the world. The buildings of the Malabar Mine were all around him. A little distance down the slope from where he stood the wife of the company auditor came out on her back step and called something across a small white fence to the wife of the surface engineer in the yard adjoining. It was Paul's first day on the job and already he was close to being overdue on the job underground. He turned his gaze from the mountains and the buildings, to the near concrete walk leading to the main shaft head of the mine. And headed toward it, and the waiting skip.

Chapter 2

The skip slid Paul down some six hundred steeply slant-
ing feet through mountain stone. For all the romanticism
of its old-fashioned name, it was nothing more in fact
than a magnetic tube elevator. Through the transparent
walls of the tube, granite and rose quartz flickered at
him as he descended. They spoke to him as the mountains had, but in smaller voices, fine, thin, crystalline
voices with no yield, no kindness to them, and no mercy.
Between them and himself, Paul's own faint image in the
tube wall kept pace with his descent—it was the image of
a square-shouldered young man of twenty-three, already
past any look of boyishness or youth.

He was large-boned and tall, strong-featured, round-
headed, and athletic-looking. A football-player type,
but not one of the game's commoner varieties. He was
not bulky enough for a lineman, not tense enough for
the backfield. End—that was the sort of position he fitted. And, strongly calm, with long-fingered capable hands
to catch the ball, he remembered playing it well. That
had been on the first team at Colorado Institute of Mines,
where he had taken his undergraduate work.

His eyes were curiously deep, and a warm, gray color.
His mouth was thin-lipped, but a little wide and altogether friendly. His light, straight brown hair was already receding at the temples. He wore it clipped short,
and he would be nearly bald before his thirties were out,

14

but since he was not the sort of man to whom good looks are necessary, this would make little difference.

He looked instinctively in command of things. Strongly male, intelligent, physically large and strong, with a knack for doing things right the first time around. And he was all these things. It was only when people got to know him intimately that they saw past to the more complex inner part of him, the part where his own very different image of himself was kept. There were moments like this, as he suddenly caught sight of his outer self mirrored somewhere, when Paul was as startled as if he had come face to face with some stranger.

The skip stopped at Dig Level.

Paul stepped out into a bright, huge cavern filled to its lofty ceiling with the bright metal of equipment mounted ponderously on rails. The acid-damp air of below-ground struck coolly into his lungs, and the atmosphere of the mine seemed to flow into and through him as he walked down alongside the crusher to the small cleared space that surrounded the console. There, seated upon the rails, was the console itself. And at it—at the keys and stops that resembled nothing so much as the keyboard of some huge electronic organ, with the exception of the several small viewing tanks in the console's very center—a small, round-bodied, black-haired man in his forties sat winding up the duties of the shift he was just ending.

Paul came up to the edge of the platform on which the console and its operator sat.

"Hi," he said.

The other man glanced down.

"I'm the new man—Paul Formain," said Paul. "Ready for relief?"

The departing engineer made several quick motions about the console, his short, thick fingers active. He leaned back in the control seat, then stretched. He stood up to turn a tough, friendly face toward Paul.

"Paul?" he asked. "What was the last name?"

"Formain. Paul Formain."

"Right. Pat Teasely." He held out a small, square hand with a good deal of strength in its grip.

They shook. Teasely's accent was Australian—that particular accent which Australians are continually infuriated to have called cockney by inexperienced North Americans. He gave forth a personality that was as plain and straightforward as common earth. It touched soothingly against Paul, after the violence of the mountains.

"Looks like a nice clear dig for your first shift," Teasely said. "Judging by the cores."

"Sounds good," replied Paul.

"Right. No large faults in sight and the vein drift's less than eight degrees off the vertical. Watch for crowding on the ore trains going up Number One surface shaft, though."

"Oh?" said Paul. "Bug in the works?"

"Not really. They've been jackknifing and getting jammed just above Number Eight hatch, about sixty feet short of exit. The shaft's cut a little small; but no point in widening it when we'll be driving a new one in about a hundred and fifty hours. I've been up twice this last shift, though, to kick a car back on the tracks."

"All right," said Paul. "Thanks." He stepped past Teasely and sat down at the console. He looked up at the smaller man. "See you topside at the bar this evening, perhaps?"

"Might." Teasely lingered. His blunt face looked down, uncompromising, individualistic, and congenial. "You out of one of the American colleges?"

"Colorado."

"Wife and family along?"

Paul shook his head. His fingers were already moving about, becoming acquainted with the console.

"No," he said. "I'm a bachelor—and an orphan."

"Come have dinner at our place then, sometime," said Teasely. "I've got the sort of wife likes to cook for guests."

"Thanks," said Paul. "I'll do that."

"See you."

Paul heard Teasely's footsteps crunch away in the loose rubble of the cavern floor. He went back to the controls, and ran through his take-over check list. It took him about six minutes. When that was done he knew the position of every piece of equipment and how it was behaving. Then he turned to the programming section and ran a four-hour estimate and forecast.

It checked with Teasely's estimate. A routine, easy shift. For a moment he laid his fingers on the gross control tabs of the computer override and sought for the individual qualities of the machine through the little working vibrations that reached him through his finger tips. A sensation of blind, purposeful, and irresistible force at work was returned to him; like, but not identical with, the feel of all other mine controls he had touched before. He took his hands away.

For the moment, he had nothing to do. He leaned back in his bucket seat at the console and thought about leaving things here for a look at the surface shaft where Teasely had reported the ore cars had occasionally been getting stuck. He decided against it. It was best to stick close to the console until he had built up a familiarity with this new mine.

The little lights and gauges and small viewing screens showed their flickers of color and movement normally before him. He reached over and switched a Vancouver news broadcast onto the screen of his central viewing tank.

Abruptly, he looked down as if from a window onto the plaza entrance to the Koh-i-Nor Hotel, at Chicago Complex. He recognized the location—it was a hotel he had stayed at once or twice himself when he was in the Chicago area. As he looked down on it now, he saw a small knot of people carrying the cameras and equipment of reporters, gathered around three people. The view zoomed in for a shot from an apparent distance of only a few feet and Paul had a second's close-up glimpse of two of the three, who were standing a little back from the third. The two were a flat-bodied, crop-haired man of middle age, and a tall, slim girl of Paul's age, whose appearance jerked suddenly at Paul's attention before the camera moved away from her, and left him frowning over what could have seemed so remarkable about her. He had never seen either her or the flat-bodied man before.

But then he forgot about her. For the third member of the group was filling the screen. And there was something about him that would have held any viewer's attention.

He was a gaunt giant of an old man in the formal black-and-white of evening clothes. Very stark and somber in these, he bent his head a little to avoid the low edge of a candy-striped beach umbrella overhead. And, although straight enough for the years he seemed to own, he leaned heavily on the carved handle of a thick cane in his right hand. The motion spread his wide shoulders, so that he seemed to stoop above the crowd of reporters. Dark glasses obscured the expression around his eyes —but even without these, his face was an enigma. Though it stood clear and sharp on the screen before him, Paul could not seem to grasp its image as a whole. It was a collection of features, but there was no totality to it. Paul found himself staring at the straight lips and the deep parentheses of creases around the corners of the mouth as the man spoke.

". . . robes?" one of the newspeople was just finishing asking.

The lips smiled.

"You wouldn't expect a mechanic to go out to dinner in his working clothes, now would you?" The voice from the lips was deep and pleasantly sardonic. "If you people want to see me in my official robes, you'll have to make an appointment to meet me during my office hours."

"Do they have office hours in the Chantry Guild, Mr. Guildmaster?" asked another reporter. There was laughter, but not disrespectful laughter. The lips smiled with them.

"Come and find out," said the lips. Paul frowned. A small closed pocket in his memory had opened up. He had heard of the Chantry Guild—or Société Chanterie. Come to think of it, he had heard of them now and again—quite often, in fact. They were a cult group—devil-worshipers, or some such. He had always dismissed them as a group of crackpots. But this man—this Guildmaster—was nothing so simple as a crackpot. He was . . .

Frustrated, Paul put his fingers instinctively out to the image of the man before him. But the cold glassy surface of the screen baffled his finger tips. The reporters were still asking questions.

"What about Operation Springboard, Mr. Guildmaster?"

The lips quirked.

"What about it?"

"Is the Guild against an attempt to reach the nearer stars?"

"Well now, ladies and gentlemen . . ." The lips smiled. "What did the Sumerian and Semite say in the days of the older gods? I believe they called the planets *sheep that are far away.*' Did they not? Shamash and Adad were the deities responsible for that statement, as you can find by checking your ancient histories. And if habitable worlds are like sheep, then surely there must be a great many strayed around farther stars which we can find again."

And the smile stayed on the lips.

"Then the Guild is in favor of the station on Mercury? You don't object to work on methods for interstellar travel?"

"Such," said the lips, and the smile vanished, "is not my concern, or the concern of the Guild. Man may play with the technical toys and sciences as he has in the past; he may play with space and the stars. But it will only sicken him further, as it has already sickened him almost to his end. There is only one thing that concerns us of the Guild and that's the destruction that will save Man from himself."

"Mr. Guildmaster," said a voice, "you can't mean to- tal——"

"Total and absolute!" The deep voice strengthened in the speaker. "Complete. Destruction. The destruction of Man and all his works." The voice grew, sonorously near to chanting, on a note that sent a sudden wild surge of feeling through Paul, like a powerful shock from a vein- injected stimulant. "There have been forces at work for eight hundred years that would save Man from his destruc- tion. Woe to Man when that day comes, that he is safe and saved. Woe to Woman and children unborn, when the last strength to destroy himself is finally stolen from him. For by his own eternal life will he be doomed, and only by his destruction may he survive."

The buzzing of an alarm signaled the sudden jack- knifing and jamming of an ore train in surface tube *A*. Paul's hand went out automatically and slapped a fif- teen-minute break on shaft power.

"And so I charge you"—the voice rolled like drums below a guillotine from the screen before him—"that you look to the welfare of man and not to yourselves. That you turn your backs on the false promise of life and face the reality of death. That you charge yourselves with a duty. And that duty is complete—is utter—is total destruction. Destruction. Destruction! *Destruction. . . .*"

Paul blinked and sat up.

The mine was all around him. The console was before him and in its center screen the group on the plaza of the Koh-i-Nor was breaking up. The newspeople were dispersing. The old man and the girl and man with him were following a fourth man—a thin young man with black hair and a tense, driving walk—into the hotel. Paul stared. He felt that only a minute had gone by, but even that was startling. For one of the peculiar facts about him was that he was completely unresponsive to

20

hypnosis. It was a trait that had complicated matters for the psychiatrist who had worked with him following the boating accident. How, then, could he have lost even a minute?

Sudden memory of the jackknifed cars in the surface tube broke him away from his personal puzzle. A more general power shutoff of equipment would be required unless he could solve that problem shortly. He left the console and took the chain lift alongside surface shaft Number One. The telltale on the console had spotted the jam-up at a hundred and forty-three feet below the shaft mouth. He reached Number Eight trouble hatch, turned on the lights in the shaft, and crawled through into the shaft himself. He saw the trouble, almost directly before him.

The Number One surface shaft, like the skip tube, approached the surface from the mine below at an angle of roughly sixty degrees. A single powered rail ran up the bottom center of the shaft, and the fat-bodied, open-topped ore cars, filled with pebble-sized rock from below, rolled their cogwheels up the cleated rail. The cleats themselves served Paul now as hand and footholds as he climbed up to where one of the cars sat off the rail, angled against the stony wall.

Still wondering about the familiar-looking girl and the extraordinary cultist who called himself the Guildmaster, Paul braced himself against the sharp-pointed wall of the shaft and the last car. He kicked at the hitch between the two cars. On the third kick, the hitch suddenly unbound the kink it had acquired when the car had jackknifed. With a snap and a grunt from the stored power in the motorized base of each car, the train suddenly straightened out.

As it did, the lights in the shaft dimmed, then flashed up again without warning as all the motors in all the cars hummed steadily to life. The train jerked and moved up the shaft, and without thinking, instinctively, Paul leaped and clung to the final car of the train.

It burst on him then, brilliantly as mountains seen suddenly against a high spring sky, that in his preoccupation with the news broadcast he had only put a temporary fifteen-minute hold on power to the shaft. And afterward, following his little blackout, he had omitted to set the power controls for the shaft on manual.

Now he was being carried up the shaft by the last car in the train. A few inches below him, the powered rail promised instant electrocution if he touched it. And the high-sided cars, all but filling the shaft, would block any try he could make to open the emergency hatches yet between him and the surface, as the train passed them.

The walls and the roof were close.

The roof in particular pressed down near to him. Rough-chewed from the granite and quartz, it rose and dipped unevenly. At points along the shaft, Paul knew, it would all but scrape the tops of the ore cars. If he could keep low, he might be able to ride the car he was holding to, to the surface. But, clinging to the back of it as he was, he felt his grip weakening.

He pulled himself upward, flat onto the bed of ore in the car. The roof under which he was passing scraped harshly against the back of his head as the ore train, leaving the lighted section where he had put it back on the track, plunged upward into darkness. His hands pawing at the small sharp rock in the car, Paul dug furiously, burrowing himself in. Swaying and rumbling, the train climbed on. In the blackness Paul did not even see ahead the low point of the roof that was approaching. . . .

Out in the clear mountain morning the surface engineer on duty had been drawn to the mouth of the Number One shaft by the blinking of a white trouble light on his own console, and a later automatic signal that power to that shaft had been cut. He had come to the shaft mouth, only to be joined a few minutes later by the managing engineer, who had been keeping his eye on the telltales in his office, this day with a new man underground for the first time.

"There it goes," said the surface engineer, a slight man named Diego and as young as Paul, as the hum of motors echoed once more up the natural speaking tube of the shaft. "He got it fixed."

"A little slow," said the Malabar mine manager. He frowned. "Let's wait a minute here and see what the trouble was."

They waited. The humming and the clank of the cog-wheels approached. The first car poked its front out into the sunlight and leveled off on the flat.

"What's that?" asked the mine manager, suddenly. There was a shadowy outline visible in the gloom around the approaching final car.

The train trundled automatically on. The last car emerged into the sunlight and the bright illumination fell full on the shape of a man, half-buried and unmoving in the load of ore.

"My God!" said the mine manager. "Stop those cars and help me get him off there!"

But the young surface engineer was already being sick, turned away and leaning against the millhouse wall, in the early shadow of the mountains.

Chapter 3

The clerk working the afternoon division, day shift, on the room desk of the Koh-i-Nor Hotel in the downtown area of the Chicago Complex, was conscious of the fact that his aptitude tests had determined that he should find work in a particular class of job. The class was that of ornament—actually unnecessary from the point of view of modern hotel equipment. Accordingly he worked conscientiously at the primary virtue of a good ornament—being as hard to overlook as possible.

He did not look up when he heard footsteps approach his desk and stop before it. He continued to write in elegant longhand at the list of currently newsworthy guests he was making on a bulletin sheet laid down beside the guest register.

"I have a reservation," said a man's voice. "Paul Formain."

"Very good," said the clerk, adding another name to his list without looking up. He paused to admire the smooth, flowing loops in the *p*'s and *l*'s of his penmanship.

Abruptly, he felt his hand caught and held by a fist considerably larger than his own. It checked his pen's movement. The strange grasp held his hand like an imprisoned fly—not crushingly, but with a hint of unyielding power in reserve. Startled, a little scared, the clerk looked up.

He found himself facing a tall young-old man with only one arm, the hand of which was holding him with such casual power.

"Sir?" said the clerk. His voice pitched itself a little higher than he would have preferred.

"I said," said the tall man, patiently, "I have a reservation. Paul Formain."

"Yes sir. Of course." Once more the clerk made an effort to free his trapped hand. As if by an afterthought, the tall man let go. The clerk turned hurriedly to his desk register and punched out the name. The register lighted up with information. "Yes sir. Here it is. An outside single. What décor?"

"Modern."

"Of course, Mr. Formain. Room 1412. Elevators around the corner to your left. I'll see your luggage is delivered to you immediately it arrives. Thank you. . . ."

But the tall, one-armed man had already gone off toward the elevators. The clerk looked after him, and then down at his own right hand. He moved the fingers of it experimentally. It had never before occurred to him what wonderfully engineered things those fingers were.

Up in room 1412 Paul stripped and showered. By the time he stepped out of the shower, his single suitcase had emerged from the luggage-delivery chute in the wall of the room. Half-dressed, he caught sight of himself in the mirror, which gave back his lean, flat-muscled image wearing the gray-green disposable slacks he had pressed for from the room dispenser after the shower. Above the waistband of the slacks, his chest and shoulders showed a healthy tan. The fine scars left by the plastic surgery had now faded almost to the point of invisibility. It was eight months since the accident in the mine, early in a new spring, with gray skies and a March wind blowing chilly off Lake Michigan.

The stub of his left arm looked shrunken. Not so much, it seemed, because it no longer had the rest of the limb

25

to support, but in contrast to the right arm that remained to him.

The compensation development of the right arm had proceeded with unusual speed and to extremes, according to Paul's physicians. It hung now, reflected in the mirror's surface, like a great, living club of bone and muscle. The deltoid humped up like a rock over the point where clavicle toed into shoulder frame; and from the lower part of the deltoid, triceps and biceps humped like whale-backs down to the smaller, knot-like muscles above the elbow. Below the elbow, the flexors and the brachio-radialis rose like low hills. The thenar group was a hard lump at the base of his thumb.

And it was as a club that he sometimes thought of it. No—nothing so clumsy as a club. Like some irresistible, battering-ram force made manifest in flesh and skeleton. In the three-quarters of a year since the mine accident, through the long process of hospitalization, operation, and recuperation, that invincible part of him which sat in the back of his mind seemed to have chosen the arm for itself. The arm was *that* part of Paul, the part that doubted nothing, and least of all itself. Nor had time to waste on the posing of a hotel clerk.

Obscurely, it bothered Paul. Like a man testing a sore tooth continually with a tongue, he found himself frequently trying the arm's strength on things, and being disturbed anew each time by the result. Now, standing before the mirror, he reached out and closed his hand around the single ornament in the starkly modern hotel room—a tulip-shaped pewter vase about nine inches high, with a single red rose in it, that had been sitting on the dresser top. The vase fitted easily into his grasp, and he lifted it, slowly tightening the grip of his fingers.

For a moment it almost seemed that the thick metal walls would resist. Then slowly the vase crumpled inward, until the rose, pinched halfway up its stem, toppled to one side, and water, brimming up over the rim of the vase, ran down onto Paul's contracting hand. Paul relaxed

26

his grasp, opened his hand, and looked down at the squeezed shape of the vase lying in it for a second. Then he tossed the ruin—vase, flower, and all—into the waste-basket by the dresser and flexed his fingers. They were not even cramped. With that much strength the arm should already be becoming muscle-bound and useless. It was not.

He finished dressing and went down to the subway entrance in the basement of the hotel. There was a two-seater among the empty cars waiting on the hotel switchback. He got in and dialed the standard 4441, which was the Directory address in all cities, centers, and Complexes over the fifty-thousand population figure. The little car moved out into the subway traffic and fifteen minutes later deposited him forty miles away at the Directory terminal.

He registered his credit card with Chicago Complex Bookkeeping, and a routing service directed him to a booth on the ninth level. He stepped onto the disk of a large elevator tube along with several other people and found his eye caught by a book a girl was carrying.

The book was in a small, hand-sized portable viewer, and the book's cover looked out at him from the viewer's screen. It gazed at him with the dark glasses and clever old mouth of the face he had been watching that day in the mine. It was the same face. Only, below the chin instead of the formal white collar and knotted scarf, there was the red and gold of some ceremonial robe.

Against this red and gold were stamped the black block letters of the book's title. DESTRUCT.

Glancing up from the book, for the first time he looked at the girl carrying it. She was staring at him with an expression of shock, and at the sight of her face he felt a soundless impact within himself. He found himself looking directly into the features of the girl who had stood beside and a little behind the Guildmaster in the viewing tank of the console at the mine.

"Excuse me," she said. "Excuse me."

She had turned, and pushing blindly past the other people on the disk stepped quickly off onto the level above that level on which Paul had entered.

Reflexively, he followed her. But she was already lost in the crowd. He found himself standing in the heart of the musical section of the Directory library. He stood, brushed against by passers-by, gazing vainly out over the heads of the crowd for the sight of her. He was only half a pace from a row of booths, and from the partly-open door of one of these came the thin thread of melody that was a woman's soprano singing to a chimed accompaniment in a slow, minor key. . . . .

In apple comfort, long I waited thee

The music ran through him like a wind blowing from far off, and the pushing people about him became distant and unimportant as shadows. It was the voice of the girl in the elevator just now. He knew it, though he had only heard those few words from her. The music swelled and encompassed him, and one of his moments of feeling moved in on him, on wings too strong for love and too wide for sadness.

And long I thee in apple comfort waited.

She was the music, and the music was a wind blowing across an endless snow field to a cavern where ice crystals chimed to the tendrils of the wind. . . .

In lonely autumn and uncertain springtime
My apple longing for thee was not sated. . . .

Abruptly he wrenched himself free.

Something had been happening to him. He stared about him, once more conscious of the moving crowd. The music from the booth was once more only a thread under the shuffle of feet and the distant sea-roar of conversations.

He turned around and saw nothing on every side but the prosaic music section of a library floor in the directory. The magic was gone.

But so was the girl.

Paul went on up to the ninth level and found an open booth. He sat down, closed the door, and punched for a list of local psychiatrists, giving his now-registered credit number. As an afterthought, he added a stipulation that the list be restricted to those psychiatrists who had been interested or concerned with the problems of amputees in the past. The board before him flashed an acknowledgment of the request, and a statement that the answer would require about a ten- to fifteen-minute wait.

Paul sat back. On impulse he coded the title of the book the girl had been carrying with a purchase request, and a second later a copy in a commercial viewer was delivered to the desk in front of him from the delivery chute.

He picked it up. The face on the book's cover seemed to be staring at him with a sardonic expression, as if it amused itself with some secret it was keeping from him. The imaged face was not as he had seen it in the viewing tank at the mine, when the features had seemed to refuse to join in a clearly observed face. Now Paul saw the whole face, but something else was wrong. It was not so much a face but a wax mask. Something lifeless and without meaning. Paul punched the trip that would change the cover picture to the first page within.

On the white expanse of paper shown, the title leaped at him once again.

DESTRUCT, by *Walter Blunt*

Paul turned the page. He found himself looking at the first page of an introduction written by someone whose name he did not recognize. Paul skimmed through its half-dozen pages.

Walter Blunt, he read, was the son of rich parents. His family had owned a controlling interest in one of the great schools of bluefin tuna that followed the circle migratory route between North and South America and Japan. Blunt had grown up brilliant but undisciplined. He had lived the life of the wealthy who have nothing important to do, until one day when with thousands of other hunters he had been caught in an uncontrolled freak early-winter blizzard, while out stalking deer in the Lake Superior Range.

Four others in Blunt's party had died of exposure. Blunt, equally city-bred and unprepared, had in a wry moment conceived of the Alternate Forces of existence, and offered to trade them his life's service for the protection of his life itself. Following this, he had walked unerringly out of the woods to safety and arrived warm and unexhausted at shelter, in spite of the sleeting wind, the dropping temperature, and the fact that he was wearing only the lightest of hunting clothes.

Following this experience, he had dedicated himself to the Alternate Forces. Over a lifetime he had created and organized the Chantry Guild, or Société Chanterie, composed of students of, and graduate workers with, the Alternate Forces. The aim of the Chantry Guild was universal acceptance of the positive principle of destruction. Only by destruction could mankind signify its adherence to the alternate Laws, and only the Alternate Laws remained strong enough to save mankind from the technical civilization that was now on the verge of trapping mankind like a fly in amber.

The delicate chime of a response counter drew Paul's attention to the screen before him. He looked at a double list of names, addresses, and call numbers. He turned his attention to the typewriter-like keyboard below the screen and tapped out a message to all the names on the list.

My left arm was amputated slightly over seven months ago. My body has to date rejected three attempts to graft on a replacement. No reason for the intolerance can be discovered in the ordinary physiological processes. My physicians have recommended that I explore the possibility of a psychological factor being involved in the causes of the intolerance, and have suggested that I try my case among psychiatrists of this area, where a large amount of work with amputees has been done. Would you be interested in accepting me as a patient? Paul Allen Formain. File No. 432 36 47865 2551 OG3 K122b, Room 1412, Koh-i-Nor Hotel, Chicago Complex.

Paul got up, took the book he had just purchased, and headed back toward the hotel. On the way back and after he had returned to his room, he read on into Blunt's writing. Sprawled out on his hotel-room bed he read a collection of wild nonsense mixed with sober fact, and an urgent appeal to the reader to enlist himself as a student under the instruction of some graduate Chantry Guild member. The reward promised for successfully completing the course of instruction was apparently to be a power encompassing all wild dreams of magical ability that had ever been conceived.

It was too ridiculous to be taken seriously.

Paul frowned.

He found himself holding the book gingerly. It did not stir in a physical sense, but a vibration came from it that seemed to quiver deep in the marrow of Paul's bones. A singing silence began to swell in the room. One of his moments was coming on him. He held himself still as a wolf come suddenly upon a trap. About him the walls of the room breathed in and out. The silence sang louder. The place and moment spoke to him:

DANGER.

Put the book down.

Louder sang the silence, blinding the ears of his sensing. . . .

Danger, said the invincible part of him, is a word invented by children, and is essentially meaningless to the adult.

He pressed the button to turn the page. A new chapter heading looked up at him.

ALTERNATE FORCES AND REGROWTH. THE REPLACE-MENT OF MISSING LIMBS, OR EVEN OF THE BODY EN-TIRE.

The reparative regeneration of parts of the human body by epimorphosis, or regrowth beginning from a regeneration bud or blastema formed at the wound surface, is a property capable of stimulation by the Alternate Forces. It has its justification and instigation in the intended action of self-destruct. Like all use and manipulation of the Alternate Forces, the mechanism is simple once the underlying principles are grasped. In this case, they are the Non-Evolutionary (blocking to the Natural Forces) and the Regressive (actively in reversal of the Natural Forces). These principles are not merely statically negative, but dynamically negative, so that from the fact of their dynamism derives the energy necessary for the process of regeneration. . . .

The call note on Paul's room telephone chimed, breaking the spell. The room fled back to naturalness and the book sagged in his hand. From the bed he saw the screen of the phone light up.

"A Directory report on your query, sir," said a canned voice from the lighted screen.

The screen dissolved into a list of names with medical and mental science degrees after them. One by one the

names winked out until only one was left. Paul read it
from the bed.

DR. ELIZABETH WILLIAMS

A moment later the word *accept* was printed beside it.
Paul put the book aside where it could be picked up
later.

Chapter 4

_____

". . . How do you feel?"

It was a woman's voice. Paul opened his eyes. Dr. Elizabeth Williams was standing over the chair in which he sat. She put the hypodermic spray gun down on the desk beside him, and walked around to take her seat behind the desk.

"Did I say anything?" Paul sat up straighter in his chair.

"If you mean, did you reply to my questions? no." Dr. Williams looked across the desk at him. She was a small, square-shouldered woman with brown hair and an unremarkable face. "How long have you known about this strong resistance of yours to hypnosis?"

"Is it resistance?" asked Paul. "I'm trying to co-operate."

"How long have you known about it?"

"Since the sailing accident. Five years." Paul looked at her. "What _did_ I say?"

Dr. Williams looked at him.

"You told me I was a foolish woman," she said.

Paul blinked at her.

"Is that all?" he asked. "I didn't say anything but that."

"That's all." She looked at him across the desk. He felt curiosity and a sort of loneliness emanating from her.

34

"Paul, can you think of anything in particular that you're afraid of?"

"Afraid?" he asked, and frowned. "Afraid . . . ? Not really. No."

"Worried?"

He thought for a long moment.

"No—not worried, actually," he said. "There's nothing you could say was actually worrying me."

"Unhappy?"

He smiled. Then frowned, suddenly.

"No," he said, and hesitated. "That is, I don't think so."

"Then why did you come to see me?"

He looked at her in some surprise.

"Why, about my arm," he said.

"Not about the fact that you were orphaned at an early age? Not that you've always led a solitary life, with no close friends? Not that you tried to kill yourself in a sailboat five years ago, and tried again in a mine, less than a year ago?"

"Wait a minute!" said Paul. She looked at him politely, inquiringly.

"Do you think I arranged those accidents to try and kill myself?"

"Shouldn't I think so?"

"Why, no," said Paul.

"Why not?"

"Because . . ." A sudden perfect moment of understanding broke through to Paul. He saw her sitting there in complete blindness. He stared at her, and before his eyes, looking back at him, she seemed to grow shrunken and a little older. He got to his feet. "It doesn't matter," he said.

"You should think about it, Paul."

"I will. I want to think over this whole business."

"Good," she said. She had not moved out of her chair, and in spite of the assurance of her tone, she did not seem

quite herself since he had looked at her. "My receptionist will set up your next time in."

"Thanks," he said. "Good-by."

"Good afternoon, Paul."

He went out. In the outer office the receptionist looked
up from a filing machine as he passed.

"Mr. Formain?" She leaned forward over the machine.
"Don't you want to make your next appointment now?"

"No," said Paul. "I don't think so." He went out.

He went down a number of levels from Dr. Williams'
office to the terminal in the base of the building. There
were public communications booths nearby. He stepped
into one and closed the door. He felt both naked and
relieved. He dialed for a listing of the Chantry Guild
members in the area. The screen lighted up.

Walter Blunt, *Guildmaster* (no listed phone number)
Jason Warren, *Necromancer,* Chantry Guild Sec-
retary, phone number 66 433 35246
Kantele Maki (no listed phone number)
Morton Brown, 66 433 67420
Warra, *Mage,* 64 256 89235
(*The above list contains only the names of those
requesting listing under the Chantry Guild heading.*)

Paul punched 66 433 35246. The screen lighted up
whitely, but it was half a minute before it cleared to show
the face of one of the people Paul remembered from the
television broadcast in the mine a year before, the face
of a thin, black-haired young man with deep-set, unmoving eyes.

"My name is Paul Formain," said Paul. "I'd like to
talk to Jason Warren."

"I'm Jason Warren. What about?"

"I've just read a book by Walter Blunt that says the
Alternate Forces can grow back limbs that are missing."

Paul moved so that the stub of his left arm was visible to the other.

"I see." Warren looked at him with the movelessness of his dark eyes. "What about it?"

"I'd like to talk to you about it."

"I suppose that can be arranged. When would you like to talk to me?"

"Now," said Paul.

The black eyebrows in the screen went up a fraction. "Now?"

"I was planning on it," said Paul.

"Oh, you were?"

Paul waited.

"All right, come ahead." Abruptly the screen went blank, but leaving Paul's vision filled with the after-image of the dark face that had been in it looking at him with a curious interest and intent. He rose, breathing out a little with relief. He had moved without thinking from the second of perception that had come to him in Elizabeth Williams' office. Suddenly he had realized that her education and training had made her blind to understanding in his case. She had not understood. That much had been explosively obvious. She had been trying to reconcile the speed of light with the clumsy mechanism of the stop watch she believed in. And if she had made that error, then the psychiatrist at San Diego, after the boating accident, had been wrong in the same way, as well.

Paul had reacted without thinking, but, strongly now, his instinct told him he was right. He had labored under the handicap of a belief in stop watches. Somewhere, he told himself now, there was a deeper understanding. It was a relief to go searching for it at last with an unfettered mind—a mind awake.

Chapter 5

As Paul entered through the automatically-opening
front door of Jason Warren's apartment, he saw three
people already in the room—a sort of combination office-
lounge—he found himself stepping into.

Two of the three were just going out through a rear
door. Paul got only a glimpse of them—one, a girl who
with a start Paul recognized as the girl with the book he
had encountered earlier at Chicago Directory. The other
was a flat-bodied man in middle age with an air of quiet
competence about him. He, too, had been with the girl
and Blunt on the broadcast Paul had witnessed in the
mine a year before. Paul wondered briefly if Blunt, also,
was nearby. Then the thought passed from his mind. He
found himself looking down, slightly, into the dark, mer-
curial face of Jason Warren.

"Paul Formain," said Paul. "I phoned———"

"Sit down." Warren waved Paul into a chair and took a
facing one himself. He looked at Paul with something of
the direct, uninhibited stare of a child. "What can I do
for you?"

Paul considered him. Warren sat loosely, almost
sprawled, but with his thin body held in the balance of a
dancer or a highly trained athlete, so that a single movement might have brought him back to his feet.

"I want to grow a new arm," said Paul.

"Yes," said Warren. He flicked a forefinger toward

the phone. "I punched information for your public file after you called," he said. "You're an engineer."

"I was," said Paul, and was a little surprised to hear himself say it, now, with such a small amount of bitterness.

"You believe in the Alternate Laws?"

"No," said Paul. "Truthfully—no."

"But you think they might give you an arm back?"

"It's a chance."

"Yes," said Warren. "An engineer. Hard-headed, practical—doesn't care what makes it work as long as it works."

"Not exactly," said Paul.

"Why bother with the Alternate Laws? Why not just have a new arm out of the culture banks grafted on?"

"I've tried that," said Paul. "It doesn't take."

Warren sat perfectly still for a couple of seconds. There was no change in his face or attitude, but Paul got an impression as if something like a delicately sensitive instrument in the other man had suddenly gone *click* and begun to register.

"Tell me," said Warren, slowly and carefully, "the whole story."

Paul told it. As he talked, Warren sat still and listened. During the fifteen minutes or so it took for Paul to tell it all, the other man did not move or react. And with no warning, even as Paul was talking, it came to Paul where he had seen that same sort of concentration before. It was in a bird dog he had seen once, holding its point, one paw lifted, nose straight and tail in line with the body, as still as painted Death.

When Paul stopped, Warren did not speak at once. Instead, without moving a muscle otherwise, he lifted his right hand into the air between them and extended his forefinger toward Paul. The movement had all the remote inevitability of a movement by a machine, or the slow leaning of the top of a chopped tree as it begins its fall.

"Look," Warren said slowly, "at my finger. Look at

the tip of my finger. Look closely. Right there at the end of the nail, under the nail, you can see a spot of red. It's a drop of blood coming out from under the nail. See it swelling there. It's getting larger. In a moment it'll drop off. But it's getting larger, larger——"

"No," said Paul. "There's no drop of blood there at all. You're wasting your time—and mine."

Warren dropped his hand.

"Interesting," he said. "Interesting."

"Is it?" asked Paul.

"Graduate members of the Chantry Guild," said Warren, "can't be hypnotized, either. But you say you don't believe in the Alternate Laws."

"I seem to be a sort of free-lance, then," said Paul.

Warren rose suddenly from his chair with the single motion Paul had expected. He walked lightly and easily across the room, turned, and came back.

"In order to resist hypnosis," he said, standing over Paul, "you must make use of the Alternate Laws, whether you recognize them as such or not. The keystone of the use of the Alternate Laws is complete independence of the individual—independence from any force, physical or otherwise."

"And vice versa?" asked Paul, smiling.

"And vice versa." Warren did not smile. He stood looking down at Paul. "I'll ask you again," he said. "What do you expect me to do for you?"

"I want an arm," said Paul.

"I can't give you an arm," said Warren. "I can't do anything for you. The use of the Alternate Laws is for those who would do things for themselves."

"Show me how, then."

Warren sighed slightly. It was a sigh that sounded to Paul not only weary, but a little angry.

"You don't know what the hell you're asking," said Warren. "To train whatever aptitude you have for use of the Alternate Laws, I'd have to take you on as my apprentice in necromancy."

40

"Blunt's book gave me to understand the Guild was eager for people."

"Why, we are," said Warren. "We have an urgent need right now for someone comparable to Leonardo da Vinci. We'd be very glad to get someone with the qualifications of Milton or Einstein. Of course, what we really need is someone with a talent no one has conceived of yet—a sort of X-Genius. So we advertise."

"Then you don't want people."

"I didn't say that," said Warren. He turned and paced the room and came back. "You're serious about joining the Guild?"

"If it'll get me my arm."

"It won't get you your arm. I tell you, no one can put that arm back but you. There's a relation between the Alternate Laws and the work of the Guild, but it isn't what you think."

"Perhaps I'd better be enlightened," said Paul.

"All right," said Warren. He put his hands in his pockets and stood with shoulders hunched slightly, looking down at Paul. "Try this on for size. This is an ill world we live in, Formain. A world sick from a surfeit of too many technical luxuries. An overburdened world, swarming with people close to the end of their ropes." His deep-set eyes were steady on Paul. "People today are like a man who thought that if he made his success in the world, everything else that makes life good would come automatically. Now they've made their success—the perfection of a technological civilization in which no one lacks anything in the way of a physical comfort—and they find themselves in a false paradise. Like an electric motor without a load upon it, the human spirit without the weight of the need to achieve and progress is beginning to rev up toward dissolution. Faster and faster, until they'll fly apart and destroy this world they've made."

He stopped.

"What do you say to that?" he asked.

"It might be the case," said Paul. "I don't really believe that's the situation we're in, myself, but it might be the case."

"All right," said Warren. "Now try this: In a climate of confusion, one of the surest ways of confounding the enemy is to tell him the plain truth. And the Guildmaster has stated the plain truth plainly in his book. The Chantry Guild is not interested in propagating the use of the Alternate Laws. It only wants to train and make use of those who can already use the Laws, to its own end. And that end's to hurry the end that is inevitably coming, to bring about the destruction of present civilization."

Warren stopped. He seemed to wait for Paul to say something. But Paul also waited.

"We," said Warren, "are a small but powerful revolutionary body with the aim of driving this sick world into complete insanity and collapse. The Alternate Laws are real, but most of our structure is completely fake. If you come in as my apprentice, you'll be committed to the job of destroying the world."

"And that's my only way to a use of the Alternate Forces?" asked Paul.

"For you to accept the Guild's philosophy and aim, yes," said Warren. "Otherwise, no."

"I don't believe that," said Paul. "If your Alternate Forces exist, they'll work for me as well as all the Chantry Guild put together."

Warren dropped into a chair and stared at Paul for a long moment.

"Arrogant," he said. "Completely arrogant. Let's see. . . ." He rose lightly to his feet, crossed the room, and touched a spot on one of the walls.

The wall slid back, revealing an area which seemed half modern laboratory and half alchemist's den. On the table in its center were earthenware containers, some metal jars, and a large flask full of dark-red liquid.

Warren opened a drawer in the table, and took out something which his body hid from Paul's view. He closed the drawer, turned, and came back carrying a rather decrepit-looking conch shell, brown-stained and polished by handling and age.

He put the shell down on an occasional table a few feet from Paul's chair.

"What does that do?" Paul asked, looking at it curiously.

"For me," said Warren, "it does a lot of things. Which is no advantage to you except that we might say it's been sensitized to the action of the Alternate Laws. Let's see if this arrogance of yours can do anything with it."

Paul frowned. He stared at the shell. For a second the situation was merely ridiculous. And then it was as if a thread of brightness ran through him. There was a sudden weird sensation, as if a great, deep gong sounded, somewhere deep inside him. And then a rushing, back in the depths of his mind, as if a host of memories long forgotten ran and beat upon a locked door held shut to them since he could not exactly remember when.

The conch shell stirred. It rolled to a point of balance and hung there. The bright daylight lanced through a far window of the room and a faint wisp of some light music sounded from the apartment next door. A thin, reedy voice spoke faintly but clearly from the shell.

"From greater dark into the little light. And then once more to greater dark he goes."

The beating on the locked door in Paul's mind dwindled away into silence. The shell lost its balance and fell over, still, on one side. Across from Paul, Warren drew a deep breath and picked up the shell.

"You may be a natural," he said.

"A natural?" Paul looked up at him.

"There are certain abilities in the province of the Alternate Powers which can be possessed by those who know nothing of the true nature of the Alternate Powers. Mind reading, for example. Or artistic inspiration."

"Oh?" said Paul. "How do you tell the difference between people with that, and your Alternate Power people?"

"Very simply," answered Warren. But the tone of his voice and the way he held the shell and continued to watch Paul did not imply simpleness. "For such people their abilities work spasmodically and unreliably. For us, they always work."

"For example, mind reading?"

"I'm a Necromancer," said Warren, shortly, "not a seer. Besides, I used the common, recognizable term. I'm told minds aren't so much *read* as experienced."

"When you go into someone else's mind, you lose your own point of view?"

"Yes," said Warren, "you must be a natural." He took the conch shell back across to the cabinet and put it away. He turned around and spoke from where he was.

"You've got something," he said. "It may be a valuable aptitude, and it may not. But I'm willing to take you on as a probationary apprentice. If I think you have promise after a while, you'll be taken fully into the Guild on an apprenticeship basis. If that happens, you'll be required to assign everything you own and all future personal income to the Guild. But if it reaches that point, you needn't worry about material things." Warren's lips twisted slightly. "The Guild will take care of you. Study and learn, and you'll be able to grow your arm back one day."

Paul stood up.

"You guarantee me an arm?" he said.

"Of course," said Warren. He did not move from where he stood, watching Paul across the widths of laboratory and apartment room with unmoving gaze.

Chapter 6

Shuttling through the many-leveled maze of the Chicago Complex's streets and buildings in a one-man subway car, Paul leaned his head back against the cushions of the seat and closed his eyes.

He was exhausted, and exhaustion, he now suspected, had its roots in something besides the physical efforts he had been put to today. Something almost physical had taken place in him following his recognition of the ridiculousness of the psychiatric approach to his situation. And the business with the shell had also drained him.

But the exhaustion was something that rest could cure. More important were two other things. The first of these was a clear recognition that too many things were happening around him and to him for them all to be accidents. And accidents, once the notion that he was subconsciously bent on self-destruction had been discarded, had been the obvious alternative answer.

The second was the fact that the Necromancer, Warren, had called him arrogant.

Disturbed by this, Paul for the first time faced the fact that such disturbance was unusual with him. Now that he stopped to consider the fact, in spite of all that had happened to him it had never before occurred to him that he might be at the mercy of any other force than that of his own will. Perhaps, he thought, this was arrogance, but the idea did not ring true. Above all else, he trusted his own feelings, and he did not feel arrogant. All that came to him when he reached back into himself for reasons was a calm feeling of certainty. It was that invincible element in him which took all things calmly.

For, thought Paul, leaning back with his eyes closed, above all he must not be arrogant. He was like a man peering through the glass-clearness of still water into the secret life of a tide pool on an ocean beach. Wonderful things were happening just a little before him, and would continue to happen as long as the pool was not disturbed. But a touch of wind or a dabbled finger, a ripple across the water's surface, and the life going on under his nose would no longer be isolated, pure, and complete. Gentleness was the watchword. Gentleness and extreme care. Already he had begun to separate and identify elements: by a hint of movement, a change of color, an emerging shape. . . .

Leaning back with his eyes closed, Paul lost himself in a half-doze and a dream of things half-seen.

Sudden deceleration of his small car pulled him upright in his seat. The car jerked to a stop. He opened his eyes and looked out through the unopaqued bubble of the car's top.

He was at a mid-level intersection of streets. Above and below him were residential and business layers of the great three-dimensional community that was Chicago Complex. On his own level his car had halted part-way out into an intersection the four corners of which were occupied by small shops and offices, beyond which was a large recreation area, parklike with trees. But no people were visible. The shops were empty. The park was empty. The streets were clear and still.

Paul once more leaned forward and pressed for the terminal at the Koh-i-Nor Hotel. The car did not move. He punched for the transportation control center, malfunction division.

The communications tank above the car's dashboard lighted up.

"Sir?" said a woman's canned voice. "Can I help you?"

"I'm in a one-man car that won't move," said Paul. "It's stopped at the intersection of—" he glanced at a street-corner sign—"N Level 2432 and AANB."

"Checking," said the canned voice. There was a moment's wait and the voice spoke again. "Sir? Are you certain of your location. The area you report yourself in has been closed to traffic. Your car could not have entered it in the last half hour."

"It seems to have anyway." Paul broke off suddenly. He seemed to have heard something odd. He got out of the car and stood up alongside it. The sound came thinly but more clearly to his ears. It was the noise of people chanting, and the noise was approaching.

"The area you report yourself in," the tank in the car was saying, "has been cleared to allow for a public demonstration. Would you please check your location again? If it is the location you have already reported, please leave your car at once and ascend one level immediately to find another. Repeat, leave your car *immediately*."

Paul swung away from the car. Across the street from him was an escalator spiral ramp. He reached it and let himself be borne upward. It swung up and out over the street he had just left. The chanting now came clearly to his ears. It was not words, but sounds without meaning.

"Hey, hey! Hey, hey! Hey, hey! . . ."

Puzzled, he stepped off the upward-moving surface of the ramp and looked out over the chest-high siding. Down around a curve of the cross street to the one on which his car had stalled he saw people pouring toward him in a sort of orderly mob, twenty abreast, and filling the street solidly from curb to curb.

They came quickly. They were at jog trot. Young men and women for the most part wearing blue slacks, white shirts, and green-colored, odd, cocked hats. They ran with arms interlinked, in step with the rhythm of their chanting.

Abruptly, Paul identified them. They represented, evidently, one of the so-called marching societies. Such groups gathered together for no other purpose than to run through the streets perhaps once or twice a month. It was a sort of controlled and channeled hysteria, or so Paul remembered reading. Such exercises blew off a lot of emotional steam safely, said the societies' advocates. For unless the group ran directly into some obstacle, they did no harm and were not harmed.

They came on now and Paul could see their eyes, which were all fixed straight ahead. But their gazes were not glassy, as of people drunk or drugged. Rather, they were clear, but fixed, as with people undergoing a moment of exaltation or frenzy. They were almost below Paul, now. Almost to the intersection.

Suddenly, Paul realized that his one-man car, stalled where it was, would be in their way. They were practically upon it now. The cadenced slapping of their river of feet was shaking the ramp on which he stood. It was making, it seemed, the whole structure of the city Complex, level on level, vibrate to a high, almost supersonic singing. A wave of heat struck up to them from their onrushing bodies, and the louder, ever-louder yelping of their chant rocked on his ears like the unnatural amplification of sounds heard in a fever. Whirlpooled about by noise and heat, Paul saw their first ranks run into his empty car and, without halting, like a stampede of mindless cattle, tumble it, rolling, over and over until it bounced at last to a railing overhanging the level below. Paul watched it mount the railing and drop from sight, the ultimate noise of its impact below lost in the encompassing noise of the running crowd.

He looked back along the road, in the direction from which they had come. The river of people was unended, still passing out of sight around the curve. But now, as he watched, the final ranks began to thin and quieten, and over the other sounds he heard the thin wail of ambulance sirens following slowly after.

Paul went on up to the level above, found a two-man car that was empty on a siding, and returned to the hotel.

When he got to his room, the door was open. A small gray man in a business suit rose smoothly from a chair as Paul entered, and offered an opened wallet cardcase for Paul's inspection.

"Hotel security, Mr. Formain," said the small man. "My name's James Butler."

"Yes?" said Paul. He felt his tiredness like a cloak around him.

"A routine matter, Mr. Formain. Maintenance discovered a vase in your room that had been rather bent out of shape."

"Put it on my bill," said Paul. "Now, if you don't mind——"

"The vase isn't important, Mr. Formain. But we understand you have been seeing a psychiatrist?"

"A Dr. Elizabeth Williams. Today. Why?"

"As a routine matter, this hotel asks for and is notified if any of its guests are currently under psychiatric care. The Chicago Complex Public Health Unit permits us to refuse occupancy to guests who might disturb the hotel. Of course, no such refusal is anticipated in your case, Mr. Formain."

"I'm checking out in the morning," said Paul.

"Oh? I'm sorry to hear that," said James Butler evenly. "I assure you there was no intention to offend you. It's just one of the management rules that we inform our guests that we have been notified about them."

"I was leaving anyway," said Paul. He looked at the man's unchanging face and motionless body, and James Butler's personality came clearly through to him. Butler was a dangerous little man. An efficient little machine of suspicion and control. Underneath, though, was something repressed, something guarded by an inner fear. "Right now, I want to turn in. So if you don't mind . . ."

Butler inclined his head slightly.

"Unless, of course," he said, "there's something more."

"Nothing."

"Thank you." Butler turned and walked smoothly to the door. "Feel free to call on hotel services at any time," he said, and went out, closing the door behind him.

Paul frowned. But weariness was like a great load on him. He undressed and dropped into the bed. And sleep closed down about him like great, gray wings, enfolding.

He dreamed that he walked a cobbled road, in darkness under the stars, alone. And the cobbles grew as he went until they were great boulders to be climbed. And then that dream vanished and he dreamed that he was paralyzed, drifting upright through the nighttime streets of the Chicago Complex. He drifted along without touching the ground and after a while he came on an arc light on its pole that had been changed into a monstrous candy cane. And just beyond it a store front had been turned from plastic to ice, and was melting.

In the morning he woke feeling as if he had slept fourteen years, rather than fourteen hours, packed, and went down to the main lobby to pay his bill.

He cut through one of the hotel bars on his way down to the basement terminal. At this early hour it was all but deserted except for a plump middle-aged man who sat alone at a table with a small tulip-shaped glass of some purplish liquid before him. For a moment, passing, Paul thought that the man was drunk. And then he caught the scent of cinnamon from the glass and saw the man's eyes had pinpoint pupils. And looking behind this, he caught sight of Butler, seated in the darkness of a corner, watching. Paul went over to the hotel security man.

"Are you notified about drug addicts, too?" Paul asked.

"Our bars stock the non-habit-forming synthetics," said Butler. "It's quite legal."

"You didn't answer my question," said Paul.

"The hotel," said Butler, "feels a certain responsibility to certain guests." He glanced up at Paul. "That's legal,

50

too. And any extra charges are quite reasonable. If you hadn't already planned to leave, Mr. Formain, I could have told you what services we had available."

Paul turned and went on. He found a one-man car at the terminal, and, getting in, punched for Warren's apartment. The first demand the Necromancer had made of his probationary apprentice was that Paul should move into the apartment, where Warren could have him under constant observation.

He found Warren waiting for him. The Necromancer turned over one of the bedrooms in the apartment to him, and then to all intents and purposes left Paul to his own devices. For the rest of the week Paul hardly saw the intense young man.

It was five days later that Paul, thoroughly bored with the apartment by this time, happened to be going through the music Warren had listed in his apartment player. Abruptly, he came across a title which caught his attention.

IN APPLE COMFORT . . . vocal. Sung by *Kantele*

Kantele. Suddenly the mental connection was made. It had been there in the list of local members of the Chantry Guild. *Kantele Maki.* And he remembered now, there was a girl who sang professionally under the single name *Kantele.* She was the girl with the book that he had first seen on the news broadcast, and after that at the Directory. He pressed the small black button alongside the initial letter of the song title.

There was the barest second of a pause, and then the chimed music rose softly ringing from the player, interspersed by the cool, shifting silver of the voice he recognized.

*In apple comfort, long I waited thee
And long I thee in apple comfort waited.
In lonely autumn and uncertain——*

51

A sudden gasp from behind him made Paul shut off the player abruptly and turn about. He found himself facing the girl herself.

She stood a little to one side of a bookcase of old-fashioned volumes. But the bookcase, to Paul's surprise, was swung out from its usual place, revealing not a wall behind it, but an entrance to a small room furnished and equipped like an office. Seeing his gaze go to it, Kantele broke suddenly out of the rigidity that had been holding her, and, putting out a hand, pushed the bookcase back into position, closing the entrance. They stood, looking across the room at each other.

"I didn't know . . ." she said. "I forgot you were living here now."

He watched her, curiously. She was noticeably pale.

"Did you think I was someone else?" he asked.

"Yes. I mean"—she said—"I thought you were Jase."

She was one of the kind who lie defiantly. He felt her untruthfulness across all the distance separating them.

"You've got a fine voice," he said. "I was playing that song of yours——"

"Yes. I heard you," she interrupted. "I—I'd rather you wouldn't play it, if you don't mind."

"Would you?" asked Paul.

"It has associations for me. If you don't mind . . ."

"I won't play it if you don't want me to, of course," said Paul. He walked toward her and then stopped suddenly, seeing her reflexively take the one step back from him that the wall behind her allowed.

"Jase . . ." she said. "Jase will be here at any minute."

Paul watched her, frowning a bit. He felt puzzled and a little exasperated by her, but also oddly touched, as he might be by anyone or anything defenseless that did not realize he meant it no harm. And that was odd too, because Kantele did not give the impression generally of defenselessness, but of wire-like courage. Paul was reaching to approach this problem in words when the sound of the opening front door of the apartment brought both their heads around in its direction.

Warren and the flat-bodied, crop-haired man Paul had seen in the news broadcast, and again leaving the apartment with Kantele the first time he had come to see Warren, had just come in. They headed straight for Paul and Kantele.

Chapter 7

"You didn't answer the door," said Warren, stopping before them and looking at Kantele.

"You didn't ring," said Paul.

"He means me—my apartment, next door," said Kantele, but without looking away from Warren to Paul. "I forgot he was here, Jase. I heard noise and I knew you were out. I stepped in from the office."

"Yes," said Warren. His thin, dark, bright face looked from her to Paul without smiling. "Well, you'd have met anyway. You know each other now? This is Paul Formain, Kantele. Paul, Kantele Maki."

"How do you do?" said Paul to her, and smiled. She gave a little spasm of a smile back.

"And this is Burton McLeod."

"McCloud?" echoed Paul, shaking hands with the flat-bodied man.

"Spelled McLeod, pronounced McCloud," said McLeod. His voice was mild and a little husky. His handgrip was dry and firm. His brown eyes were the lonely, sad, and savage eyes of a hawk on leash and perch. A week before, the hotel security man, Butler, had impressed Paul as dangerous. McLeod radiated dangerousness of a different order. If Butler was like a stiletto, needle-pointed and polished, then this man was scarred and heavy as some ancient broadsword.

While Paul and McLeod had been shaking hands,

Warren and Kantele had held each other's eyes for a long second. Now, suddenly, Warren turned away from her with a quickness that was almost like a shrug and took a small box from his pocket. He opened it in front of Paul.

Paul saw neat rows of white gelatin capsules within. Warren took one out and handing the box aside to Mc-Leod, broke it and poured a white powder from it into his palm.

"Taste," said Warren. Paul frowned.

"It's quite harmless," said Warren. He dipped a finger in the powder himself, and put it to his tongue. Paul hesitated a second and then followed suit. He tasted sweetness.

"Sugar?" said Paul, looking at Warren.

"That's right." The Necromancer dusted off his hands over a nearby ash tray. "But to the man you'll be giving it to it'll be cocaine. I said"— Warren stared at Paul tightly—"it'll *be* cocaine. The minute you let the box into anyone's hands but your own. I mention this so that you'll realize you're legally in the clear in delivering it, as long as you keep it in your pocket until the last moment."

"You want me to deliver it?" asked Paul. "Who to?"

"You know how the Koh-i-Nor's laid out. I want you to take this box to suite 2309. Don't ask directions from the desk clerk or anyone else. Give it to the man you find there. If you run into any trouble . . ." Warren hesitated and glanced for a second at Kantele. "I don't expect you will. But if you do, there's a chess tournament going on on the sixtieth level in the banquet rooms there. Go up there and look for Kantele. She'll get you out."

He stopped talking. There was a moment of silence in the room.

"If it was cocaine," said Paul, "of course I wouldn't take it."

"You'll be carrying sugar," said Warren. His thin face seemed to flash for a second like a drawn blade in the brightness of the sunlight coming through the far windows of the room. "It'll be transmuted into the drug only after you deliver it. You can believe or not believe, go or part company with me, just as you like."

"I'll take it," said Paul. He held out his hand. Mc-Leod gave him the box. "Twenty-three-o-nine?"

"Twenty-three-o-nine," said Warren. The eyes of all three followed him, Paul could feel in the muscles of his back, as he took the box and left the apartment.

The desk clerk he passed at the Koh-i-Nor was a stranger and did not look up as Paul went by. Paul took the elevator tube to the twenty-third level.

It turned out to be a level of modern-décor, semi-VIP suites. The type of establishments that would require income in excess of forty thousand a year to be supported without strain by their occupants. Paul walked down the wide, tiled hallway, coolly lighted by the high, blue-curtained windows at each end of it, until he came to a door marked with the numerals 2309. Below it in small letters were the two words *service entrance*.

Paul touched the door. It was not only unlocked but ajar. It swung noiselessly back into its wall recess at his touch. He stepped into the kitchen of the suite.

Voices broke on his ear from elsewhere in the suite. He stopped dead, and with a faint noise the door slid closed again behind him. One of the voices was an incisive, middle-aged tenor, sharp with emotion. The other was thick and deeper in tone, stumbling, sullen.

". . . pull yourself together!" the tenor voice was saying. The deeper voice muttered something unintelligible.

"You know better than that!" said the tenor. "You don't want to be cured, that's what it is. The substitutes were bad enough. But your monkeying around with real drugs makes you a danger to the whole Department, if not the whole Division. Why didn't you take psychiatric leave when I offered it to you last March?"

The heavy voice muttered something, it seemed to Paul, about the soup, or super.

"Get that out of your head!" said the tenor. "You've

let the statistics on mental health get you to seeing ghosts in the woodwork. Electronic equipment is electronic equipment. No more. No less. Don't you think that if there was anything more there, *I'd* know it?"

"Unless . . ." muttered the heavy voice, "got you already."

"For your own sake"—the tenor was disgusted—"see your physician. Get yourself committed. I won't investigate your Department for the next four days. That'll give you time to get safely into a hospital room where you can decently refuse to answer questions. That's it, now. It's up to you." There was the sound of footsteps walking across hard flooring and a door button snapped to unlatch. "Four days. I won't give you an hour more."

A wind of sudden suspicion blew coolly through Paul, chilling him. He turned quickly himself, stepped silently back through the door he had just entered, and out into the hall. There was a small alcove in the wall about six feet to his left. He stepped to it and pressed himself, back to its wall, deep in its shadow, looking along the hall to 2309's main entrance.

It opened immediately. A small, sparely erect man with thin gray hair came out, closed the door behind him, and went away from Paul toward the far set of elevator tubes at the other end of the hall. For a second as he turned to the elevators, Paul saw a sparrow-like profile against the blue illumination from the curtain windows, and recognized the man. In the suite the tenor voice had sounded vaguely familiar, and Paul had thought it might be the security man, Butler, speaking. But he saw now that there was another reason he had half-recognized the voice.

The man by the elevators was Kirk Tyne, World Complex Engineer. He was the executive head of the theoretical machinery that correlated the activities of the interlocking Complexes of technological devices that made modern life possible about the planet. In theory he and his Division of Engineers performed the functions of a sort of super-computing element, since sooner or later mechanical decisions had to find their ultimate authority and review in human ones. He reached out his hand now to open the elevator tube.

He had not quite touched it when a fair portion of the blue illumination from the window was suddenly occulted by the dark, wide-shouldered body of a tall man who stepped off the downshaft alongside the one toward which Tyne was reaching.

"Well, Kirk," said the tall man. "Didn't expect to see you here."

His voice struck and reverberated on Paul's listening ear like the little echoes chasing each other, on and on, from the sound of a gong struck in some deep and stony cave. It was the voice of Walter Blunt. Almost involuntarily, Paul stepped forward to the edge of his recess to get a better look at this head of the Chantry Guild. But Blunt was standing just so slightly turned that his face was shadowed and averted from Paul.

"Got off here by mistake," replied Tyne, sharply and smoothly. "I was headed for the chess matches upstairs. How about you, Walt?"

"Why," Blunt leaned on his heavy cane, and his voice had a humorous note in it, "I saw you and stepped out to say hello. Headed for the lobby myself for a moment, to meet someone. You look good, Kirk." He laid aside his cane, leaning it against the wall of a tube, and offered his hand. Tyne shook it.

"Thank you, Walter," said Tyne, shaking hands. He added, drily, "I imagine we'll both live a while, yet."

"Why, no, Kirk," said Blunt. "The instrument of Armageddon is already at work. I intend to survive the conflict when it comes, but I don't expect you will."

Tyne shook his head.

"You amaze me, Walt," he said. "You know very well I'm the one man who knows all about your little sect—right down to the fact that it numbers only a little more than sixty thousand members, scattered all over the globe.

Yet you keep on insisting to my face that you're about to take over the world. And what would you do with it, once you'd taken it over? You can't run things without the very Complex technologies you claim you intend to destroy."

"Well, now," said Blunt, "there're a lot of different versions of this world of ours, Kirk. You've got one, with your Complexes of equipment—a nice steady-ticking world. The only pity is, it won't stop growing and complicating itself. Then, there's the world of the fanatics, the people who go in for dangerous sports, wild cults, and marching societies. And then again, there's a vague, gauzy world of the spiritually inclined, and the world of the asymbolic pioneers, artist and scientist. There's the world of those to whom tradition and an anchored existence are the only worthwhile basis for life. There's even the world of the psychotics, the neurotically crippled."

"You talk," said Tyne, "as if these other . . . attitudes, had an equal value with normal civilized society."

"But they have, Kirk, they have," said Blunt, looming over the smaller man. "Ask anyone who belongs to one of them. Don't look at me, man. This is your world—the world you boys made out of the industrial revolution three hundred years ago. To put it somewhat crudely, if this here's heaven, how come we still got stomach-aches?"

"We got stomach-aches," said Tyne, stepping a little aside toward his elevator tubes. "But we also got doctors to physic 'em. Which we didn't always have before. If you'll excuse me, Walt, I want to get upstairs to the chess matches. Are you coming back up?"

"Right away," said Blunt. Tyne stepped onto a disk floating up the tube beside him, with one foot. The disk checked itself. "And how's Mrs. Tyne been?" asked Blunt.

"Excellent," said Tyne. He stepped completely onto the disk and was borne upward out of sight.

Blunt turned, stepped through the open door of the

down tube onto a descending disk, and disappeared himself.

Paul came out from the shadow, still looking toward the elevators where the two men had stood. They were gone now, but Blunt's stick was still leaning where he had placed it before shaking hands with Tyne. Paul remembered abruptly how Blunt had stood, half-turned away from the alcove. It came to Paul that he had never got a square look at the head of the Chantry Guild. Before, this had been only a minor omission in the back of his mind. But suddenly it moved to the forefront.

Paul was suddenly conscious of something that most of the time he merely took for granted. That for him to meet someone was automatically to gain a great deal of insight into them. And Blunt was an enigma. But an enigma with whom Paul's life had become considerably entangled. With Blunt, as with the Guild itself, there seemed to be considerably more going on than met the eye. Deciding, Paul strode out from his alcove, down to the elevators, and picked up the stick. Blunt could hardly avoid facing the man who returned his walking stick to him in person.

Paul came back to suite 2309, the main entrance this time, the one through which he had seen Tyne leave. He pressed the door button. It was unlocked and opened at his touch. He stepped inside, closing the door behind him, and found himself in the sitting room of the suite, and facing the man he had seen drugged and under watch by Butler in the hotel bar, the morning of his leaving.

The sound of the closing door brought the man's head around. He had been half-turned away, blowing his nose on a tissue. At the click of the door's latching, he jerked about to face Paul. And then he went backward across the room, mouthing and stumbling like a creature scared out of all common, ordinary sense, until the high, wide window of the room stopped him.

He stood, trapped and staring, blinking, shivering, pushing against the window as if he could shove himself through it into the twenty-three levels of unblocked air that separated him from the ground level before the hotel.

Paul checked instinctively. And the wave of sick fear emanating from the man crested and broke over Paul like solid ocean surf. Paul stood, momentarily and in spite of himself, stunned. He had never thought a thinking being could go so bad.

The man's eyes flicked and bored into Paul. The eyes themselves were watering, and the nose sniffled uncontrollably. The man's face was gray and rigid. Something mangled whimpered within him.

"It's all right," said Paul. "All right . . ." He came gently toward the man, Blunt's stick tucked under his right arm and the box of capsules in his single hand outstretched. "Here . . . I'm just bringing you these. . . ."

The man continued to stare and sniffle spasmodically. Paul, now within arm's length of him, laid the box down on a table. As an afterthought, he opened it with two fingers and took out one of the white capsules.

"See?" he said. "Here . . ." He held it out to the man, but the other, either jerkily reaching for it, or jerkily pushing it away, knocked it from Paul's fingers. Automatically, Paul bent to pick it up.

His head was still down when warning rang loud within him. He straightened up suddenly to see the drug addict facing him now, a small handgun black and deadly in one trembling hand. The pinhole of its muzzle wavered at Paul's chest.

"Easy," said Paul. "Easy . . ."

His voice seemed not even to reach the ears of the other man. The drug addict stepped forward and Paul automatically stepped back.

"It sent you," said the man, hoarsely. "It sent you."

"Nothing sent me," said Paul. "I came to bring you that box on the table. There it is." He nodded toward it.

The man did not look at it. Moving out into the room, he began to circle Paul, while keeping gun and eyes aimed at Paul.

"I'm going to kill you," he said. "You think I won't kill you, but I will."

"Why?" asked Paul. And that monosyllable, he thought, should at least have made the other pause, but again it seemed the drug addict did not even hear him.

"It sent you to kill me," said the man. "It can't kill. It isn't built to allow itself to kill. But it can fix things so some other factor does the dirty work."

"I don't want to hurt you," said Paul.

"It's no use," said the man. Paul could sense the will to pull the trigger accumulating in the mind opposite him. The man's back began to straighten with something like pride. "I understand, you see. I know all about it."

The man was almost between Paul and the room's entrance, now. He was at a distance of about eight feet, out of arm's reach. Paul made a move to step toward him and the tiny muzzle of the gun came up sharply.

"No, no!" said the man. *"No!"*

Paul stopped. He became conscious suddenly of the hard roundness of Blunt's walking stick under his arm. It was a good three feet in length. Paul began to let the stick slip down into his hand.

"Just a little," said the man. "Just a moment more . . . It thought you'd find me alone here. It didn't know I had a gun. When you steal something, there's no way for it to know. No record—*what're you doing?"*

The last three words came out in a scream, as the man noticed the end of the walking stick slide into Paul's hand. The pinhole muzzle leaped up and forward. Paul jumped aside and forward. There was no time to throw the stick as he had planned. He saw the man swinging to bring the gun's aim upon him. The other was close.

"Now!" screamed the man. The walking stick leaped in Paul's grasp and he felt it connect solidly. The man fell away from him.

The man fell and rolled over on his back on the carpet. The small gun tumbled foolishly out of his hand. He lay, looking in terrified accusation at the ceiling.

Still holding the walking stick, Paul stepped forward. He stared down at the drug addict. The man lay still. His bloodshot eyes did not focus upon Paul. Paul lifted the stick in his hand and stared at it. The dark wood was dented and splintered a little but in no way broken or weakened. Paul looked back down at the man on the floor, letting the heavy weight of his unnaturally muscled right arm, holding the stick, drop limply at his side.

Among the sparse black hair on the man's skull, the blood was beginning to flow, slowly and darkly. Paul felt emptiness inside him, as if he had deeply inhaled on nothingness. The broken skull looked as if it had been stricken almost in two by some heavy sword.

Chapter 8

The man's dead, thought Paul. He took a deep, shudder-
ing breath, but the emptiness inside him did not go away.
Why don't I feel anything more than this?

Once he would have expected an answer from the
unconquerable element back in the depths of his mind.
But with the overgrowth of his right arm, and the decision
in the psychiatrist's office, that part of him seemed to
have melted into the rest of his consciousness. He was all
of one piece now. Still, he could almost imagine he heard
the ghost of a whisper replying to his thought.

Death, it whispered, *is a factor also.*

The stick was still poised in his hand. Paul opened his
hand about it and a small object fell onto the carpet. He
bent and picked it up. It was the capsule he had offered
the dead man, flattened and bent now from being between his palm and the walking stick. He put it in his
pocket. Swiftly he turned and went out of the suite.

He closed the door behind him and was halfway to
the same elevator tubes which Tyne and Blunt had taken,
when his mind started working sensibly again. He
stopped dead.

Why should he run, he asked himself? He had only
acted in self-defense on being attacked by what
amounted to an insane man waving a gun. Paul went
back into 2309 and used the phone there to call the hotel's security office.

The office answered without lighting up the vision tank. A voice spoke to him from out of blank grayness.

"Who is calling, please?"

"Suite 2309. But I'm not a guest of the hotel. I want to report——"

"One minute, please."

There was a moment of silence. The tank still did not light up. Then suddenly it cleared and Paul found himself looking into the neat, expressionless features of James Butler.

"Mr. Formain," said Butler. "I was informed twenty-eight minutes ago that you had entered the hotel by the plaza entrance."

"I was bringing something——"

"So we assumed," said Butler. "As a matter of routine, our hall monitor cameras are lighted to follow nonguests under conditions when we haven't been notified of their visit in advance. Is the occupant of suite 2309 with you now, Mr. Formain?"

"Yes," said Paul. "But I'm afraid there's been an accident here."

"Accident?" Butler's voice and expression stayed invariable.

"The man I met here threatened me with a gun." Paul hesitated. "He's dead."

"Dead?" asked Butler. For a second he merely looked at Paul. "You must be mistaken about the gun, Mr. Formain. We have a complete file and check on the occupant of 2309. He did not own a gun."

"No. He told me he stole it."

"I don't mean to argue with you, Mr. Formain. But I must inform you that in accordance with police regulations this conversation is being irreversibly recorded."

"Recorded!" Paul stared into the tank.

"Yes, Mr. Formain. You see, we happen to know that it would have been impossible for the resident in 2309 to steal any kind of weapon. He has been under constant surveillance by our staff."

"Well, your staff slipped up!"

"I'm afraid that's impossible, too. The only way a gun could have entered the suite where you are now would have been if you had carried it in yourself."

"Just a minute." Paul leaned down toward the tank. "Mr. Kirk Tyne, the World Complex Engineer, was here just before I came."

"Mr. Tyne," said Butler, "left the North Tower lobby at 14:09 by up tube on the elevators and arrived at the chess tournament on the sixtieth level at 14:10. Our hall monitors show no one entering 2309 in the past six hours but you. Accordingly . . ."

The barest flicker of Butler's eyes to the side woke Paul suddenly to the nearness of the trap into which he was sliding. The hotel security agent was no mean hypnotist himself. The dead monotony of his voice, the expressionless face that classed all things with the dull unimportance of a lost hotel key or misdirected luggage, would have been lethal against anyone who lacked Paul's inherent immunity.

Without waiting even to shut off the phone Paul moved, letting his reflexes take over. He was at the door and through it into the hall before Butler had time to stop talking. The hall outside was empty.

Moving swiftly, Paul turned from the elevators and raced down the hall to a heavy fire door. He pulled it open and passed through into the concrete shaft of a stairway. He found himself on a small landing with steps leading up from one end and down from another. The edge of another fire door recessed in its slot in the wall stood level with the first step of the down flight of steps.

Paul ran down the stairs. He was quiet about it, but the stair shaft itself was as silent as something that had been sealed for eternity. He made four floors without a hint of danger. Then, when he reached the landing of the fifth level below where he had started, he saw the staircase fire door closed, barring further progress.

He turned to the door leading out into the hallway of that level and went through it, onto soft carpeting.

"Mr. Formain?" asked a polite voice in his ear. "If you'll just come . . ."

A security agent, a young man by his voice, had been standing back by the side of the door where the latch was, his back to the wall alongside and waiting for Paul to come out. As Paul stepped through, the agent spoke and stepped forward to take hold of him. Paul felt the left hand of the other man expertly seeking the twin nerves just above his elbow and the man's right reaching out to catch his thumb and bend it back wristward in that unobtrusive hold long familiar to police people, known as the "comealong."

The searching hands of the security man failed of their mark, for no fault of the man himself, but for two reasons he could not have expected. The first was that his pinching left hand missed its mark completely, the seeking thumb and middle finger not finding the nerve-points they sought since they were hidden under the greatly overdeveloped muscles of Paul's arm, just above the elbow. The second was that Paul was no longer thinking his reactions out in conscious terms, but in this emergency abandoning himself to that invulnerable part of him that had earlier claimed his overdeveloped arm as its own. So, what actually happened was that even as the security man reached out to take him prisoner, even as he felt the man's hands upon him, Paul was already in movement.

At the other's touch, all in a split second, he checked, balanced, moved a fraction of an inch to the right, and drove the point of his elbow backward with all the natural strength of his arm.

It was a move executed with a hesitationless smoothness and accuracy that would have made it lethal against a trained fighter. It was aimed to be lethal. The elbow-point was fired with impossible accuracy into the unprotected area just below the man's breastbone, and driving upward.

It would have torn lungs, crushed arteries, and possibly burst the heart. The only reason it did not do so, and did not kill, was that at the last split second Paul realized what was about to happen and managed to slightly deflect the aim.

Still, it lifted the man and slammed him back against the hallway wall, from which he fell forward and lay on his side, eyes half showing under fallen lids, legs a little drawn up and twitching with little spasmodic movements. Even as it was, he had been severely damaged.

And so almost, it seemed, had Paul.

It was nearly as if the blow he had just struck had recoiled on him with most of its original force. He doubled up as if he had been the target. A washback of emotion shuddered through his whole body, and he staggered blindly down the hall, dizzy, nauseated, half-blinded, and bent over. Still moving, however, he got himself under control. Somehow he sought for and found the control in him that was necessary, and it was like pushing a button. So swiftly that it almost seemed he had never felt it, the reaction vanished from him and he straightened up.

He found himself now at the end of the hall, by more tall, curtained windows. The elevator tubes were close and there was no place else to go. He remembered that in case of trouble he was to seek out Kantele on the sixtieth level, and he stepped onto a disk floating up the up tube.

It carried him up with it. Over his head the bottom of the immediately superior disk closed him off into a little tube-shaped enclosure of which the bottom was his own disk, with him filling the tube. For the moment he was safe. Looking out through the transparent wall of the tube, he saw the various levels dropping past him, but though he saw occasional figures in the halls and standing by the tubes, none of them seemed to pay any special attention to him.

If the hotel security men were waiting for him anywhere, he thought, it would be at the roof-garden top of the hotel where the small-craft landing pad was. But that was thirty levels above the floor where he intended to get off.

He was at the fifty-eighth level now. He moved forward to the edge of the disk, and as the sixtieth level approached, he stepped off.

He stepped almost immediately into a hallway crowd of people coming and going, and standing around in small, talkative groups. He pushed his way through them and stepped into the first entrance to a banquet room he found. Within were tables at which chess matches were going on, here and there with a few watchers clustered around some special pair of players. Kantele was not in view. He left the room and went on.

In the third room he visited he found Kantele. She was with several other people who were watching an individual match across the room from the entrance, and not too far from the French windows which indicated an outside balcony or terrace beyond the banquet room. She was standing behind the chair of a man who, with a sudden quickening of his pulse, Paul recognized to be Blunt. Blunt sat leaning forward, absorbed in the condition of the board he was observing, and Kantele stood with one hand on his wide shoulder.

It occurred to Paul that he was going to have the chance of facing Blunt sooner than he had expected. He started toward the table where Blunt and Kantele watched, and abruptly stopped.

He no longer had the walking stick.

Paul stood still, and for a second the hum and movement of the room faded almost out of his consciousness. His hand was empty. But he could not remember either dropping the stick or laying it aside. All that occurred to him was that he must have let go of it in the reaction that followed his elbow-jabbing of the security man. Well, if that was the case, Blunt might have something to explain to the police—and then he might not. It might be that, as in the case of Tyne's visit to 2309, hotel security would, on finding the stick, politely cover up for him.

At any rate, Paul intended to face the Chantry Guild head *now*. Paul went forward again.

But he was already too late. Kantele, he found, had already looked up and seen him. Her face unnaturally expressionless, she shook her head at his advance and then gestured with a nod at the French windows. Paul hesitated for a second, then turned and obeyed.

He passed the tables and stepped through one of the French windows, closing it behind him. He found himself, as he had expected, on a long and fairly narrow terrace with a waist-high parapet of ornamental stone around it. Beyond the parapet he could see the rooftops of lower surrounding buildings, and beyond them the farther levels of Chicago Complex. The afternoon had turned out to be almost cloudless, and the bright sun lanced warmly across the white, round tables and translucent, single-legged chairs on the terrace. He walked to the parapet and looked over.

Below him the side of the Koh-i-Nor's North Tower fell sheer in an unbroken pattern of alternate window glass and marbled tile to the top level of commuter traffic, sixty stories below. Postage-stamp-size directly underneath him was the main concourse in front of the tower, and, a narrow two hundred yards away across it, some sort of office building with a single aircar on its landing pad, and the highly-polished surface of the building's construction tile reflecting the utter blue of the sky.

He turned back from the parapet. On the white table top nearly beside him was a brightly-illustrated throwaway magazine left by some earlier visitor to the terrace. The breeze across the terrace ruffled and tried to turn its pages. He glanced at the titles in colorful type on its cover. The lead one jumped at him.

NECROMANCER

WAS GANDHI'S WAY RIGHT?

And under this, in slightly less bold print:

The Psychotics of Our Overcrowded Cities

The author of this later article, he noticed with interest, was the same Dr. Elizabeth Williams, psychiatrist, he had encountered only the week before.

He reached for the magazine to turn to the article.

"Formain," said a voice. He looked up and turned.

Facing him from about fifteen feet away, his hand on the half-open French door through which he must just have stepped out onto the terrace, was Butler. The small hotel security man stood with one hand thrust into the right pocket of his barrel-cut jacket. His face was as polite as ever.

"You better come along quietly with me, Formain," he said.

Paul let go of the magazine. The fingers of his single hand flexed reflexively. He took a casual step in Butler's direction.

"Stop there," said Butler. He took his hand out of his pocket, revealing a small finger gun. Paul stopped.

"Don't be foolish," said Paul.

Butler looked at him with the closest approach to a flicker of emotion in his face that Paul had yet seen.

"I think that's my line," Butler said. "Don't be foolish, Formain. Come along quietly."

Paul looked across the short distance separating them. His first impulse, as it had been with the agent in the hallway, had been to go into action. He had checked that. And now a part of him waited critically to see what the other part of him might do. He looked at Butler, trying to narrow down his mental field of vision. Trying to see the man as something individual, unique, limited by the forces that tied him into his environment, by the very elements that made him dangerous.

71

Anyone can be understood, Paul told himself. Anyone.

For a second, Butler's image seemed to swim in Paul's retina with the effort Paul was making, like a figure seen through the bottom of a drinking glass. Then the image cleared.

"I don't intend to be foolish," said Paul. He sat down on the edge of the table beside him. "I'm not going with you."

"Yes," said Butler. He held the finger gun steady.

"No," said Paul. "If you take me in, I'll tell the police that you were the source of supply for the drugs of the man in 2309. I'll tell them you used to be a drug addict yourself."

Butler gave a small, tired sigh.

"Come along, Formain," he said.

"No," said Paul. "To take me, you'll have to shoot me first. If you kill me, there's bound to be the kind of investigation you don't want. If you do less than kill me, I'll tell them what I just told you I'd say."

There was a moment's silence on the terrace. While it lasted, they could both hear the leaves of the magazine rustling in the breeze.

"I am not a drug addict," said Butler.

"No," said Paul. "But you were until some fanaticism, some particular blind faith gave you the strength to kick the habit. You're not afraid of the fact being found out so much as the fact that an investigation into the fact would cause you to be cut off from this source of strength. If I mention it, the police will have to investigate the matter. So, you're going to let me go."

Butler regarded him. The security man's expression was as unreadable as ever, but the finger gun jerked for a second as his hand trembled momentarily. He hid the hand back in the pocket of his jacket.

"Who told you?" he asked.

"You did," said Paul. "Being the sort of man you are, the rest had to follow."

Butler watched him for a second more, then turned toward the French door behind him.

"Someday I'll make you tell me who told you," he said, and went back into the banquet rooms where the chessmen were at war.

The French door had barely closed behind him when one of the other doors opened and Kantele stepped through, quickly closing the door behind her. She came quickly over to Paul, her fine-cut features pale and her lips a little compressed above the square blue shoulders of her tailored jacket and the tooled-leather strap of the heavy handbag cutting into one of them.

"How did you—no, don't tell me," she corrected herself as she met him. "There isn't time. There are a dozen more hotel men going through the banquet rooms. Here . . ."

She lifted her large handbag onto one of the tables and pressed it at certain points. It opened out like a slow-motion jack-in-the-box. It was a one-man parachute copter, of the emergency type used by aircraft and fire departments. She unbuckled the straps that would fit around his shoulders and helped him into it.

"As long as the air-traffic police don't spot you, you'll be all right," she said, tightening the straps upon him. "Head for the rooftop of that building opposite."

The sound of one of the French doors opening made them both turn. It flew open, smashing against one of the tables, and two men catapulted onto the terrace, drawing guns from their jackets.

Paul did not hesitate. With one sweep of his powerful arm he snatched up the table alongside and threw it, as if it had been a balsawood mock-up of itself, at the two charging men.

They dodged, but not quickly enough. They went down before it. And Paul, sweeping Kantele up in his grasp, took one long step to the top of the parapet, and another off into sixty levels of emptiness.

Chapter 9

They fell like a stone, while Paul's hand, restricted by the fact that his arm must keep its hold on Kantele, fumbled with the controls of the parachute copter. He located them finally and switched them on, and suddenly it was like a heavy brake being applied against the force of gravity as the spinning blades blurred into action to break their fall.

"I'm sorry," he said to Kantele. "But they'd seen you with me. I couldn't leave you behind to face the music."

She did not answer. Her head lay back and sideways against his shoulder and her eyes were closed. Her face was like the face of someone who has surrendered completely to some superior force.

Paul turned his attention to guiding the copter toward the building across the concourse from the hotel. He was only partially successful. The copter, powerful enough to handle a two-hundred-and-fifty-pound individual, was fighting a losing battle in trying to uphold the combined weights of a man and woman both well above the average in size. They were drifting off and down at a long slant, the way the winged seed of a maple tree flutters to earth in fall winds.

"The rooftop, you said?" asked Paul. Her eyes remained closed. He joggled her a little. "Kantele!"

She opened her eyes, slowly.

"Yes," she said. "What's that noise?"

There were faint, piping noises around them. Looking back over his shoulder, Paul saw the two men he had bowled over with the table, leaning on the parapet with their forearms, almost casually. But the fists of both held dark objects. They were shooting at Paul and Kantele.

The anesthetic slivers of metal which were the missiles of their weapons could not be too accurate at the present and steadily increasing range. Air police were the greater danger. Paul fingered the controls and they rotated slowly through a hundred-and-eighty-degree angle.

To the north of them and about five hundred feet up, were two specks approaching rapidly. Kantele saw them as Paul did, but she said nothing.

"And after we land on the roof, what?" asked Paul. He looked down into her face. She had closed her eyes again.

"Jase is waiting, on the floor below." She answered almost dreamily, and her head was back against his shoulder again.

"The floor below?" Paul was puzzled and nearly provoked by her. She seemed to have given the matter completely over into his hands. "We haven't time for the roof. I'll try for a window."

"If he has it open," she said dreamily, without opening her eyes.

He understood what she meant. They were falling swiftly, even though at a slant. If Jason Warren did not see them coming and get the window open in time, they would most certainly smash themselves against the unbreakable glass, bending their copter blades and ending in an unchecked drop to the traffic level thirty or forty stories below. There would be no hope for them.

"He'll have it open," said Paul. She did not disagree.

The police cars were swelling in size visibly with the swiftness of their approach. But the building before them was close now, too. Looking down, Paul suddenly saw one of the top level's larger windows slide back.

He angled the copter toward it.

For a moment he thought that he would be falling too rapidly to make it over the open sill. Then it leaped up before him. He jammed the controls on to full braking power, ready to burn the copter's small motor out now that it had served its purpose.

The last burst of effort from the device saved them. The copter shot them through the window, checked itself in the midst of its own suddenly enclosed hurricane, and froze its bearings with an ear-splitting screech. Paul and Kantele dropped less than three inches to land on their feet, upright upon an office floor.

The hurricane with its floating documents and light objects blew itself suddenly out, and the Necromancer came toward the two of them from a far corner of the room. Kantele opened her eyes and looked about her; then, suddenly stiffening, pushed herself almost violently away from Paul and, turning her back, walked several steps from him until a desk blocked her path. Paul looked after her, frowning.

"Get that copter off," said Warren. But Paul was already shrugging out of the straps. The piece of ruined equipment fell heavily to the floor.

"Well, Jase?" asked Paul. The minute he had said it the name sounded oddly on his tongue. For the first time he realized that he had always thought of the Necromancer in terms of his last name. That he had called him by the name everybody else who knew him used, was like cracking a barrier. He saw the other man glance at him for a moment, oddly.

"We're located, now," said the man called Jase. "We're probably surrounded already. We'll have to take another way out with you."

"Why bother?" asked Paul. Jase looked at him again, oddly.

"We take care of our own people, of course," Jase said.

"Am I one?" asked Paul.

The Necromancer stopped dead and looked at him.

"Don't you want to be?" he asked. He nodded toward

the door of the office. He added, dryly, "If you want to walk out there, I won't stop you."

"No," said Paul, and to his own surprise found himself smiling a little sadly, "no, I'm one of you, all right."

"Good." Jase turned briskly to a desk and swept it clean of papers, desk pad, and office instruments. "Shut the window," he said, and Kantele went across the room to it. As the window closed, Jase lifted a brief case from below the table and opened it.

He took from the brief case a large, hooded, black cloak which, when he put it on and pulled the hood over his head, covered him almost completely. In the shadow of the hood his face lost something of its identity. Kantele had come back to the table. He took also from the brief case what looked like three good-sized cones of incense, and lighted them. They immediately began to pour forth a dense, heavy smoke which quickly started to obscure the room. The smoke, to Paul's senses, had a sweet, almost cloying smell and evidently something narcotic about it, for he felt himself getting light-headed with the first few inhalations.

They were all standing close around the desk. The room was a fog of dark smoke now, in which Paul's drugged senses were already having difficulty focusing on nearby objects. Across the desk from him the Necromancer's voice came suddenly, deeper-toned than ordinary, measured, chanting. . . .

"This ae nighte, this ae nighte, everie night and alle . . ."

Kantele's voice, from another quarter of the table, chimed in. And what had been pure doggerel recital from Jase's lips acquired a touch of music with the addition of her voice.

"Fire and sleete and candlelight, destruction take thee alle."

The Necromancer produced one more item and put it on the desk. At the sight of it Paul's mind went suddenly white with an awareness of danger. He would have been a poor sort of mining engineer not to have recognized it. What Jase had just put on the table was a cotton block of blasting jelly two inches on a side, enough to reduce the office and everyone within it to uncollectable fragments. It was topped with no more than a ninety-second fuse, and as Paul peered through the gathering smoke, the Necromancer pinched the fuse and started it burning.

Jase chanted alone:

"If from hence away thou'rt past"

And Kantele's voice joined him in chorus:

"Everie nighte and alle . . ."

"To Whinny-muir thou comest at last," Jase chanted alone.

"Destruction take thee alle." Kantele joined again.

He should not have recognized what they were chanting, but it happened that Paul did. From where or how it came to him, he could not in that smoke-fogged moment remember. But it was a somewhat changed version of one of the old north-of-England corpse chants, sung at wakes with the corpse under the table and a dish of salt on its breast. It was a ritual with its roots going back beyond Christianity to the ancient Celts, to a time when small dark men crept together in the forests to sing their dead kinsman on his road of shadows, in the first nights after his departure. And the version Paul heard now had none of the solemn music of its seventeenth-century shape, but was nearly back to the harsh atonal chant of the original primitive, cold as winter stones and unsparing as the wind across them. On it went, with Jase speaking alone and then Kantele joining in the chorus. It was a "lyke-wake dirge":

"If ever thou gavest roof and flame,
  Everie nighte and alle . . .
Pass thee by the standing stane,
  Destruction take thee alle.

"The standing stane, when thou art past,
Everie nighte and alle . . .
To empty airt thou comest fast,
Destruction take thee alle.

"If ever thou feddest fish or fowl,
Everie nighte and . . ."

Distantly, through the chanting and the swirling smoke, came the sound of a loud-speaker from beyond the closed window.

"Formain! Paul Formain! This is the police. We have you completely surrounded. If you do not come out within two minutes, and those with you, we will force an entrance." There was a momentary pause, and then the speaker once more rattled the window. "Formain! Paul Formain. This is the police. We have you. . . ."

Meanwhile, in the office the smoke was now so thick that even the cotton block of blasting jelly and its rapidly diminishing fuse was hidden from Paul's eyes. He seemed to hear the chanting of Jase and Kantele mounting in volume:

"From empty airt when thou'rt past
Everie nighte and alle . . .
To Alleman's Ende thou comest at last,
Destruction take thee alle."

Something was happening now. The fuse was shortening fast. A pressure was building up about the three of them and the desk between them. Paul felt a sudden deep-moving urge to join with Kantele in the chorus of the chant. He heard the fuse fizzing. A part of him shouted that in seconds he would be blown to pieces. But another part watched, detached and curious, and checked the chant in him before it reached his lips.

"And if thou holdest to any thinge
Everie nighte and alle . . .

79

The Ende thou canst not enter in,
Destruction take thee alle."

Jase's and Kantele's voices were all around Paul now, like a loop of rope holding them all together and drawing tighter. The fuse must be all burned down now.

"But if thou guardest nae thing at all,
Everie nighte and alle . . .
To Alleman's Ende thou'lt passe and falle
And Destruction'll take thee alle!"

Suddenly, Jase and Kantele were gone, and almost in the same fraction of a second the world lighted up around Paul and he felt the sudden slam of enormous pressure against him, as if he were a fly clapped between two giant hands. He was aware, for one tiny moment of perception, of the office flying to pieces around him as the blasting jelly exploded, and then he himself seemed to fly off into nothingness.

Book Two: SET

By stony staircase, hall, and pier,
Those shadows mazed around me there,
Wove doubt on doubt, and—fools!—broke out
That part in me that feared no doubt.

The Enchanted Tower

Chapter 10

With the situation fully and correctly understood, it becomes entirely reasonable that the very small fraction of a second preceding a violent death could be a trigger to speculative thought.

Ninety-three years after Paul was caught by the explosion of the block of blasting jelly, the phenomenon of *no-time*—that is, of a state of existence in which time is lacking—was finally and fully explained. It had been made use of, of course, even by people preceding the Chantry Guild. On a hit-and-miss basis. But with the development of the phase-shift form of transportation that permitted the interstellar expansion of the human race, it became necessary to understand the a-time state which was basic to the phase shift. Briefly and crudely, the explanation was that there is a reciprocal relationship between time and position. And if time becomes nonexistent (perhaps *nonoperative* would be a better word) then the choice of position becomes infinite.

There are, of course, practical difficulties limiting the use of this, which arise when the problem of exactly calculating the desired position arises. But that has been explained in a different place.* Once more, in the future and again in a different place, the problem of no-time will be entered into once again when the philosophical

*Dorsai!—Commander-in-Chief II

82

aspects of it become relevant. But for now, to return once more to the historical moment of the exploding blasting-jelly cube, the important thing is that for vulgar practical purposes, no-time can be taken merely to mean sufficient, uncounted time.

No one—literally, *no one*—is immune to error. It had been an error for Paul to linger behind Jase and Kantele in their departure and be caught by the first edge of the explosion. Having been caught, there was only one way out. He went instinctively into no-time to escape being destroyed, as lesser individuals have done before him. Nearly everyone has heard of the authenticated instance of the man who walked around the horses of his coach into nonexistence, and there are many others.

In no-time he remained conscious, and was triggered into a sudden awareness that since the original boating accident, at no time had he ever been without some element of awareness. Even his sleep had been given over either to periods of asymbolic thought on the subconscious level or to dreams. And his dreams, in fact, seemed a fine mill in the complex of his mental machinery. A mill which took the results of the crude data that had been mined from the solid substances of his daytime surroundings by the tools of his senses, then rough-crushed by the intellectual upper processes of his intelligence, and now were ground to fine powders and begun on the obscurer process that would separate out the pure valuable elements of comprehension.

Other than this he did not approach any letting go of his awareness. It had occurred to him that this might be the basic cause of his unyielding refusal to accept hypnosis. But this explanation failed to completely satisfy him in that area of his perception in which he was most sensitive—it did not *feel* like the complete answer. If the recognizable processes by which he attempted to understand and control his environment could be compared to the mechanical, this last could be best compared to something chemical. And this was so powerful and effective a tool in its own way that for practical purposes it blinded him to the common channels of reasoning. It was extremely difficult for him to add two and two and get four. It was exceedingly simple and natural for him to contemplate two by itself, as an isolated element, and find four as an implied, characteristic possibility of it.

He looked out on all existence through a window that revealed only unique elements. He approached everything in terms of isolates. Isolates and their implied possibilities of characteristics. All time, for example, was implied in any single moment that he might choose to examine. But the moment itself was unique and unalterably separated from any other moment, even though the other moment also implied all of time.

It followed that it was almost impossible for him to be tricked or lied to. Any falsity palmed off on him almost immediately collapsed like fraudulently understrength construction under the natural weight of its own proliferating possibilities. It also followed, and this was not always an advantage, that he was almost impossible to surprise. Any turn of events, being implied in the moment preceding its taking place, seemed perfectly natural to him. As a result he did not question a great many things that he might normally have been expected to question.

He had not, therefore, questioned the abilities the Chantry members seemed to claim for themselves. It had seemed—to this part of him, at least—quite reasonable that Jase and Kantele should attempt to make their escape with him by means of narcotic smoke, archaic corpse chant, and a block of blasting jelly with a short fuse. He had, however, allowed himself to get so interested in what was going on that he found himself left behind and caught in the first microsecond of the explosion.

He was driven out to the very edges of his consciousness, but no farther. He was aware of himself moving very swiftly and at the same time being driven by the explosion away down into the impossibly tiny end of something like an enormous funnel. He flew through this into all but complete unconsciousness, fighting for survival. He was an infinity of fathoms deep in darkness, but somewhere above him was light and life.

He came up, fighting.

His mind was quicker to react to full consciousness again than his body. He woke to find himself plunging clear across some sort of small, bare room with a circular, raised stage in the center of it, and carrying four men along with him as they attempted to restrain him. He was headed for the door to the room.

He checked, understanding. And, after a second, the men holding on to him let go. As they cleared away from in front of him, Paul caught sight of himself in the mirror surface of a far wall. His clothes were torn, apparently by the explosion, and his nose was bleeding slightly. He got a handkerchief tissue from his pocket and wiped the blood away from his upper lip. The nose stopped bleeding. Jase and Kantele watched him from across the room.

"I don't understand this," said one of the men who had been holding him, a small, brisk-looking man with a shock of brown hair over a sharp-featured face. He looked at Paul almost challengingly. "How did you get here? If Jase brought you, why didn't you come with Jase?"

Paul frowned.

"I seem to have been a little slow," he said.

"Never mind," spoke up Jase from across the room. "If you're all right now, Paul, come on."

He led the way out of the room, Kantele following with a momentary, troubled glance in Paul's direction. Paul went after them.

He caught up with them in a hall outside the room. It was a blank wall without windows, and it led them up an incline until they stepped suddenly around a corner and emerged into open air. Paul looked curiously around himself. They had emerged onto a vast field spotted with the raised white concrete pads from which space-going vehicles fitted with their great collars of lifting equipment took off. Beyond were the snow-topped peaks of a mountain range Paul did not recognize.

It was no commercial field. The uniformity of the constructions about the field and the khaki coveralls of the personnel about spoke clearly to the effect that this was a government installation.

"Where are we?" asked Paul. But Jase was already striding away with Kantele to a pad occupied by the squat, almost bulbous shape of an outer-space vessel looking like an ancient artillery shell many times enlarged, and fitted with its spreading soup-plate collar of atmosphere engines, ducted fans in the outer ring, ramjets in toward the center. Paul caught up with Jase and Kantele.

"Where are we?" he asked again.

"Tell you after we're aboard," said Jase economically. They walked along together, Jase staring straight ahead toward the ship, his face like a knife edge, Kantele with her wordless gaze down and ahead, so that she looked at the treated gravel surface of the field on which no green grew, just before her as she walked. Paul felt a sudden small rush of sorrow that human beings should be so locked away and separate in their body and mind, so bound to different wheels. And, with a sudden soundless shock, it occurred to him that out of all the real universe the one class of isolates who strove and threatened to burst the bounds of their separateness was people.

This realization, simple as it appeared in bald statement, exploded in Paul like a pan of flash powder set off before a man in a vast and complex city, standing lightless under the stars. It blinded, rather than illuminated, but its light left an afterimage printed on the retinas of the explorer in the dark, and would be permanently remembered. With his mind washed clean of other matters for the moment, Paul walked automatically into the base tunnel of the take-off pad, rode the elevator up through pad and collar, and paid little attention to anything until the whine of the outer ring of fans began to impinge on his consciousness. He came back to present awareness to see that he was seated in a convertible acceleration couch-chair, in a passenger compartment of the ship. In front of him he could see the black top of Jase's head just showing above the top cushion of the next couch-chair, and across the aisle from Jase, up against the rounded wall enclosing the elevator-tunnel running up the center of the ship, he saw the profile of Kantele.

The ship lifted. After a little the sound of the fans was drowned out in the beginning thunder of the jets, which mounted the ladder of volume into silence. A little after that, the viewing tank in the wall beside Paul lighted up, and, looking into this illusion of a window, he saw the lifting collar of atmosphere engines, their earth-bound clumsiness all left behind, fall away gracefully like some enormous soaring bird toward the cloud-laced earth far below.

"Couchback, all passengers," announced a speaker system somewhere above Paul's head. "All passengers, couchback now."

The chairs tilted and leveled into horizontal position. Deep cushioning buffers moved in about his body. There was a moment of silence and then the space engines fired, and their mighty thrust threw the blunt body of the ship, with Kantele, and Jase, and Paul, and all within it, out between the stars.

Mercury, Paul discovered, was a five-day run. The ship had four cross levels between the pilot room in the nose and the engines in the rear. The passengers were restricted to two of them. Evidently because it was government procedure, they were required to take mild sedatives during the actual flight. These made Kantele and three other passengers whom Paul did not know sleepy. They spent most of their time dozing with their couch-chairs in a reclining position. Jase had disappeared early up into the crew's section and Paul had not seen him after that for the first four days of the run. Since Kantele seemed to reinforce the effect of her sedatives with an obvious disinclination to have anything to do with Paul, once more that left Paul solitary.

To Paul's unusual set of mental and physical reactions, the sedatives brought a bodily lethargy, but an increase in mental speculation and introspection. Jase had escaped early before Paul could question him again, but a tall, stiff-backed man, in the seat behind Paul and across the aisle which with the two rows of seats circled the central elevator shaft, had replied to Paul's question.

"Operation Springboard," he had said sharply. He stared almost fiercely at Paul out of middle-aged eyes above a neat white mustache that contrasted with the brown tan of his face. "You know about the project to reach the Arcturian planets, don't you? Apprentice, are you?"

"Yes," said Paul.

"Ask your master, boy! He'll answer you. Who is he? Necromancer Warren?"

Secretly a little amused to be addressed as "boy," a term he had not had used to him since he was fourteen, Paul nodded.

"That's right," he said. "Do you happen to be a Necromancer, too?"

"No, no," said the man. "Sociologist—what they call 'untitled.' Don't have the patience for the rigmarole. But it's fine work for a younger man like yourself to get into." He grew fiercer, suddenly. The white mustache seemed to bristle. "A good work!"

"Necromancy?" asked Paul.

"All of it. All of it. Think of our children . . . and their children."

A man of about the same age as the white-mustached speaker leaned out of a couch-chair farther back on Paul's side of the circular aisle.

"Heber," he said.

"Yes, yes," said the white-mustached man, sinking

back into his seat. "You're right, Tom. Don't ask me questions, boy; ask your master. I've got to take my medication now, anyway." He reached into the little compartment in one arm of his chair, and Paul, giving up that avenue of information, turned and sat back in his own place.

He had plenty to occupy his mind. He let his attention go free among it.

It was a type of mental activity having its own element of actual built-in pleasure reward, a pleasure to which, he had lately come to realize, it would be quite possible to become addicted, if it were not for the fact that the basic drive to accomplish forbade too much loitering on the pathway from means to end. It was the sheer pleasure of turning the questioning spirit loose in the great dark city of all personal knowledge. For those who panicked easily in the dark, it was no occupation. But for those without fear and the true night-sight of understanding, there was no pleasure like that of wandering some strange and intricate part of that city, until out of shadow rose shapes, and out of shapes, plan, and out of plan—original purpose. Only then, at last with original purpose encompassed and understood, came— perhaps—the greater occupation of putting that knowledge to work in new building.

So for five days Paul all but lost himself in a new part of his city of knowledge. It was only shortly before landing on Mercury that he was abruptly called back from it, and the one who called him back was Kantele.

"I wasn't going to ask you why," she said. He awoke to the fact that she was standing in the aisle before his seat, looking down at him. "But I just can't. . . . Why did you do it? Why did you have to kill Malorn?"

"Kill who?" asked Paul. For a second she and her question was still mixed in with the shapes of his thoughts. Then the shapes faded and he became aware that they were, at least as far as he could see on this side of the elevator shaft, alone on the level among the couch-chairs.

"Kevin Malorn—the man at the hotel."

"Kevin Malorn," echoed Paul. For a part of a second the only thing that was in his mind was a feeling of un-utterable sadness that he should have been the instrument of the man's death and never until now known the name under which other people had known him alive.

"You won't tell me," said Kantele, when he did not answer immediately. He looked up at her pale, set face.

"Yes," he said. "But you probably won't believe me. I didn't kill him. I don't know why he died."

She stared at him for a moment longer, then whirled about and walked off around the elevator tube. Following a little later, he discovered all the other passengers one level up in the lounge, watching in the large tank there the ascent of the landing collar, with chemical engines fueled by native Mercury products, that would carry them safely down to that planet's surface.

Chapter 11

It was a strange tumbled landscape through which they all walked the half mile from the ship to the reception dome of Station Springboard. The sky was white to the right and dark to the left, and cloudless. There was enough of an atmosphere here on the surface of Mercury's twilight zone to scatter the light in this direction. The resulting illumination seen through the face windows of Paul's protective suit was like the yellow glare before a thunderstorm back under the kinder sky of Earth. In this all-pervasive, unchanging light, the terrain appeared to be peopled with the split and damaged fragments of fantastic sculptures. It would be the temperature changes of alternating dark-side and light-side storms that had caused this, and the volcanic action along the line of weakness in Mercury's crust that the Twilight Zone represented. But still it looked like a country out of a dream of unreality, a garden out of a nightmare, set up and despoiled by witches.

They entered the dome and stepped through a lock into an elevator which sank for a quite noticeable distance. Paul guessed that he might now be in the neighborhood of forty to sixty levels underground, for the elevator had been a large mechanical, rather than magnetic, one, and the descent had been uncomfortably swift. As the elevator halted, a further door opened and they passed into a desuiting room.

From the desuiting room they were herded into separate cubicles for what Jase informed Paul were purposes of decontamination. Paul found himself instructed by a wall speaker to strip, pass through a shower area, and a further door where new clothes for him would be waiting.

He did so and came out into another cubicle, this one not much more than an area hacked out of the solid granitic rock. On a concrete bench there a pile of clothing was waiting for him.

He set about putting it on and found it to be of a peculiar style. There were soft leather shoes, pointed at the toe, fawn-colored; what seemed to be long green stockings; shorts; a green smock with a loose belt to cinch it up, and a sort of half-sleeved leather jacket.

It seemed likely to Paul that the Chantry Guild was given to dressing for dinner, so to speak, here on Mercury. He put the clothes on—the left arm of smock and jacket had been designed sleeveless and all the clothes were in his size—and stepped through the further door of the second cubicle.

He checked instinctively.

He had emerged into a single, low-ceilinged room, crudely hollowed out of the rock and lighted by two flaring torches in heavy wall brackets of some metal-like blackened iron. The floor itself was roughhewed of rock and pressed hard against the soles of his feet through the soft leather of his shoes. Beyond the torches was darkness and he could see no far wall.

He turned quickly, back the way he had come. And stopped. There was no door behind him, through where he had stepped a minute before. He faced more of the hewn-rock wall, only that. He reached out and touched it with his hand. It felt as solid as judgment day.

He turned back to the light of the torches. Between them now, he saw standing the man called Heber, the torchlight sparkling on his white mustache. Unlike Paul, he was clothed in a single scarlet robe and hood. The hood threw a shadow across his forehead and the long sleeves of the robe fell together from his hands, which were joined together before him.

"Come here," said Heber. His lips trembled a second after the last word, as if he could just barely restrain himself from adding "boy!" Paul walked up to him and stopped. Heber was looking past him, the older man's shadowed eyes seeming fantastically deep-socketed in the shadow of the hood.

"I am here to sponsor this apprentice," announced Heber, "to his initiation into the Société Chanterie. It is required that there be two sponsors, one visible and one invisible. Is the other sponsor here?"

"I am," said the voice of Jason Warren, startlingly at Paul's right ear. He turned and saw nothing but the walls of the room. But he could now feel the presence of Jase beside him.

Paul turned back to Heber. The white-mustached man, he saw, was now holding in one arm a heavy, leather-bound, archaic-looking book. In the other hand he held by the middle a snake about four feet in length, which twisted and writhed.

"To the jurisdiction of the Alternate Laws you have come," said Heber. "To the jurisdiction of the Alternate Laws are you now committed and sealed. And to the jurisdiction of the Alternate Laws will you be bound, for all time past or present, and beyond time until the Alternate Laws cease their effect."

"I witness this," said the voice of Jason, at Paul's shoulder.

"Take then your spear," said Heber. He held out the snake toward Paul's single hand. Paul reached for it, but at the first touch of his fingers around it, it ceased suddenly to move and live. He found himself holding, in fact, a tall wooden spear with a dully gleaming metal point.

"Take then your shield," said Heber, stepping forward with the book. But it was a kite-shaped metal shield, with leather grips riveted to a wooden frame, that he hung from Paul's armless left shoulder by a wide leather strap.

"Now follow me," said Heber. He strode off into the darkness beyond the torches. And Paul, following after, found himself proceeding down slanted tunnels and around corners in the rock until he came finally to a small, square, carved-out room where two more torches burned on either side of what looked like a stone altar, more long than wide. Along the top of the altar were laid out, from left to right, a small toy sailboat with the tiny figure of the toy sailor within it spilled out as the boat lay over on one side, a toy model of the console of a mine, a stained and weathered conch shell, and a three-dimensional snapshot of the head of Malorn, the dead drug addict, showing the broken skull.

Heber and Paul stopped before the altar.

"Let the other sponsor now instruct the apprentice," he said. Jase's voice spoke from Paul's other side. He looked at empty air.

"The apprentice is an apprentice in the art of Necromancy," his voice said. "Therefore we have brought him to the root of the tree. Let the apprentice look."

Paul turned his attention back to the altar. A massive tree root now emerged from the rock and arched out over the objects on the altar, down to his feet and Heber's.

"This," said the voice of Jase, "is the well Hvergelmer, in the realm of death. The root is the first root of the ash, Yggdrasil, which is the tree of life, knowledge, fate, time, and space. During the period of his vigil here, it is the duty of the apprentice to defend it, and the parts of his life which are on the altar. It may be that the apprentice will not be attacked during his time of vigil. But it may be that the dragon Nidhug and his brood will come to gnaw at the root of the tree. If the tree and the parts of his life are attacked, the apprentice may call on the Alternate Forces or not, as he chooses; but if he does not conquer Nidhug, Nidhug will devour him."

Jase ceased speaking. Heber spoke, and Paul turned his head to the white-mustached man.

"The tree," said Heber solemnly, "is an illusion. Life is an illusion. Nidhug and his brood are an illusion, as is all the universe, eternity, and time. Only the Alternate Forces exist, and time, space, and all things within them are merely toys of the Alternate Forces. Know this and know yourself unconquerable."

"You shall keep vigil," put in the sound of the Necromancer's voice, "until the third sounding of the gong. With the third sounding of the gong, you will be freed from the realm of death, back to the world of light and life once more. Now I leave you, until the third ringing of the gong."

Paul felt a void suddenly beside him. He turned instinctively toward Heber. The white-mustached man was still standing beside him.

"I leave now, too," said Heber. "Until the gong rings for the third time." He stepped past Paul, back toward the entrance to the room; and as he did, Paul caught the ghost of a wink from the man's near eye, and a *sotto voce* mutter, "Rigmarole."

Then Heber was gone.

Silence held the room.

It was the silence of the rock where the rock is igneous in nature and far below ground. Here there was no water dripping, only the still cold. Even the torches flared in silence. Paul's breath went out in a frosty plume in that red, dancing light, and vanished with each fresh inhalation.

But he began to become aware.

About him was stone, the mineral flesh of Mercury, in all directions. The rough, cut stone underfoot pressed sharply against his feet, the cold wrapped him like a chilly cloak. The minutes passed in solemn procession, all but identical one with the other. Time piled up in the quiet of the room, the strap of the shield cut into his shoulder and his fingers grew a little cramped around the wooden shaft of the spear. He held it with its butt on the floor, its point elevated, angled a little out from him like a Roman sentry. An hour went by, and then another. And then, perhaps, another. . . .

The solemn, brassy note of a deep gong struck once, reverberated through the entrance to the room, and beat about his ears. It rang away into silence, leaving a memory behind it in the noiselessness of the room until that, too, was buried and smoothed over by the marching minutes.

Paul's mind drifted out to an unconscionable distance. He leaned on his spear, now, and the shield had swung forward with its own weight. He thought of mountains whose stony sides and slopes were constructed of empty space, and of the twinkling illuminations of distant habitations upon the mountain peaks, which were the lights of the farther stars, stars not seen from Earth. A bittersweet emotion of sorrow and desire stirred in him like faint smoke from burning incense. Love and hunger pulled against each other within him. . . .

And then suddenly, distant in the back of his mind, came a chime of warning.

He came back to the stony room. It was as it had been before. The torches still flared upward and his breath smoked peacefully on the still air. But now there was something more. While he had daydreamed, the deep waters of some unseen danger had welled up to the very entrance of the room. It lapped now in the darkness just beyond the reach of his sight. And in those deep waters, there was something stirring.

It was Nidhug and his scaly brood.

They were not real. They were an illusion, as was the deep mass of waters making a beleaguered island of this room. Paul recognized this with a sure and certain swiftness. Those minds among the Chantry Guild who were capable of such tricks were flooding the solid (but to these productions of their minds, transparent) rock with the emanations of fear, pictured as heavy, secret waters. And through the fear, in the guise of a monstrous, scaly

96

worm and its litter, they were now lifting the image of self-doubt. These things were fantasies, but nonetheless dangerous. Fear can be a deadly danger to the mind, and self-doubt can cause an organism to destroy itself, as Paul knew. Knowledge could be a shield and wisdom a weapon, but it took something uniquely human to use them.

He braced himself. The rising tide of fear was already flooding into the room. If he allowed his senses to yield to the fantasy, he could see it, like a gray, quicksilver tide, pushing its sullen rivulets into this and that small indentation in the rough floor. Nidhug and his children were very close.

The gong rang for a second time.

The waters crested suddenly, swirling into the room. They mounted up to his knees, surged to his waist, and in seconds eddied about his throat. They swelled over his head. And touched the ceiling. The room was drowned.

One massive body length below the unblocked opening of the room, Nidhug gave his final surge of approach. He lifted like a demon out of darkness, and a second later his hideous mask blocked the entrance to the room.

Leveling his spear, hunching his shoulder behind the shield, Paul went to meet him. As in a nightmare, the heavy waters of fear slowed his thrust to a dreamlike slowness. The point of his spear slid deliberately through the impending medium and glanced off the tortured dragon-face.

But the overdeveloped muscles of Paul's arm, like what they represented in Paul himself, were something more than ordinary strength. The spear point, glancing off, dug a deep furrow from the twisted jaw to the staring eyes, and a flood of deep, luminescent, reddish blood stained and clouded the atmosphere of the room.

In this murk the battle became obscure. It became drearily a matter of Paul's thrusting back what came at him again and again. Gradually there broke on him the understanding that this was a contest that he perpetuated by the very act of fighting in it. The way to victory here was to deny the enemy. He laughed.

He threw away both shield and spear.

Like an express train, Nidhug leaped upon him. Paul stood still. And the gaping jaws, monstrous before him, closed as if on the invisible substance of an inch-thick wall between them. And the creature vanished.

The waters began to slowly ebb from the room. Far away the first shivering sounds of the third striking of the gong reached out to Paul's ears.

And in that moment, that tiny piece of a second, with the dragon vanished and the waters failing, something real and deadly reached through and struck.

It came from a distance to which the distance to the farthest stars was like a step to a long day's journey. It came with a speed beside which the speed even of thought was too slow to be measurable. It came along the dark and cobbled road of which Paul had dreamed on returning to the hotel after he had first seen Jase. It was blind and young and not yet fully formed, but it recognized its still-unarmored foe by sure instinct. And it struck.

It brought Paul to his knees as a giant might strike down a baby with a sword of steel—but it clashed like steel on steel against his invincible self behind. For a moment the forces hung together, and then the crest wave of the sounding gong finished closing the door through which the unknown had reached for a microsecond, for almost no time at all. And Paul knelt, free, but numb and blinded on the hard rock floor.

Paul's sight returned to show him the white ceiling of a room above the cot on which he lay. He was vaguely aware that they had carried him here.

Jase's face loomed over him. It was as keenly honed as ever, but there was a touch of friendliness there Paul had not seen before. Beside him was the white-mustached face of Heber showing concern.

"Quite a reaction you had there," said Jase, "after it

98

was all over. We didn't expect to see you go down like that."

Paul focused on the Necromancer.

"You didn't?" he said. He frowned. "You certainly didn't expect me to stay on my feet?"

It was Jase's turn to frown, slightly.

"Why not?" he said. "If you'd stood up to things while it was going on, why collapse after it's all over?"

Paul faced it then. Jase and the other watchers had remained unaware. He closed his eyes wearily and a little bitterly, for he felt the beginnings of some sort of understanding seep into him at last; and understanding, he was discovering, like money, does not always bring happiness.

"Of course. Why not?" he agreed. "You must be right. I'm still suffering from the reaction."

Chapter 12

Dressed in ordinary jacket and slacks, one week later Paul sat with three other journeymen Chantry Guild members in a conference room of the orthodox part of Station Springboard. Talking to them was a brisk athletic young man with a short haircut and no older than Paul. Younger, in fact, than two of the journeymen, who looked disconcertingly like overfed salesmen in their thirties, except that one, who smelled strongly of after-shaving lotion, was twice as tall as the other.

"You can't *teach* the Alternate Laws," the instructor had begun by saying, as he half-perched on the edge of a table, facing the low, comfortable chairs in which the four sat. "Any more than you can *teach* the essential ability to create art, or the essential conviction of a religious belief. Does that make sense to you?"

"Ah, teaching!" said the fourth member of the journeymen group, a pleasant-faced, brown-headed young man, in an entirely unexpected, bell-toned bass. "What crimes have been committed in thy name!"

Since he had not spoken previously, the rest—even including the instructor—appeared somewhat startled, not only by his pronouncement, but by the volume and timbre of it. The young man smiled at them.

"True enough," said the instructor, after a slight pause. "And very true to the Alternate Laws. Let's simplify the Laws to a ridiculous extreme and say that the point they express is that as a rule of thumb, if it works best one way for everybody else, chances are that way won't be the best for you. In other words, if you want to get to the top of a mountain and you see a broad, well-marked, much-traveled road headed straight for it, the last route you should choose to the top of the mountain would be up that road."

He stopped talking. They all looked at him expectantly.

"No," he said, "I'm not going to tell you why. That would be teaching. Teaching is good only for learners, not for discoverers. Right now is the one and only time in the Chantry Guild that you're going to encounter anything like a question-and-answer period." He looked them over. "You're at liberty to try and tell *me* why, if you want to."

"Ah," said the large salesman sort with the shaving-lotion smell. He got the interjection out hurriedly, and it was at once noticeable to all his audience that his voice, though loud and determined, was neither bass nor bell-toned. "I—ah—understand that the Alternate Laws are parapsychological in nature. Can it be that involvement with the ordinary, that is to say—ah—scientific, laws has an inhibiting effect upon the person's—I mean the different sort of person who is able to take advantage of the powers of the Alternate Forces?" He drew a quick breath and added quickly, "I mean, his essential difference, so to speak?"

"No," said the instructor, kindly.

"No? Oh," said the other. He sat back, cleared his throat, crossed his legs, got out a handkerchief, and blew his nose loudly.

"The area of parapsychology," said the instructor, "is only a small part of the universe of time and space. The Alternate Laws cover all this and more."

"They mean what they say, don't they?" asked the smaller salesman-type unexpectedly. "Alternate Laws— other laws. And the only way to find the other ways is by deliberately avoiding the established way."

"That's right," said the instructor.

"Creative," rang the young man with the bass voice.

"And that's very right," said the instructor. He ran his glance from right to left over them. "None of you here would have got this far if you hadn't each demonstrated some capability in the area of the Alternate Laws. That capability may be parapsychological—say, teleportation. Or it might be an ability to write truly creative poetry, say. It might even be a particular sensitivity to the needs of growing plants. Not that I mean to give you the impression that creativity is all of the Alternate Laws, or even the key to them."

"Ah," said the large salesman, uncrossing his legs determinedly, "you certainly don't expect us just to write poetry or grow plants, or even teleport."

"No," said the instructor.

"Then—ah—can it be that you mean," said the large salesman, perspiration beginning to stand out on his brow, "that these things—whatever they may be—are a part, only a part, of the Alternate Laws? And it's the rest we have to go after? We have to try? We have to get?"

"Yes," said the instructor. "That's very good. It's not a full answer by any means——"

"No, no, of course not," said the large salesman, flushing and smiling, and pulling out his handkerchief. He blew his nose again as if it were a soldier's bugle.

"—a full answer by any means," said the instructor. "In fact, if there is a full answer, I don't know it. Everyone, in this, is on his own. And now," he said, standing up, "I think you've already had enough discussion about an inherently undiscussable subject to last you a lifetime. If indeed we haven't already done the damage of setting up some artificial concepts. Remember"—his whole voice and manner changed abruptly; it was almost as if he had reached out and wrapped some invisible cloak about him—"life is an illusion. Time and space and all things are an illusion. There is nothing, nothing but the Alternate Laws."

He ceased speaking suddenly. The journeymen got up automatically and began to file out. As Paul walked past, however, he felt his arm touched by the instructor.

"Just a minute," the instructor said. Paul turned. The other waited until the three other journeymen were out of the room. "You didn't say anything at all."

"Yes," said Paul. "That's right. I didn't."

"Mind if I ask why?"

"If I remember rightly," Paul said, "the key word of Walter Blunt's book is *destruct.*"

"Yes, it is."

"And we," said Paul, looking down at the instructor from his own greater height, "were talking about creativity."

"Mmm," said the instructor, nodding his head thoughtfully, "I see. You think somebody's lying?"

"No," said Paul. He felt a sudden weariness that was not physical at all. "It's just that there was nothing to say."

The instructor stared at him.

"Now you're the one who's baffling me," the instructor said. "I don't understand you."

"I mean," said Paul patiently, "that it's no use saying anything."

The instructor shook his head again.

"I still don't understand you," he said. "But that's all right." He smiled. "In the Guild it's: To thine own self be true, thou needst not then explain to any man."

He patted Paul on the shoulder.

"Go, man!" he said, and on that note they parted.

Returning to his room, as Jase had warned him to do when not otherwise occupied, Paul passed along the catwalk above the relay room in the orthodox part of the Station. He had only a vague notion of what went on in the three-step accelerator that stretched through nearly a quarter mile of the vast cavern five levels high, with thirty- and forty-foot banks of equipment surrounding its tube shape. From news and magazine accounts he had acquired the general knowledge that its function was a matter of shuttling a point of higher-level energy back and forth along a line of constantly lower energy until the point's speed was just under the speed of light. At which time it "broke" (i.e., disappeared) and became instead a point of no-time, following the same path. This point of no-time, if perfectly synchronized with a point of no-time back in the laboratory building of World Engineer's Headquarters Complex, created a path for instantaneous, timeless transmission between the two points.

Since the point of no-time had universal dimension, it could, by a complicated technical process, be used to transport objects of any size from the primary station on the Earth to the secondary station here on Mercury Station. For some reason there had to be a critical minimum distance between stations—Mars and Venus were too close to Earth. Stations there had been tried and had failed. But theoretically at least, by this method Springboard could have been directly supplied from World Engineer's Complex, with anything it needed. It was not, in practice, because its function on Mercury was to tinker and experiment with its end of the transmission path. Instead, most of the Station's solid needs were met by resolution of materials from Mercury's crust.

It was also not only theoretically possible, but practically possible, to send living creatures including humans by the same route. However, those who tried it flirted with insanity or death from psychic shock, and even if they missed both these eventualities, could never be induced to try it again. Apparently what was experienced by the transmittee was a timeless moment of complete consciousness in which he felt himself spread out to infinite proportions and then recondensed at the receiving end. It did no good to use present known sedatives or anesthetics—these merely seemed to insure a fatal level of shock. Medicine was reported working on a number of drugs that showed some promise, but no immediate hope of discovering a specific was in sight.

Meanwhile drone ships had been started off at sub-light velocities for some of the nearer stars known to have surrounding systems. The ships bore automatic equipment capable of setting up secondary receiving stations on their arrival on some safe planetary base. If and when medicine came through, the transportation setup would be already established.

All of this touched Paul only slightly. He recognized it and passed on, noting only that in passing by and over the equipment, as he was doing now, he received from it an emanation of mild, pleasurable excitement. Like the so-called "electric" feeling in the air before a thunderstorm, which comes not only from an excess of ions, but from the sudden startling contrast of dark and light, from the black thunderheads piling up in one quarter of a clear sky, the mutter and leap of sheet lightning and thunder along the cloud flanks, and the sudden breath and pause of cooler air in little gusts of wind.

He passed on and entered the area of smaller corridors and enclosures. He passed by the double airlock doors of the transparent enclosure that held the swimming pool. With the relative preciousness of water, this had been set up as a closed system independent of the rest of the station and supplied with a certain amount of artificial gravitation for Earth-normal swimming and diving. Kantele was all alone in the pool. As he passed, he saw her go gracefully off the low board. He paused to watch her swim, not seeing him, to the side of the pool just beyond the glass where he stood. She did not look so slim in a bathing suit, and for a moment a deep sensation of loneliness moved him.

He went on, before she could climb out of the pool and see him. When he got to his room there was a notice attached to the door: "Orientation. Room eight, eighteenth level, following lunch, 1330 hours."

Orientation took place in another conference room. The man in charge was in his sixties and looked and acted as if he had been on an academic roster for some time. He sat on a small raised stage and looked down at Paul, the three men who had been with him for the meeting with the instructor on the subject of Alternate Laws, and six other people, of whom one was a young woman just out of her teens, not pretty, but with an amazingly quick and cheerful expression. The man in charge, who introduced himself as Leland Minault, did not begin with a lecture. Instead he invited them to ask him questions.

There was the usual initial pause at this. Then one of the five men Paul had not met before spoke up.

"I don't understand the Chantry Guild's connection with Project Springboard and the Station, here," he said. Leland Minault peered down at the speaker as if through invisible spectacles.

"That," said Minault, "is a statement, not a question."

"All right," said the speaker. "Is the Chantry Guild responsible for Station Springboard, or the work on a means of getting out between the stars?"

"No," said Minault.

"Well then," asked the other, "just what are we doing here, anyway?"

"We are here," said Minault deliberately, folding both hands over a slight potbelly, "because a machine is not a man—beg pardon"—he nodded at the one woman in the group—"human being. A human being, if you bring him, or her, say, to some place like Mercury, to an establishment that seems to be completely at odds with his purpose in being there, will sooner or later get around to asking what the connection is."

He beamed at the man who had spoken.

"Then," Minault went on, "when you give him the answer, it's liable to sink in and promote further thought, instead of merely being filed as a completed explanation. Which is what is likely to happen to it if you just volunteer the information."

There was a general round of smiles.

"All right," said the one who had asked, "any one of

us could have been the patsy. And you still haven't answered me."

"Quite right," said Minault. "Well, the point is that human beings react this way because they have an innate curiosity. A machine—call it a technological monster—may have everything else, but it'll be bound to lack innate curiosity. That is a talent reserved for living beings."

He paused again. Nobody said anything.

"Now our world," Minault said, "is at the present time firmly in the grip of a mechanical monster, whose head —if you want to call it that—is the World Engineer's Complex. That monster is opposed to us and can keep all too good a tab on us through every purchase we make with our credit numbers, every time we use the public transportation or eat a meal or rent a place to live—that is, it can as long as we stay on Earth. The Complex of sustaining equipment at Springboard here is officially a part of the Complex-Major back on Earth. But actually there's no connection beyond the bridge of transportation and communication between these two planets." He smiled at the group.

"So," he went on, "we hide here, under the cloak of Springboard. Actually, we control Springboard. But its work is not our work—it merely serves us as a cover. Of course, we're an open secret to those Springboard workers who aren't Chantry Guild members as well. But a machine, as I say, doesn't react as a human being would. If it doesn't see anything, it simply assumes nothing is there—it doesn't poke and pry into dark corners, because it *might* find enemies."

A hand was up. Turning his head slightly, Paul saw it was the cheerful-looking young woman.

"Yes?" said Minault.

"That doesn't make sense," she said. "The World Engineer's Complex is run by men, not machines."

"Ah," said Minault. "But you're making the assumption that the World Engineer and his staff are in control. They aren't. They are controlled by the physics of the society of our time, which in turn is controlled by the Earth Complex—to give it a convenient name—without which that society couldn't exist."

She frowned.

"You mean"—she wavered a moment on the verge of plunging into the cold waters of the wild statement —"the Complex-Major has *intelligence?*"

"Oh, I'm pretty sure we can say that," replied Minault cheerfully. "Fantastic amounts of knowledge, of course; but a sort of definite rudimentary intelligence as well. But I don't think that's what you meant to ask. What you meant to ask was whether the Complex-Major—Super-Complex, I understand a lot of people have begun calling it lately—has an ego, a conscious identity and personality of its own."

"Well . . . yes," she said.

"I thought so. Well, the answer to that, lady and gentlemen, is astoundingly enough, Yes, it has."

The group in the room, which had settled back to listen to a Socratic dialogue between the young woman and Minault, woke up suddenly and muttered disbelief.

"Oh, not in the human sense, not in the human sense," said Minault, waving them back to calmness. "I don't mean to insult your credulity. But surely you all realize that sooner or later a point of complication had to be reached where a certain amount of elementary reasoning power was necessary to the machine. In fact, why not? It's a very handy thing to have a machine that can reason, and consequently protect itself from falling into its own errors."

"Ah," said Paul's large salesman-type companion from the earlier gathering. "In that case I fail to see—that is, the implied problem was one of control, which we wished to avoid. Wasn't it?"

"I was," said Minault, peering at the large man, "explaining the personality of the Complex-Major."

"Ah, I see," said the large man, sitting back. He blew his nose.

"Your question was a good one," said Minault, "but slightly premature. For the moment, you must understand what I mean by a machine ego. Think of the growing Complexes of computer-directed equipment back on Earth as if they were an animal whose purpose is to take over more and more of the work of keeping mankind alive and well. It grows until it is *the* means by which mankind is kept alive and well; it grows until a certain amount of independent reasoning ability must be built into it, so that it doesn't provide fine weather for California when that action will later on cause hailstorms on the Canadian wheat crop. Given this much of a thinking creature, what's the next evolutionary step?"

"An instinct for self-preservation?" asked the girl quickly, while the large man was clearing his throat preparatory to another "ah."

"Quite right."

"Ah, I should think it would regard human actions not in line with its reasoning—ah—like grit in a smooth-running motor, so to speak?"

"Would it have that much power of imagination?" asked the girl. She and the large man were both looking at Minault, who sat relaxed, peering at them.

"I did not mean actual imagination. Ah—it was an illustration."

"A rather good one," said Minault, as the girl opened her mouth again. "The Complex-Major is a sort of benevolent monster whose only desire is to choke us with a surfeit of service and protection. It has a sort of mechanical intelligence with no specific locus, but an instinct to protect itself and its ability to go on taking over control of human caretaking. And it does regard not only us in the Chantry Guild, but all those whose independence manifests itself in the taking of drugs, joining of cult societies, or any non-machine-planned action, as a sort of grit in its smooth-running motor. A grit that one day must be neatly cleaned out."

He glanced toward the back of his group of auditors.

"Yes?" he asked.

Paul, turning, saw a young, swarthy-skinned man in the back putting his hand back down.

"It seems," said this man, "almost silly to be going to all this trouble just to oppose a pile of equipment, no matter how complicated."

"My dear young friend," said Minault, "we in the Chantry Guild are not opposing a pile of equipment. We're opposing an idea—an idea that has been growing for some hundreds of years—that happiness for the human race consists of wrapping it tighter and tighter in the swaddling bands of a technological civilization." He stood up. "I think that should be enough to chew on for the moment. I suggest you all think the situation over."

He got down from the platform and headed toward the door of the room. His audience rose and also began to move out, and the orderly manner of the room dissolved into a babble of conversation and people slowly swarming out the exit. As Paul pushed his way out the door behind Minault, he caught sight of the girl, who had just buttonholed the large man.

"I think you're quite wrong about the power of imagination you implied to the Complex-Major," she was saying, severely.

Chapter 13

"You've handled explosives before?" asked the lean instructor with the sun-leathered face above the open collar. He was holding a package of plastic, adhesive blasting jelly with a three-minute pinch fuse.

"Yes," said Paul.

Paul stood on one cliff-edge of a remarkably realistic simulation of a mountain gorge some five hundred feet wide, across which had been thrown the thin long web of a temporary snap-to arch bridge of magnesium-alloy sections. The bridge-end by which Paul and the instructor stood, just the two of them, had been anchored in a local timber cradle, or box, filled with loose rock. And the cradle extended its wooden underarms in support about fifteen feet out from the lip of the cliff.

"This amount of jelly," said the instructor, hefting it, "can be carried inconspicuously in a brief case and still leave room for enough other material to make it look as if the brief case is full. It's powerful enough to cut two or three of those timbers or one or two of the metal members you see there. How would you go about completely knocking out this bridge with it?"

Paul looked again at the bridge. In the past nine days since his first class he had been put through a number of *sessions*—that was the only word to describe them. They appeared to be classes, on a strange variety of subjects, some of which appeared to bear no relation to the

111

Chantry Guild. The longest of them had lasted not much more than twenty minutes, and the information imparted by each of them had been obscure. In fact, it had not been quite clear whether the intent of the sessions had been to inform or to test the journeyman audience, which seemed to consist of different individuals from session to session. Paul was privately of the opinion that the intent had been both to inform and test—and probably, as well, to stimulate and confuse. Some of the journeymen, he was sure, were ringers. Some of the sessions had been nonsense.

And this session—himself alone with the instructor, the explosive, and the simulated bridge in the mountains on Earth. Was it instruction, test, nonsense—or something else?

The simulation was a magnificent job. For the scene it pretended to show was clearly an impossibility, here deep under the surface of Mercury's rocky hide. What Paul's eyes saw was a gorge at least eight hundred feet in depth, up from which came the distant sound of a narrow mountain river in its gallop to lower levels. The air was the thin, dry air of high altitudes. The sky was cloudless.

The question was, How much was real and how much false? For if the blasting-jelly block was real, and it was to be set off in the reality of a small underground room of the size Paul had had his sessions in lately, then it would take Alternate Laws indeed to show cause why Paul and the instructor should survive the explosion. Paul laid his hand on the timber cradle and looked over the cliff edge. His gaze plunged away into spray-misted depths. There was distance down there, by any test of his feelings. Just how much, he could not be sure. But it *felt* deep below the cliff. On the other hand, under his hand the materials of the bridge felt solid but deceitful.

"Well," said Paul, "I'm no expert on bridges. But I imagine the trick would be to break this end loose, so that it falls. If this end goes down, it'll tear the other end loose and it'll all drop into the gorge."

"Good enough," said the instructor. "How'd you go about breaking this end loose?"

"I think," said Paul, pointing to where the end of the cradle met a magnesium I-beam, fifteen feet out above the gorge's depth, "if we blew it loose just there, cutting that stringer, or whatever the proper term is, that runs along the left side of the travel-surface of the bridge, the weight of the rest of it would cause it to sag and twist, and tear the other stringer loose. Then this whole end would drop."

"All right." The instructor handed the block of jelly to Paul. "Let's see you do it."

Paul looked at the bridge again. Then he stuffed the block of jelly inside the waistband of his slacks and began to climb out along the timbers of the cradle. The lack of a second arm hampered him but not so much as Paul thought it might have seemed to the instructor. The strength of his remaining arm was such as to lift the weight of his body from angles clearly impossible to an ordinary climber. When he got to the end of the stone enclosing the timbers, Paul paused, ostensibly to rest, but actually to reach some sort of conclusion.

The bridge still felt deceitful. He quietly loosed a splinter from the timber on which he rested, and dropped it. It floated down until he lost sight of it some thirty or forty feet below. So, that much of distance under him at least was real. He looked once more at the spot where he would stick the explosive.

It was at a point just above the single final timber of the supporting cradle. He would have to stand on that timber and place the jelly above the upright at the timber's end, where that upright met the magnesium I-beam. He began to move again. He climbed on up to the I-beam and out onto it until he was above the timber. Hanging to the I-beam, he cautiously let his feet down until they rested on the timber.

Then, as unobtrusively as possible, he increased his

hold on the I-beam and pressed down with both feet on the timber.

There was a sudden screech of tearing wood. The timber ripped away from beneath him, and he dropped suddenly to the length of his arm, and hung there sustained only by his grip on the I-beam. Below him he saw the falling timber on which he would have stood tumbling and shrinking until it vanished suddenly fifty or sixty feet below him. Still hanging, he looked across to the point where the underfoot timber had been joined to the upright by a metal collar held by four thick magnesium rivets.

There were no rivet-hole marks or broken rivet ends in the wood of the upright at all. What was visible was the snapped end of a quarter-inch-diameter wooden dowel rod.

Paul pulled himself easily back up on the I-beam. The bridge stood firm and secure—it had been balanced, evidently, somewhat differently than it appeared to be, on its supports. He climbed back to the instructor, on solid ground, and handed the jelly block back to the man.

"Now what?" Paul said.

"Well," said the instructor, "we'll go up to the front offices. I don't know what your master will say, and of course it's up to him. But as far as I'm concerned, I'd say you've graduated."

They left the simulated scene in the mountains and went out into the Station proper, and took an elevator up a good number of levels. Paul had the impression that they were almost to, if not right at, the surface. And this impression was justified a second or two later when they entered a large lounge-office with, not a vision tank, but an actual window looking out on the yellow twilight and the witches' garden of Mercury's surface around the Station.

Jase was there, along with Heber, the white-mustached unlisted member, and a couple of men Paul did not recognize. The instructor had Paul wait while he went over and talked to the three for a few minutes in a voice too low for Paul to hear. Then Jase came over alone, and the instructor, with the other two men, went over to one of the desks at the other end of the room and began going over what, judging from their quite audible conversation, were the files of journeymen currently undergoing tests.

"Come on over to the window," said Jase. Paul followed him. The slim, dark young man was as relaxed as Paul had ever seen him, though he still walked with the prowling balance of a cat. "Sit down."

Paul sat, in a low, comfortably overstuffed chair. Jase took one opposite.

"To all intents and purposes," said Jase, and his deep-set, clear brown eyes watched Paul closely, "you're a Chantry Guild member now. Before you first came to me, you'd gotten the psychiatric viewpoint on yourself and your missing arm. Now, I'll tell you the true situation from the point of someone like myself who is acquainted with the Alternate Laws."

He stopped.

"—You were going to say something," he said.

"No," said Paul.

"All right," said Jase, "here it is, then. You have an ability under the Alternate Laws which is probably parapsychological in nature. I told you when I first met you —and I've an ability myself where it comes to judging character—something to the effect that your arrogance was astounding."

Paul frowned. He had all but put aside the memory of the Necromancer calling him arrogant. It was the one thing he could not accept about himself.

"I understand now better why you should be so arrogant," Jase was saying. "I've no idea, none of us have in the regular membership, about the possibilities or limitations of your ability. But we've no doubt about its essential nature. Your ability is to make use of the Alternate Laws for purposes of almost total defense. We've done everything but try to kill you outright and without reservation. You've come through beautifully. Tell me, do you think you could explain to me in words just how you came to suspect that bridge timber just a little while ago? I'm not asking you to explain, I'm asking you if you think you *could* explain it to me."

"No," said Paul, slowly. "No, I don't think so."

"We thought as much. Well, what you want to do with your ability from here on out is up to you. I myself think that the reason a grafted arm won't take on your left side there, is because this defensive ability of yours sees some danger to you in an arm graft. If you find what that danger is, maybe you can discover another counter to it, and the next arm you have attached to you will live instead of dying. But, as I say, that's up to you. However, there's something else."

He stopped. There seemed to be almost a touch of indecision in his manner, for the first time since Paul had met him.

"As I say," said Jase, not quite as quickly as he usually spoke, "in all but name now, you're a member. We haven't only been active with you up here, but we've been active for you back down on Earth. If you go back, you'll have to stand police investigation in connection with the death of Kevin Malorn, that man in the Koh-i-Nor you took the drug to."

"I was wondering about that," said Paul.

"You needn't wonder any longer," said Jase. "The purchase desk in the music section of the library at Chicago Complex Directory now has among its records one showing that you purchased a song tape there at the same time that Malorn was being killed. You will simply have to show up and add your testimony to the evidence of the record. Since the records are machine-made and regarded as untamperable, you'll be clear of any connection with Malorn's death an hour or so after arriving back in Chicago."

"I see." Paul nodded. "The song tape—it isn't one of Kantele singing something about *'in apple comfort time,'* is it?"

Jase frowned.

"Yes," he said. "As a matter of fact it is. Why?"

"Nothing," said Paul. "I've heard it, but not all the way through."

"It's a natural choice," said Jase. "The record shows my credit number—you were buying it at my request. That's reasonable enough, since Kantele and I are old friends and the song was written for her by Blunt."

"Blunt?"

"Why yes." Jase smiled a little at him. "You didn't know the Guildmaster wrote music?"

"No."

"He does a great many things," said Jase, a little dryly. "However, the point is you can go back to Earth as free as you ever were. Except that as a Guild member you'll be required to take orders from the masters, like myself."

"I see," said Paul, a little grimly.

"Do you?" replied Jase. He sighed. "I don't think you do. Not by a damn sight. Would you listen with an open mind for about five minutes?"

"Of course," said Paul.

"All right," said Jase. "Modern man got his motor to turning over with the Renaissance. At that time two things were initiated. One was the attitude of enlightened inquiry that began people on the road to a technological society and civilization. The road that sought to build a man a home and keep him well fed and happy within it by use of the machine."

"Which was bad?" said Paul.

"No, no," said Jase. "There's nothing wrong with a prosthetic appliance if nothing else is available. But you'd rather have a flesh-and-blood arm just like your own grafted on, wouldn't you?"

"Go on," said Paul.

"However, the original role of the machine started to

get perverted around the time of the industrial revolution. It came to be regarded not as a means to a desired end, but as part of the end in itself. The process accelerated in the nineteenth century, and exploded in the twentieth. Man kept demanding more in the way of service from his technology, and the technology kept giving it—but always at the price of a little more of man's individual self-contained powers. In the end—in our time —our technology has become second thing to a religion. Now we're trapped in it. And we're so enfeebled by our entrapment that we tell ourselves it's the only possible way to live. That no other way exists."

"I——" began Paul, and checked himself.

"Yes, 'I,'" said Jase. "The arrogant 'I,' with the built-in survival qualities. But other people aren't like you."

"That wasn't what I was going to say," observed Paul.

"It doesn't matter," said Jase. "The point isn't you, but the world, which is at the mercy of an ever-growing technological system."

"Which the Chantry Guild wishes to attack."

"Attack?" said Jase. "The Chantry Guild was formed by Walt Blunt to protect its members against the attack of the technological system."

"What you're saying," Paul said, "is that your members grew up out of something other than the technological system."

"That's quite right," said Jase calmly. "They did. And so did you."

Paul looked searchingly at the Necromancer, but the dark face was as full of honesty as Paul had ever seen it.

"I said, two things were initiated at the time of the Renaissance," said Jase. "One was the roots of the single system that has given us our technological civilization, that says there is only one way for Man to live, and that's swaddled by the machine. And the other was all other systems—the principle of freedom which lies at the base of the Alternate Laws. The first would make

118

Man an inferior, the second acknowledges his superiority."

He looked at Paul as if expecting a protest.

"I'm not in disagreement with the idea of superiority," said Paul.

"Side by side, but not noticed except by a few," said Jase, "while everybody and his Uncle Charlie was engaged in making a god out of the machine, a few talented people were proving that Man had already reached that level of deity and wasn't even started yet. Genius was at work in every generation—and genius works with the Alternate Laws. Only, after a while the machine got enough muscles so that it started crowding genius—and that brings it down to our time, Paul."

"We do seem to end there, all the time," said Paul, and could not stop himself from smiling a little.

"I thought you promised me an open mind," said Jase.

"I'm sorry."

"All right, then," said Jase. "Answer me something. Suppose you're a person in any generation up to about fifty years ago whose abilities and inclinations make him inclined to have something more or something different than what's available to the mass of people in his time. What happens?"

"I'm listening," said Paul, "with an open mind."

"He can go under to the general attitude and be essentially destroyed by denying his own possibilities. Or he can rise above the general attitude and keep afloat by sheer dint of extra ability-muscle. Agreed?"

Paul nodded.

"In other words, he can lose or win his own personal battle with the mass-opinion of his time. In either case he's resolved his problem." Jase looked at Paul. Paul nodded again.

"But in our time," said Jase, "such a person isn't up against the opinions and attitudes of his fellows. He's up against an attitude brought to life and resolved into a mechanical monster that can't be reasoned with, and can't be adjusted to. He can't win for the same reason he can't outwrestle a bulldozer with his bare hands. And he can't submit because the bulldozer doesn't understand submission. It only understands a complete job."

Jase leaned forward with his hands on both of his knees. The emotion in the man came at Paul as sharp as an arrow.

"Don't you understand?" asked the Necromancer. "The Chantry Guild was established because the technological system of our own time was trying to kill these people who belong to the Guild—each and every one of them, and any more like them—kill them off." His eyes blazed at Paul. "Just as it's been trying to kill you!"

Paul looked back at him for a long moment.

"Me?" he asked, at last.

"The weather warning you didn't get when you were out sailing," said Jase. "The temporal disorientation that caused you to be caught by the starting ore cars in the shaft of the mine. The misdirection of the subway car that stranded you in the middle of a street cleared for use by a marching society. Yes," he added, as Paul's eyebrows raised slightly, "we had a tracer on you from the time you first left my place. That's usual." He looked a little thin-lipped for a moment. "It's part of the war between us and it."

"I see," said Paul, his mind running back over a number of things.

"You're in it, on the side of the Guild, whether you like it or not. We'd like your active, working co-operation. If your ability under the Alternate Laws is what it seems to be, you'll be more valuable to your fellow Guild members than anyone else could be."

"Why?" asked Paul.

Jase shrugged a little angrily.

"I won't tell you that—*now,* of course," he said. "How could I? You've got to commit yourself to the Guild— that is, try for the rank of Necromancer, a master in the Guild. We'll put you to the test. If you come through all right, then some time in the future you'll learn what you can do for the Guild. You'll hear it from the only man who can give you commands once you're a master—the Guildmaster himself, Walt Blunt."

"Blunt!"

Paul felt the name slide into place with the events here on Mercury at Springboard. He felt a rage of passion remembered, and a lonely sorrow, and then the hard, driving core of his determination to bring this man Blunt face to face.

"Of course," Jase was saying. "Who else could there be to give orders to the master rank? Blunt's our general."

"I'm committed," said Paul, quietly. "What do I do?"

"Well," said Jase, taking his hands off his knees and sitting up straight, "I told you it's this ability of yours we want to determine. I said we'd done everything but try to kill you outright and without reservation. We'd like to take that last step now—make a serious effort with the resources of the Guild behind it and no safety hatch—and see if you survive."

Chapter 14

Master and Necromancer in name only, and under the shadow of a sometime attempt to be made upon his life, Paul returned to Earth and the Chicago Complex—ostensibly from a canoe trip up in the Quetico-Superior wilderness park area along the Canadian border near Lake Superior. He was picked up at the Complex Outer Terminal, taken to Complex Police Headquarters, and gave his statement concerning his whereabouts at the time of Malorn's murder by person or persons unknown. A police-beat reporter for one of the newssheets questioned him perfunctorily as he was leaving after his release by the police.

"How does it feel?" asked the reporter, matching strides with Paul as Paul walked toward the waiting cars at the Police terminal, "not to be facing a possible sentence of death?"

"You tell me," said Paul, as he got in a two-man car and went off. The reporter considered a moment and erased the reply from his hand recorder. It had been too flippant, he thought.

" 'I am relieved, of course,' " dictated the reporter into the recorder. " 'However, knowing modern police methods and equipment I never had any real doubt they would find out I hadn't done it.' " He put the recorder back in his pocket and returned to the booking desk inside.

Paul, reporting to Jase, who also had returned, was told to rent himself an apartment not too far from Suntden Place and amuse himself for the present. Paul did so. There followed several weeks of idleness in which Paul slept late, wandered around the Complex soaking up the feel of it and its crowds, and generally waited for his personal ax to fall.

It did not fall. Paul seemed almost forgotten—pensioned off and put aside by the Chantry Guild. Yet Jase, when Paul checked in with the Necromancer, and Kantele, on the one or two brief glimpses Paul had of her, seemed caught up in a smoothly constant, high-temperature state of activity. On one of his visits Paul had attempted to find out how he might get in touch with Blunt. Jase had told him quite bluntly that when Paul needed to know such information, it would be given to him. Blunt, Paul gathered, had no fixed address. His location at any time was a matter for his own immediate decision, and known only to those like Jase and Kantele, who were close to him.

The first week in May, on a Monday, found Paul up around the Wisconsin Dells, ostensibly squirrel-hunting. He had largely given over any conscious watch for the attack he had been promised by Jase, but that anterior part of his mind which took care of such things had not forgotten. Midday found him seated with his back to the trunk of a silver maple, half drowsy with the warmth of the strong spring sun out of a blue sky, and lost in a collection of newspapers and periodicals. However, his gun was across his knees, a steep fifty-foot cliff of loose gravel fell away behind the maple, and before him he could see clear down through a small grove of maple, pine, and poplar to a wide field of black earth faintly dusted with the new green of coming corn plants. It was an automatically perfect defensive position.

There were gray squirrels in the trees down the slope. They had taken care not to get too close when Paul had first settled himself against the trunk of the maple, but,

Sciurus carolinensis not being known for any lack of curiosity, they had been allowing themselves to work and play closer to where he sat in motionlessness. Now, after about two hours of Paul's sitting and reading, one slim youngster had grown so swashbuckling as to slip out from behind a narrow poplar trunk not fifteen feet from the human and sit up boldly to stare.

Paul was aware of these small attentions, but he felt a certain definite pleasure in letting them go on uninterrupted. The last thing from his mind was the desire to kill. He had more than a moral conviction against it, he was discovering. He almost regarded it as a sort of self-performed amputation. Particularly at this moment when he had allowed himself to go deep into the life and stir of the small section of the world at the moment around him. He let himself float in the sensation of the warming earth, the light and movement surrounding, and gave the full attention of his thinking processes to the reading material he had brought with him.

The material was merely a chance selection among the many publications currently on sale or merely available for the picking up. But they struck hard upon him. He found himself wondering how, with such a universal voice of unhappiness sounding in the world, he had failed to be overwhelmed by it before.

The publications were full of the statistics of distress. Testing of grade-school children revealed that seven per cent of those under the age of eight were headed for major mental illnesses. The world crime rate had been climbing steadily for fifty years and this last year had jumped twenty-three per cent again. And this in a world in which nobody needed to lack for the necessities, and even most of the luxuries, of life. The world suicide rate was climbing sharply. Cultism was commonplace. Hysteria such as the marching societies exemplified was growing steadily. The birth rate was down.

Article after article either explored the situation, or offered some self-help method of individual adjustment to it. And yet—Paul went back through the pages before him again—there was enough of other topics, of sports, news, humor, art, and science, so that someone like himself who had not suffered individually could ignore the notes of trouble in the general symphony of modern achievement otherwise.

And still—Paul frowned a little. He did not believe what he read, or what people told him. He believed only what he himself could check against the touchstone of his feelings, and it occurred to him now that he seemed to sense something about the catalogue of unhappiness. A faint tone as of something whining. Or was he being unfair?

He pushed the newssheets and periodicals aside, and half-closed his eyes to the sunlight coming through the young leaves. He was conscious of the weight of the gun across his legs as well as the peaceful rustlings of the woods. The adventurous squirrel had been followed into the open by two of his fellows, but the first one, the one with guts, was still in the lead. As Paul watched without stirring, the adventurous one made a sudden dash right up to the toe of Paul's left hiking boot, and examined it with a quivering black nose.

The other two followed after. Man, thought Paul slowly, proceeds by dashes like the squirrel, and each new discovery is the one which is going to turn the world upside down. Each new setback seems to threaten eternal night. He looked at the squirrels. All three were now examining the rifle-stock of the gun where it projected out into the air beyond his right knee on a level with their small, black, fascinated eyes. He tried to feel what it was like to be one with them, and for a second his point of view flooded into a fantastic, pillared world of attack and defense, sleep, hunger, and the unknown.

Another squirrel raced suddenly toward him from the cover of the nearest tree. Suddenly there was concerted movement. As the newcomer reached the two followers, all three with unnaturally perfect teamwork threw their squirrel-weights suddenly against and on top of the projecting rifle stock. The gun tilted and swung, the muzzle of the barrel coming up thump against the left side of Paul's chest.

And at the same moment the adventurous squirrel leaped fair and true for the trigger button of the gun.

All in one explosive instant, it happened. And all in one movement of coldly swift and certain reaction, Paul's arm had galvanized into movement with the first rush of the fourth squirrel across the dappled earth. His long fingers met the leaping squirrel in mid-air, caught him, and broke his neck.

There was a scuttling rush away in all directions. Then silence. Paul found himself standing on his feet with the spilled gun, the scattered throwaway publications at his feet, and no other living creature in sight. He held the dead squirrel still in his hand.

Paul's heart thumped once, savagely, in his chest. He looked down at the dead squirrel. The small, black, animal eyes were squeezed tightly shut, as they might have been in any living being forced into risking all, in one wild tourney with the unknown.

The wound of an amputation bled somewhere in the depths of Paul. His eyes dimmed. The sun had lost its way momentarily behind a cloud, and the forest floor was all one color. Paul laid the small gray body gently down at the foot of the silver maple and smoothed its rumpled fur. He picked up his gun by the cold, slickly-machined metal of its barrel, and went off through the trees.

When he got back to his apartment in the Chicago Complex, Jase was already inside it and waiting for him as he entered.

"Congratulations," said Jase, "—Necromancer."

Paul looked at him. Involuntarily, Jase stepped back.

Chapter 15

Paul was, he learned in the next few days, now a part of the more or less "Cabinet" group in the Guild, which operated directly with and under Blunt himself. The other Cabinet members consisted of Jase, Kantele, Burton McLeod—the heavy broadsword of a man Paul had met earlier in Jase's apartment—and an elusive gray wafer of a little man whose name was Eaton White. White, it seemed, was posted high on the personal staff of Kirk Tyne, and the first thing he did was take Paul in to see Tyne about a job in the World Engineer's office.

"I suppose," asked Tyne, when he had shaken hands with Paul in the clear morning sunlight coming through the high windows of a luxurious office lounge two hundred levels above the Chicago traffic, "you wonder why I seem so little hesitant to have a member of the Guild on my personal staff? Sit down, sit down. You, too, Eat."

Paul and Eaton White took comfortable chairs. Tyne also sat down, stretching his slim legs before him. He looked as fit as a well-kept bowstring, and as unfrayed by the demands of his work. His eyes, glancing directly into Paul's under neat brown eyebrows, were startlingly perceptive.

"I was a little surprised, yes," said Paul.

"Well, there's a number of reasons," said Tyne. "Did you ever consider the difficulties of changing the present?"

"Changing the present?"

"It's impossible," said Tyne, almost merrily. "Though very few people stop to think about it and realize the fact. When you pick up an inch of the present to move it, you also pick up several thousand miles of history."

"I see," said Paul. "You mean, to change the present you'd have to first change the past."

"Exactly," replied Tyne. "And that's what reformers invariably forget. They talk about changing the future. As if doing so was some new and great feat. Nonsense. Our main business as living human beings is changing the future. In fact, that's all we can change. The present is the result of the past; and even if we could monkey with the past, who'd dare to? Change one tiny factor and the result in the present might well be the whole human race blown apart. So your reformers, your great changers, are kidding themselves. They talk about changing the future, when what they really mean is that they want to change the present, the present they're living in right at the moment. They don't realize they're trying to move furniture that's already nailed down."

"So you think the Chantry Guild is made up of furniture movers?" asked Paul.

"Essentially—essentially," said Tyne. He sat forward in his chair. "Oh, I want you to know I have a high opinion of the Guild, and the Guild members. And I have something more than a high opinion of Walt Blunt. Walt awes me, and I don't mind admitting it. But that doesn't alter the fact that he's barking up the wrong tree."

"Apparently," said Paul, "he thinks the same of you."

"Of course!" said Tyne. "He'd be bound to. He's a natural revolutionist. I'm a real revolutionist. I know the present can't be changed, so I concentrate on changing the future. Really changing it—by hard work, discovery, and progress; the way it actually gets changed."

Paul looked at him interestedly.

"What's your idea of the future?" asked Paul.

"Utopia," said Tyne. "A practical utopia that we've

all adjusted to. That's all that's really wrong with the present, you know. We've achieved, through our science and technology, a practical utopia. Our only trouble is that we aren't adjusted to it yet. We keep feeling there must be a catch somewhere, something to be fought against and licked. That's Walt's trouble, incidentally. He can't help feeling he ought to be revolting against something intolerable. And since he can't find anything intolerable, he's gone to a great deal of trouble to work up a revolt against what's not only tolerable, but infinitely desirable—the very things we've been working for for centuries. Comfort, freedom, and wealth."

"I take it," said Paul, and frowned for a second as the ghost of a small gray squirrel scampered for a moment unbidden across his thoughts, "you don't worry too much about the increases in crime, suicides, mental disorders, and so forth?"

"I consider them. I don't *worry* about them," said Tyne, leaning forward with argumentative relish. "In the Super-Complex—I mean by that, the reconciling units here in the Headquarters building—we've got the greatest tool ever forged by Man for solving all Man's problems. It'll take a few generations, no doubt, but eventually we'll iron out the essentially emotional reaction that's causing these things you talk about."

"Emotional reaction?" asked Paul.

"Of course! For the first time in the history of Man, for the first time since he first stuck his nose out of a nice safe hole in the ground, people have absolutely nothing to be afraid of, nothing to worry about. Is it any wonder that all their little individual quirks and idiosyncrasies sprout wings and fly off with them?"

"I can't believe," said Paul slowly, "that the causes for what I read about in the newssheets and periodicals now are caused just by idiosyncrasies in the individual."

"Well, of course, it isn't that simple." Tyne sat back in his chair. "There are strong group elements in the human character. Religion, for one—that's at the root of all these sects and cults. The tendency toward hysteria and mob action that's been the cause of the marching societies. We're getting a social fragmentation. But just because Utopia's new, and there's no reason not to run hog wild. As I say, a generation or two will see us settling back down."

He stopped talking.

"Well," said Paul, when it seemed to be up to him, "this is all very - interesting. I take it you're trying to convert me."

"Exactly right," said Tyne. "As I say, I don't agree with Walt, but he recruits some of the best material in the world. Eaton here's an example. And poor Malorn was a Guild member."

"Malorn!" said Paul, looking closely at the World Engineer.

"Yes—in a way you might say I owe you something for having been unfairly accused in connection with his death. It was a breakdown misfunction in the police machinery, and I'm responsible for the smooth working of all machinery."

"But that isn't why you'd give me a job?"

"Not by itself, of course. No. But Eat here speaks highly of you and says you don't seem to be completely blinkered and blinded by all those theories of Walt's. I'm willing to take a chance on talking you over to my point of view, if you're willing to take the chance of being talked. And of course, Walt will be tickled to have you on the inside, here. You see, he thinks he's outsmarting me by being completely open and aboveboard about planting his people on me."

"And you," said Paul, "think you're outsmarting him."

"I know I am," said Tyne, smiling. "I have an intelligent friend who tells me so."

"It seems to be settled, then," said Paul. He stood up. Tyne and Eaton rose with him. "I'd like to meet your intelligent friend, sometime."

"Some day, you might do that," said Tyne. They shook

hands. "In fact, I imagine you will. It was this friend's recommendation that rather clinched this matter of taking you on here."

Paul looked at the World Engineer sharply. With his last words something had come and gone so swiftly in the other man that it was impossible now to say what it might have been. It was as if a metal edge had shown itself for a moment.

"I'll look forward to it, then," said Paul. And Eaton led him out.

Outside the World Engineer Complex Headquarters they parted. Eaton went back in to work. Paul went on to Jase's.

As he stepped through the entrance to Jase's apartment and put his key back in his pocket, he heard voices. One was Jase's. But the other—he stopped at the sound of it—was the deep, resonant, and sardonic voice of Blunt.

"I realize, Jase," the voice of Blunt was saying, "that you find me a little too much of a playboy at times. It's something you'll just have to bear with, however."

"I don't mean that at all, Walt!" The younger man's voice was charged and grim. "Who's going to lay down rules for *you*, of all people? It's just that if I find myself having to take over, I want to know what you had in mind."

"If you take over, it's your own mind you'll follow, and that's the way it should be," said Blunt. "Let's cross such bridges when we come to them. You may not have to take over. Who just came in?"

The last words coincided with Paul's stepping around the corner from the entrance hall into the main lounge of Jase's apartment. The wall entrance to the office in Kantele's apartment next door was open, and through it Paul now saw the wide shoulders and back of Blunt, with the dark, startled visage of Jase beyond.

"Me. Formain," answered Paul, and he walked toward

the office. But Jase stepped swiftly past Blunt and came down into his own lounge, closing the office entrance behind him.

"What is it?" asked Jase.

"It seems I'm now on the immediate staff of the World Engineer," said Paul. He looked past Jase at the closed wall. "That's Walter Blunt in there, isn't it? I'd like to speak to him."

He stepped around Jase, went to the wall, and opened it. Within, the office was empty. He turned back to Jase.

"Where did he go?"

"I imagine," said Jase, dryly, "if he'd wanted to stay and talk to you, he'd have stayed."

Paul turned again and went on into the office. He went through it into the farther reaches of Kantele's apartment. It was a feminine dwelling, but empty. Paul paused by its front door, but there was no clue about it to signal whether Walter Blunt had walked out through it in the last few minutes.

He went back to the office, and through it. Jase was no longer in his own lounge. He seemed to have left the apartment. Paul was about to leave, too, in a mood of puzzled disturbance, when the entrance to Jase's apartment clicked open—he heard it—and someone came in.

Expecting Jase, Blunt, or both, he was turning toward the entrance hall when Kantele came out of it, carrying some sort of package, and stopped.

"Paul!" she said.

It was not a happy, or even pleased, sounding of his name. Rather, it was on a note of dismay that she said it.

"Yes," he said, a little sadly.

"Where's"—she hesitated—"Jase?"

"And Walter Blunt," he said. "I'd like to know where they disappeared to, and why, myself."

"They probably had to go someplace." She was ill-at-ease. It showed in the way she held the package to her.

"I hadn't realized," he said, reaching for a neutral

132

topic, "that Blunt wrote that 'apple comfort' song of yours. Jase told me."

She looked abruptly a little sharply at him. Almost challengingly.

"That surprised you, did it?" she asked.

"Why—" he said. "No."

"It didn't?"

"I don't know," he said, "exactly whether to call it 'surprise.' I didn't know the Guildmaster wrote songs, that was all. And—" He stopped, feeling her bristle.

"And what?"

"Nothing," he said, as peaceably as he could, "I only heard the first verse before you came in that day, and the one time I heard it before. But it seemed to me more a young man's song."

She strode angrily past him. He got the impression that she was rather pleased than otherwise to find something to get angry about. She punched buttons on Jase's music player and swung about with her back to it.

"Then it's time you heard the second verse, isn't it?" she asked. A second later her own voice swelled from the player behind her.

> In apple comfort, long I waited thee
> And long I thee in apple comfort waited.

"Young man's song," she said bitingly.

> In lonely autumn and uncertain springtime
> My apple longing for thee was not sated.

The clear, mountain rivulet of her recorded voice paused, and then went on into the second verse. She looked across at him with her eyes fixed and her lips together.

> Now come thee near anigh my autumn winding.
> In cider-stouted jugs, my memories

Shall guard thee by the fireside of my passion,
And at my life's end keep thy gentle lees.

The music shut off. He saw that she was profoundly moved by it and deeply unhappy. He went to her.

"I'm sorry," he said, standing before her. "You mustn't let what I think disturb you. Forget I had any opinion at all."

She tried to take a step back from him and found the wall behind her. She leaned her head back against the wall, and he put out his long hand to the wall beside her, half-convinced for a moment that she was about to fall. But she stood with her shoulders against the wall and closed her eyes, turning her face away to one side. Tears squeezed from under her closed eyelids and ran down her cheeks.

"Oh," she whispered, "why won't you leave me alone?" She pressed her face against the wall. "Please, just leave me alone!"

Torn by her unhappiness, he turned and left, leaving her still standing there, pressed in sorrow against the wall.

Chapter 16

In the days that followed, Paul did not see her again. It was more than obvious that she was avoiding him, and she must at least have spoken to Jase about him, for the Necromancer made it a point one day to speak about her.

"You're wasting your time, there," Jase said bluntly. "She's Walt's."

"I know that," said Paul. He glanced across the table at Jase. The other man had met him for lunch near World Engineering Headquarters, bringing him a long and curious list of cults and societies with which, as Jase put it, the Guild had some "influence." Paul was supposed to learn the names and habits of these groups against some future date when the Guild might want to cultivate them. Paul accepted the list without protest. In spite of the fact that he was theoretically supposed to take orders only from the Guildmaster, he had yet to meet Blunt. Jase brought him all his instructions. Paul had decided not to make an issue of this for the moment. There was too much to be learned even as things were.

There were about sixty thousand members in the Chantry Guild. Of these, perhaps fifteen hundred had dramatic parapsychological talents. Even in a world which accepted such things—even though mostly as interesting parlor tricks or talents on a par with wiggling one's ears —fifteen hundred people represented a pretty remarkable pool of potential ability. Paul was supposed to learn all about each one of the fifteen hundred odd: who could do what, and when, and, most important, who was improving his powers by exploring them in the curious, mystical, long-way-around light of the Alternate Laws.

In addition, there were other aspects of the Guild for Paul to learn, like the list Jase had just brought over on Paul's lunch hour. And all the work connected with the World Engineering Complex, where Tyne had Paul studying procedure like any executive trainee.

Weather all over the world had been freakishly bad. In the southern hemisphere the winter had been stormy and cold. Here, the summer days were muggy and sweltering, but no rain fell. The Weather Control Complex found itself in the position of having to rob Peter to pay Paul—moisture diverted to one needy section of the Earth left other sections either twice as arid or drowned in torrential, flooding rains that caused widespread damage. It was no crisis, but it was annoyingly uncomfortable. The internal climate of the great city Complexes held the outside weather at arms length, but the emotional impact of the season's aberrancies came through even into air-conditioned interiors like this one where Paul and Jase sat at lunch.

"It's just as well you realize she does belong to Walt," said Jase. For perhaps the first time since Paul had met him, there was a gentleness in Jase's voice. "She's Finnish, you know—you know where her name comes from?"

"No," said Paul. "No, I don't."

"The Kalevala—the Finnish national epic. Longfellow wrote his Hiawatha poem from it."

"No," said Paul, "I didn't know."

"Kaleva—Finland," said Jase.

(Wind across snow fields. Tinkling among the icicles of a cavern—I knew it the first time, thought Paul.)

"Kaleva had three sons. Handsome Lemminkainen,

136

the art-smith, Ilmarinen, and the ancient Väinämöinen."
Paul watched Jase with interest; for the first time the
drive and rush of the man was gone. He spoke the names
of the old legend with the lingering love of a scholar in
his voice. "Väinämöinen invented the sacred harp—
Kantele. And she is a harp, our Kantele. A harp for
the hand of gods or heroes. That's why Walt holds her,
old as he is, unyielding as he is to anything but his own
way of doing things." Jase shook his head across the
table. "You may be arrogant, Paul. But even you have to
face the fact that Walt's something more than us ordinary men."

Paul smiled a little. Jase, watching him, laughed shortly. Abruptly the Necromancer was his own hard, glitter-
ing self again.

"Because you don't think you can be killed," said
Jase, "you think you can't be defeated, either!"

Paul shook his head.

"I'm quite sure I can be killed," he answered. "It's the
defeat I doubt."

"Why?" asked Jase, leaning forward. Paul was a little
surprised to see that the man was seriously asking.

"I don't know. I—feel it," said Paul, hesitantly.

Jase let the breath out through his nose with a faint,
impatient sound. He stood up.

"Learn that list," he said. "Burt said to tell you he'd
pick you up tonight after you're through at your office,
if you weren't otherwise tied up. You might give him a
call."

"I will," said Paul, and watched the other man leave,
moving lithely and swiftly among the tables of the restaurant.

Burton McLeod, two-handed broadsword with human
brain and soul, had become the nearest thing to a close
friend Paul could ever remember having in his life. And
this just in the past few weeks and months.

McLeod was in his early forties. Occasionally he looked

immeasurably older. Sometimes he looked almost boyish. There was a deep, unvarying sadness in him, which was there as a result of the violence he had done, but not as a result of the ordinary reactions.

He did not regret the killing he had done. His conscience saw no reason why an enemy should not die. But deep within him, it saddened him that battle was not sanctified. Surely there had been something right and holy at one time about a flat field, a fair fight, and a fair death? He would never have thought to ask quarter for himself, and it embarrassed him that the world in which he lived insisted upon the concept of unvarying quarter for all, even for those he regarded as needing killing. He was a kind and gentle man, a little shy with those of the human race he considered worthwhile, in which class, along with Blunt, Kantele, and Jase, Paul was pleased and embarrassed in turn to find himself numbered. His mind was brilliant and he was an instinctive bookworm, and his essential moral code was so innate that there seemed to be a wall between him and any possibility of dishonesty.

Like Paul, his life had been solitary. That might have been part of what drew them together. But a mutual honesty and a lack of ordinary fear played a part, also. It began with Paul being sent for some rudimentary tutoring in unarmed self-defense, as part of his Guild teachings, and went on from there with Paul's and Mc-Leod's mutual discovery that Paul's overdeveloped arm was not amenable to ordinary training, or susceptible to ordinary attack and disablement.

"It's speed that does it," Mc Leod had said, one evening in a gym, after several unsuccessful attempts on his part to lock and hold Paul's arm. "Given speed and leverage, you don't need much in the way of muscle. But you've got the muscle, too." He examined Paul's arm with interest. "I don't understand it. You ought to be slow as a truck. But you're as fast or faster than I am."

"A freak," said Paul, opening and closing his fist to watch the muscles in his forearm bulge and retreat.

"That's it," agreed McLeod, without any overtone of comment. "That isn't just an overdeveloped arm. It's just a properly developed, trained arm for somebody six inches bigger than you. Someone rather lean, but in top shape, and about six-seven or so. Was your other arm as long as this one?"

Paul dropped his arm down by his side. To his intense and sudden interest, he saw that the tips of his fingers hung down almost to his kneecap.

"No," he said. "This one wasn't, either."

"Well," said McLeod, shrugging. He began to put on the shirt he had taken off to instruct Paul. "We didn't really work up a sweat. I'll wait until I get home to shower. Buy you a drink?"

"If I can buy the second," said Paul. And that was the beginning of their friendship.

It was late July of the summer that Jase made his call, left the list of the cults and societies for Paul to learn, and the word about McLeod seeing Paul after working hours that evening.

Paul called up the other man from back at the office and agreed to meet McLeod in the bar of the same restaurant where he had had lunch with Jase. He spent the rest of the afternoon *running the charts,* as the office phrase was, down in the heart of the huge two-hundred-level building that was the core of the world's machinery, actually in the Super-Complex, itself.

This duty was one which everyone on Tyne's staff, including Tyne, had to perform for himself about once a month. The equipment of the Super-Complex was semi-self-adapting. Changes were constantly being made in it to keep it in line with changes being made in the ultimate mechanisms out in the world with which it was in contact and control. Also, within certain limits, it was capable—and exercised that capability—of making changes in itself. Accordingly, everyone on Tyne's staff had the obligation of keeping up their own portfolio of charts and information about the Super-Complex. You started out with a thick sheaf of notices of alteration, and went 'down among the working levels, checking the actual changes and seeing they were entered in your portfolio. Without these, there might have been a number of shifts in responsibility from one recording, computing, or controlling element to another, and the human staff might have found itself trying to initiate changes through automatic channels that had already been closed.

It was simply the homework connected with the job of being on the World Engineer's staff, the necessary duty of keeping up-to-date in your own field of endeavor.

Nonetheless, in Paul's case he found it to be much more than the routine duty it was supposed to be. Moving about through chance corridors allowed by the mobile units of the Super-Complex itself, surrounded level by level by the impossible intricacies of softly humming and clicking equipment, Paul could now understand why someone like the weak, drug-fogged Malorn could have been pushed over the unstable border of his mind by moving around here. There was life, all right, in this steadily operating maze of understanding and control; Paul felt it certainly and surely. But it was not life in the human sense of the living, and it did not face him directly. Rather, it slid behind the massed equipment, hid in a corridor closed a second before by a unit moving to block a path that had once been open.

The two previous times he had been down to bring his portfolio up to date he had not seemed to notice so much purposefulness to the feeling of mechanical life about him. He wondered if he was becoming sensitized, perhaps in the same way that Malorn had.

The idea was ridiculous. The moment he held Malorn's broken personality up alongside his own for purposes of comparison, that much became immediately plain. Malorn had been afraid.

Paul stood still for a moment on the sixty-seventh level, looking about him. Far down the open corridor in which he was standing, a tall gleaming bank of units slid across the opening, blocking it, and a new path opened up, angling off to the right. It was like being down in among the moving parts of some engine. An engine equipped to be careful of crushing any small creature climbing about within it as it moved to break old connections between its parts, and make new connections.

Paul turned back to his portfolio with a suddenly inquiring eye. It had not occurred to him before to consider areas within the levels of equipment. He, like all other staff members, simply went to the point where it was necessary to check on a change, checked on it, then took the most direct route to the next closest change point. But the portfolio was simply a history of changes running back to the general chart put out at the beginning of each year. He glanced through it.

The forty-ninth to the fifty-second level, he saw, showed no changes whatsoever since the beginning of the year. In this area the chart showed the Earth terminal of the no-time connection with Station Springboard on Mercury, and the equipment dealing with the relationship of this project to Earthside economy, social factors, and science. Paul frowned over the immediate chart of that area. It seemed incredible that an area dealing with research and discovery should have failed to show a multitude of changes in seven months, let alone showing none.

It occurred to Paul, abruptly, that information about the changes in that area might be restricted to certain qualified people. Perhaps to Tyne himself. The World Engineer had, not once but a number of times in the past weeks, recommended that Paul ask about anything that puzzled him. Paul lifted his wrist phone and buzzed the office on the two hundredth level.

"Nancy," he said to the receptionist, "this is Paul. Do you know anything about any area down here I'm not supposed to go into or know about?"

"Why, no," said the girl. In the small tank of Paul's wrist phone, her face was slim, cheerful, but puzzled. "Staff members from this office can go anywhere in the Supe."

"I see," said Paul. "Could I talk to Mr. Tyne?"

"Oh, he just went down into the Supe himself, about five minutes ago."

"Portfolio?"

"That's right."

"He's wearing a phone, isn't he?"

"Just a minute." She glanced at her board. "I guess he must have left it on his desk here. You know he doesn't like wearing one." She grinned at Paul. "It's just the rest of us have to follow rules."

"Well," said Paul, "I'll catch him later after he's back."

"I'll tell him you called, Paul. 'By."

" 'By, Nancy." Paul clicked off his phone. He thought for a second and then headed himself for the unchanged area between the forty-ninth and fifty-second levels.

He found it no different on the forty-ninth level than on other levels in the Supe, until he came suddenly upon the long, looming roundness of the three-step accelerator tube. He passed around the end of this and found himself crossing the small open area that was a counterpart of the contact point he had seen at Springboard. This was one end of the no-time pathway that abolished the distance between terminals.

As his first step came down on the highly polished surface of the area, the alarm of a sudden warning rang loudly in his inner sensitivity. He almost checked himself. But just at that moment something attracted his attention otherwise.

The sound of a conversation came to his ears. Both voices used the deeper, male register of tones, and one was the voice of Kirk Tyne. The other voice was unnatural.

They reached Paul's ears down an angled corridor between high units of equipment. Paul went quickly and, he did not think why, quietly up the corridor toward them.

He turned the angle of the corridor. And stopped, finding himself shielded behind the angle of a projecting unit some eighteen or twenty feet high. Just beyond this angle he looked out into a fairly good-sized open space, almost a square, surrounded by units a good two levels in height. Their lower levels were lighted for the benefit of those living people who might need to work among them, as all units were lighted. But their upper part projected up into the dusk where lights were not. All around the square of open space they loomed like finely machined and polished idols in a temple. Tiny below them, facing one wall of these great shapes, stood Tyne.

"There's no doubt about it," Tyne was saying, "the weather—all this rioting and upset. The world situation is abnormal."

"It has been recorded." The voice came from somewhere in the wall of units facing the World Engineer. "It has been symbolized and integrated with the base situation. No apparent need for extraordinary measures is now indicated."

"There's an atmosphere of unrest. I can feel it myself."

"No concrete indications have been signalized or recorded."

"I don't know," said Tyne, almost to himself. He raised his voice slightly. "I think I may override you on this."

"Override," said the voice, "would introduce an uncalculable factor rising to a peak unit influence of twelve per cent and extending over an eighteen-month period."

"I can't simply ignore the situation."

"No situation is ignored. Ordinary measures are in process to correct the aberrancies."

"And you think they'll prove sufficient?"

"They will correct."

"By which you mean, you think they'll correct," said Tyne, a little harshly. "Sometime I'm going to take a summer off and design an honest element of self-doubt for you."

The other voice did not answer.

"What should I do?" asked Tyne, finally.

"Continue normal routine."

"I guess," said Tyne. He turned suddenly and strode off toward an opposite side of the square. Before him, a corridor opened up. He went away down it, and it closed behind him.

Paul was left watching in silence.

Quietly, he came out into the square and looked about him. The units he looked at were in appearance no different than the larger computer elements on other levels. He walked over to the side where Tyne had stood. But he could not even discern a loud-speaker element in the faces of the units he was observing.

A slight sound behind him made him glance over his shoulder. He turned completely around. The corridor by which he had come to this spot was now closed. The units stood looming, side by side, unbroken around him.

"Paul Formain," said the voice that had spoken to Tyne. Paul turned back to the units he had just been looking over.

"Your presence at this point in space and time is unjustified within the symbolic structure of human society. Accordingly, your removal may now justifiably be effected."

Book Three: **PATTERN**

Emerging on that final plain,
Once more the watch-bell tolled again.
—Twice! Thor's soul and mine were one,
And a dragon shape had crossed the sun.

The Enchanted Tower

Chapter 17

"Set!" said Paul.

The word went out and was lost in the shadowy stillness above and behind the metallic shapes of the huge units standing over and around Paul. There was a slight noise behind him. He glanced toward it and saw a corridor opening once more in the general direction from which he had reached this area on the forty-ninth level. In the opposite direction a single unit slid out to fill most of the open space, and turned toward Paul. It rolled slowly toward him. He backed up and saw he was being forced into the newly opened corridor.

"So you can do violence to people," said Paul.

"No," said the voice that had spoken to Tyne. Now it seemed to come from the unit that was crowding Paul backward.

"You're doing violence to me right now."

"I am correcting a misplacement," said the voice. "Your value is external and false. It is perverting the symbological matrix of society at this moment."

"Nonetheless," said Paul, "you have a responsibility to me, as well as to society."

"More latitude," said the unit, forcing him back along the corridor, "is possible with those not sane, who are not responsible."

"I'm not sane?"

"No," said the machine, "you are not."

"I'd like," said Paul, "to hear your definition of sanity."

"Sanity," replied the voice, "in the human being is a response to natural instincts. It is sane to sleep, to eat, to seek to feed oneself, to fight if attacked, to sleep if no occupation is at hand."

Paul's shoulder blades came up against something hard. Turning around, he saw he had reached a turn in the corridor down which he was backing. The unit rolling toward him on invisible smooth-turning cylinders had not paused. He changed direction and backed away again.

"How about thinking? Is that sane?"

"Thought is a perfectly sane process, as long as it follows sane paths in the human brain."

"Such as those concerned with feeding and sleeping?"

"Yes."

"But not," said Paul, "those concerned with painting a picture or discovering a new method of interstellar travel?"

"Such thinking," said the unit, "is a response to abnormal irritations in the environment of the human concerned. Perfectly sane human beings have no need to do more than live and propagate, all under the conditions of greatest comfort."

"By those standards," said Paul, still backing up, "most of the human race is insane."

"You are quite wrong," said the voice, "roughly eighty-five per cent of the human race has had no real desire outside the framework I mentioned. Of the remaining fifteen, only about five in any generation have made any real effort to put their insanities into practice. Perhaps two per cent have some effect on future generations and one-tenth of one per cent are later admired even by the sane."

"I won't argue your figures," said Paul, feeling his left shoulder brush a unit, unyielding as the brick wall against which a man stands before a firing squad. "Even though I could. But don't you think the fact that your final category is admired even by the sane, as you put it, is some kind of an indication that maybe others had something besides insanity at work for them?"

"No," said the voice.

"Forgive me," said Paul. "I think I overestimated you. Let me say that again in terms you might be able to handle. Once you achieve an ideal existence for the human race, what's going to become of the arts, scientific research of all kinds, and the exploration of the natural universe?"

"They will be abandoned by the sane," said the machine.

Paul, backing up, saw the flanking units on either side of his corridor suddenly give way to open space. At the same time, the unit which had been herding him forward rolled level with the mouth of the corridor and stopped, so that Paul now found himself facing a final wall. He turned and looked about him. He stood, completely hemmed in by a wall of units, upon the contact area at the end of the three-step accelerator. The end of the tube, the terminal that could tear him from this spot off into the universal ubiquity of no-time, loomed high above his head like a cannon mouth over the head of a sparrow which, in its muzzle, had taken refuge from a hawk.

"And the insane, at that time?" asked Paul.

"There will be no more insane," said the voice. "They will have destroyed themselves."

Paul saw nothing to give him any impression, and heard nothing; but deep within his flesh and bones he felt the accelerator warming to life. Even now, back and forth over flashing yards of distance, the point of no-time to be, was warming to life. Paul thought of Springboard, and of the emptiness of space.

"You tried to get me to destroy myself, didn't you?" said Paul, remembering what Jase had said. "In the mine; in front of the marching society that day."

"Always," said the voice, "the way has been open for you to destroy yourself. It is what works best with the insane. The sane are easy to kill. The insane fight very hard against being killed, but are more susceptible where it comes to the opportunities of self-destruction."

"Do you realize," asked Paul, feeling the accelerator warming to life over him, "your definition of sane and insane is completely artificial and wrong?"

"No," said the machine, "I cannot be anything but correct. It is impossible for me to be incorrect."

"You ought to see," said Paul, "that one false assumption used as a basis for later decisions could cause all your conclusions to be in error."

"I know this. I also know I contain no false assumptions," answered the voice. Above the looming curve of the accelerator the dusk of the dark higher up seemed to be pressing down on Paul. Almost, the voice seemed to descend also, becoming confidential. "My assumptions must stand the test of whether the structures built upon them guarantee a safe and continued life to mankind. This they do. I am humanity's guardian. You, in contrast, are its destroyer."

"I——?" asked Paul, staring up into the darkness.

"I know you. You are the destroyer of mankind. You are the warrior who will not fight and cannot be conquered. You are proud," said the machine. "I know you, Necromancer. Already you have done incalculable damage, and created the first blind living form of the inconceivable enemy."

A barrier went down in Paul's mind. What was beyond it, he could not at this moment see; but it brought him relief and strength. It was as if a soldier, after long waiting, had at last received definite orders commanding him upon a long and desperate journey.

"I see," said Paul quietly, as much to himself as to the machine.

"To see is not enough," said the voice. "It is not enough excuse. I am the living wish of mankind expressed in solidity. I have the right to direct people. You have not. They are not yours. They are mine." The tones of the voice did not vary, but Paul got an impression of total effort being directed against him. "I will not let you lead mankind blindfold through a dark maze to an end they cannot conceive of, and final destruction. I cannot destroy you, or I would. But I can put you aside."

The voice paused slightly.

Paul was suddenly aware of a slight humming from the great cylinder head beside and above him. The acceleration was nearing the point of break into no-time which, like a sudden spark jumping, would contact and remove him from the point where he stood. He had just time to remember that he had been through no-time before, on the heels of Jase and Kantele when they escaped the police in the office across the concourse from the Koh-i-Nor. But that had been like running down a flight of stairs, while this would be like being thrown down them. He had just time to brace his awareness.

"*Now,*" said the machine.

And Paul was ripped from the position he held in time and space and spread out to the uttermost reaches of the universe.

Chapter 18

Paul was not immediately delivered at the destination to which the machine had sent him.

From the psychic point of view the action of the accelerator upon him was like that of hurling him down an endless flight of infinitely stretching stairs. But even as he tumbled, that invincible part of him, like the reflexes of a superbly conditioned athlete, was instinctively gathering his feet under him, regaining his balance, and stopping his fall. It checked him, got him upright; but the conscious part of him was for the moment stunned and dazed, out of action. Instinctively in action, like a half-knocked-out fighter too well trained to stay down, he fought clear of the push of the accelerator and wandered, as it were, off sideways along one of the stair surfaces.

The situation was entirely different from when he had gone through no-time on the heels of Jase and Kantele, when he and they had been escaping the air police across from the Koh-i-Nor Hotel. The way by which they had entered no-time then, had been by a much more bearable emotional route. The accelerator method (lacking the medication that was yet to be discovered) was simply and plainly brutal.

It achieved its desired end by sheer savagery of action. It was this that had caused effects ranging from severe nervous breakdown to death in early Springboard volunteers transmitted to the terminal from which Paul had left. In essence, under the accelerator method, the individual's identity fled the immediate level of no-time to escape the suddenly intolerable conditions under which it had been forced to experience real time and space. Inanimate objects, of course, had no such difficulties. But the human psyche could not have retained its orientation under a full experiencing of conscious dispersal to universal dimensions and later reassembly. In instinctive self-protection it made the great step upward into the subjective universe.

Now, experiencing this, Paul suddenly understood the operation of the Alternate Laws, which were naturally entirely subjective in nature. However, at the moment this understanding could make no contact with the operative areas of his mind, which were still stunned. These wandered the subjective dimension of that line of endeavor to which the greater part of his being was dedicated.

There was no shape or dimension to the subjective universe in which he now wandered. It was, however, subject to the reality imposed on it by the symbolic processes of Paul's deeper self. Consequently, to him now, it took on the appearance of a vast, pebbled plain, with the pebbles growing in size in the distance. It was the plain of which he had dreamed on returning to the hotel after his first meeting with Jase.

Before, he had toiled over it as if walking. Now he skimmed rapidly just above its surface. Gray, black, rubbled, and bleak, the plain stretched off about him in all directions, not to any horizons, but to a great but finite distance. An emptiness of spirit, a sense of desolation, made up the atmosphere around him. He chilled in it, even while the unstunned part of him struggled to remind him that it was all subjective, all interpretative of the job he had, at a great distance in time and space, once dedicated himself to do.

"Arrogant," murmured a wind across the larger pebbles with the voice of Jase.

"These are my people, not yours," whispered a metallic breeze from another direction. And then, from a little farther off, and fainter even: *"I know you, Necromancer. . . ."*

He went quickly from the voices. The pebbles grew to boulders, to huge and mammoth shapes, to vast mountains with darkness between them. Then, at last, over the farthest and largest of these, he came to the final edge of the plain.

He went swiftly to it. From a point above the last and most mountainous boulder shapes he hung and looked down, out, and up at the same time upon a shifting infinity of darkness.

It was a gulf beyond which he felt there was light. But he could not see it, for the closer darkness. And in the darkness, something stirred.

It was barely living yet. It was an embryo, an amoeba, with only so much of consciousness as had allowed it to sense his existence when he had been under initiation, deep in the rock of Mercury. And only so much of reaction as had allowed it to make that one reactive, whiplash attack in his direction. Its growing was all yet before it.

And it was all in the way of evil that the Super-Complex had said it was. And Paul had created it. Without him it would never have been, but now it lived, and grew in power and understanding.

A terrible desire came over him then, to attack it now and settle the matter once and for all. But when he moved to go beyond the edge of his plain, he found something invisible there that would not let him pass. It was the barrier of the laws under which he had created what stirred out there. The laws that protected it from him as much as he from it, until the time when both he and it should be strong enough to break all barriers. And suddenly his dazed mind cleared, and he realized that if he should meet and conquer it now, nothing would be proved. Nothing accomplished. There would have been no point in its creation in the first place.

Abruptly, his mind was clear again. He retreated swiftly from the edge of the plain. He returned to the area where the boulders were again down to the size of pebbles. And here, close to where he had wandered astray, he found something like a cairn, or stony pile, new-built. It was about three times his own height, and the chance crevices between its stones gave an errie impression of tiny arrowslits or windows, though he felt instinctively that there was nothing alive about it as yet, nothing within. Standing beside it, he looked once more about the plain, and saw now that here and there at the farthest limits, this subjective landscape of his seemed to have elevated itself slightly, as if in the beginnings of hills, in a circle, surrounding him.

With that, he gave in to the original impulse that had brought him here and went forward to his destination.

He came to ordinary consciousness again in what looked like a small apartment. He had one brief glimpse of it before his legs—he had come through standing in the same position in which he had faced the Supe—crumpled under him and the full shock of what had been done to him took its price from his physical body. He pitched to the floor.

Here again, as always, he did not go completely under into unconsciousness. By all ordinary standards he should have gone completely out, but in actuality he only passed into a foggy, uncertain state which was the physical equivalent of his dazed condition while he had been wandering the subjective universe. During the succeeding several days in which this state gradually wore itself out, he was vaguely conscious of the fact that he had dragged himself from the floor to a nearby couch, and that he had once or twice drunk from a water dispenser that was nearby. Otherwise, he had not eaten or slept, or even fallen into the half-active dream-filled state that was his ordinary slumber.

He did not suffer in a physical sense. He had in no meaning of the term suffered any physical damage as a result of being transmitted to this spot. What had been torn about and attacked in him was his essential, immaterial identity. And the effect was similar to that of an attack of profound depression. He was perfectly capable physically of getting up and examining his surroundings. The act of will required to do so, however, was like that of lifting his own body's weight to a man drained of blood almost to the point of death.

Gradually, however, he recovered.

He became aware first that the apartment was shaped like a section of a cylinder, its bottom curve having a floor built across it. It was fitted with the compact luxury of an ocean-going submersible liner. Between the curved walls were couch and easy chairs, tape cabinets, music player, bar, kitchen—even some finger-sculptures, and a couple of interesting stochastic paintings, one in oils, the other in red, black, and yellow clays.

There was also the cleared area, floored in polished black, which had been the terminal point of his arrival.

It was sometime on the third day that he found himself staring at the paintings, as he had for some hours now, like a man stupefied. His feeble but certain perception made the connection immediately, and he laughed weakly. He had suddenly realized the existence of a plasma that could in part replace the psychic blood of which he had been drained.

He struggled wearily up from the couch and went clumsily on hands and knees across the room to the music player. From there he went to the tape cabinets, and to some adjoining shelves where he found a reference printer.

Twenty minutes later found him back on the couch. The fine, golden threads of *Il Trovatore* were spinning themselves out of the speakers of the music player, the rich canvas of Rubens' "Adoration of the Magi" was displayed in the tank of the tape cabinets, and the solemn heartbreak of Milton's sonnet on his blindness tolled like a slow and shadowed bell from a printer sheet in Paul's hand:

> *When I consider how my light is spent*
> *Ere half my days in this dark world and wide . . .*

Paul lay there, changing art, music, and poetry for mathematics, philosophy, medicine, and all the fields of man's endeavor. And slowly the life of those who had had something to give to life seeped back into his own drained being, and his strength came back to him.

By the fourth day after his arrival he was back to normal. He got himself a large meal out of the kitchen, and then set about exploring the limits of this prison to which he had been sentenced.

It was about thirty feet in length, and about that same height and width at its greatest points of those two dimensions. Either end of it was a great circle flattened off at the bottom by the chord-line of the floor. One circle overlooked the terminal area of his arrival. The other merely filled up the far end of the living space.

It was this second circle that Paul looked over with interest. The first, overhanging the terminal point of his arrival, presumably simply hid the business end of an accelerator. The second might, however, be blocking the way to an escape route. When he looked closely, he discovered that the second in fact did appear to be something in the nature of a removable cover, held in place by a simple magnetic lock.

He unlocked the cover and the lower half of it swung away from him like half of a huge Dutch door. He walked through it and found himself in a farther extension of the cylinder, three times as big as the living quarters and filled with crated equipment and tools. He let his gaze settle over the tools and crates, and the answer he was looking for became easily apparent to him. This was the material with which the accelerator terminal here could be fitted to transmit as well as receive. He paused to glance at the tickets attached to some of the crates, but they were punch cards notated in a technician's shorthand that he did not know. He went on to the still farther circular wall that ended this division of the cylinder.

This had been sealed with a running bead of plastic weld all around its rim. It was evidently intended to be easily removed, but only by someone who knew how to do so, and why he was doing it.

Paul turned back and searched the second room once more, but there was no message or instruction list in sight.

He went back into the living quarters, and proceeded to make a methodical search of that area. He excavated drawers and investigated files and cabinets. There was no instruction sheet or manual. Evidently, whoever this place had been designed for had been expected to have that sort of information in his head. Paul was standing in the middle of the living-area floor and looking about for some hiding place he might have overlooked, when there was a sound from behind him, from the direction of the terminal area.

He looked. There on the bare and polished surface he saw a newssheet lying, still slightly curled from the printer. He went to it and picked it up.

For a moment he could not imagine what reason had caused the Supe to send it through to him. The headings of the various stories on the front page screamed of riots, panics, and earthquakes. Then, sliding his eye up one column and down the next in automatic speed-reading, Paul saw a small item: WORLD ENGINEER GIVEN EXTRAORDINARY POWERS.

By an unprecedented world-wide register vote, the World Engineer yesterday was awarded authority to freeze the credit numbers and deny all Complex services to rioters and those suspected of disturbing the peace. The Complex-Major tabulated an almost

inconceivable 82 per cent of the total voting popula-
tion, with 97.54 per cent of those voting registering
in favor of awarding the additional authority to the
World Engineer.

A tiny item. But Paul frowned. Highly important it
was, but that did not seem to him sufficient cause for the
Supe to send him the newssheet. Nor—he glanced back
at the other stories upon the front page—was the news of
widespread emotional disturbances and rioting sufficient.
The machine was not equipped to gloat, and surely with
Paul imprisoned here as he was, there could be no other
reason for informing him about events he was powerless
to have an effect upon.

Still puzzling, Paul opened the newssheet to its second
and third pages. Then he saw it.

By some apparent freak mishap, the printer had failed
to bring out the printing on these two pages otherwise
than as an unreadable blur, except for one item as small
as the front-page item Paul had just frowned over. That
one stood out as if framed.

DRONE LOST

The Complex-Major today noted the information
that one of its Springboard drones, carrying auto-
matic terminal receiving equipment to the planet
known as New Earth, fourth world of the star Sirius,
has suffered a malfunction of the directing system
and been lost in space. This drone, which three days
ago was noted as being in position to land shortly on
New Earth, apparently missed its landing and has
fallen beyond that planet under conditions of move-
ment which will carry it out of the Sirian system.
There can be no hope of reestablishing contact, notes
the Complex-Major, or of recovery of the drone.

Paul dropped the newssheet and, spinning about, strode
swiftly back into the farther room. Seizing a tool like a

chisel, he attacked the plastic weld around the rim of the circular end wall. The plastic peeled up under his gouging and a thin edge of the metal was revealed. He forced the chisel edge in under the edge of the revealed metal. For a moment there was resistance, and then the chisel plunged through. There was a sudden whistling insuck of air past Paul's hand, the plastic weld cracked loose halfway around the rim, and the lower half spanged sharply on a deep bass note. Before Paul's eyes a horizontal crack ran across the metal, and the lower half of it broke clean from the top and fell into the room.

Paul caught it. It was a thin sheet of light magnesium alloy. He bent it inward and laid it flat on the floor. Then he stepped one step forward and looked out, through heavy glass.

Before him was a rolling landscape under a slightly yellowish sky, an atmosphere hazed with fine dust. Something like tiny, close-packed fern leaves covered the ground and grew thickly and a little larger about an occasional boulder or outcropping of granitic rock. Farther back were low, broad trees whose trunks and limbs looked as if they had been shaped out of dark, twisted cable. The brilliant white points of two Ao-type stars, so close they seemed at the moment to be swimming into each other, peered burningly through the dust haze and made the illumination for the day outside.

From the sight of these and the landscape they lighted —a landscape rich in promise for the yet infant science of terraforming—Paul had no difficulty making the connection between his present location and one of the worlds described in popular articles as destinations for the Springboard drones.

The double star in the sky out there could only be Sirius and its close companion. Which meant that this was New Earth, and the message of the newssheet the Supe had sent him was clear. Paul, and this drone in which he found himself imprisoned, had been deliberately and officially "lost" from the records.

For a moment Paul leaned his forehead wearily against the cool pane of the glass. The long palm and fingers of his single hand pressed uselessly against the glass' thick surface. Out there beyond its protection was, according to all official reports, an atmosphere suffocating with hydrogen sulphide. Behind him was crated equipment he had not the education and training to assemble.

Suddenly he stiffened. His hand slipped down from the glass and he raised his head to look sharply out through the transparency.

Leaning against a boulder on this alien world a little more than a dozen feet from the drone and incongruous against the small, carpeting ferns, was a heavy cane of dark wood; Walter Blunt's cane, one end of which was cracked and splintered as it would have been from being used to smash a human skull.

Chapter 19

"I see," said Paul quietly to the empty room and the land-scape beyond the glass. "Of course."

It was like driving through a strange city at night and being convinced that north lay on your right hand. Then, suddenly, a chance-glimpsed street sign, some small but undeniable scrap of information, brings suddenly the un-deniable orientation that places north on the left. Abrupt-ly, silently, without real physical movement, the universe swaps ends and you realize that all this time you have been heading west, not east.

Suddenly the pattern about Paul had become clear and correct, down to the last detail.

It was Blunt, of course. As he had instinctively felt all along, it was Blunt—this man who would not turn and show his face openly and clearly—who was the demon. Paul spoke out loud again, but not to Blunt.

"Get me out of here," he said.

No, came an answer from deep inside him, from the invincible part in the back of his mind.

"You mean," asked Paul, "we end here, you and me? The two of us?"

No.

"Then——?"

There's only one of us.

"I see," said Paul again, quietly. "I should have known that."

I can do anything you want. But if I do it, what's the use? We won't have found any way other than force. Our work will all have been wasted, as the living darkness we created beyond the boulders would have been wasted if you had killed it then, or if you kill it now, while it's ungrown. It's up to you now to find the different way.

"Not the machine's way," said Paul. "Not the way you moved me out of that office just behind Jase and Kantele that time? A different way than either of those?"

Yes.

"I don't know where to start."

Perceive. Recapitulate. Feel.

"All right," said Paul. He looked out at the cable trunks and limbs of the trees beyond the window, and at the cane. "There is only one thing common to both the objective and the subjective universe. This is identity."

Yes. Go on.

"The objective universe can be expressed in its lowest common denominators as an accumulation of identity isolates, both living and nonliving."

That's right.

"The isolates, however, in order to live—that is, to have function along the single dimension of the time line— must pass in and out of combinations which can be called sets."

Continue, Brother.

"The sets, in order to create the illusion of reality in objective time and space, must at all times arrange themselves into a single pattern. The pattern may vary, but it can't be abandoned or destroyed without also destroying or abandoning the illusion of reality."

Entirely correct. And very good for a partial identity that is restricted to reasoning by use of emotion and response. We can be proud of you. Go on. The next step?

Paul frowned.

"Next step?" he asked. "That's all."

Application.

"Application? Ah!" said Paul, suddenly. "Of course.

The so-called Alternate Laws"—he glanced once more at the cane against the boulder beyond the window—"and the talents deriving from them are merely methods of altering the pattern so that the illusion of reality temporarily permits actions ordinarily not permitted." He thought for a second. "Blunt doesn't understand this," he said.

Are you certain of that?

Paul smiled a little in the empty silence of the room.

"That's my department, isn't it? Understanding."

I submit myself. Go on.

Paul hesitated.

"Is there more?" he asked.

You wanted to get out of here. You have perceived and recapitulated. From here on you leave me for your own territory. Feel.

Paul closed his eyes. Standing with the yellow light from outside showing faintly through his lids, he tried for a total contact with all that surrounded him—room, drone, planet, suns, space. It was like attempting to make some delicate last connection with blind fingers at arm's length, out of sight inside a piece of complicated equipment. Only, Paul's effort was completely nonphysical. He was reaching out to feel fully and correctly the great pattern of the objective universe, so that he could fit his own identity perfectly into pivot position within its structure.

For a moment he made no progress. For a fraction of a second he felt the completely stripped feeling of total awareness, but lacking even a single point of contact as he floated free, swinging into position. Then, suddenly, it was like the moment of orientation that had followed his seeing the cane beyond the glass, but much greater. And mixed with it the sensation of melting together, like but greater than that which had come to him to finish his interview with the psychiatrist Elizabeth Williams.

In one sudden moment of no-time, Paul and the invincible part of him fused irreversibly together.

It was as if he had stood on a narrow stage and suddenly, on all sides, great curtains had been raised, so that he found himself looking away in all directions to enormous distances. But now—alone.

"*Ave atque vale,*" he said, and smiled a little sadly. "Hail and farewell." He turned back to the glass of the window. "Destruct," he said. "Of course. Blunt planted that for me, and in his own limited way, he was right."

Paul turned back to the tools behind him. He chose a heavy sledge hammer and took it to the window. His first blow bent the metal handle of the sledge but merely starred the glass. But his next blow sent the sledge crashing through and the whole wall of glass fell out in ruins.

He took three rapid steps toward the boulder where the cane leaned, as the acid, choking atmosphere numbed his sense of smell with the assault of its odor and filled his lungs. He reached the cane and seized it even as his eyesight began to sear and blur with tears. Almost, he could hear Blunt chanting, as he had chanted in the vision tank back there underground at Malabar Mine while Paul watched.

"Destruct! The ultimate destruct! The creative destruct that will rescue Man from being saved forever . . ."

Then Paul felt his knees strike the ground as he fell. And with that his identity quit his body forever and left it there, fallen and dying in the suffocation of the yet-untamed atmosphere of the world which would be called New Earth, with a splintered walking stick clutched in its single fist.

Chapter 20

Full twenty-fathoms times five, thy body lies. Of its bones is ocean debris made. . . .

Thirty miles due west of La Jolla, California, which is a few miles up the coast line from San Diego, on a sandy underwater pleateau six-hundred-odd feet below the surface of the ever-moving blue Pacific, Paul's bodiless identity hovered above a skeleton of a man wrapped and weighted with half-inch chain. This place had not been his original intended destination, but he had detoured here to settle a purely emotional point in his own mind. Now, hovering above the chain-wrapped skeleton, he sensed with relief that the body it once supported had died a natural death. It was not that he doubted that Blunt had been willing to murder to gain the results he wanted. It was just that he wished the ledger sheet on which he and Blunt were totaled up together and against each other to be as clean as possible.

He left the white bones in the peace of their eternal darkness, and went his way.

His way—the way Blunt's cane on New Earth had been designed to send him—led him to an awakening in something like a coffin. He lay, legs together, arms at his sides, on his back, and tightly enclosed in a metal container. His eyes were open but they saw nothing but blackness. His pattern-linked perception, however, recognized that he was in a sort of cold-storage vault—something very like the slide-out six-and-a-half-foot drawers for unclaimed bodies in a public morgue. The body he now inhabited was identical with the one he was used to, except that it had two good arms. However, it seemed completely paralyzed.

It was paralyzed, he recognized with a sudden grim humor, because it was frozen stiff. The container in which he lay was surrounded with refrigerator coils and his body's temperature was a little more than twenty degrees below zero, Fahrenheit. The body would first have to be thawed before any life could be brought to it.

Paul surveyed the surrounding pattern. It would be surprising if Blunt, who had made so many arrangements where Paul was concerned, had not also made some here. Sure enough, the container lay on tilted tracks and was held inside the freezing unit by the bare hooking of a catch. Paul made the necessary slight alterations in the pattern and the catch failed. He slid out into the light of a brightly illuminated room without windows.

As he emerged into the room, the temperature rose sharply and suddenly from close to freezing to seventy-six degrees Fahrenheit. Lying at a tilted angle that put his feet close to the floor below the container and his head several inches higher, Paul saw it was a small room with a single door and no furniture, tiled in white.

The single item of interest in it was a message neatly printed in large letters on the wall opposite Paul. It read:

> *Paul: As soon as you find yourself able,*
> *come and join us in suite 1243, at the Koh-i-Nor.*
> *—Walt Blunt*

Paul's container had gone into action on its own now. It was beaming deep, gentle heat into the very center of his frozen bones and tissues. It would take—what? Half an hour, perhaps longer, to bring him up to a living temperature so that his identity could take over command of his new body in the ordinary sense. Of course, almost un-doubtedly Blunt had planned that Paul would help and hurry the process along. In any case it was rather fine scheduling, and showed an attitude toward other people and the universe that was far from modest. For the first time—in such small unexpected ways, thought Paul, do past things of minor importance explain themselves—Paul received a sudden extra insight into Jase's repeated accusation of arrogance. Over the years Jase must have become well acquainted with arrogance, in the person of Blunt.

Yes, thought Paul, he would hurry things along. But in a way in which Blunt, with his less complete awareness of the pattern, could not expect. Blunt would not expect that the message on the wall would be a clear warning to Paul that the Chantry Guild had already made its move. Outside this room the world would be trapped in a war—a strange, weird war such as it had never known before. And Blunt, general of the attacking forces, would have timed the entrance of Paul upon the battlefield for the most effective moment from Blunt's point of view.

Only Paul would come early.

He reached into the pattern and to the invincible knowledge that had become a part of him with his own individual ability. He cut certain lines of causal relation-ship, and established new ones. The pattern altered, in the immediate identity area of the body. And the body itself floated upright out of its container.

It floated toward the door. The door opened. Skimming just above the steps, it mounted a flight of stairs and passed through a farther door into a small hallway. Be-yond, was a third door, a transparent door to the traffic level, on a street Paul recognized as being less than a dozen blocks from the Koh-i-Nor. It was night beyond this last door, and for some reason the Complex without seemed darker than it should be.

Paul's body floated to the last door. It opened and he floated out into the hot July night. The Complex Internal

Weather Control seemed to have failed in its functioning, for the temperature outside here was in the high nineties at the very least and humidity must be close to a hundred per cent. The still air of the Complex seemed to hang heavily in the unusual shadows between structures, and its heat wrapped itself steamily around Paul's icy body.

No vehicles were in motion. And here, at least, the streets seemed deserted. Paul swung about and skimmed off along the concrete walk in the direction which he knew would take him to the Koh-i-Nor.

The streets were as empty as if the people in the Complex had locked and barred their doors against some plague or roaming madness. In the first half block the only sound Paul heard was the insane, insect-like buzzing of a defective street light. He looked up at its pulsating, uncertain glow, and saw at least part of the reason it did not do well. Its pole had become a monstrous cane of red-and-white striped candy.

Paul floated on. At the next corner he passed a closed door. From the crack beneath it, however, a flood of red fluid remarkably like blood in its color and viscosity was flowing. One block farther on, Paul turned down into a new street and saw his first living person of the night.

This was a man with his shirt half torn off, who was sitting in a doorway and turning a kitchen knife over and over in his hands. He looked up as Paul came toward him.

"Are you a psychiatrist?" he said. "I need——" His lifted eyes caught sight of Paul's feet and the space between them and the pavement. "Oh," he said. He looked down at his hands and went back to playing with his knife again.

Paul paused. And then he realized that his body could not speak. He went on, and as he did so he reached once more into the pattern. It was possible, as he had suspected Blunt had intended, to hurry things up. Living cells could not be thawed quite as crudely as dead meat, but borrowing heat uniformly from the general surroundings was even more efficient than the deep-heating mechanism of the storage container had been. Slowly, but at the same time much more rapidly than might have been expected, a living warmth came to Paul's body as he proceeded on toward the Koh-i-Nor.

He passed other things of the night which bore little relation to normality. A monument in the center of one street crossing was slowly melting down as he passed, like wax in a warm oven. The stone head of a lion, at the corner of a heavy balcony running around one large building, dipped its heavy muzzle and roared down at him as he passed below. In the center of one street he passed a circle of blackness—a hole of nothingness that showed, not the level below, but a spatial distortion on which the human eye was not equipped to focus. No cars were running—Complex Transportation must have been as inactive or powerless as Internal Weather—but occasionally Paul saw other people, alone, on foot, and at some distance. None of them stayed to talk when they saw him coming, but hurried off rapidly.

Life was rapidly taking over Paul's body. He had started the heart early. By the time he reached the concourse his temperature was at ninety-six and a fraction of a degree, pulse and respiration almost normal. He could have walked it, but he waited until he actually reached the entrance to the North Tower of the hotel before he put his feet to the ground.

He walked into a dim-lit lobby illuminated only by emergency lighting, and empty of guests. A white face stared at him from well back of the desk counter. It was the clerk with the elegant longhand. Paul paid him no attention, but walked on around the corner to the elevators.

These, being a balanced system running on stored power, had been unaffected by the obvious curtailment of services otherwise. Silently, gently, efficiently, as if the human race were already dead and only a mechanical duty remained, the disks floated one after another in regular, spaced intervals, up and down the transparent tubes of their shafts. Paul stepped onto a disk ascending the up shaft.

He slid smoothly up, past a succession of empty hallways, barely lighted by the red emergency light above the door to the stairs on each level. Only once did he see someone. That was in passing the ninth level. It was a woman—a young woman, almost a girl. At the sight of him passing up the elevator tube, she turned hastily and ducked into a doorway.

He went on up.

The twelfth level of the hotel, in contrast to the rest of the world Paul had seen that night, was fully lighted. Its illumination seemed almost garish in contrast to the surrounding dark. But no one stirred about its corridor, either. More than this, Paul received from the closed doors he passed an impression of darkness and emptiness beyond, as if suite 1243 toward which he walked was the only space with life within it on this bright level.

When he turned a last corner of the corridor and approached 1243, he saw its door was ajar. It stood three-quarters of the way rolled back into its wall socket, and the sound of a voice came audibly through the opening.

The voice was that of Kirk Tyne.

". . . your blind spot," he was saying. "That's what I can't understand, Walt. A man of your intelligence who thinks the present can be changed *in* the present, without going back and altering the predisposing factors of the past. And so you let loose this madness on the world."

Paul stopped just short of the entrance. He had heard this argument from Tyne before, at the time when Tyne had taken him onto the World Engineer's personal staff. Now it struck Paul as interesting to know what Blunt's answer to it would be.

"You've sold your birthright for a mess of circuits," answered Blunt's voice. "You don't think, Kirk. You parrot what the Supe tells you. If the past can't be changed, the present must. For the future's sake."

"Will you use a little logic?" asked Tyne. "I tell you the present *cannot* be changed without changing the past. Even the Supe, with all its stored knowledge, wouldn't be able to calculate the ultimate possibilities of a single insect's life pattern being altered in the past. And that's the easier way. What you're trying here, now, tonight, is the harder."

"Kirk," said Blunt's voice. "You're a fool. The predisposing factors leading up to this hour have been laid and set up for centuries now. All that's necessary for us is to recognize them and use them."

"I tell you that's not true!"

"Because your Supe . . ." Blunt was beginning, with hard irony forming a cutting edge to his resonant voice, when Paul stirred himself again. He stepped forward, entered the doorway, and walked into the main lounge of what was probably one of the best suites the Koh-i-Nor had to offer its guests.

Around this large room seven people stood in tableau. Close and on Paul's left was Kantele. Just beyond her, half turned away from the entrance, was Blunt, an odd tall hat on his head and a heavy black cape with purple facings rippling down from his wide shoulders. Beyond Blunt stood Burton McLeod, who of all seven showed the least concern, and Jase, also in cape and hat. His back to the blue curtains closed across the wide, far window wall of the room opposite the door, stood Eaton White, like a small, colorless silhouette. To White's left, on the opposite side of the room, stood the Koh-i-Nor Hotel's security agent, James Butler. But the bizarre touch was upon him, too. He wore the all-black jumper and slacks of one of the better-known marching societies, an outfit that left only face and hands whitely exposed; and in one of those white hands, he held a slim, lethal police handgun which had had its front sight removed. In place of the sight gleamed a small, blue metal cross.

He and McLeod stood across from each other with perhaps a dozen feet of carpet between them. The police handgun casually covered the chest of McLeod, and both men stood untensely, but as if aware of no others in the room besides themselves.

Closest of all, on Paul's right, stood Tyne. He faced the half-turned-away Blunt, and so was, like the colorless and motionless Eaton White, the first to see Paul as he entered. The sudden widening of his eyes made Blunt check his speech. The rest all turned, even Butler and McLeod. And Kantele gasped. They, all except Blunt, stood like people who witness a basic violation of the natural laws by which they have lived all their lives.

But Blunt leaned upon the straight silver knob of a new walking stick and smiled. As perhaps the Athenian pole-march Callimachus smiled on that day in late September, twenty-five hundred and forty years previous, on seeing in the cool bright sunlight between clouds, the dust of his reinforced Greek wings close in on the Persian horde on the plain of Marathon.

"You're a little early, not too much," he said, looking at Paul. "Kirk here hasn't quite been softened up enough yet. But come on in—myself."

And Paul, walking into the suite, seeing Blunt full and clearly face on for the first time, saw indeed—himself.

Chapter 21

Paul strode into the suite. The eyes of all of them were fixed on him, but none showed more shattering from the blow than the blue eyes of Kantele. For, of course, she alone of them all had felt it from the beginning, even though she would not admit it to herself. It was the reason she had been so drawn to Paul, and had denied being drawn so fiercely. Paul had not blamed her then; and understanding as he did now, he blamed her less. Even for him, as he stopped, facing Blunt from the distance of a few feet, the experience had its unnatural elements.

To those standing watching, he knew, it must be worse. For it was not a physical resemblance that he shared with Walter Blunt. They were both tall, wide-shouldered, long-boned, with strong facial features. But there the similarity of the flesh ceased. Their common identity was all the more jolting to the emotions because it was a matter of nonphysical duplications. They should not have looked alike. But they did.

It was weirdly as if the same man wore two different costumes and disguises. The surface appearances were totally different, but identically the same way of standing, the same balance of movement, the same mannerisms and attitudes, glowed through the outer shells like the same candle-flame through two differently ornamented lanterns.

"You understand," said Blunt conversationally to Paul, "why I've dodged you all this time?"

"Of course," said Paul.

At that, Kirk Tyne finally found his voice again. And a note that rang clearly in it witnessed to the fact that for the first time the World Engineer was seriously shaken in his convictions.

"What kind of unnatural devil-thing is this, Walt?" he burst out.

"It's a long story," said Blunt. He still leaned on his cane, examining Paul almost the way a connoisseur might examine a particularly valued work of art. "But that's what I brought you here to hear, Kirk."

Kirk glanced from Paul to Blunt and back, as if magnetically attracted against his will.

"I don't believe it," he said.

"Neither the world nor I," answered Blunt, without shifting his gaze off Paul, "will care what you think after tonight, Kirk."

"Satan!" said a voice. Those in the room, including Paul and Blunt, all looked. It was James Butler, the hotel agent, and he was lifting the gun in his hand. The blue cross on the end of its barrel centered on Paul, wavered, and swung over to point at Blunt. "Denier of God."

Something black flickered through the air of the room. There was the sound of a soft impact, and Butler staggered and dropped the gun from his suddenly limp grasp. The polished haft of a leaf-shaped, hiltless knife stood out from the muscles of the agent's shoulder. McLeod came walking calmly across the room. He bent to scoop up the gun and tucked it into his waistband, and then taking hold of Butler's shoulder with his left hand, he pulled out the knife with his right. He pulled a self-adjusting pressure bandage from his pocket, put it around Butler's shoulder to cover the wound, and lifted the crippled arm across Butler's chest into the grasp of Butler's other arm.

"Hold that," he said. Butler looked at him. The agent

had not made a sound. McLeod went back to his position beyond Blunt.

"Now," asked Kirk, out of a white face, "you sick your hoods on me, and decent people?"

"You call that fanatic decent?" asked Blunt, nodding at the blackclad Butler. "How decent would he have been if he'd shot me, or Paul? As he would have, if Burt hadn't stopped him."

"It makes no difference," said Kirk. Before their eyes, with a remarkable effort of will, they saw the man pull himself together. He repeated himself more calmly. "It makes no difference. None of this makes any difference. There are still only sixty thousand of you. That's not enough to wreck the world."

"Kirk," said Blunt, "you know I enjoy arguing with you. You make such a fine straight man."

"The credit goes to you as the comic," said Kirk, dryly.

"Now, that's more like it," said Blunt, nodding his head thoughtfully. "You see, Kirk, I want to break you. If I can get you nicely broken, I can enlist you in tearing this civilization up by the roots and get it done twice as fast. Otherwise, I wouldn't waste time talking with you like this."

"I assure you," said Kirk, "I don't feel the least bit broken."

"You aren't supposed to—yet," said Blunt.

"All I see so far," said Kirk, "is a series of adult-scale Halloween tricks."

"For example?" asked Blunt. "Paul, here?"

Kirk glanced at Paul and for a moment hesitated.

"I don't believe in the supernatural," he said.

"Nor do I," said Blunt. "I believe in the Alternate Laws. Under their power, I created Paul. Didn't I, Paul?"

"No," said Paul. "Creation isn't that easy."

"I beg your pardon," said Blunt. "Let me put it this way then—I built you. I brought you to life. How much do you remember?"

"I remember dying," said Paul. "I remember a tall

175

figure wearing the cape and hat you're wearing now, who brought me back to life."

"Not brought you back," said Blunt. "The real Paul Formain is dead—you knew that?"

"I know it now," said Paul. "I investigated."

"I had tracers on a number of youngsters like him for over fifteen years," said Blunt, "waiting for an opportunity. Odds were with me. Sooner or later one was bound to die under convenient conditions."

"You could have rescued him from that sailboat while he was still alive," said Paul.

"I could have," said Blunt. He looked squarely at Paul. "I think you know why I wouldn't do such a thing. I got to him in time for the moment of his death. I got several cells from his body, living cells. Under the powers of the Alternate Laws, I regrew from each of those cells a living body."

"More?" ejaculated Kirk, staring in something like horror at Paul. Blunt shook his head.

"Living," he said, "but not alive, any more than the dying body I took them from was alive in the true sense. The conscious personality of a living human being is something more than an arithmetical total of the consciousness of its parts." He gazed at Paul for a second without speaking, then said slowly, "Under the Alternate Laws I sparked his life with a portion of my own."

There was a silence in the room, so complete that it seemed that for a moment everyone there had ceased breathing.

"I made another *me,*" said Blunt. "His body, his memories, his skills were those that belonged to the boy who had just died. But in essence, he was me."

"In one essence," corrected Paul, "I was you."

"The most important essence, then," said Blunt. "That was why your body wouldn't take an arm graft. Your body's cells had used up their ability to make large adjustments and repairs in forming you."

"He has two arms now," said Kirk.

"This isn't the original body I started him in," said Blunt. "I assume he had to leave the first one on New Earth?" He looked inquiringly at Paul.

"By your cane," said Paul.

"Yes," said Blunt. "That cane."

"What cane?" asked Kirk.

"The cane that killed Malorn," said Paul. He gazed with a still face at Blunt. "The cane with which *he* killed Malorn."

"No," said McLeod, from behind Blunt. "I did it. It took someone who knew how to handle it like a single-stick. Walt just twisted the Alternate Laws to let me do it."

"But why?" cried Kirk. "Murder, canes, New Earth! I don't understand." He stared. "To educate Paul in——" He broke off.

"You're breaking very nicely, Kirk," said Blunt, turning his head briefly toward the World Engineer and then coming back as always to look at Paul. "You see how little you know? Even your Supe didn't inform you that it had used the accelerator down in its guts to ship Paul off to a planet circling Sirius and its companion star. I'll tell you the rest now and we'll see how you stand up to it." He nodded at the curtained window. "Open that," he said to Eaton White.

The colorless little man hesitated.

"Go ahead," said Kirk, harshly.

White reached in among the folds of the curtains, and down. They drew back revealing a wall-wide window above a low ledge about two feet high.

"All the way," said Blunt.

White reached and pressed again. The whole window slid down into and through the ledge. The hot air of the steamy night outside welled into the conditioned coolness of the room.

"Look!" said Blunt. "Listen out there." He pointed with his stick at the bulking darkness of the Complex outside, lighted here and there dimly. On the hot still air came the sound of chanting, the *"Hey-ha! Hey-ha!"* of a marching society. And from closer by, out of sight somewhere twelve stories below the window ledge, came a long drawn-out howl from something human that had gone a long ways back toward the animal.

"Look," said Blunt. Turning, he threw his cane out the window. Wheeling, spinning about the axis of its center point, the two rotating ends blurred themselves into scalloped, raking wings. The center acquired a rodent body, and a bat-shape instead of what had been a stick beat upward blackly against the dim glow of the Complex, turned and swooped back, gliding into the room to end up a stick in Blunt's hand again.

"Sixty thousand, you said," said Blunt to Kirk. "The unstable groups, organizations, and elements in this world of ours total nearly one-fifth the world population. For forty years the Chantry Guild has primed them for this moment of final breakdown. One-fifth of the world is out of its senses tonight, Kirk."

"No," said Kirk. "I don't believe it. No, Walt."

"Yes, Kirk." Blunt leaned on his cane again. His dark eyes under the eaves of his aging eyebrows bored in on the other man. "For centuries now you and your kind kept the hound of Unreason chained and locked away from the world. Now we've set him loose again—loose for good. From now on, there'll be no certainty to existence. From now on there'll always be the possibility that the invariable laws won't work. Reason and past experience and the order of the community will fail as guides, and the individual will be left with nothing to anchor to, only himself."

"It won't work," said Kirk. "Those streets out there are mostly empty. We moved too fast for you, my staff and the Super-Complex. Lack of light, lack of comfort, lack of services—people are hiding in their rooms now, because we forced them there. They can only hide so long; then the basic needs—hunger, reaction against boredom—will take over. They'll come out in the daylight and see how little your Halloween tricks have changed the essential structure of their lives. They'll adjust and learn to live with the necessarily small percentage of your magic in the same way they live with the small possibilities of other freak accidents or being struck by lightning."

"*You* moved too fast!" said Blunt. "You only reacted with all the fine obedience of one of your machines. The streets are dark because I wanted them that way. The heat is driving people to huddle apart from each other, alone with their fears, each in his own room, because these are the best breeding grounds for Unreason. Tonight is not something to which people can become accustomed, it's only the first battle in a war that will go on and on, waged with new weapons, fought in different ways, waged on altering battlefields, until you and your kind are destroyed."

Blunt's hard old jaw lifted.

"Until the final moment of destruct!" His voice rang through the room and out into the night. "Until Man is forced to stand without his crutches. Until his leg irons are struck off him and the bars he has built around him are torn down and thrown away! Until he stands upright and alone, free—*free* in all his questioning, wandering spirit, with the knowledge that in all existence there are only two things: himself, and the malleable universe!"

Blunt's heavy shoulders swayed forward over the cane on which he leaned, almost as if he was about to leap on Kirk Tyne where he stood. The World Engineer did not retreat before Blunt's words, or that movement, but he seemed to have shrunk slightly and his voice was a trifle hoarse when he answered.

"I'm not going to give in to you, Walt," he said. "I'll fight you to the bitter end. Until one of us is dead."

"Then you've lost already," said Blunt, and his voice was almost wild. "Because I'm going on forever." He pointed aside at Paul. "Let me introduce you, Kirk, to a younger, stronger, greater man than yourself, and the continuing head of the Chantry Guild."

He stopped speaking, and as the sound of his voice ceased, a sudden violent silence like summer sheet lightning flashed across the room. On the heels of it came an abrupt, instinctive, inarticulate cry from Jase.

"No," said Paul, "it's all right, Jase. The Guild will go to you. My job is something different."

They stared at him.

"Something different?" asked Blunt, dryly. "What is it *you* think you're going to do?"

Paul smiled at him and at the others a little sadly.

"Something brutal and unfair to you all," he said. "I'm going to do nothing."

Chapter 22

For a moment they merely looked back at him. But in that moment something inevitable, and not at all unique, happened. It has taken place before at gatherings that those present arrange themselves in a social pattern oriented around the strong point of one individual present. Then, something is said or something takes place. And suddenly, though none present have made an actual movement, the strong point is displaced to a different individual. The pattern reorients itself, and though nothing physical has happened, the emotional effect of the reorientation is felt by everyone in the room.

So with Paul, at that moment. He had reached out and touched the pattern, and like one drop melting into another, abruptly he was the focus for the emotional relationships in the room, where Blunt had been, a moment before.

He met Blunt's eyes across the little distance that separated them. And Blunt looked back, without expression, and without speaking. He leaned still on his cane, as if nothing had taken place. But Paul felt the sudden massive alertness of Blunt's genius swinging to bear completely on him, in the beginnings of a recognition of what Paul was.

"Nothing?" asked Jase, breaking the silence. Sudden alarm for the Chantry Guild, in this breakdown of whatever Blunt had planned for it, was obvious upon Jase, obvious even to others in the room besides Paul.

"Because," said Paul, "if I do nothing, you'll all go your separate ways. The Chantry Guild will continue and grow. The technical elements in civilization will continue and grow. So will the marching societies and the cult groups. So"—Paul's eyes, ranging backward in the room, met for a moment with Burton McLeod's—"will other elements."

"You want that to happen?" challenged Tyne. *"You?"*

"I think it's necessary," said Paul, turning to the World Engineer. "The time has come when mankind must fragment so that his various facets may develop fully and unaffected by other facets nearby. As you yourself know, the process has already started." Paul looked over at Blunt. "A single strong leader," said Paul, "could halt this process temporarily—only temporarily, because there would be no one of his stature to replace him when he was dead—but even in temporarily halting it, he could do permanent damage to later development of fragments he didn't favor."

Paul looked back at Kirk. There was something like horror on Kirk's face.

"But you're saying you're *against* Walt!" stammered Kirk. "You've been against him all along."

"Perhaps," said Paul, a little unhappily, "in a sense. It'd be kinder to say that I haven't been *for* anyone, including Walt."

Kirk stared at him for a moment, still with an expression varying from shock almost to repugnance.

"But *why?*" Kirk burst out finally. *"Why?"*

"That," said Paul, "is a little hard to explain, I'm afraid. Perhaps you might understand it if I used hypnosis as an example. After Walt first brought that last body of mine to consciousness, I had quite a period in which I didn't really know who I was. But a number of things used to puzzle me. Among them the fact that I couldn't be hypnotized."

"The Alternate Laws——" began Jase, from back in the room.

"No," said Paul. "I think someday you Chantry people are going to discover something to which your Alternate Laws bear the same relation alchemy does to modern chemistry. I couldn't be hypnotized because the lightest form of hypnosis requires the giving up of a certain portion of the identity, just as does really complete unconsciousness, and this is impossible to me." He looked around at all of them. "Because, having experienced a shared identity with Walt, it was inevitable that I should come to the capability of sharing the identity of any other human with whom I came in contact."

They all looked back at him. With the exception of Blunt, he saw, they had not fully understood.

"I'm talking about understanding," he said, patiently. "I've been able to share identities with all of you, and what I've found is that each one of you projects a valid form of the future of human society. But a form in which the others would emerge as stunted personalities if they managed to live in it at all. I can't further any one of these futures, because they'll all be coming into existence."

"All?" asked Kirk, just as, at the same moment, Jase also asked, "All?"

"You, yourself, were aware of the situation, Kirk," said Paul. "As you told me yourself, society is going through a necessary stage of fragmentation. It's only a matter of time, now, until a medication is devised that makes Springboard's work into the basis of a practical transportation system. As people spread out to the stars, the fragmentation will be carried further."

He stopped speaking to let that point sink in.

"None of you," said Paul, "should be wasting time fighting each other. You should be busy hunting up your own kind of people and working with them toward your own separate future."

He paused, to give them a chance, this time, to answer.

No one seemed disposed to do so. And then, from perhaps the most unexpected quarter, came the protest.

"There's no reason to believe any of this," said Eaton White, in his thick, dry voice from beside the open window.

"Of course not," said Paul reasonably. "If you disbelieve me, you only have to have the courage of your convictions and ignore what I've said." He looked around at them all. "Certainly you don't believe I'm trying to talk you into anything? All I want to do is step out of the picture and go my own way, and I should think the rest of you would want to do likewise."

He turned back to meet Blunt's eyes.

"After all," he said, "this has been a transition period in history, as Kirk has, no doubt, often told other people besides myself. It's been a time of stress and strain, and in such times things tend to become dramatic. Actually, each generation likes to think of itself as at the pivot point in history, that in its time the great decision is made which puts man either on the true road or the false. But things aren't really that serious. Truthfully, the way of mankind is too massive to be kinked, suddenly; it only changes direction in a long and gradual bend over many generations."

Paul turned to the World Engineer.

"Kirk," he said, "as I say, I'm not trying to convince anyone. But certainly *you* can see I'm talking sense?"

Kirk Tyne's head came up with decision.

"Yes," he said sharply, "I can." He looked at Blunt and back to Paul. "Everything you say makes sense. Everybody has one person who can put the Indian sign on them. With me it's always been Walt." He turned to Blunt. "Because I always admired you, Walt. I wanted to believe in you. And as a result you were able to con me into thinking that the world was upside down and just about to be inside out. It took someone with his feet on the ground, like Paul here, to bring me back to Earth. Of course, our centuries-old technical civilization wasn't the sort of thing that could be hoodooed out of existence by black magic overnight. But you almost had me thinking it could."

He stepped up to Paul and held out his hand. Paul took it.

"Everybody owes you a lot," said Kirk, shaking Paul's hand. "But I, most of all. I want you to know I haven't any doubts where you're concerned. I'll get the services back in action immediately. Come on, Eat." He turned to Blunt, hesitated, shook his head, and turning away again, walked toward the door. Blunt smiled grimly after him.

Eaton White came forward from his position at the window. As he passed by Paul, he hesitated, turned to Paul, and opened his mouth as if to speak. Then he turned and went on out, after Kirk. Jase followed.

"Jim," said Paul gently, looking across at the black-clad hotel agent, still holding his helpless arm across his chest with his other hand, "you probably have responsibilities calling."

Butler snapped his head around at the sound of his first name like a man coming out of a dream. His eyes were like gun-muzzles trained on Paul.

"Yes," he interrupted. "Responsibilities. But not the sort you think. You've been the instrument of a revelation to me—the revelation of the New Jerusalem. The future may hold more than many think."

He turned and walked upright away, still holding his arm, until he passed through the door, and turning, vanished.

"Good-by, Walt," said a voice. Paul and Kantele turned to see that McLeod had come up and put his hand on Blunt's shoulder. Blunt, still leaning on his cane, turned his face sideways toward that hand.

"You, too?" he asked a little huskily.

"You'll be all right, Walt," said McLeod. "Truth is, I've been thinking of it for some time."

"For the last six weeks—I know," said Blunt with a

wolf's grin. "No, no, go on, Burt. There's nothing to stay here for now, anyway."

Burt squeezed the caped shoulder, looked across it compassionately at Paul, and went toward the door. The three who were left watched him out in silence.

When Burt had gone, Blunt swung about a little on his cane and looked sardonically at Paul.

"Do I have to love you, too?" he asked.

"No," said Paul. "No, of course not! I wouldn't ask that."

"Then, damn you," said Blunt. "Damn you and may you rot in hell until judgment day!"

"Paul smiled sadly.

"You won't tell me why?" asked Blunt.

"If I could," said Paul, "I would. But it's a matter of language. I don't have words for you." He hesitated. "You could take it on faith."

"Yes," said Blunt, suddenly and heavily as if the strength had gone out of him. "I could take it on faith, if I were bigger." He straightened up suddenly and looked with a deep, penetrating curiosity at Paul.

"*Empath,*" he said. "I should have suspected it sooner. But where did the talent come from?"

"From your plans for me," said Paul. "I told the truth. It's a high wall that separates the inner parts of one identity from the inner being of another. From having the experience of no wall between you and me, I could learn to tear down the walls between myself and all others."

"But why?" said Blunt. "Why would you want to?"

Paul smiled again.

"Partly," he said, "because unlimited power or strength is a little like credit. In the beginning it seems that enough of it would do anything. But, when you achieve it, you find that it, too, is limited. There are areas in which it's helpless, like other things. Can you hammer out a roughness in a delicate piece of carved jade?"

Blunt shook his head.

"I don't see how it applies," he said.

"It's just that I have some things in common," said Paul. "And Kirk was very nearly right. It's not possible to change the future except by changing the present. And the only way to change the present is to return to the past and change that."

"Return?" asked Blunt. "Change?" Blunt's eyes had lost their earlier hardness. They were now fully alive. He leaned on his cane and looked directly at Paul. "Who could change the past?"

"Perhaps," said Paul, "someone with intuition."

"Intuition?"

"Yes. Someone," Paul said, "who could see a tree in a garden. And who knew that if that tree were to be cut down, then some years in time and some light-years in distance away, another man's life would be changed. A man, say, who has conscious intuitive process and can immediately realize all the end possibilities of an action the moment he considers it. Someone like that could step back into time, perhaps, and make changes without risk of error."

Blunt's face was perfectly still.

"You aren't me, at all," Blunt said. "You never were me. I think it was you who animated Paul Formain's body, not me at all. Who are you?"

"Once," said Paul, "I was a professional soldier."

"And an Intuit?" asked Blunt. "And now an Empath as well?" His voice was a little harsh. "What next?"

"An identity," said Paul slowly, "needs to be a dynamic, not a static, quantity. If it is static, it becomes helpless within the pattern of its existence. This is a lesson man eventually will have to learn. But if it is dynamic, it may direct its existence as a mining machine is directed, through the otherwise impassable fusion of rocky elements known as reality. From being dominated and imprisoned by them, it can pass to dominating and making use of them, and with its existence plow through, pulverize, and handle reality until it separates out those uniquely real and valuable parts of it which the identity wishes to make its own."

Blunt nodded, slowly, like an old man. It was not clear whether he had understood and was agreeing, or whether he had given up the attempt to understand and was merely being agreeable.

"They all would have their futures," he said. "That's what you told them, wasn't it?" He stopped nodding and looked at Paul for the first time with eyes that were a little faded. "But not me."

"Of course, you," said Paul. "Yours was the greatest vision, and simply the one furthest from realization, that was all."

Blunt nodded again.

"Not," he said, "in my lifetime. No."

"I'm sorry," said Paul. "No."

"Yes," said Blunt. He took a deep breath and straightened up. "I had plans for you," he said. "Plans rooted in ignorance. I had everything set up for you." He glanced at Kantele. "It was almost like having a——" He checked himself, threw back his head, and took a firmer grip on his cane. "I planned to retire after tonight, anyway."

He started to turn away. As he turned, he stooped a little. He hesitated and looked back at Kantele. "I don't suppose. . . . No," he said, interrupting himself. He straightened up once again, so straight the cane merely brushed the surface of the rug underfoot. He threw back his shoulders and for a moment towered in the room, as if he were young again.

"It's been an education," he said, and saluted Paul with the cane. Turning, he strode out. Behind his back, Kantele made a little gesture after him with her hands, and then let her hands and gaze drop. She stood, her head bent, her eyes on the carpet at her feet, like a maiden, captive to the stranger's bow and spear.

Paul looked at her.

"You love him," he said.

"Always. Very much," she said, almost inaudibly, not looking up.

"Then you're a fool to stay," he said.

She did not answer that. But after a moment she spoke again, uncertainly, her gaze still on the carpet.

"You could be mistaken," she said.

"No," said Paul; and she did not see the centuries-old pain that came into his eyes as he said it. "I never make mistakes."